James Joyce's Painful Case

THE FLORIDA JAMES JOYCE SERIES

UNIVERSITY PRESS OF FLORIDA

Florida A&M University, Tallahassee
Florida Atlantic University, Boca Raton
Florida Gulf Coast University, Ft. Myers
Florida International University, Miami
Florida State University, Tallahassee
New College of Florida, Sarasota
University of Central Florida, Orlando
University of Florida, Gainesville
University of North Florida, Jacksonville
University of South Florida, Tampa
University of West Florida, Pensacola

James Malton, "View of Dublin from the Magazine, Phoenix Park," 1795. *A Picturesque & Descriptive View of the City of Dublin* (London: Malton, 1799).

James Joyce's Painful Case

Cóilín Owens

Foreword by Sebastian D. G. Knowles

University Press of Florida
Gainesville/Tallahassee/Tampa/Boca Raton
Pensacola/Orlando/Miami/Jacksonville/Ft. Myers/Sarasota

22 21 20 19 18 17   6 5 4 3 2 1

First cloth printing, 2008
First paperback printing, 2017

Library of Congress Cataloging-in-Publication Data
Owens, Cóilín.
James Joyce's Painful case / Cóilín Owens ; foreword by
Sebastian D. G. Knowles, series editor.
p. cm.—(Florida James Joyce series)
Includes bibliographical references and index.
ISBN 978-0-8130-3193-4 (cloth: acid-free paper)
ISBN 978-0-8130-5471-1 (pbk.)
1. Joyce, James, 1882–1941. Painful case. I. Title.
PR6019.O9Z776 2008
823'.912—dc22   2007027538

The University Press of Florida is the scholarly publishing agency
for the State University System of Florida, comprising Florida A&M
University, Florida Atlantic University, Florida Gulf Coast Uni-
versity, Florida International University, Florida State University,
New College of Florida, University of Central Florida, University of
Florida, University of North Florida, University of South Florida, and
University of West Florida.

University Press of Florida
15 Northwest 15th Street
Gainesville, FL 32611-2079
http://upress.ufl.edu

To the forbearing Julianne: I pray that you not be disappointed.

But we always keep the dearest things to ourselves.
—Letter to Henrik Ibsen, March 1901

Contents

Figures

Foreword

This is a much-needed casebook on "A Painful Case," wherein every possible angle, from manuscript study to religion to music to the influences of nineteenth-century literature and philosophy, is given a thorough and definitive treatment. Lesser mortals would assemble and edit a volume of essays with such an encyclopedic scope: Cóilín Owens has quite miraculously done it all himself. From the opening apple in Mr. Duffy's desk to the final worm that winds through the night at the story's close, the significance of all things in "A Painful Case" is beautifully laid out. Owens responds to every cue in the story, right down to the books in Duffy's bookcase, which include not just the Friedrich Nietzsche that everyone remembers but the works of Arthur Schopenhauer, William Wordsworth, and the *Maynooth Catechism*. We may have been onto the connection with Richard Wagner's *Tristan und Isolde*, but now we are shown how James Joyce overlaid the songs of Wolfgang Amadeus Mozart and the music of Christoph Willibald Gluck and John Field onto Richard Wagner's *Tristan*, giving the story a much richer aural density than it had before, and bringing "A Painful Case" into the canon of Joycean texts, like "Araby," "The Dead," and "Sirens," that cannot be understood without attention to their musical dimension. In all aspects of this book, the author shows himself to be Joyce's ideal reader for the story.

But *James Joyce's Painful Case* is not just a work of dissection; it is a work of love: Owens presents the characters with such wit and empathy that no one could ever take him for Mr. Duffy. Even more than this, *James Joyce's Painful Case* is a work of art, written with such elegance and intelligence that every page brings new delight. We discover that there was an original James Duffy who printed devotional manuals in the 1840s, manuals that included imaginary love letters between a communicant and Jesus: these letters, we are told in a deadpan voice, are "saccharined over with the pale cast of piety." In a spectacularly innovative move, the central quibble of "A Painful Case" is turned into a *casus conscientiae*, or a case in a Jesuit handbook of complex moral conundrums: "Is James responsible for Emily's death?" Not content with this, the author drafts the problem in Latin, so that "Jacobus" is put in the dock for the death of Mrs. Sinico: "Utrum Jacobus de morte Ameliae rationem reddet?" In the section stunningly titled "Full Astrakhan Jacket," the author demonstrates seven ways in which "A Painful Case" draws from *Anna*

Karenina, and in keeping the train on the tracks throughout the argument shows himself to be not only a master rhetorician but also a person with the organizational genius of a railway traffic controller. This is a book anyone would want for their bookcase: one can only hope that the Owens treatment for the other fourteen stories in *Dubliners* is not far behind.

Sebastian D. G. Knowles
Series editor

Preface and Acknowledgments

Nine years elapsed between James Joyce's completion of *Dubliners* and its eventual publication (1916). By then Yeats's "terrible beauty" had been born. The tectonic shifts in Ireland between 1914 and 1922 changed the country, the subject, and the mental habits of the readers that Joyce might have envisaged when he made his original scrupulous prescriptions. Despite the substantial and protracted attention given these stories, professional commentaries still suffer from a paucity of historically informed inspections of Joyce's passport and cultural baggage. This is particularly true of the aspects of his sensibility that (however much he struggled against their respective restrictions) are deeply conditioned by his ethnicity, sect, and prewar manners. Out of admiration for his accomplishment, for the intellectual challenge, the sheer pleasure of it, and the confidence that there will be a payoff, I have therefore attempted to assume the position of an Irish Catholic reader of a century ago.

To develop the case in its full efflorescence, I have had to set aside many of the received ideas about Joyce and this, one of his least favored creations, "A Painful Case." The work took me through a "defamiliarization" process with a text I had known—and read about—for a long time: to read afresh this subtle, understated, and allusive story, pursuing its intertextual implications wherever they led. The argument of the book therefore examines how its incidents and idiom are embedded in the cultural life of Dublin between 1899 and 1904, and how they are refracted through Joyce's subsequent personal experience: familial, literary, and spiritual. It will therefore take readers through the conditions of its genesis, composition, revisions, and apparent abandonment. Even at this early stage of his career, Joyce's rhetorical mastery is evident in his management of an abundance of "cultural texts" (geographical, historical, musical, literary, dramatic, legal, and theological), which constitute the pointillism in the imaginative universe of this deceptively plain tale. The James Duffy that James Joyce imagines is a well-read and cultured man who feels that he must choose between Christ and Schopenhauer. His case requires careful unraveling, from the style in which he conducts his daily affairs through his reading and leisure, in order to discern the noumenal myths that vie for the mastery of his soul.

In this study, then, I argue that the emotional dilemma faced by James Duffy is the product of an early modern Irishman's encounter with what we now call a "post-Christian" world. A man who in childhood accepted the Catholic assumptions about the perfectibility of nature "with the help of God" (grace), and having abandoned the spiritual discipline enjoined by his religious tradition to achieve that end, finds himself disabled from the prospect of any engaging human bond. To adopt such a line of criticism is neither to advance nor criticize Catholic belief in particular, but seeks to understand how an intense commitment to such an ethos, when surrendered, affects a sensitive and intelligent personality in a destructive way. The particular variant on general apostasy that Joyce is concerned with in this story is known in Irish folklore as a "spoiled priest": the man who rejects the gift of a priestly vocation. "A Painful Case" is its classic articulation in the literature of Ireland.

Through many years of duties as a teacher of writing and literature and participating in professional conferences in Irish and Joyce studies, the central idea of both *Dubliners* and *A Portrait of the Artist as a Young Man* has been clarifying itself in the privacy of my mind. That is the implied author's argument between the world as imagined according to the Christian paradigm of nature completed by grace alone, or only by an open-minded and alert observer enlivened by a historically and mythically informed natural imagination. With extraordinary brilliance Joyce enters into this fundamental dialectic. This study of "A Painful Case," which began as a chapter, because it sketches but one phase of the larger idea, grew into the present book. The research and writing took the best part of one year's full-time work, the first fruit of a somewhat premature retirement. The rest will come, DV, later.

In one sense the work on this book began forty years ago when an earnest seminarian, reading Ludwig Feuerbach, first contemplated the issues faced by Duffy (resolving them differently, however, as would Joyce). The book concluded in March 2006 (after much homework, and with a heavier tread) as I followed in the literal footsteps of Joyce's imaginary walkers through the environs of Chapelizod, the Phoenix Park, Golden Lane, Baggot Street, Merrion Road, and Sydney Parade (see fig. 2.2). I had returned to pace an already heavily interpreted cityscape. The surges of the impetuous traffic and the cascades of eager faces worn by today's throngs seemed a faery host by contrast with the solitary walkers and irreducible geography rendered in Joyce's indelible account. At the same time I was struck by the corollary speculation: that the sensuous force of the teeming present makes ordering and judgment seem impossible. Joyce, of course, is the genius of both sides of the paradox: he was the keenest observer of the life of his native city, and at the same time a cartographer of its many contours, linguistic, historical, mythological. It is as if he were observing his own pedestrian progress along its sidewalks from

Dedelian and Augustinian heights. The assured distance between Trieste and these streets, in the event, facilitated his inimitably Eblanaphile art. A careful reading of Joyce's work, in its various parallaxes—visual, linguistic—enables us to not only view the present moment vividly, but also to remember it historically, imagine it mythically, and contemplate its spiritual mystery.

As the research and writing progressed, I became more and more moved by the grandeur and punctilio of Joyce's imagination, revealed even in this the apparently least favored of his fictional works. As the argument in the following pages implies, there is continuity between "A Painful Case" and *Ulysses*. In one sense, his creation and rejection of Mr. Duffy liberated him to imagine Bloom. But in another, the technical brilliance of *Ulysses* is not substantially different from what we can discover in careful rereadings of "A Painful Case." In tackling this story, then, I am taking advantage of an unwarranted complacency on the part of critics who have interpreted Joyce's dissatisfaction with it as a sign of its unworthiness as an object of systematic critical investigation. It is an anguished, highly personal, and in some ways private, work; an early foray of a widely read and ambitions writer. It is a failure only by contrast with its author's technical capacities and grand aspirations.

Joyce is not a philosopher or a historian. He is first and last a poet who read the masters and measured his work against theirs. Out of respect—and some measure of understanding—of what this means, I approach his work not in order to illustrate some political or social position or theory of language, but to explore the imaginative world of which his work is an expression. This requires an appreciation of his literary language, his apparently eclectic allusiveness, and his classical appetite for design. A systematic elucidation of these elements takes us closer to an appreciation of its high seriousness and beauty. We cannot be in a hurry elsewhere.

This study could not have been undertaken without the work of many scholars including those cited in the bibliography. I am but one student of these magisterial critics: Richard Ellmann, Father Robert Boyle SJ, Hugh Kenner, and Fritz Senn.

In memoriam these particular Joyceans: Augustine Martin, who started it all; Bernard Benstock, acute reader and mentor; Nathan Halper, spirited correspondent; Janet Dunleavy, advisor and patron; and generous friend and neighbor, Mary Reynolds.

Thanks for encouragement and help to these scholars: Maria Tymoczko, Bob and Tina Mahony, Jin Di, Maureen Murphy, Lee Jacobus, Maurice Harmon, Joe Sendry, Hilton Landry, Bobby Smith, and Sebastian Knowles. Thanks to Dom Columcille O'Toole OCSO and Father John Ford CSC for their exemplary teaching. Thanks to Eric Molin, Roger Lathbury, Bob Nadeau, Winnie Keaney, David Williams, Amelia Rutledge, and Chris Thaiss, George Mason colleagues true and dear.

For practical help with various aspects of the project, thanks (again) to Roger Lathbury, Gerry Maloney, Connie Milner, and Father Paul Smith OFM.

Thanks to members of the Association of Literary Scholars and Critics, the American Conference for Irish Studies, and the James Joyce Foundation for fellowship, encouragement, and occasionally lively exchanges, including David Wright, John Gordon, Mary Power, Paul d'Andrea, Murray Beja, Stanley Sultan, and Marc Connor.

Thanks to Sue Baldwin, Beth McDonald, Amy Gorelick, and Michele Fiyak-Burkley of the University Press of Florida for their guidance of this project to completion.

The extensive citation of the text of "A Painful Case" was accommodated with the permission of the Trustees of the James Joyce Estate.

Finally, to my loving wife, Julianne, and sons, Seamus and Conor, for their tolerance of my absorption in (and occasional venting about) this project: *go raibh maith agaibh*!

Abbreviations

For almost all of the following abbreviations cited parenthetically in the text I have followed the standard conventions of the *James Joyce Quarterly*. I add several other items that are frequently cited. Unless otherwise noted all references are by page and line.

CDD   Stanislaus Joyce, *The Complete Dublin Diary*, edited by George H. Healey (Ithaca and London: Cornell University Press, 1971).

CM   James Joyce, *Chamber Music*, edited by William York Tindall (New York: Columbia University Press, 1954).

CW   James Joyce, *The Critical Writings of James Joyce*, edited by Ellsworth Mason and Richard Ellmann (New York: Viking, 1959).

D   James Joyce, *Dubliners*, edited by Robert Scholes with Richard Ellmann (New York: Viking, 1967).

Dircks   *Essays of Schopenhauer*, edited by Mrs. Rudolph Dircks (London: Walter Scott, 1897).

FW   James Joyce, *Finnegans Wake* (New York: Viking, 1939).

JJII   Richard Ellmann, *James Joyce: New and Revised Edition* (New York: Oxford University Press, 1982).

JJA   *The James Joyce Archive*, edited by Michael Groden et al. (New York and London: Garland, 1977–78). I follow the *JJQ* guide for citing volumes and pages.

JJQ   *James Joyce Quarterly*

Letters   James Joyce, *Letters of James Joyce*, vol. I, edited by Stuart Gilbert (New York: Viking, 1966). Volumes II and III, edited by Richard Ellmann (New York: Viking, 1964).

MBK   Stanislaus Joyce, *My Brother's Keeper: James Joyce's Early Years*, edited by Richard Ellmann (New York: Viking, 1969).

MK   Gerhart Hauptmann, *The Dramatic Works of Gerhart Hauptmann*, 7 vols., translated by numerous translators, edited by Ludwig Lewisohn (New York: B. W. Huebsch, 1913–29).

P   James Joyce, *A Portrait of the Artist as a Young Man*, corrected text by Chester G. Anderson and edited by Richard Ellmann (New York: Viking, 1968).

P&P   Arthur Schopenhauer, *Parerga and Paralipomena: Short Philosophi-cal Essays*, 2 vols., translated by E.F.J. Payne (Oxford: Clarendon Press, 1974). References in the text are to volume and page number.

SH   James Joyce, *Stephen Hero*, edited by Theodore Spencer, John J. Slocum, and Herbert Cahoon (New York: New Directions, 1963).

U   James Joyce, *Ulysses*, edited by Hans Walter Gabler et al. (New York: Random House, 1986).

World Arthur Schopenhauer, *The World as Will and Idea*, 3 vols., trans-lated by R. B. Haldane and J. Kemp (1883) (London: Routledge and Kegan Paul, 1948). References in the text are to volume and page number.

Introduction

"obvious remarks"

In my works there is a good deal of talk about religion. Many people think I am a spoiled priest. I profess no religion at all. Of the two religions, Protestantism and Catholicism, I prefer the latter. Both are false. The former is cold and colorless. The second-named is constantly associated with art; it is a "beautiful lie"—something at least.

These conversational remarks made in 1918 are instructive regarding one of James Joyce's most underestimated but personally revealing stories, "A Painful Case" (Potts, 71). They help explain the grounds of his dissatisfaction with and ambitions for a minor work upon which he labored with unusually protracted care.

The thesis of this book is that James Duffy bears not only the guilt of a Catholic apostate but also of a man who had rejected a vocation to the religious life, that is, to that of a priest or monk. He has attempted to compensate for the resultant spiritual void by doing the decent Victorian thing: cultivating his own garden with the ersatz consolations of music, literature, and philosophy. The impressionable youth who was once moved to regulate his life in obedience to the call of Jesus Christ that "I am the way and the truth and the life" (John 14: 6) has in his adulthood adopted Arthur Schopenhauer's view that Christianity is a *pia fraus* (a pious fraud).[1] A financially secure, health-conscious, and personally independent man, James Duffy is Joyce's depiction of what we might today call a graying yuppie. His brief friendship with Mrs. Sinico is a catalyst in his intellectual development and spiritual decline: it moves him from a general subscription to Schopenhauer's notion of metaphysical Will to a thoroughgoing Nietzschean nihilism and spiritual despair.

James Duffy is a sensitive and reflective man. A genuine intellectual, he is a uniquely severe representation of his creator. Duffy's efforts to become a secular free spirit founder on his ineluctable sense of personal soul. The dream of spiritual perfectibility inculcated in his school days and which pursued him through his second score of years now dogs him through the routines into which he has in adulthood settled: his days at the bank and evenings of solitary leisure. All of his disciplined efforts at personal liberation—his solitary walks, his disdain of urban fads, his strenuous attachments to German high culture, and his reading of "advanced" thinkers—collapse when he realizes that in turning away from Mrs. Sinico's offer of erotic love he was repeating his earlier rejection of divine grace. The corresponding irony at the heart of this story of a soul within the story of adultery manqué is that the very idea of perfect love, which animated him in the first place, is in the second, the source of his inability to give or accept a personal love that is within the compass of any normal person. A further and complementary corollary is that while a premise of the story is an implied criticism of the hegemony of Catholic clericalism in Irish life, the narrative exhibits Duffy's despair as a caution to those who would consider themselves free thinkers: "noh man liberty is" (*FW* 611.11).

This book examines the knot of relationships between the minds of the implied narrator and James Duffy, the idea of a priestly vocation as the cornerstone of the cultural institution of Irish Catholicism, in contrast with the figure of Schopenhauer, the nineteenth century's boldest atheist and the éminence grise behind the multiple literary ghosts who shimmer through this story: Wagner's Tristan, Gerhart Hauptmann's Michael Kramer, Leo Tolstoy's Konstantine Levin (*Anna Karenina*), and Ivan Turgenev's Tchulkaturin ("Diary of a Superfluous Man").

"A Painful Case" is a deceptively simple story of disappointed love. But as with his major works, the pursuit of its technical labyrinth leads to its deposit of ideas and an appreciation of the Joycean sensibility. The pen of a man with a singularly discerning ear, the practiced punctilio of a grocer's assistant, an obsessive observer of congruencies between various spheres of personal experience, and correspondences between them and literary precedents, could not but inscribe a maze. Recommending the Irish tenor, John Sullivan, whose career he promoted in 1930, Joyce offered this testimony: "I have been through the score of *Guillaume Tell* and I discover that Sullivan sings 456 G's, 93 A flats, 92 A's, 54 B flats, 19 C's, and 2 C sharps. Nobody else can do it" (Gorman, 346). Nobody indeed.

Every detail in "A Painful Case" is accountable both as a naturalistic narrative and a fine amalgam of images and ideas forged around the idea of disappointed spiritual hope. These minutiae, drawn consciously or unconsciously from his disturbed personal and family history, his prescribed formal education, and his canny observation of his acquaintances, he enlarged imaginatively by his voracious reading of literature, philosophy, and music. Joyce did not lead a personally adventuresome life (unlike his friend Ernest

Hemingway, he hunted no lion or marlin), but his encyclopedic reading enabled the expanding universe of his imagination. In some material ways he is dependent on the works of others, as he admitted to Stanislaus (February 11, 1907, *Letters* II: 212). But he inimitably assimilates these works to his own vision in a manner that was technically sophisticated and deeply serious.

"A Painful Case" is partly an adultery story, partly a ghost story, partly a love-death story, but first and last it is the story of a spoiled priest. It is a turning point in the overall design of *Dubliners*. As Hugh Kenner (ever the progenitor of pregnant phrases) remarked, "A Painful Case" is "the heart of the matter": the midpoint of the book and "in terms of ideas almost equal to 'The Dead'" (*Dublin's Joyce*, 58). It plays variations on the loneliness and cultural aspirations of Tommy Chandler ("A Little Cloud"), Farrington's automatism ("Counterparts"), and Maria's living death ("Clay"). It reiterates and refines some of the themes of "Counterparts" (alienating labor, the law) and its immediate predecessor in order of composition, "The Boarding House" (marriage, music, and work), and to both of these in the masterful management of free indirect discourse. Prospectively, it is the first of several late stories in which a ghost—an emissary from the world beyond rational apprehension or explanation—makes an appearance. Like many other stories in *Dubliners*, its epiphany beams through a slip in an amateur performance. Its self-criticism anticipates the major epiphany of "The Dead."

As a critique of would-be atheism, "A Painful Case" mediates between "The Sisters" and "The Dead," which limns a movement from agnosticism to an epiphany of Christian grace. Duffy's ambivalence condemns him to eternal waiting, "beyond the city lights," like Belacqua Shua. In this way it anticipates the bolder self-criticism implied by the portrait of Gabriel Conroy. In another way (and in contrast with "The Dead") it looks past Gabriel's age and further into its author's possible future, because Mr. Duffy is about eighteen years older than his creator (as would be the yet unconceived Leopold Bloom). In these ways, "A Painful Case," uniquely among the stories of *Dubliners*, anticipates the project that was to become *Ulysses*. Humane Bloom, whose lips were never twisted in prayer, shrugs past the apostate's guilt.

A would-be priest, James Duffy mediates between the duo of dead clerics with which *Dubliners* opens (Father Flynn of "The Sisters"—and the deceased priest of "Araby") and the complementary clerical pair, superseded by the narrators, with which it ends (Father Purdon of "Grace" and Father Constantine Conroy of "The Dead"). In this respect, James Duffy is a variant upon the major theme of hieratic absence in *Dubliners*. "A Painful Case" gives a singular articulation to one of the major themes of the work: the relationship between the order of nature and "that other world" of grace mediated, in the Catholic tradition, by the Church in its doctrine, its moral discipline, its sacraments, its apostolic succession, and its priests. The first paragraph of "The Sisters" establishes this theological theme: where the gnomon represents the relationship between incomplete (because "fallen") nature and the infinitely near-and-far square of perfection to which it, without grace, forever fruitlessly "aspires." Father Purdon's sermon, with which *Dubliners* originally ended, is a parody of an inept but official attempt to convey the idea of grace to "men of the world." In Joyce's revised ending to the book, at the conclusion to "The Dead," the symbol of the snow enveloping all of the natural universe expresses a serious Christian parable of the miracle of grace: God's continuous creation. The concealed narrator, a lay Christian poet, takes the place of Gabriel Conroy's unaccountably absent clerical brother. In this way it anticipates the self-criticism implied in the portrait of Gabriel Conroy.

The radar of the Joyce industry, which for over fifty years has been so searchingly trained on *Dubliners*, has not gone much beyond detecting "A Painful Case" as an embarrassment: among so many clear masterpieces a fuzzy disappointment. This imperception may be partly rationalized by the dissatisfaction with the story that Joyce expressed, even after several revisions of the manuscript: one of his "two worst stories" (November 6, 1906, *Letters* II: 189). Its apparent weaknesses of narrative control have been the subject of acute analysis (for example, Beck, 219–36); but some of the commentary has been condescending, begrudging, or opportunistic, and too much has been merely illustrative of sophisticated theoretical paradigms rather than genuinely respectful towards or illuminative of Joyce's polyvalent language, the complexity of his designs, the cultural moment, and the elusive larger implications of his texts. The most sensitive and instructive readings, those by John William Corrington (1966), Michael West and William Hendricks (1977), and Fritz Senn (1988), are not recent. Most of the published discussion (numbering about fifty items) is insufficiently historicized or attentive to Joyce's engagement with literary, philosophical, and religious cultures. As this study will attempt to demonstrate, the principal difficulty that Joyce encountered in "A Painful Case" was that the subject was too capricious and far-reaching for the necessarily enthymemic constraints of the short story form. Too much of what is essential to understanding Mr. Duffy's frame of mind depends upon a few allusions and oblique citations. They are insufficient, by themselves, absent freight of character and dramatic torque, to bear their intended weight.

This study makes no theoretical pretense beyond attempting to constitute Joyce's ideal contemporary Irish reader. Even if he is no more than half reliable, Stanislaus had good reason to tell his BBC listeners that his brother "always thought that his stories could interest only Dubliners and [he] struggled desperately to have his book published in Dublin" (*The Listener,* March 25, 1954). How might Joyce have expected this story to be understood by purchasers of the projected Maunsel edition of 1909? Joyce's texts make many assumptions that we do not today accept and are thronged with information that would have been unremarkable among his contemporary readers. A century later, Dubliners and non-Dubliners are alike in that they share few of the religious, political, or cultural assumptions that governed the lives of Joyce's former fellow citizens. In that respect, we are better equipped than were his contemporaries to appreciate the report of this "ideal informant": one who, as Margaret Mead puts it, is aware of the assumptions that everyone else in the culture accepts as self-evident. On the other hand, their very familiarity with Edwardian Dublin's "street furniture"—an inventory of which Joyce bore with him through the cities of Europe—is as often as not for Dubliners are blind to Joyce's larger purposes (as the current commodification of Joycean Dublin makes all too clear).

Our remove in time, distance, and culture offers, in different respects, both advantages and disadvantages to us as readers of Joyce's work: because his critical position is generally well understood, it is easier for us to appreciate his unmasking of the assumptions of his fellow citizens, even though we are not directly familiar with the local evidence. The matter is complicated further by the by now largely unexamined acceptance of certain of Joyce's critical stances towards his native city as he was writing *Dubliners,* when some were serious and longstanding while others were rhetorical, temporarily held, intended as *en famille,* or were dissipated among their momentary contingencies. Similarly, the language of Joyce's art is partially authorized by the literary tradition, partially companioned by the streets he walked, and partially tuned by the tensions between personal, fraternal, and filial bonds.

While appreciating the "cultural moment," this study is more interested in how and why Joyce's story takes its immemorial shape. It therefore attempts to peer into the Joycean well from which it is drawn. To accomplish this task, I have tried to capitalize on what I have in common with him—his ethnicity, religion, education, and musical tastes—developing a sympathy for his literary aims by reading much of what he did before he set pen to paper in Trieste in the middle of the summer of 1905. What follows, then, is a historicization of the story, a reconstruction of its conception and genesis with special attention to the surviving manuscripts, and a series of tandem rereadings of the story against an array of texts—literary and cultural—that were among the imaginative baggages he brought on board as he embarked on the composition of "A Painful Case." The hope is that such a genealogical study will enable the catholic reading that this story deserves. These unravelings of the skeins of Joyce's imaginative character required forensic perusal and beg patient reading. Their justification—not perhaps always evident while in transit—is in what they illuminate of Joyce's apparently miraculous verbal art.

The most frequently observed biographical point about "A Painful Case" is its genesis in an incident recorded in Stanislaus Joyce's diary (now alas lost), his brief conversation with a genteel lady at a concert in 1901–2 (*MBK* 158–60). A subsequent chance encounter with her on the street—which went no further—provided Joyce with the cue for the faux-adultery plot of "A Painful Case." The story draws on an unrelated historical event that occurred some two-and-a-half years later, and was reported in the *Illustrated Irish Weekly and Nation*, a train accident at the Sydney Parade Station on July 14, 1904, resulting in the death of one Mrs. Sarah Bishop (Jackson and McGinley, 99–100). Joyce imagines the action of the story, however, as commencing in the autumn of 1899 and ending four years later (since Leopold Bloom was among the mourners at Mrs. Sinico's funeral on October 17, 1903, *U* 17.1454). The personal circumstances under which Joyce undertook the writing of the story in July 1905, as Nora Barnacle was about to confer upon him the numinous name of "father," are also relevant to an understanding of "A Painful Case." The mutual relationships among these three events inform the penetrating reflections on sexual love, death, alcoholism, musical performance, and paternity and the rejection of the gift of faith that are the serious issues given concentrated consideration in "A Painful Case."

Written in Trieste in 1905–6, the story's imaginary four years synthesize a number of apparently unrelated historical events four years previously. In May 1900, poking around in an ashpit at their latest residence (8 Royal Terrace, Fairview), Stanislaus stumbled on a collated edition of the Gospels (*MBK* 100). His perusal of the four accounts of Christ's life provoked a skepticism about the inerrancy of sacred scripture that he shared with his older brother. This sent the pair on a course of reading and discussion, over the next couple of years, in what would later be called "the search for the historical Jesus." Together they read Ernest Renan's *Life of Jesus*, comparing and contrasting its interpretation (which they considered a sentimental projection) with the spiritual testimonies of figures like Saint Augustine (*Confessions*), Tolstoy (*The Fruits of Enlightenment*), Henry Olcott's *A Buddhist Catechism*, the Catholic mystics (*MBK* 131), and evidently, some of the works of Schopenhauer and Nietzsche. They consulted the new English translation of the Bible (the American Standard), which appeared in 1901.

Meanwhile, Joyce participated in public meetings at which were discussed Canon Patrick Sheehan's novel *My New Curate* and Thomas à Kempis's *The Imitation of Christ*. During that summer, Joyce was making his first concerted literary efforts, writing the lyrics entitled *Shine and Dark* (some of which graduated into *Chamber Music*), and while in Mullingar (July–August) translating Hauptmann's plays *Michael Kramer* and *Vor Sonnenaufgang* (*Before Sunrise*). Returning to Dublin, he received the announcement that William Butler Yeats and George Moore were about to mount their collaborative play *Diarmuid and Graine*, provoking his "Day of the Rabblement" (October 15). This broadside attacked the provincial direction the Irish theatre was taking, and en passant, chastised Moore's collection of novellas, *Celibates* (1895). Joyce was also sufficiently interested in Irish nationalist affairs to attend some of Patrick Pearse's classes on the Irish language and occasional meetings of the Gaelic League. He was therefore in a position to appreciate the import of the column in the *United Irishman* (October 19) on the links between Chapelizod and the Celtic myth that were the subject of Wagner's opera, and attend the John F. Taylor speech on the revival of the Irish language (October 23).

Shortly thereafter, on the "West Briton" side of the ledger, Stanislaus Joyce attended a concert given by Clara Butt, the young English contralto, at the Rotunda Concert Hall (*MBK* 158–59). The vocal sensation of 1901, she had sung "Abide with Me" at Queen Victoria's funeral (February 2) and the national anthem at the coronation of Edward VII (June 26). Her tour of the British provinces the following season included the Dublin appearance attended by Stanislaus at which she sang "*Che farò*" (Gluck), "*Mon Coeur s'ouvre à ta voix*" (Camille Saint-Saëns) (*MBK*), and "*Il segreto*" (Gaetano Donizetti). The second musical event relevant to "A Painful Case" was the Carl Rosa production (November 1901) of *Tristan und Isolde*, the libretto of which was among James Joyce's literary possessions at the time.

Walking the city streets from the new Joyce domicile at Glengariff Parade (the thirteenth address in James's nineteen years) to his classes at Earlsfort Terrace, this son of a home ruined by alcohol passed notices promoting the highly effective campaign for sobriety, then in its third year, the Pioneer Total Abstinence Association. The tragic death of George, their young brother, the following spring (May 3, 1902), brought to a head and into the open the apostasy of the brothers Joyce. The following pages will demonstrate that the imaginative world conjured up by the text of "A Painful Case" accommodates these (and many other) odd bedfellows. Thus, when Joyce writes indignantly that "It is not my fault that the odour of ashpits . . . hangs round my stories" (June 23, 1906, *Letters* I: 63–64), he may be telling Grant Richards that he is a realist, but the image that floats in his private mind is also of the "ashpit book" recovered at 8 Royal Terrace five years before.

Had Joyce's earliest efforts to publish *Dubliners* been less troublesome, we would know little about his intentions. For example, he told Grant Richards, "I have written my book with considerable care, in spite of a hundred difficulties and in accordance with what I understand to be the classical tradition of my art" (April 26, 1906, *Letters* I: 60). The naturalistic or social action of his works—"hemiplegia of the will" and all that—is but a pretext for the deeper agenda of these early works. As an imaginative representation of moments of social paralysis, however, there is much more "going on" than the plain sense of the texts admits. So while no doubt these stories can be examined for what they exhibit of an aspiration to social liberation (economic, nationalist, feminist, et cetera), as a careful examination of Joyce's reading at the time in conjunction with the finely signaled allusions and structures permeating his texts shows, his persistent concerns are perennial: death, providence, fate, freedom, and faith.

So while the social themes comment on the relationships between men and women, the social classes, the generations, and between nations, the radical pleasure of Joyce's text arises from his capacity to release the latent energy of language to express the relationship between humanity and the gods: in a word, it is "theologicophilological" (*U* 9.762). This is the import of his remark to Grant Richards that "the special odour of corruption" hangs about them (October 15, 1905, *Letters* II: 123). He has minted this phrase from the familiar figure from hagiographic literature, *odor sanctitatis* (the odour of sanctity), and Saint Paul's eloquent contrast of the hope for salvation—wherein our natures are ultimately perfected—and the corruption of the flesh: "Seminatur in corruptione, surget in incorruptione" (It is sown corruptible; it is raised incorruptible) (1 Cor. 15: 42).

Once the course was set, Joyce was single-minded about his stories. His letters to his brother and the testimony of his friends at the time indicate that he was a voracious reader of serious literature before he attempted to publish anything. He prepared himself for this task through determined and systematic reading of what he considered conducive to his singular purpose. By the time he wrote "A Painful Case," he had read widely in the works of practitioners of the short story, Irish and Continental, and had a cultivated appreciation of philosophical and theological questions, operatic literature, vocal music, several European languages, English literary history, and Irish popular and political culture. One of the pleasures of his work is the feeling produced by the harmony of tongues: the tenor of his Dublin voice against the tones of those he esteemed enough to mimic. With form comes substance. Thus, a "high literacy" is one of the prerequisites to get to "the heart of the matter." A handful of modish phrases borrowed from a latter-day (and presumably superior) theoretical position will not do. Joyce is always smarter, and usually better read, than any cohort of his readers.

Literary scholars have intimated or explored several intertextual relationships of "A Painful Case," some substantial, some superficial: with Turgenev's novella, "Clara Militch" and Guy de Maupassant's "Promenade/A Little Walk" (West and Hendricks, 715–16), with Henry James's "The Beast in the Jungle" (Reid; Zlotnick), Wagner's *Tristan und Isolde* (R. Jackson), with Nietzsche and Hauptmann (Magalaner), Tolstoy's *Anna Karenina*, and naturally, with Gustave Flaubert's *Madame Bovary*. To the uninitiated, these relationships may seem tendentious (and indeed a couple are nothing but superior guesswork). But even to readers familiar with Joyce's extraordinary linguistic and readerly retentiveness, his ability to amalgamate a multiplicity of different texts to his apparently simple narrative is dizzying. The dense intertextuality of his literary method induces, as has often been remarked, a sense of critical vertigo. The "texts" of the natural world he knew—his family, friends, Dublin, Ireland—are a small minority among the sum total of those which inform his stories. As we shall see, besides literary antecedents, the disciplines of music, philosophy, and theology have a substantial bearing on our reading of "A Painful Case."

To sketch this caricature of himself as he might become (*Dubliners* is a retrospective and prospective arrangement of his personal *futurabilia*), Joyce designs a highly nuanced and allusive account. The hypothesis upon which he constructs "A Painful Case" is Mr. Duffy's inability to transcend his childhood faith. The unintended consequences of his rejection of that naïve faith have sent him upon a career of displaced renunciations, leading to his final complete unhappiness. The items in Mr. Duffy's library are the mileposts of that descent: the *Maynooth Catechism*, Wordsworth's *Complete Poetical Works*, Mozart's music, Schopenhauer's *World* (implied), Hauptmann's *Michael Kramer*, and Nietzsche's *Thus Spake Zarathustra* and *The Gay Science*.

The implied narrator comes to his task in a larger company of creative figures who have already marked the territory with monuments great and small. George Moore, his immediate role model and rival on the Irish literary scene, but also Yeats and some minor figures such as Canon Sheehan and William Carleton had already superficially surveyed the course taken by the spoiled priest. Behind them are the three Continental masters, Wagner, Tolstoy, and Turgenev. The story owes a major structural and thematic debt to Wagner's *Tristan und Isolde,* and makes miniature subscriptions to Tolstoy's masterpiece of adultery and Christian conversion, *Anna Karenina,* and to Turgenev's novellas of alienation, disappointed love, and paranormal experience, "Diary of a Superfluous Man" and "Clara Militch." The common philosophical patron of these works, bequeathing to each of them variously his metaphysics of music, his atheism, his pessimism, or his ur-psychology, is Schopenhauer. This same philosopher has contributed to the intellectual character of Mr. Duffy, accounting for his attitudes towards politics, sexuality, music, and Christian faith.

Joyce's cast of characters includes but five intellectuals—men whose reading, rather than their communal relationships, determines their values—Stephen Dedalus, Gabriel Conroy, Richard Rowan, Shem, and James Duffy. His celibacy thus renders Duffy a unique Joycean figure. He lives outside the orbit of the five-figure family cell that composes the sphere of Joyce's social world. A man in middle age who began his spiritual life as a pious and conventional Irish Catholic, the role models of his early life were clerical. The ascetic orderliness of his life when we meet him bears witness that he still retains a self-image shaped by the dedicated life to which he once aspired. But turning away from that early attraction, he became a nineteenth-century skeptic while retaining emotional ties with his former belief through temporary allegiances to pantheism, Schopenhauerean idealism, and following his separation from Mrs. Sinico, Nietzschean nihilism. Despite these efforts at disengagement from the past, he is still haunted by the guilt of having rejected the grace to ascend to the altar and become the instrument of God's love for mankind. In short, he is a spoiled priest. In this respect, he is what Stephen Dedalus, who has confused himself with Lucifer and other fallen angels, could become (*P* 239.6), without his human savior, Leopold Bloom.

Temperamentally disposed towards a meditative life, James Duffy withdraws from social and emotional engagement. An intelligent and sensitive man, the formative trauma of his youth was the loss of the faith that animated his childhood. Joyce's fine-grained text intimates this hegira through a terrain of explicit and oblique references to the call to grace and its attendant perils. Irish Catholic culture of the late nineteenth century directed his aspirations towards the Christian ideal of the perfectibility of the soul. This required a dedication, in the name of Jesus, to a moral life, ascetic discipline, spiritual or pious reflection, and dedication to the service to others. In this reading of the story, Duffy passed from this early indoctrination as an Irish Catholic (of which his resewn *Maynooth Catechism* is a memento), to a romantic pantheism (via Wordsworth's poetry), to an adult reading of Schopenhauer (whose misogynistic encomia he translates), and thence to Nietzsche, the prophet of modern despair.

Like many nineteenth-century cultural elites, he considered that the arts—especially music—succeeded prayer and religious meditation as the language of the soul. For Mr. Duffy, Ludwig van Beethoven (whose death mask is the central icon of Hauptmann's *Michael Kramer*, which he has translated) and Mozart (whose piano and vocal music draw him to his landlady's instrument and to public concerts) are the masters of his discerning, but solipsistic, soul. For James Duffy (as for Karl Barth's angels), Mozart's music expresses the soul untouched by original sin. It is at this point in his intellectual and spiritual development that we meet him. As we shall see, at the heart of the Sinico-Duffy relationship are some of Mozart's songs, the memory of which remind Duffy of the closest he ever gets to the happiness to be found in the love of another. The dense intertextuality of the story expresses the aspirations of the soul conceived in analogous theological and musical terms. There is a relationship between Mr. Duffy's rejection of his Christian vocation and of Mrs. Sinico's offer of love. Mozart's music is the primary vehicle of mediation between the realms of the divine and human. He rejects each on a similar premise: the detachment of the contemplative from Christian love is replayed with the detachment of art from its subject. Both the presumed basis of his relationship with Mrs. Sinico—the celebration of music as the art uniquely expressive of the noumenal—and its failure—misogyny—can be traced to his reading of Schopenhauer.

His reading of Nietzsche subsequent to Mrs. Sinico's dismissal reassures him of his predispositions, and he sinks more deeply into social isolation and spiritual despair. The littérateur in him was, no doubt, attracted by the brilliant energy of Nietzsche's writing, his biting parables, and the verve of his paradoxical aphorisms. In the figure of this same philosopher, whose youth was also spent in a religious environment and who entertained aspirations towards the Lutheran ministry, and whose works have been permeated by biblical tropes, Mr. Duffy met a fellow traveler. Each, to coin a phrase, was supersaturated with that which he rejected.

As a spoiled priest, pianist, and translator, Mr. Duffy is close to, but at a small but significant distance from the full realization of religious or artistic aspirations. He consequently regards detachment as a virtue. Mr. Duffy's disengagement from the life of the city, and even his own body, is reflected in the implied narrator's detachment from Mr. Duffy. Joyce himself wore such a mask in his youth as well as in his maturity. Witnesses to his Literary and Historical Society addresses at the National University attest to the detachment of his demeanor; and he often wore the same mask during his later life in Europe. Casual acquaintances (though not his closest friends) report of his excessive politeness, impersonality, and formality. Barbara Sloan has identified this literary stance—signifying the pose of a deliberately self-exiled poet—as a Joycean borrowing from Gabriel D'Annunzio's *Il Fuoco*. Fritz Senn's sophisticated essay takes this argument to the next step, brilliantly elucidating the many ways in which Joyce's refined diction and syntax express Duffy's assiduous self-management. The limitations of this emotional principle are put to the test when he meets Mrs. Sinico. His neurotic inability to literally "get in touch" with her is his signal moral failure. The ethical conundrum Duffy faces in Mrs. Sinico's offer of an adulterous yet salutary love is the casus conscientiae that the poker-faced narrator, in the guise of a moral casuist, poses for his reader. Duffy rationalizes his withdrawal by appealing to the convention that a relationship would be adulterous. Yet at the same time he professes to hold social convention in contempt. He has become so practiced in the mode of renunciation that it seems to him both natural and right.

In developing a naturalistic story with an ingenious subscription to Wagner's treatment of a Celtic myth, Joyce is at once remaining true to his own emerging vision and sensibility while also emulating the practice of Yeats's followers in the Irish Literary Revival: by giving voice to what remained of Ireland's indigenous imaginative tradition. The technical sophistication of "A Painful Case" articulates both a Celtic myth (the romance of Tristan and Iseult) and a cultural type with which he was acquainted from his own familial experience and Irish popular culture: the type of the spoiled priest and its variants that he found in Yeats's Owen Aherne, George Moore's John Norton, and Sheehan's anonymous figure. Mr. James Duffy is a reverse image of the romantic lover Tristan and a direct expression of this familiar clerical figure. This reading will therefore refine Stanislaus Joyce's characterization of Mr. Duffy as "the type of the male celibate" (*MBK* 159).

The analysis of the text of "A Painful Case" implies three distinguishable but interrelated systems of reference. First are the historical and biographical circumstances bearing upon its composition: his brother's account of the Clara Butt concert (the Gluck aria in particular) and the other cultural events contemporary with it; the events in Joyce's life from the same period, such as his declaration of apostasy; the circumstances under which "A Painful Case" was written in Trieste; his abandonment of the *Chamber Music* poems to their fate in his brother's hands; the birth of Giorgio; his public lecture in Trieste on English poetry; and his feelings of guilt for his abandonment of his father.

The second system of reference is in the mind and weltanschauung of the narrator of "A Painful Case." This detached voice delivers with brittle economy the brief and sad story of a Dubliner at the turn of the twentieth century though with evident awareness of how he is similar to other figures in other places and times, and even in ancient myth and popular folklore. This narrator, therefore, allows us to observe his selective but systematic borrowings from various nineteenth-century and contemporary Irish writers, including de Maupassant, Tolstoy, Wagner, Turgenev, Moore, and Yeats. This narrator allows us to infer, in addition, that he is familiar with the writers that Duffy reads, notably Nietzsche and Schopenhauer. The narrator implicitly invites his readers to savor the manner in which he has adapted various masterworks— such as Wagner's *Tristan und Isolde* and Tolstoy's *Anna Karenina*—and minor fictional experiments—such as Turgenev's "Diary of a Superfluous Man" and Moore's "John Norton"—providing for a rich cross-cultural aesthetic experience. The narrator is highly attuned to his own narrative manner and diction, savoring his ability to ventriloquize the language of the priest, the moralist, and the newspaper reporter.

Third, we are allowed to see James Duffy as he sees himself. He is a keen and constant self-observer. He is not a traveled man, but his mind is well stocked between his early education and two decades of serious reading. Although he thinks of himself as possessed of an emancipated mind—witness his appetite for German culture—his mental habits and private language show that he thinks more in the idiom and image of the Gospel of Saint Matthew than of the banking business he endures. He admires the Germanic genius; and no passive consumer, he plays Mozart's music, translates Hauptmann, and keeps a daybook into which he enters reflections drawn from German intellectuals. The effect of this disciplined acculturation shows in his self-absorption, his detachment, and the formality of his own mental language, which the narrator occasionally parodies.

In the imagined world of "A Painful Case," Mr. Duffy's story is of a failure of the heart: in the first place to respond to the offer of God's love, and in the second to respond to that of Mrs. Sinico. The music of Mozart and Wagner—by allusion and by structure in the text of the story—represents the prospects and the failures of love. Nietzsche's rejection of Wagner's romanticism—implied by Mr. Duffy's reading—is also an issue here. It is one of the devices by which he is held to account in the implied differences between the structuring work, *Tristan und Isolde*, and his personal situation. At this stage in his life, Joyce is implicitly choosing the spirit of this opera over Nietzschean cynicism. Therefore, just as the story is a self-criticism of his youthful flirtation with Nietzschean nihilism and his consequent callousness, it is also a self-criticism of the aestheticism of which the young Stephen Dedalus is possessed. "A Painful Case" is a powerful expression of the relationship between spiritual nihilism and other forms of self-deception.

The story finally comes down to this: Christian love is both spiritual (the love of God experienced by the contemplative soul) and social (the love of humankind). Duffy is offered both, temporarily practices each, and then on the rational grounds of disbelief and artistic detachment, rejects each in turn. He chooses Nietzsche over Christ and music over the subject of music. As with his Christian vocation, so with Mrs. Sinico: he could have had contemplation with Christian engagement (the workmen's group) as he could have had both music and love. The story is therefore an account of a soul in retreat from grace: a depiction of its declivity into damnation.

Although this direction may appear liberating, considering Joyce's own vector during this period of his life,[2] the unhappy conclusion of the story—that Mr. Duffy's final state is worse than his first—urges us to be cautious about such easy judgments. This reading of the story—that it is about the rejection of grace—therefore shows that if Joyce considered the effects of Catholic hegemony in Ireland the source of paralysis—the standard received view—then the embrace of a reactive skepticism is similarly paralyzing. The story is a caution to freethinking. We must also bear in mind what Stanislaus—no friend of Catholic piety—wrote about his brother's attitude towards spiritual questers independent of a tradition guided by the Holy Spirit through the Reformation, the Enlightenment, and the Industrial Revolution:

> Jim professed a great contempt for the morality of the Irish Mystics. He said their leaving the churches was useless and nominal, for when they left them they tried to become latter-day saints. Even as such they do not compare either for consistency, holiness, or especially charity with a fifth-rate saint of the Catholic Church. (CDD 156–57)

Joyce grew up in the only Catholic nation that, so far as he could judge, actually practiced what it preached and had not sold its Celtic birthright for a mess of (Anglo Saxon and Protestant) pottage (CW, 166). He was aware of the generosity bequeathed on Ireland by that inherited culture. Despite centuries of colonial exploitation, systematic impoverishment, and persecution, the Catholic Ireland that he knew had an energetic missionary outreach to the English-speaking globe, renewing a tradition that had a precedent on the European continent during the early middle Ages.

Most of the evidence and the conclusions are original. I have eschewed fashionable attitudes towards Joyce's work. Contemporary theories, for all their striking of liberating postures, admit more about the state of academic cultural politics than about the exquisite pleasures of Joyce's work. Neither the axes ground by the cultivators of modish political complaints nor Occam's austere razor will cut it. The theorists who matter here are those who are agents in Duffy's moral world. Respect for Joyce's meticulous text—trivial and quadrivial—requires that (unless the reader has a memory better than mine) page and line references be used throughout. In developing this argument, I hope therefore to escape Cranly's censure, "—I can see, he said, that you are about to make obvious remarks" (*P* 235.1–2).

2

The Dublin-Trieste Cradle

Delivery

The seventh story in the order of composition, "A Painful Case" is the eleventh of the fifteen stories of *Dubliners*. The last of the adult group, it looks both forward and backward to the stories of the thwarting of private aspirations and the disappointments in the spheres of social and public life. Written from the perspective of a concealed narrator, it employs the technique of free indirect discourse of which Joyce was by this point a sophisticated practitioner. The opening sentence, for example, must strike unsuspecting readers as a curious mixture of imprecision and posturing: "Mr James Duffy lived in Chapelizod because he wished to live as far as possible from the city of which he was a citizen and because he found all the other suburbs of Dublin mean, modern and pretentious" (*D* 107.2–5). Its awkward and apparently tone-deaf repetitions ("lived . . . live . . . city . . . citizen . . . suburbs . . . Dublin") clash with the formality of its opening ("Mr James Duffy") and the sententiousness of its close ("mean, modern and pretentious"). This does not betray any degree of ineptitude on the narrator's part, but rather exhibits his ability to ventriloquize his subject. Without any rhetorical cues, we overhear some of the tics of Mr. Duffy's interior monologue, its repetitions suggesting his mental habit of regarding his fellow citizens with condescension. In the same stroke we are listening to the officious tones—drawn from the culture of print—in which (on behalf of his bank) he has become accustomed to address others.

Like many of these stories, it arranges the action in a dialectical sequence of three scenes (the portrait of Duffy, the Duffy-Sinico moiety, and Duffy's reaction to Mrs. Sinico's death). These broad structural divisions comprise five sections, the last of which has three phases:

1: Four paragraphs. The exposition, establishing Duffy's character and circumstances (*D* 107.2–109.16).
2: Eight paragraphs and one direct quotation. The dramatic development, describing the Duffy-Sinico relationship (*D* 109.17–112.11).
3: One paragraph. The four-year interlude (*D* 112.12–27).

4: Two narrative paragraphs. Mr. Duffy's first reaction and the newspaper report (*D* 112.28–115.14).

5: Seven paragraphs comprising three movements:

a. Mr. Duffy's second response, in his room (*D* 115.15–116.2)

b. Mr. Duffy's third response, in the pub (*D* 116.3–33)

c. Mr. Duffy's final response, in the Phoenix Park (*D* 116.34–117.34).

The most obvious structural point to be made is that the final seven paragraphs complement the opening four in their treatment of Mr. Duffy as a solitary. Section 1 offers the thesis of Mr. Duffy's purported self-sufficiency and social detachment, section 2 presents the antithesis of his foray into personal engagement (for example, we do not learn of his relationship with the Irish Socialist Party until he subsequently tells Mrs. Sinico, *D* 110.31–111.8), and section 5 is the synthesis of a deeper and comprehensive disengagement from "all the living and the dead."

As readers would have come to expect at this point in *Dubliners*, the deceptive simplicity of the story engages in a few remarkable narrative tricks. Whereas sections 1 and 2 follow a "normal" narrative sequence (building from the introduction of the characters into a sequential narrative), after recounting the rupture of the Duffy-Sinico relationship, the narrative changes pace and order. First, there is the "fast-forward" interlude, which in fifteen lines moves through a four-year period (*D* 112.12–27). Next comes section 4, which reverses the time sequence: we read Mr. Duffy's reaction to a newspaper article of which we have not yet been apprised. Part 5 slows the action to provide for a searching dilation of Mr. Duffy's thoughts and feelings before the pace of the narrative comes to a complete stop.

At this point, the most general observation is that Joyce's favorite physical exercise—learned from his father and shared with his brother Stanislaus—informs the relationship between the form and content of "A Painful Case": walking. The Joyces were inveterate long-distance walkers: John Stanislaus in the course of his duties as collector of rates, and the brothers on weekend excursions, which ranged the whole city of Dublin, its suburbs, and nearby Wicklow mountains. The appetite for and intimacy with Dublin topography that Joyce acquired from his father made this propertyless pair Dublin's mental landlords. In this story, Joyce endows his alter ego, James Duffy, with a similar taste for healthy exercise; an activity that, despite his personal alienation from the life of the city, earns him the name "citizen" (*D* 107.3–4) in this particular Joycean sense.

Of this pastime there is much in "A Painful Case" and at different speeds: Duffy's "roaming" about the suburbs, striding "firmly" and "quickly" from the city, "wandering" about the Phoenix Park with Mrs. Sinico, or haltingly and in reverse, while rehearsing, in the final three paragraphs, the occasion that ended their "walking out." Walking thus metaphorically carries the action forward. There is an implied formal analogy between the narrative ordering and pacing of "A Painful Case," with its variations, pauses, and reversals, turning around the consequences of a pedestrian's fall (at that oxymoronic place of antipodal perambulation, Sydney Parade). Such formal expressiveness—in which there is an analogy between the action described and the formalities attending the description—was to become one of the hallmarks of Joyce's writing, especially in *Ulysses*. In this particular respect, "A Painful Case" anticipates the "peristaltic" technique of "Lestrygonians."

The story features one of Joyce's favorite literary devices: the insetting of one text within another, as a kind of expanded allusion (André Gide's *mise-en-abyme*). The technical and stylistic contrasts between the Joycean narrative and the one it encloses provide the pleasure, puzzlement, and meaning of the entire work. The hellfire sermon (117.10–124.26) and villanelle (223.17–224.2) in *Portrait* are major examples, and John F. Taylor's speech in *Ulysses* (7.828–69) a minor one. *Dubliners* has two full and express examples: Mr. Hynes's poem in "Ivy Day in the Committee Room," and the *Dublin Evening Mail* news item that Mr. Duffy reads in "A Painful Case."

Stephen Donovan has examined this paragraph in "A Painful Case" with attention to the paradoxical proposition that it is the occasion of Duffy's consternation as to its content and condescension to its vulgar style (which Donovan summarizes as "the inferior epistemological value of newspaper text," 26). He correctly notes that while its journalistic clichés reinforce Mr. Duffy's sense of his cultural superiority and isolation, it also gives him the unwarranted impression that her death was a suicide. Maria's partial song and the excerpted Father Purdon's sermon are similarly complex thematic and aesthetic presences in "Clay" and "Grace," respectively. On a decreasing scale are the expressly cited, outside the surface text but present to the mind and feelings of one or another character or of the implied narrator: Byron's "The Prisoner of Chillum" ("A Little Cloud"), Tom Farrington's "Hail Mary" ("Counterparts"), and "The Lass of Aughrim" ("The Dead").

These examples are but express representatives of an allusive method that permeates Joyce's literary procedures, the implications of which are the major object of this study of "A Painful Case." Its surface narrative sits upon an enormous, encyclopedic, and largely occluded body of cultural texts, only some of which it expressly indicates. Almost every sentence Joyce writes contains a reference to another text and writer; and the force of his text depends in large part on the relationship between the apparently "plain sense" of the prose and the thickened and deepened sense it has when the citation is apprehended, comprehended, and felt. Joyce's works are built from multilevel combinations of quotations from other works of literature, music, religion, philosophy, popular culture, history, and linguistic usages, high, low, and middle. From that point of view none of it is original. The originality is in the brilliant coalescence of scores of texts in his deceptively simple accounts of minor incidents in the lives of ordinary people. His literary genius resides in the mastery of language and narrative technique that enables him to bring a designed illumination to the opacity of deceptively transparent events. The reading of Joyce's texts is therefore a literary exercise, and the experience affords a pleasure particular to the arts.

As most readers of Joyce know, "A Painful Case" is loosely based on an incident in the life of his brother, Stanislaus, where he had a chance encounter with a lady whom he had previously met at a concert (*MBK* 158). His brother's account of that evening and its sequel, however, unwittingly conceals as much as it recounts of the original occasion, as we shall see; and it is possible to peruse his account in conjunction with the historical record to elucidate "A Painful Case." His transformation of materials from his then seventeen-year-old younger brother's diary and conversation into the experience of the forty-year-old James Duffy is radical in several ways, not the least of which is its anticipation of the imaginative feat of representing the contrasting experiences of young Stephen Dedalus and middle-aged Leopold Bloom in *Ulysses*.

As his letters to Stanislaus during the spring and summer of 1905 show, the story took shape in his imagination along with three others during that time. In February James chides him for his taciturnity and solemnity: "no more bile beans, brother John" (February 7, 1905, *Letters* II: 81), cited in the story. Beginning sometime in late July or early August ("Counterparts" was finished on July 15), he produced the first draft by the middle of August (*Letters* II: 105).[1] This manuscript, minus a sheet or two, has survived (*JJA* 4.95–134). It is in Joyce's hand, bearing the original title, "A Painful Incident," written in ink on twenty sheets, numbered 1 to 20, on the back of the first of which is a list of laundry that Nora had evidently taken in. He moved on directly to "Ivy Day in the Committee Room" and "An Encounter," before returning to the manuscript in late September. Around September 24 he wrote to Stanislaus to enquire about some historical details regarding the administration of police and ambulance services (*Letters* II: 109).[2] On October 10, he got his first critical review of the story: Stanislaus reported that "A Painful Case" was their

Aunt Josephine (Murray's) favorite story, but in the correspondent's opinion it is too big for the form (*Letters* II: 115). Ten months later, when Joyce was in Rome, he returned to this story, and between August 12 and the end of the month added "about five pages" (*Letters* II: 148, 151, 153). Some of these additions can be seen, in the form of marginalia to the original manuscript. He returned, once again, to "A Painful Case" in mid-October, 1906 (*Letters* II: 182), but even three weeks later, was still dissatisfied (*Letters* II: 189). By this time, he had turned over the manuscript of *Chamber Music*—"a record of my past"—to Stanislaus for his arrangement and publication (*Letters* II: 182). He had come to realize that his future lay in prose fiction: "A page of 'A Little Cloud' gives me more pleasure than all my verses" (*Letters* II: 182). By contrast with "A Little Cloud," however, which he had finished in early 1906, he was still worrying about "A Painful Case" the following November, admitting to Stanislaus that "After the Race" and "A Painful Case" were "[t]he two worst stories" in *Dubliners* (*Letters* II: 189).

In addition to the apparently first full draft we have a fair copy of this second draft, on twenty-three numbered pages incorporating the marginalia, additional pages, and other internal changes to the first draft (*JJA* 4.136–79). Although this major revision was done, therefore, during August and September 1906, it bears the date upon which he evidently completed the original draft, August 15, 1905. The surviving proofs of the 1910 and 1914 attempted publications and the Grant Richards (1914)/Huebsch (1916) printed editions indicate that Joyce made some further emendations to the text of "A Painful Case" (*JJA* 5.237–41; *JJA* 6.130–43; Slocum and Cahoon, A8). The reference in "A Painful Case" to Sydney Parade was among the issues to which George Roberts objected, holding that it was potentially libelous. The impression that these repeated references in Joyce's correspondence and the surviving manuscripts give is that he had unusual difficulties with this story. The surviving manuscript record from this period in Joyce's life is spotty, however, and therefore unreliable as an indicator of his compositional methods.[3] One effect of his well-recognized dissatisfaction, however, is that the story has not received the close respect and attention it deserves both for its technical virtuosity and for its significant place in the development of *Dubliners* and as the harbinger of one of the many potential books that *Ulysses* ousted from Joyce's expanding imaginative ambitions.

Revealing Revisions

Joyce's composition of "A Painful Case" is the best documented among the stories in *Dubliners*. Almost all of the original draft manuscript and Joyce's revisions of it (*JJA* 4.95–134), another subsequent, and complete, handwritten draft (*JJA* 4.136–79), partial late page proofs for the aborted 1910 Maunsel publication (*JJA* 5.237–42), and the complete 1914 page proofs survive (*JJA* 6.130–43). An examination of the process through which the text of "A Painful Case" comes to us produces a few insights into his methods and discipline as a writer.[4] The original complete draft is evidently the transcription from some rougher version or collection of notes. This can be inferred from the occasional skipping of a word and the variations between the compression and loose scrawl in the handwriting. The manuscript record shows Joyce's familiar preference for French dashes before and after direct quotations and his growing antipathy to hyphenated words, except where predominant usage required them. Thus we get "phrasemongers" (1914 proofs, but not before then), "bookcase," and "handmirror."

The first draft shows that he had from the beginning a very clear idea of the design of the story: the five-stage organization including the fast-forward intermission (*D* 112.12–27), and the several stages of Duffy's conflicted reaction to the story in the *Evening Mail*.[5] Even the placement of the paragraphs preceding the newspaper story remains much as originally committed to paper. He was from the start very clear about the dramatic structure and ironic cast that his narrative was to take. The first draft also shows that he had a surer sense of its overture than of its closure. The portrait of Mr. Duffy is practically unrevised from first to last drafts, whereas two of the latter stages gave him much trouble. The first of these, the inquest report in the newspaper, is considerably expanded from the brief first version. He was for a long time displeased with his effort to reproduce the proper tone of a newspaper report: the draft has many changes and revisions. The second of these, the manner in which Mr. Duffy responds to the news of Mrs. Sinico's death, he had to revise several times, with many indications of changes in language and emphasis. He struggled to find the language which judiciously represented Mr. Duffy's intellectual self-awareness and to assert an appropriate tension between the narrative voice and Mr. Duffy's own idiom.

He revised extensively the newspaper account of the inquest. While some of these changes are acknowledgments of the historical record (the implications of some of which will be discussed below), he adjusted the fictional names in a manner consistent with the social composition of the cast of characters. The Deputy Coroner and the solicitor representing the railway company, Mr.

Leverett and Mr. H. B. Patterson Finlay, have conspicuously Anglo-Saxon names (the Dublin City Coroner in 1904 was named Sir Henry L. Harty; and in the original MS, the company lawyer bore the Irish Catholic name, H. B. Higgins). In the first two manuscript drafts, before Stanislaus informed him that the City of Dublin Hospital ambulance served Sydney Parade, he had a Dr. Cosgrave of Vincent's Hospital give medical evidence. This was a nod to Joyce's friend at the time, Vincent Cosgrave, who was studying medicine at Saint Vincent's Hospital. The clever inscription did not survive the necessary change of hospitals (or Joyce's subsequent break with Cosgrave), so that in the 1914 proofs a Dr. Halpin succeeds to the role of medical examiner. Like this pair, the names of all of the lower functionaries in the story are native Irish Catholics: Lennon, Dunne (Kilbride in the original MS), and Croly. The railway porter in charge of the Sydney Parade Station bears the name "P. Dunne." Were he to be relieved of the semianonymity of his Christian initial, he would, most likely, emerge as no more than just another "Paddy Stink." He suffers, in addition, the indignity of bearing one of the commonest Irish Catholic surnames (Ó *Duinn*, "brown," is the 27th such, according to Mac-Lysaght, 132–33). Within the verbal universe of *Dubliners*, moreover, where "Browne is everywhere," he is a figure of death, and in this instance of the motif with a particularly apt and ironic frisson. According to the *Evening Mail* report, Mrs. Sinico's body was removed from the tracks first to the platform, and thence, "apparently dead," to the station waiting room, pending the arrival of the ambulance (*D* 114.10–14). The Sydney Parade Station, under the supervision of the said P. Dunne (which Joyce changed from the historical Henry Bishop; see *Thom's Official Directory*) thus becomes the figurative *Tech Duinn*, "Dunn's House," the assembly place of those housed within that zone of antipodal wanderings, the Celtic otherworld. There they await, as Joyce would have read in Alfred Nutt's *The Celtic Doctrine of Rebirth* (1895–97), their subsequent metempsychosis (Tymoczko, 44–45, 185–86; MacKillop, s.v. "Otherworld, *Tech Duinn*").

Joyce's elision of "Kilbride" in favor of Dunne, thus accords with his design of "A Painful Case" as a redaction of the Celtic myth of Tristan and Iseult to which he was, by virtue of Mr. Duffy's domicile and his would-be liaison with another's bride, committed to develop.[6] Sergeant Croly of the Dublin Metropolitan Police (DMP) (added in the second full MS) endures the obloquy of having his name misspelled (or is perhaps the victim of an unintentional historical interference from the singular George Croly, a Protestant divine from the early nineteenth century). In contrast with the Royal Irish Constabulary, the police force in the Irish provinces, Irish Catholics were attracted to the DMP, which was regarded as a more benign fraternity, although, of course, loyal to the crown. Large numbers of Irish Catholics thus ascended into the higher ranks of the DMP. In this instance, the court reporter for the Unionist/Protestant *Evening Mail* does not recognize the Irish Catholic name "Crowley" when he hears it, and his copy editor does not either. Joyce dilates this kind of journalistic slip in *Ulysses* (L. Boom, 16.1260 et cetera); but here it is also a sly comment on the sectarian myopia of the *Evening Mail* when it reports the affairs of "mere Irish" Catholics.

The second draft makes some corrections of spelling (surprising, indeed) in the original manuscript: "sollicitude/solicitude," and "Leveret/Leverett;" and it is not until after the 1914 proofs that "*In Secretis*" is properly rendered "*Secreto*." Even so accomplished a writer as Joyce could still write, "she became his confessional to the full" (*JJA* 4.105), correcting it to "she became his confessor" (*JJA* 4.151). He vacillated, too, on the shape of the clause, "the city the lights of which seemed all that was human and hospitable" (original MS, *JJA* 4.131), which he turned into "the lights of which burned humanly and hospitably" (second MS, and 1914 proofs, *JJA* 4.177, *JJA* 6.142), before settling on "the lights of which burned redly and hospitably" (*D* 117.10–11). The original manuscript exhibits the non sequitur of having Captain Sinico hail from the inland Udine (adjusted to the seaport Leghorn), and the sentence serving a mélange of metaphors "During these years Mr Duffy retreated more into himself as the accentuated lines on his face testified" (*JJA* 4.111), subsequently withdrawn. One peculiar and uncharacteristic departure from Joyce's magisterial control comes in the penultimate paragraph of the original MS. He has Mr. Duffy gaze towards the Dublin city lights in the "august and inhospitable and inhuman night" (*JJA* 4.131). With this quotation from the execrable Sir William Watson (1858–1935), author of a collection of poems with the title *The Man Who Saw* ("The august, inhospitable, inhuman night, / glittering magnificently unperturbed"), an allusion of a veritably Chandlerian cast, Joyce nods, coming close to traducing Duffy's dry but good taste.

Most of the corrections are directed towards careful stylistic variation in the service of economy. For example, "The proprietor prepared the glass himself and took great pains to earn his customer's thanks" (first draft, *JJA* 4.125), became by the second, "The proprietor served him obsequiously" (*JJA* 4.173) where it remains, concisely drawing the unsuspecting barman into the funereal occasion in Mr. Duffy's mind. Similarly, the paragraph describing the drift of Mr. Duffy's reflections during his moiety in the public house begins with these three sentences:

As he sat there, living over his life with her and evoking alternately the two images in which he now conceived her, he realised that she was dead, that she had ceased to exist, that she had become a memory. He began to feel ill at ease. He asked himself what else could he have done. (*D* 116.22–26)

The length and syntax of the initial sentence are appropriate to its atomic weight. It contrasts Duffy's living presence with Mrs. Sinico's absence through death. It begins with three iterations of the existence to which he clings uncomfortably ("he sat," "living," and "life"), and ends with three reiterations that insist, in apparent disbelief, on her nonexistence. Embedded within this major contrast are the two images of Mrs. Sinico in Mr. Duffy's mind: the sympathetic companion and the drunken derelict. The suspension of the "and" that normally follows the second comma (after "exist") is a favorite Joycean syntactic arrangement, denoting, in this case, Duffy's repeated attempts to come to grips with Mrs. Sinico's removal. The second and third sentences, brief and parallel, express his attempts at psychic relief and moral release from these entanglements.

The original mansuscript presents an interesting contrast with this narrative clarity. It reads:

As Mr Duffy sat, living over all his life with her and evoking alternately the two images in which she came to his mind, the he realized that she was dead, that she had ceased to exist, that she was a memory. The thought fact discomposed him because his own statement of it to himself seemed something of an accusation. He asked himself what else could he have done—. (*JJA* 4.127–29)

This is surprisingly inept: it is too convoluted and repetitive ("him . . . his own . . . himself . . . himself") and pointlessly legalistic or diplomatically evasive ("statement . . . seemed something of an accusation"). Besides, if "thought" and "fact" refer to Mrs. Sinico's death, then "discomposed" is too close to "decomposed" to avoid an unfortunate near pun. Rather than extract Mr. Duffy from the embroilments of the first sentence, it snares him and the readers still further. What became the third, and short, sentence, began with another long listing following the dash. Between the first and second drafts, however, he spotted these inadequacies, and tidied them forthwith.

Joyce's revisions show his careful attention to the distinctions between the tones of the narrative voice and those of Mr. Duffy, while indicating their occasional interfluence. He refined, on one hand, the narrator's control of metaphor in describing Mr. Duffy's lodgings as "somber" rather than "gawky" (*D*

107.5) to accord with his "saturnine" temperament (first draft, *JJA* 4.95, 97). He excised overstatements of Mr. Duffy's self-rule like he "never yielded to any love" (*JJA* 4.109), and Mr. Duffy's overcommitment to the use of "squalid." On the other, he usually struck oil at the first plunge, as when recording Mr. Duffy's reaction to Mrs. Sinico's impulsive gesture in breaking their unspoken platonic troth. There is a paragraph break, and then "Mr Duffy was very much surprised. Her interpretation of his words disillusioned him" (*D* 111.33–34). This pair of sentences, following the momentary pause, perfectly catches the idiom of Duffy's studied self-righteousness. Joyce worked to fine-tune the narrator's tone, balancing familiarity with formality, detachment with judicious irony. For example, from the first draft, he gave the two evening newspapers their street names (recognizable to newsboys and sophisticates alike), while turning the original colloquial error "water-croft"—inappropriate in the vocabulary of the superior narrator—into the proper "water-carafe" (*D* 112.31). He sharpened the expression of Mr. Duffy's observation that "the interest they [the workmen] took in the question of wages" from the trite journalese of "excessive" (*JJA* 4.107) to the precise clerical Duffyism, "inordinate" (*D* 111.5). Similarly, the revision of the sentence characterizing Captain Sinico's dismissal of his wife from his "gallery of pleasures" as "sincere" rather than "thorough" raises the narrator's detached irony a palpable notch.

In all of these revisions, we see his balance of idiomatic nuance and metaphoric consistency. A nice example of this is his revision of the sentence describing Duffy's diplomacy in arranging his parting from Mrs. Sinico: "As he did not wish their last interview to be troubled by the influence of their ruined confessional they met in a little confectionery shop near the Parkgate" (*JJA* 4.109–11). This sentence remained intact from first to last except that "confectionery shop" became "cakeshop" (*D* 112.1–4). The "ruined confessional" moves them from her room, the site of the crisis in their relationship, to the public space, the shop by the Parkgate. The substitution of "cakeshop," then, avoids a euphemism Mr. Duffy is unlikely to employ, while also silencing the too-close echo between "confessional" and "confectionery" potentially amplified by the image of enclosure.

These manuscripts provide ample evidence, therefore—if we need it—that Joyce was a careful reader of his own work. The seeming innocence and spontaneity of the written script is deceptive, however. There is much more "going on" behind its apparent diffidence. What the revisions show, however, is that even in a story he considered unsatisfactory, to paraphrase Hugh Kenner's remark about *Chamber Music*, "he worked hard to prevent it from writing itself" (28).

Constable 57 E

As Joyce was completing the first draft of "A Painful Case," Nora's first pregnancy was nearing its fruition (Giorgio was born on July 27). Meanwhile,
the relationship between James and Nora was going through its first serious
crisis: they were in continuous financial straits and considered separation; he
was drinking a lot, and she was given to bouts of weeping, depression, even
threatening suicide.[7] Writing frankly to Stanislaus in apprehensive anticipation of the approaching birth in the middle of these dire circumstances, he
admits, "I do not know what strange morose creature she will bring forth
after all her tears" (July 12, 1905, *Letters* II: 95). These are the immediate circumstances under which he brought the melancholic Duffy and his tearful
Mrs. Sinico into the world (even in her late pregnancy, Nora was taking in
washing to meet domestic needs, *JJA* 4.96). He produced the original draft of
"A Painful Case" between July 15 (when "Counterparts" was completed) and
approximately one month later, that is, within the first three weeks of his son's
birth, in early August (*Letters* II: 105; *JJII* 765 n. 30). On July 29, 1905, he reported to Stanislaus: "The child appears to have inherited his grandfather's
and father's voices. He has dark blue eyes. He has a great taste for music"
(*Letters* II: 101). In the original manuscript of "A Painful Case" completed
on August 15 (*JJA* 4.179) he bequeaths two similar portions of the Joyce inheritance on Mrs. Sinico: her "very dark blue eyes" and her musical talent
(*JJA* 4.103).

As he viewed his own infant son, he was evidently struck with renewed
force by feeling for his own father, bereft (by a year's exile) of his firstborn and
(by three years' decease) of his fourth son, George Alfred. He compensated
for the latter loss by naming his firstborn Giorgio. These feelings were to be
revisited twenty-six years later when with the death of John Stanislaus and
Stephen's birth, he wrote the most heartfelt of his poems, "Ecce Puer": "May
love and mercy / Unclose his eyes" (*JJII* 642–46). A surprising but quintes-
sential Joycean detail indicates that when the following year he returned to
the manuscript of "A Painful Case," his father's paternity was very much on
his mind.

"A Painful Case" gave Joyce a lot of bother. The manuscripts that survive
from these years are unrepresentative, so it is hard to tell whether this was
unusual or not. These MSS show that he redrafted and emended the impersonal passages describing the inquest and Mr. Duffy's personal grieving.
One passage—deceptively innocuous—gave him particular difficulties. It
reads:

Police Sergeant Croly deposed that when he arrived he found the deceased lying on the platform apparently dead. He had the body taken to the waiting-room pending the arrival of the ambulance.

Constable 57 E corroborated. (*D* 114.10–14)

Now, the original draft of the newspaper account of the inquest makes no reference to any police testimony or to the removal of the body for medical examination.[8] The scrawled crossouts and marginal additions are evidence that Joyce inserted these few sentences in a couple of stages and after some revealing vacillations. A careful examination of *JJA* 4.117 provides evidence of this reconstructed sequence of additions and changes (*D: Text and Criticism* 230). Transcribed *verbatim*, it reads:

Constable 43 D corroborated. The evidence of the f the evidence forego-ing evidence, saying that he had the body removed to the waiting-room of the station. Police sergeant Croly Constable 43 D said that when he arrived he found the deceased lying on the platform. He had the body taken to the waiting-room pending the arrival of the ambulance. Con-stable 42 D corroborated. 457 D

In the order of composition, the passage begins in the middle of the page ("Constable 43 D . . . ambulance"), goes to the top ("Constable 43 D . . . Po-lice sergeant Croly"), and concludes at the bottom ("Constable 42 D . . . 457 D"). These additions introduce the police testimony into the proceedings. The testimony came from one constable, serial number 43 D. His testimony corroborates the previous witness, P. Kilbride of the railway company. Con-stable 42 D—otherwise silent—corroborates his colleague's testimony. The DMP patrolled in pairs, at least at night, as their appearance at this time and place indicates. They are numbered sequentially like the night watchmen in *Ulysses*, 65 C and 66 C. The letter signifies that this latter pair belongs to the C Division, headquartered at Store Street, and charged with patrolling the North Side inner-city streets including Bella Cohen's address (*U* 15.4336). In assigning the pair of constables in "A Painful Case" to the D Division, then, he was guessing that Sydney Parade Station lay within their purview. Some five weeks after finishing the first draft of the story he enquired of Stanislaus whether Sydney Parade was in fact under the jurisdiction of the D Division of the DMP, and which hospital served the same area (ca. Sept. 24, 1905, *Letters* II: 109). In his reply (October 10, 1905, *Letters* II: 115), Stanislaus did not answer the question about the division, but indicated that it was part of the Pembroke Council area. So "D" it remained through the 1906 second fair copy of the story (*JJA* 4.165). The relevant pages in the 1910 galleys, which Joyce himself had attempted to steer through to publication with George Roberts, and would have been able to correct for himself, are lost. In any event, the reference is adjusted to the historically accurate E Division by the 1914 proofs (*JJA* 6.139). The E Division of the DMP patrolled the Rathmines and Pembroke suburbs, including Sydney Parade (J. V. O'Brien, 182).

So much for scrupulous fact. We have also to account, however, for the change in the constables' numbers. Returning to the adjustments to the first draft, we can see that at some point in the first set of revisions, he decided to insert Mrs. Sinico's age at death, which was first "42 years" (*JJA* 4.117, 163) and subsequently, "forty-three years" (in the 1914 proofs, *JJA* 6.138, and *D* 113.23). He then apparently realized that he had more of a stake in Mrs. Sinico's age than in the constables' serial numbers (42 and 43 respectively), and to remove the pointless coincidence, changed one of these numbers from 42 D to 47 D (the faded ink of each of these entries indicates that they were done in the same stroke).

In subsequent revisions he replaced one of the constables with Sergeant Croly (no serial number) and again changed the remaining constable's number, this time to 57 E (the manuscript clearly betrays the 4 overwritten in fresh ink into a 5). This final number—to all appearances arbitrary, but arrived at through several reconsidered adjustments, as we have seen—meant something to Joyce. A constable with the same serial number, 57 C, appears in *Ulysses* (10.217). Now, we know from his letters to Stanislaus from Rome during August of 1906 (*Letters* II: 148–53) that Joyce had returned to the "A Painful Case" manuscript about which he was dissatisfied and that had lain untouched for a year. By the time he was making these and many other changes and additions, Giorgio Joyce was one year old, and his father, John Stanislaus Joyce, who was born on July 4, 1849, had recently turned fifty-seven. The clear inference is that Joyce here inscribes an allusion to John Stanislaus Joyce, who, despite his many faults, had in a singularly redeeming instant, begotten the author of "A Painful Case." The extirpation of the coincidences between Mrs. Sinico's ages (42 and 43) and the constables' serial numbers may have suggested the link with his father's recently begun fifty-seventh year. This hypothesis is supported by the evidently simultaneous insertion of "Leoville" into the manuscript as the name of the Sinico residence in Sydney Parade (*JJA* 4.119): the Joyces lived for a year at "Leoville," 23 Carysfort Avenue, Blackrock, 1892–93 (*Letters* II: lv). In this arch filial birthday greeting, therefore, Joyce has his own father corroborate a story about the false consciousness of celibate detachment.

These aspects of the narrative framework illuminate the would-be Father Duffy's fear of the sorrow that human bonds engender. He is a perfunctory member of the Duffy family (if anyone calls him "Uncle James" on his Christmas visits, it doesn't register, *D* 109.10–11), his father's death receives a notice that does not surpass the retirement of a junior partner (*D* 112.23–24), and Mary Sinico merits no recognition beyond "the daughter" (*D* 110.22). With his dismissal of Mrs. Sinico he had also the prospect of his own paternity. These considerations have a bearing on Mr. Duffy's reflection on Mrs. Sinico's sad and lonely decline: "His life would be lonely too until he, too, died, ceased to exist, became a memory—if anyone remembered him" (*D* 116.31–33).[9] Whatever immortality his literary or intellectual interests might have conferred—his Hauptmann translation (unpublished), his ideas (unwritten)—is unrealized. Neither the readers of the National Library catalog or the back-files of newspapers will rescue his name even temporarily from oblivion. He lacks what Joyce had in addition to their works and valued above them: a son.

One of the constants in Joyce's creed is the mystical bond between father and son. His Paris Notebook contains this sentence copied from Aristotle, "the most natural act for living beings which are complete is to produce other beings like themselves and thereby to participate as far as they may in the eternal and divine" (*JJII* 204 n). His letters during this period express his profound pride in his paternity. At the end of September 1905, for example, he declared that "[p]aternity is a legal fiction" (*Letters* II: 108), later telling his sister Eva that "the most important thing that can happen to a man is the birth of a child" (*JJII* 204). Many years later he told Louis Gillet, "I can't understand households without children. I see some with dogs, gimcracks. Why are they alive? To leave nothing behind, not to survive yourself—how sad!" (*JJII* 204 n).

Touched by Her Voice

Between his reading the account of Mrs. Sinico's death in the *Evening Mail* and his fading into the obscurity of the night, Mr. Duffy's adjustment to the news of her death passes through four distinct phases. The manuscript record reveals that the broad development of these stages was from the outset clear in Joyce's mind.

The first (4) runs from Duffy's first readings of the account in the restaurant, through his quick walk home, and to his rereading of it yet again, on reaching his bedroom (*D* 112.28–115.14). The impersonal, dissociated usages, implying mechanical motion, and a suspended consciousness, "his hand stopped. His eyes fixed themselves" (*D* 112.29–30), indicate Mr. Duffy's instant and, indeed, protracted frazzle (this period of the action takes approximately two hours: from 4:30 to about 6:30 p.m.). Dumbfounded, denying, yet transfixed, he gives the column several readings. He is so abstracted by the news that he forgets his dinner chilling on his table.

Until apprised of the contents of the newspaper paragraph (*D* 113.19–115.14), readers are similarly denied access to Mr. Duffy's thoughts and feelings, or even what he has reread with such concentration. They might, in retrospect, realize that they passed by some premonitions of the subject of the newspaper report in the images of the "cold white grease" (*D* 113.3), Mr. Duffy's breath "condens[ing] in the wintry air" (*D* 113.13), and "the failing light" (*D* 113.16) that attended its fictional reader. Most actual readers would have to, like Mr. Duffy, "read the paragraph over and over again" (*D* 113.1–2) to recognize the import of these oblique directions. In an effort to steel his denial of what he has just read, Duffy reverts to the discipline he has practiced for so many years: a prompt and bracing walk.

The second stage (5 a.) shows Duffy gathering his self-possession and rereading the account in his bedroom. Brooding on the brutal physical description of Mrs. Sinico's end, he works himself up to a paroxysm of Nietzschean revulsion at her weakness of will (*D* 115.15–116.2). The free indirect discourse of this paragraph implies Mr. Duffy's penchant for obsessive self-righteousness by the use of repetitions, "The whole narrative of her death revolted him and it revolted him to think" (*D* 115.18–20), and "Not merely had she degraded herself; she had degraded him" (*D* 115.24–25). In delivering himself of this harsh and unfeeling judgment (never pausing to utter even a perfunctory RIP), he replicates in death her husband's cruelty in life. The unconsciously nautical images by which Duffy rehearses her decline—"she had been unfit . . . one of the wrecks . . . how could she have sunk . . . ?" (*D* 115.28–32)—enable the narrator to echo Captain Sinico's "dismissal [of her] . . . from his gallery" (*D* 110.19–20), thus intimating the unwitting collaboration between the males in her life. Poor Mrs. Sinico is twice condemned by would-be Nietzschean Supermen.[10] Duffy's bout of tough-mindedness does not have sufficient stamina to sustain this iron judgment, and so he turns to the public house to escape his solitary self. This moiety seems to run for about an hour, taking him to the twilight's last gleaming, around 7:30.[11]

Third (5 b.), in the Chapelizod bar, with the help of some clarifying whiskey, he tries to draw closer to the existential mystery (*D* 116.3–33). Despite his attempted abstraction from his drinking companions, their physical presence, their production and erasure of their spits, and their discussion of an imagined real estate (a paradox parodied by its remove in space and social class from their sawdust floor and heavy boots), he is so disconcerted that he begins to hallucinate: "he thought her hand touched his" (*D* 116.4). Bracing himself against this attack on his nerves, he regains his rational objectivity, distinguishing between memory and trustworthy observation. The narrator's steadying voice conveys the assurance that the workingmen are as reliably examples of physical reality as the newspaper report is of the accident at Sydney Parade. Mr. Duffy reassures himself with the unavoidable, objective inference that "she was dead, that she had ceased to exist" (*D* 116.23–24). This epistemological examen produces the moral self-questioning about the relationship between his choices and that nonexistence. A brief spasm of sympathy for her unhappiness—the loneliness that drove her to alcohol and death—takes him back to himself.

Fourth (5 c.), on his walks to and from the Magazine Hill (*D* 116.34–117.34), he retraces, in part, the last perambulation with Mrs. Sinico four years previously. During this walk the hallucination returns: he has a growing sense of her presence. Whereas in the bar "he thought her hand touched his" (*D* 116.4), he now—about one hour later ("after nine o'clock," *D* 116.34)—apprehends it more proximately and in images that the lapse of four years has not erased: "At moments he seemed to feel her voice touch his ear, her hand touch his" (*D* 117.4–5). This presence he verifies by the very aspect that in life repelled him so: her touch. Now he seems to feel the touch of her hand and the sound of her voice—singing and speaking (a point subliminally impressed on the readers in that hers is the only voice they hear directly in the narrative). He now thinks that out of a probably exaggerated sense of his own significance in her life that he has "sentenced her to . . . death" (*D* 117.17). He acknowledges his simultaneous aesthetic recoil from the "venal and furtive" act of sex, which revulsion he also rationalizes as evidence of his moral rectitude. The lovers lying by the wall compose for him an image of what he and Mrs. Sinico could have become (they had sought out "the most quiet places" for their rendezvous). This morally self-deceiving repugnance for physical love has made him, he thinks, complicit in a murder. But by regarding the surrender of his personal independence as an "entanglement" like this, he has not really changed, but reverted to the type of the spoiled priest. Whether or not he has substantially contributed to her death, he is no murderer. His is a greater, and indeed the only unforgivable sin: despair.

In these final six hours of "A Painful Case" then, as he reviews his potential moral culpability, Mr. Duffy pursues a series of attempts to verify the seemingly impossible news of Mrs. Sinico's death: by carefully rereading the newspaper account, by contemplating the fact of death, by re-examining his previous conclusion of her nonexistence, and, apparently, by encountering something like her ghostly spirit accompanying him part of the way (in a pattern of discernment similar to that pursued by the boy in "The Sisters"). Now, while the manuscripts indicate that Joyce had an assured sense of the direction in which he was steering Duffy through this dense moral argument, one of the sentences—indeed, the climactic one in this sequence—seems to have given him some trouble. Originally, it read: "At moments in the stillness her voice seemed to touch touched his ear so and he stood still. to listen" (*JJA* 4.131). Revised, it reads: "At moments he seemed to feel her voice touch his ear, her hand touch his. He stood still to listen" (*D* 117.4–6). His revisions lay stress on the image that has been dormant for four years in Mr. Duffy's memory: the touch of Mrs. Sinico's hand. The trauma of this evening's news has reawakened, we might say, this repressed and traumatic memory. Yes. But the scene that Joyce has set before his readers' imaginations is more nicely honed than this. It calls for another look.

Here is the grieving Mr. Duffy, rehearsing his last intimate walk with Mrs. Sinico, recalling with vivid clarity her touch and her voice, precisely twenty-four hours after her death: he left the bar for his hour-long walk through the Phoenix Park "after nine o'clock" (*D* 116.34), and she was killed by the previous evening's "ten-o'clock slow train from Kingstown" (*D* 113.26–27). She had met her bodily end (separated from her "spirits") on a November night (*D* 113.6, 115.5). At this point the salience of an apparently immaterial detail arises: why does Joyce schedule the inquest within twenty-four hours of the accident, and early enough in the day, moreover, to have it reported in the afternoon newspaper (*D* 113.21–24)? The manuscript revisions document Joyce's deliberate shrinking of the lapse of time between the accident and the inquest, from "Wednesday last" (*JJA* 4.117) to "yesterday evening" (*D* 113.24). Since inquests are normally held at least one week after deceases (to allow time for the performance of the autopsy, the briefing of attorneys, and the calling of witnesses), why did Joyce, a severe critic of factual lapses in others (for example, George Moore's presumption about suburban train schedules, *JJII* 193) in this case so strain verisimilitude?[12] A clue to the solution may well lie in his apparent simultaneous revision of the sentence commented on above, "At moments he seemed to feel her voice touch his ear, her hand touch his" (*D* 117.4–5). This firm and felicitous sentence is designed to leave readers in no doubt that as he walks through the park, Mr. Duffy is revisited by the hallucination he banished in the Chapelizod bar. If Mrs. Sinico's ghost temporarily accompanies him along the winding paths, reminding him again of their former intimacy, then the word upon which the story makes its exit, "alone," has a loaded account.

In popular folk culture, the ghost of a deceased person is most likely to appear following cases of violent or premature death, or of suicide. This manifestation is usually visual, but can also be in the sound of a voice, an embrace, or a touch. It occurs most frequently at the place of greatest trauma or the scene of death, and is most likely to be observed around Halloween or before interment, decreasing thereafter for about one year.[13] Joyce's partiality to such phenomena needs no special emphasis: in Stuart Gilbert's words, he "had none of the glib assurance of the late-nineteenth-century rationalist" (viii). By contrast with most of his readers a century later, he was deeply skeptical about the truth claims of science and psychology, and shared with his contemporaries deference to the occult and to superstitions.[14] He had what John Gordon calls "Orphic" propensities: "Joyce was a realist, but his reality was different from ours. He believed in things, or in the possibility of things, that most of us consider beyond the pale, and the evidence is that one of them was ghosts" (241). Such a partiality to preternatural phenomena is often found among those who can no longer subscribe to a system of supernatural belief.

There are good reasons, then, to consider Mrs. Sinico's appearance to Mr. Duffy as a particular fictionalization of an aspect of one of Joyce's most personally traumatic experiences. After tortuous and protracted suffering, May Joyce died on August 13, 1903, aged forty-four (*JJII* 136). Her death was devastating to the Joyce family, leaving so many young children dependent on an alcoholic, improvident, and, indeed abusive and violent father (see for example, *CDD* 28). Joyce felt partially responsible for her death, as he admitted to Nora (*Letters* II: 48). Despite his growing agnosticism, he accompanied his sister Margaret on the midnight after her death to await the appearance of their mother's ghost. Margaret told Father Godfrey Ainsworth—in an interview many years later—that she saw her in the brown habit (of the Third Order Franciscans) in which she was buried (Ainsworth, 6–8; *JJII* 136, 760 n. 30). His mother's death gave new force to a prophetic dream-epiphany Joyce had experienced some months before (#34, *Poems*, 194), later used in *Ulysses* (15.4203), and must have recalled another from the previous year (#23, *Poems*, 183) where he encountered the dancing spirit of his recently deceased brother George. He was predisposed to respect the paranormal.

In any event, whatever his experience in the early hours of the morning of August 14, 1903, he was sufficiently impressed to borrow from the National

Library (the following October) the most thorough and up-to-date study of paranormal phenomena at the time, Frederic H. W. Myers's two-volume book, *Human Personality and Its Survival of Bodily Death* (Costello, 212).[15] Even though the surviving version appears to have been actually written some time later, the original autograph of "A Painful Case" bears the inscription "15/8/1905" (*JJA* 4.134). Joyce was always attentive to anniversaries. Whether out of filial piety, because the story came to him on the second anniversary of the apparition, or out of a superstitious conflation of the two with the feast celebrating the bodily Assumption of the Blessed Virgin into Heaven, we do not know. It is most likely that the portion of the story that would give him the most trouble did so because it embraced such Orphic phenomena and the feelings they engendered.

Excluding the truth claims of religious revelation as unscientific, Myers sets out to subject "divine things" to objective study (II: 279). He wishes to desacralize and expand familiar religious postulates to embrace the whole range of psychical phenomena (II: 119). His immediate province is a scientific investigation of the evidence that some elements in the person survive death. His investigation of hundreds of paranormal cases is both systematic and exhaustive, running through 1300 pages. He concludes that there is a unifying principle of each personality as an indwelling soul that remains in existence after somatic death.

A descendant of Swedenborg, Myers considers that it is possible to conduct a detached study of sleep, hypnotism, genius, trance-manifestations, and telepathy. He hypothesizes that within the individual, there are different segments of the personality operating independently of and unknown to each other, and sometimes apart from the bodily organism. He proposes that we are living in two worlds. The waking personality is adapted to the needs of earthly life, while the personality of sleep maintains the fundamental connection between the organism and the spiritual world by supplying it with psychic energy during sleep. Experiments in hypnotism prove the independent operation of these different segments, with separate streams of memory and consciousness, all working through the same organism (I: xliii). Characters of genius have the capacity to draw on powers that lie too deep in this subliminal self for the ordinary person's access or control, so that an inspiration of genius comes through a subliminal uprush into the supraliminal self (I: 71). Persons of distinction (including saints) have made a sane and fruitful effort to absorb strength and grace from an accessible and inexhaustible source. Similarly, telepathic messages are direct transmissions of thought from one living person to another (I: xxv).

He postulates that the subliminal self is the principal, deepest, and the most enduring element of the self (I: xl), and that while various kinds of manifestations of the subliminal self are disintegrative, incoherent, or morbid, they also provide indications of higher faculties. Cases of telepathy exhibit the spirit emancipated from the ordinary limitations of organic life, which can be demonstrated to persist even after organic death, thus showing a relation between the subliminal and the surviving self. All subliminal action may be called automatism and regarded under the form of messages conveying information from the subliminal to the supraliminal self, in either a sensory or a motor form (I: xl).

Myers takes issue with the popular idea of a ghost as the chimera of a deceased person communicating with the living (II: 3), holding that this is but one manifestation of the general condition he postulates. We must look for, rather, "a manifestation of persistent personal energy" continuing after the shock of death (II: 4).

He cites numerous cases of telepathy between the living and those who are about to die. At the same time he admits that while there are far more cases in the record of manifestations of the spirit from those recently dead to the living, they are the least reliable and of little scientific value. There is abundant evidence of frequent appearances of spirits by relatives of the recently deceased (II: 17–19). Myers holds that in cases where the death is already known, the spirit's claimed appearance has but slight evidentiary value since such an experience might be due to the recipient's state of shock (II: 16–18). Such cases are among the most complex in nature, he claims, involving the complementary function of two unknown variables—the incarnate spirit's sensitivity and the discarnate spirit's capacity for self-manifestation (II: 19). Nevertheless, the weight of reliable evidence leads to the conclusion that souls have actually been observed in operation apart from the organism that they possess, both while those organisms are still living and after they have decayed.

He gives extensive attention to apparitions at or near the time of death, observing that while there are some that precede death (as much as by a week), they occur most frequently within the day after death, declining gradually to zero appearances by the first anniversary. A representative case is that of Mr. Dyne, in which a picture of his last scenes on earth (like the sound of the train that killed Mrs. Sinico) is impressed by a spirit on a surviving friend (I: 285). Myers reports many like that of May Joyce which occur in the middle of the night following the death.

One of the most dramatic cases in Myers's book—and which must have been of particular interest to Joyce—is reported by a Mrs. Storie from Australia. While sitting in her room in Hobart, Tasmania, at 8:30 p.m. on July 18, 1874, a certain Mrs. Storie fell asleep. She was awakened at 2 a.m., having dreamed that her brother, William Hunter, was killed by a train. One week later, she discovered that he had, indeed, been walking on the railroad tracks in Echuca, Victoria, that very same night, and had unaccountably, fallen asleep. He was fatally injured at 9:55 p.m., receiving severe injuries to his skull and ribs, precisely as his sister had simultaneously dreamed. The inquest of July 22, reported by the *Riverine Herald* and *Melbourne Argus*, concluded that death was instantaneous. In recording and analyzing this case in detail, Myers concludes it was "veridical," that is, that it was a hallucination which objective evidence confirms as corresponding to actual events, and that Mrs. Storie had experienced a genuine "psychic invasion" from her brother's disembodied spirit (I: 144–47). When the spirit seeks out a surviving friend, such a "telekinetic phenomenon" is a function of two variables: the incarnate spirit's sensitivity and the discarnate spirit's capacity for self-manifestation (II: 36–40). The conclusion from the study of many such examples is that "the kinship of souls is more fundamental than their separation" (II: 282). This is not an apologia for supernatural religion but for a preternatural order: "All life is developing itself from the primal Energy, and divinising itself into the ultimate Joy" (II: xx).

Clearly, Joyce would have been sympathetic with Myers's account of such paranormal phenomena as his own mother's appearance. The account of the Morton Prince–Sally Beauchamp case (I: 341–52), which he must have read there, may well have been Joyce's introduction to the subject that figures in *Finnegans Wake* (J. Gordon, 241), and even beyond that, to the germ of the idea realized in *Finnegans Wake*: that the sleeping state opens us to universal telekinesis. That is another day's work. In view of the coincidental elements between Mrs. Storie's case and that developed in "A Painful Case," Myers's theorizing about paranormal phenomena can justifiably be cited to illuminate Joyce's treatment of the kind of hallucination that Duffy experiences in the bar and along the walkways of the Phoenix Park. By contrast with Mrs. Storie's "veridical" hallucination, however, Duffy's was, in Myers's terms, "delusive" or "falsidical": when there is no objective counterpart within the field of vision, hearing, et cetera.

From the evidence we are given in "A Painful Case," Mrs. Sinico's emotional ties to Mr. Duffy are still sufficiently alive to enable her posthumous communion with him. The particular sensory terms in which she manifests her presence—the sound of her voice and the touch of her hand—are intimately linked with their particular relationship in life, as musical collaborators. (As we shall see, the text of the story gives us quite specific grounds for these particular, and vivid, images.) His visitation by the spirit of the departed Mrs. Sinico should have persuaded Duffy that he was wrong in holding to "the soul's incurable loneliness." His telepathic experience should have convinced him that without compromising his belief in modernity and science, he could have accepted "the existence and influence of a spiritual world" that is the common basis of both Buddhism and Christianity (Myers 2: 286–90).

Joyce's apostasy from basic Catholic spiritual doctrine and its moral corollaries was not a thoroughgoing metaphysical nihilism. It did not even go so far as an agnostic rejection of philosophical idealism regarding the prospect of life after death in some form. Whatever historical evidence that Peter Costello has that Joyce suffered from nightmares about his mother's ghost (212), it is clear that some of the more affecting moments in his fiction are those in which the living are accosted by those whose deaths they mourn (the burning of his apparently lifelong correspondence with Sister Mary Gertrude is a sad loss in what it could have yielded on this and other spiritual aspects of Joyce's personality). The text of *Ulysses* is haunted by the ghosts of Bloom's dead son and Stephen's dead mother, whose respective appearances are the most affecting moments in their fictional lives. *Dubliners* begins and ends with encounters between the living and the dead: in "The Sisters" between the spiritual son of a spiritual father (Father Flynn), and in "The Dead" between a husband and a ghostly interloper. The climactic moment in "Eveline" arises not from Eveline's relationship with the living Frank, but with her dead mother, whose "Derevaun Seraun!" is the heavily coded multilingual speech of the dead (Owens, "Eveline's Irish Swansong").

The ghostly presence of Mrs. Sinico temporarily disconcerts Mr. Duffy, for how could someone whose voice and touch he experiences so vividly be nonexistent? Had not Police Sergeant Croly deposed that Mrs. Sinico was "apparently dead" (*D* 114.11)? However, by the conclusion of the story, he has reverted to his agnostic position: that she has definitively ceased to be, as his faith in himself, and, of course, in a personal God, has ceased to be. In the final image of silence and darkness, we have a conclusion like that in "The Sisters": what began there in agnosticism here culminates in atheism.

These last paragraphs re-enact a familiar Joycean scenario—persisting from "The Sisters" to *Finnegans Wake*—of an encounter between a living character and a revenant. As do the other apparitional figures in Joyce, this one accuses the living of moral dereliction. In "A Painful Case" (the most nocturnal story of *D*), Mr. Duffy's meetings with Emily Sinico always occur in the dark or twilight or far removed from the city lights. It is again twilight when he reads of this woman who, banished from partaking in his "spiritual life" (*D* 109.9), was in the habit of going out after dark "to buy spirits" (*D* 115.5).[16] His first evaluation of her death is focused on its physicality, her "commonplace vulgar death" (*D* 115.23). However, this original positivism is disconcerted as he rehearses their final walk together—what must have been one of the major travails of her earthly existence—and their "spiritual" relationship is renewed: "She seemed to be near him in the darkness. At moments he seemed to feel her voice touch his ear, her hand touch his" (*D* 117.3–5). The emotional force of this paranormal experience so undermines his self-assurance that he feels his rational, moral, and physical natures "falling to pieces" (*D* 117.7–8). The revenant announces itself at the scene of greatest trauma during its former mortal existence, accusing wrongdoers and making a belated appeal for pity. For his part, Duffy concedes his attention, lending at this "ghosting hour conjurable . . . a divining ear" (*CM* 26). In Hugh Kenner's precise oxymoron, he "is touched by a ghost" (58). In this respect, his response is significantly different from that of the skeptical Leopold Bloom. Recalling his attendance at Mrs. Sinico's funeral, Bloom, evidently considering that her death was, like his father's, a suicide ("The love that kills," *U* 6.997), attributes this prophecy to his father: "I will appear to you after death. You will see my ghost after death. My ghost will haunt you after death" (*U* 6.1000–1001).[17]

Unlike the residually religious Duffy, that secular citizen, Leopold Bloom, does not quail at the thought. In a curious and uncharacteristic lapse of memory, Joyce has Leopold Bloom attend Mrs. Sinico's funeral on October 17, 1903 (*U* 17.1454), approximately three weeks before the climactic action of "A Painful Case" (see D. Wright, 111). Fritz Senn proposes an alternative explanation: Duffy is reading a paper that is at least a few weeks old (38 n. 5). This is very unlikely, especially in view of the narrator's phrasing of "And still every morning he went into the city by tram and every evening walked home from the city after having dined moderately in George's Street and read the evening paper" (*D* 112.24–27). The repetitions in this transitional sentence surely imply that his purchase of the *Evening Mail* is part of his daily routine (and its reading his virtual dessert). Senn's interpretation, moreover, would weaken the grounds for Mr. Duffy's ghostly encounter with Mrs. Sinico. Nevertheless, when in the end, her rejected ghost departs, he finds himself, like the boy in "The Sisters," facing a dark and silent world: in "perfect silence" he is alone (*D* 117.33–34). Exorcizing her spirit from his memory as he did her body from his life, he has rejected the last appeal to love in any form.

Constable 57 E and Mrs. Sinico's spirit are therefore an unlikely pair of flitting visitants, drawn from the familial lexicon of the Joyces and a private inscription by a prodigal son of his natural progenitors in "A Painful Case."

Durfeo ed Euridisinico

Even though it began with a chance encounter at a concert, the relationship between Mr. Duffy and Mrs. Sinico is principally sustained by their social isolation and their mutual needs for spiritual and intellectual companionship. In the account of their platonic affair, the narrator directs our attention to their discussions—or rather what we take to be her admiration for his advanced political views. It comes as a bit of a surprise, then, that the parcel returned by Mrs. Sinico contains not only his books but also his music (*D* 112.11). What music, we wonder? Rereading the story, we notice this narrative sequence:

> Little by little, as their thoughts entangled, they spoke of subjects less remote. . . . The dark discreet room, their isolation, the music that still vibrated in their ears united them. This union exalted him, wore away the rough edges of his character, emotionalised his mental life. Sometimes he caught himself listening to the sound of his own voice. . . . We cannot give ourselves, . . . The end of these discourses was that one night during which she had shown every sign of unusual excitement, Mrs Sinico caught up his hand passionately and pressed it to her cheek. (*D* 111.16–32)

In the midst of this description of Mr. Duffy's characteristic Schopenhauerean peroration there is the somewhat puzzling interpolation: "the music that still vibrated in their ears united them." Have they been attending other concerts that the narrator has neglected to identify? But surely not, since we know that they have become constant companions. So when in the final scene we read that Mr. Duffy, "seemed to feel her voice touch his ear" (*D* 117.4–5), we are a little surprised, since we have not been told much of what she has had to say. Rather than paying attention to Mrs. Sinico's opinions, he has been listening to the sound of his own voices (inner and outer). So. What is the "union" and the source of the musical vibrations of which the narrator seems to assume he has made us aware? And what precipitates Mrs. Sinico's sudden excitement and particular gesture that causes such a violation of decorum?

On the premise that the narrator has not just nodded, we review the evidence. We know that one of Mr. Duffy's pastimes is playing solo piano, although he is not sufficiently invested in it to buy one for himself: he plays on his landlady's instrument (*D* 109.4). (The Joyce households, whatever their straits, were never without this essential piece of furniture.) His musical taste, however, is curiously at odds with his personality, as we otherwise know it. Were he not religiously alienated, he should prefer the richness and control of Palestrina, Monteverdi, or Bach, to Mozart's spontaneity or (indeed) often profligate abandon upon silly subjects. But (like his creator) these tastes are not as advanced as his ideas: he prefers Mozart's operatic and concert works (*D* 109.4–5) to his contemporaries, Wolf or Mahler. He may admire Mozart's inimitable balance of exuberance and classical control, imagining himself— with many others in the late nineteenth century—as appreciating Mozart's ability to laugh through poverty and misfortune.[18] His disquisitions on this subject are likely to have passed unrecorded among the working-class materialists whose impartiality to questions of taste over those concerning wages he considered "inordinate" (*D* 111.5).

Mrs. Sinico, with an Italian husband and a daughter who is a music teacher, has a cultivated taste for vocal music. Joyce had a personal and a historical reason for giving her that name: while he was writing this story (during the summer of 1905), his voice teacher in Trieste, Francesco Riccardo Sinico, was heir to a line of music teachers in that city (McCourt, 75); the name recalled that of a soprano who appeared on the Dublin opera stages during John Stanislaus Joyce's first years there (1873–76; Jackson and McGinley, 104). This evidence, extraneous to the narrative, establishes that Emily Sinico and her daughter are most likely vocal artistes.

Although late Victorian and Edwardian Dublin had regular opera productions at the Theatre Royal and Gaiety, it was not at one of these popular and well-patronized occasions that the pair met, but at a vocal concert. The Rotunda and Earlsfort Terrace venues were, by contrast, exclusively concert halls. The historical precedent for the story—Stanislaus Joyce's meeting with a lady at a performance by the leading contralto of the day, Clara Butt and her baritone husband, Kennerley Rumford—took place in the Rotunda, not insignificantly regarding the argument here, "about the same time" as the productions of the Yeats-Moore play, *Diarmuid and Grania*, and the Carl Rosa production of *Tristan und Isolde* during the theatre season of 1901–2 (*MBK* 158–60; Jackson and McGinley, 96).

Writing about this concert over fifty years later, Stanislaus could still recall his thrill ("the music I had just heard went coursing through my veins" [*MBK* 159]). The historical record shows that the concert took place on Wednesday, April 23, 1902, and was well attended by the sizeable number of Dubliners (including Lady Cadogan) who formed what the *Irish Times* characterized as "Dublin's Butt cult." Stanislaus seemed to recall that the afternoon's program included arias from Saint-Saëns's *Samson and Delilah* and Gluck's *Orfeo ed Euridice*. We know that Stanislaus kept a diary that his brother read. We also know that James had access to an account of that particular occasion. We can therefore infer that he could imagine himself among the audience for Orfeo's despairing lament for the loss of Euridice, "Che farò senz' Euridice."

This last was evidently the pièce de résistance for Stanislaus:

Che farò senz' Euridice
Dove andrò senza il mio ben
Euridice, o Dio, rispondi,
Io son pure il tuo fedel.
Euridice, Ah! non m'avvanza
Più soccorso, ne speranza.
Ne' dal mondo, ne' dal ciel.
Mortal sillenzio
Nulla m'avvanza
Oqual mortir!
Si spezza il cor.

[Now my love has gone forever.
All my days have turned to night.
From my heart, gone forever.
Every ray of hope and light,
None can know my bitter plight.
My beloved, can you hear me?
Oh tell me, are you near me?
No sound has found me.
Silence around me!
Sorrow has crowned me.
All has ended in pain and fright.]

A paean of grief, its music and emotion ranges from the meditative to the declamatory, from lyrical intensity to wailing protest. It offered a vocalist like Clara Butt the opportunity to exhibit her considerable dramatic and expressive skills. She evidently succeeded with Stanislaus Joyce. If this, the most famous aria from Gluck's opera (1762), resonated in his memory over half a century later, he undoubtedly communicated his enthusiasm for it with his brother at the same time as he told him of the chance encounter that provided the premise for "A Painful Case." This poignant expression of emotional loss and spiritual despair, as Orpheus failed to rescue his beloved from the shades of death, seems to have also provided the cue for the resolution of the same story.

Orpheo ed Euridice was known to Dublin audiences of the 1890s (there were productions in 1893 and 1894; Reilly, 19–20), and no doubt "*Che farò*" would have been sung in the Joyce household (Joyce owned a copy of the score; Ellmann, 110). The aria is a heartrending expression of the plunge in Orpheus's emotions from a distraught bereavement to suicidal despair appreciable to those who may not be familiar with its particular placement in Gluck's opera. A survey of Raniero de' Calzabigi's libretto supports the contention that the fourth act of Gluck's opera resonated at least subliminally in Joyce's imagination when he composed the last two pages (sections 5 b. and 5 c., *D* 116.3–117.34) of "A Painful Case."

Orpheus (Duffy), a Greek musician, has lost his wife Euridice (Emily Sinico) to death by the bite of a snake ("like a worm with a fiery head," *D* 117.23). The gods—Amor and Jupiter—allow him to reclaim her from the gloom of Erebus on the single condition that he treat her detachedly: by not looking upon her. In act 4 he thus visits the netherworld in the form of a dark and labyrinthine cave obstructed by rocks and brushwood. Her shade appears by his side, and taking it by the hand, and singing to her "Ah! vieni Euridice, / Son io, del più constante amore il mio / Unico e dolce oggetto" (Oh come, Euridice, oh come! / Once more to blissful life, / To my love your return), walks beside her through the gloomy passageways.

At first puzzled, and then alarmed by her husband's unwillingness to embrace her, Euridice plaintively pleads that he at least look upon her. His anguished rejection—he is attempting to obey the gods—causes her to withdraw in anger from his companionship, claiming that death is preferable to this mental abuse. Choosing to die a second time, a victim of his apparent indifference, she falls to the ground. Distracted beyond self-control, Orpheus turns, and looking upon her, condemns her to a second, and this time irredeemable, death. He sings the distraught recitative,

Sventurato che fui!
In qual orrido abisso,
Mi gettò tal funesto amore
Cara sposa! Euridice!
Ella muor! Dì fatal!
Più il miò bnen non vedrò.
Io son, io che spensi i tuio bei di
Legge iniqua, destin crudel!
Dolor non avri eguale,
In ora sì funesta

Il mio delir, la morte
E sol quel che mi resta.

[What, great gods, have I done!
What a frightful disaster
Brought on my tortured love!
See me weeping here before you,
My beloved, I implore you!
She can hear me no more.
I have lost her again.
And I, yes, I have sealed
Her final doom!
All is over, the end has come.
I can no longer bear it.]

This leads into the "*Che farò senza*" aria, the musical and dramatic climax of the opera. The scene ends as Orpheus vainly addresses the now disappeared Euridice, "Sì la morte al tuo sen / Riconducami ancor" (Yes, I shall follow you, my love, / To the grave, and stay with you forever) and attempts to kill himself. The final scenes of de' Calzabigi's libretto void Ovid, having Amor reward Orpheus for his fortitude, and restore the pair to one another.

Joyce's subscription to act 4, scene 1, of *Orpheo ed Euridice* is both simple and complex. It accounts for Mr. Duffy's detachment from Mrs. Sinico by his acquiescence to the divinities' inhumane demands. His walk "through the bleak alleys" (*D* 117.2–3) of the park, temporarily accompanied by the spirit of the deceased Mrs. Sinico, who like Euridice, touches Mr. Duffy's hand with hers (*D* 116.4), directly parallels Gluck's libretto. Like Orpheus, who hears but cannot behold his beloved, Mr. Duffy thinks that Mrs. Sinico "seemed to be near him in the darkness. At moments he seemed to feel her voice touch his ear, her hand touch his" (*D* 117.3–5). The images upon which the scenes end— Orpheus's reflection on "Lethe's sluggish waters" and Duffy's gazing at the "grey gleaming" surface of the "shallow" Liffey (*D* 117.20–21, 107.7)—clearly reflect one another. Similarly, the anguish of personal loss leads Duffy, as it did Orpheus, into a wider and more profound despair.

Gluck's opera, moreover, may have suggested to Joyce the possibilities of more advanced plotting. Whereas Orpheus is merely playing the role of indifferent companion in order to rescue Euridice from death, Mr. Duffy is committed to a life free of emotional commitments. This sincerely held attitude, although alienated from his deeper human capacities, is the principal reason for his dismissal of Mrs. Sinico from his company (her first, and metaphoric, death), and is apparently one of the "certain circumstances" that resulted in the railway accident (her second, and literal, death). The climactic scene of the opera contributes, therefore, to the drama of the final scene of "A Painful Case." Revisiting the gloomy avenue of gaunt trees and rehearsing his dismissal of Mrs. Sinico from his life four years previously, Mr. Duffy now imagines the circumstances of her death twenty-four hours before.

The supreme irony in Gluck's opera is that whereas Euridice thinks that she is dying because she has been abandoned by Orpheus, the actual cause is that her husband is too attached to her to heed the gods' conditions for her deliverance. This irony may have contributed to Joyce's cunning management of the evidence in "A Painful Case" so that the degree to which Mr. Duffy is responsible for Mrs. Sinico's death remains indeterminate. If the historical genesis of "A Painful Case" lies in Joyce's imagining the dramatic implications of "*Che farò*," then, we have a better appreciation of the richly textured poignance of Joyce's story and of the assimilative power of his literary-musical imagination.

The part of Orpheo was written for a voice with feminine range and quality (originally for a castrato), and thus entered Clara Butt's repertoire. Clara Butt was the sensation of the 1890s for the resonance of her rich contralto, powered by her six-feet-two-inch frame, and her dramatic stage presence (Newton, 80). She made her debut, and original reputation, in the role of Orpheo. This aria therefore became her signature song for over a decade until she became Sir Edward Elgar's protégé in his *Sea Pictures* (1899). She subsequently became a figure of British national patriotism for her services to the crown: rallying the soldiers during the Great War with "Land of Hope and Glory."[19]

Stanislaus's account of the concert to his brother must have also included his impression of Saint-Saëns's Delilah's aria (from *Samson and Delilah*) recalling the resonance of Samson's voice, "Mon coeur s'ouvre à ta voix" (*MBK* 159), and Donizetti's "Il segreto" (from *Lucrezia Borgia*), even though he could not recall it many years later when writing his memoir. It is one of the great drinking songs in the operatic literature, advocating wine as the elixir of happiness: "Scherzo e beve, e derido gl'insani / Che si dan del futuro pensier" (Drink, and pity the fool who on sorrow, / Ever wastes the pale shade of a thought). Given his bitterness over the destruction that alcohol had wrought in his own household, it is no surprise that he could not appreciate with aesthetic detachment this bel canto showpiece favorite celebrating the joys of wine. The music critic of the *Irish Times* gave the palm to Clara Butt's rendition of "Il Segreto," in that it exhibited the expressive range of the contralto voice (*Weekly Irish Times*, April 26, 1902).[20] The incongruous juxtaposition of the Gluck and Donizetti arias (the forced conjunctions of tragic love and alcohol) were apparently more consonant, however, in the musical imagination that produced "A Painful Case."

Joyce's sensitivity to musical reverberations cannot be exaggerated. His mother was an accomplished pianist and his father a talented tenor: they often performed together. Similarly, Joyce's sister, Margaret, accompanied him as he sang Irish and operatic airs. She subsequently became a Sister of Mercy and deeply loved teacher of piano, violin, and voice, in New Zealand. The marked rhythms of Sister Gertrude's speech and her musical laughter struck Father Godfrey Ainsworth, who interviewed her in the early 1960s, as striking indications of the musical imagination that was her portion of the Joyce family inheritance. Similarly, Richard Ellmann records how the very performance of Germont's aria from *La Traviata* reconciled John Stanislaus with his self-exiled son (*JJII* 276–77). The bonds of love fostered and expressed through such familial musical collaboration survived the differences and distances between them, severed only by the successive deaths of John Stanislaus, James, and Margaret. Close to her own death, Sister Gertrude recalled an application of this familial gift and domestic convention to her brother's early literary efforts: when at Belvedere "James sang every line when writing his essays" (Ainsworth, 10).

When we read, then, in the final scene of "A Painful Case," that Mr. Duffy "seemed to feel her voice touch his ear, her hand touch his" (*D* 117.4–5), we are expected to recall a passage some five pages back: "he heard the strange impersonal voice which he recognized as his own. . . . The end of these discourses was that . . . Mrs Sinico caught up his hand passionately and pressed it to her cheek" (*D* 111.27–32). Duffy is (perhaps subliminally) recalling the termination, in images of reciprocal voices and ears, of his relationship with Mrs. Sinico, four years previously.

For Joyce, however, the complementary musical image would seem to reverberate too, and once again, in his brother's account of the Clara Butt concert. These repeated sentences convey a faint echo of Delilah's aria of seduction, desire, and revenge, "Mon coeur s'ouvre à ta voix." The climactic aria (which becomes a duet) of Saint-Saëns's opera, *Samson and Delilah*, it expresses in a powerfully swooning melody Delilah's conflict between her duty to avenge Philistine defeats and her attraction to Samson the man: "Ah! réponds à ma tendresse! / Verse-moi, verse-moi l'ivresse!" (Ah! respond to my tenderness! / Pour out to me the drunkenness!). The aria grows in dramatic complexity when Samson—who is similarly caught between his faith in the biblical God and his infatuation with Delila—joins her in a memorable duet. Joyce's dual citation of this aria/duet in the text of "A Painful Case" insinuates similar narrative functions. It represents the complementary conflicts racking his pair of would-be lovers: between Duffy's residual religious scruples and his natural impulses (restrained), and between Mrs. Sinico's marriage vows and her natural impulses (expressed). Whether or not consciously invoked and arranged, this item is a singular testimony to the dramatic memory and musical retentiveness of the Joycean ear. These musical allusions transmute a congeries of historical images of desire, love, music, and disappointment, heard, remembered, and fraternally rejoiced, into a fictional whole, radiant and immemorial.

The operatic arias that Clara Butt performed in Dublin that spring afternoon in 1902 were among those for which she was renowned during the first decade of her career. Stanislaus shared George Bernard Shaw's immediate infatuation. Shaw later wrote: "Witnessed her *début* as Orfeo. Loved her. Would have married her if she'd asked me."[21] Her discography indicates that she developed a popular and middlebrow repertoire—and so although such concerts did not rival opera (much less music hall), she did not perform Mozart or play to empty houses anywhere. A typical popular middlebrow concert of the period—which interposed itself between the historical Clara Butt concert and the imaginary one attended by Mr. Duffy and Mrs. Sinico—would have consisted of a mixed program of choral and solo performances, both classical and popular. John Wyse Jackson and Peter Costello's book with the suitably grandiloquent title, *John Stanislaus Joyce: The Voluminous Life and Genius of James Joyce's Father*, provides a Grand Concert Programme in which John Stanislaus appeared in 1881, which exemplifies a typical selection of operatic favorites, Irish songs, and the Twelfth Mass of Mr. Duffy's favorite composer, Mozart (120).

Mr. Duffy is a cultural highbrow. He disdains the music hall and even popular opera, reviling a society that entrusts "its fine arts to impresarios" (*D* 111.13–14). Joyce sets his standards above such pandering to popular taste and empties the hall by introducing his fictional pair to one another at a concert pleasing to patrons of cultivated musical taste. It is indeed just this quality—Mrs. Sinico's "sensibility" (*D* 109.34)—that attracts Mr. Duffy's attention. We are not informed what was on the program that evening, but if it were up to Mr. Duffy, it would most likely have included a selection of Mozart's concert arias, songs, or German lieder.

We are then led to the inference that the "union" between Mr. Duffy and

Mrs. Sinico—which began and ended in emblematic silences (*D* 109.18, 117.33)—has him accompany her song on either the piano in her little cottage in Sydney Parade or alternately in the drawing room at his boardinghouse in Chapelizod. The "vibrations" are those produced by the harmony of his piano keys and her vocal chords: in Joyce's metaphor for his own composite art, their "chamber music." And since Mozart is Mr. Duffy's favorite composer, his songs for piano and voice are sure to be among Mr. Duffy's collection of sheet music left at Captain Sinico's cottage and which she returns when the relationship breaks down.

"night's sweetmoztheart" (*FW* 360.12)

Now although Mozart's output of operatic, symphonic, choral, and instrumental music is enormous, and its technical demands require professional training, he also produced a small repertoire of art songs (forty-one, including two fragments) for domestic enjoyment. These songs do not display a creative range comparable to the song cycles of Franz Schubert or Robert Schumann; they nonetheless exemplify, in miniature, his creative development from his youth to the last year of his short life (1791). The majority of these lieder are light sketches, children's songs, or humorous throwaways. Many are delicate and playful, sentimental or pious, satiric or Masonic, and a few are serious and grave. All but one are strophic. They are written for texts in German, French, and Italian. A proportion—about twenty—appears on record labels. Of these, a handful, perhaps a half-dozen, have superior musical interest and figure in general accounts of the history of German lieder. The piano accompaniments to a small number provide densely textured relationships with the vocal melodies. Two or three of these would have most likely appealed to a man of Mr. Duffy's temperament and therefore to be among his collection of sheet music. They are the tender serenade *Das Traumbild* [The Vision] (K.530), *Abendempfindung* [Evening Thoughts] (K.523)—Mozart's serene masterpiece in this genre—and possibly *Lied der Trennung* [Song of Parting] (K.519). The K. listings indicate that these songs are the fruits of Mozart's maturity.

The circumstantial evidence suggests that Mr. Duffy and Mrs. Sinico are likely to have formed a private duet for at least these two songs together before their parting. Their first conversations would have discerned that these lieder would have comported with their common taste and complementary talents. This would have prompted Mr. Duffy to visit Pohlman's piano and music shop at 40 Dawson Street, within a short lunchtime walk from his bank, and purchase whichever German edition they had in stock. Internal evidence supports that hypothesis in the detailed ways in which they at once express a moving harmony between two voices and souls and at the same time eerily "gave distressing prophecy of failure" (*D* 109.18–19): not just of the concert—to which the narrator makes immediate reference—but of their relationship, of the conditions of its failure, of her death, and of his final desolation. These scores would then be among the music she tearfully sent him by parcel post when the relationship ended. A full registration of the poignancy of that severance depends, naturally, on an appreciation of the music and words of these songs. The premier recordings are by Irmgard Seefried (Testament SBT 1026) and Elly Ameling (Philips 22524).

The German text of *Das Traumbild* is by Ludwig Holty (1748–76):

Wo bist du, Bild, das vor mir stand,
Als ich im Garten träumte,
In's Haar den Rosmarin mir wand,
Der um mein Lager keimte?

Wo bist du, Bild, das vor mir stand,
Mir in die Seele blickte,
Und eine warme Mädcehenhand
Mir in die Wange drückte?

Nun such' ich dich, mit Harm erfüllt,
Bald bei des Dorfes Linden,
Bald in der Stadt, geliebtes Bild,
Und kann dich nirgends finden.

Nach jedem Fenster blick' ich hin,
Wo nur ein Schleier wehet,
Und habe meine Lieblingin
Noch nirgends ausgespähet.

Komm selber, süsses Bild der Nacht,
Komm mit den Engelmienen,
Und in der leichten Schafertacht,
Worin du mir erschienen!

Bring' mit die schwanenweisse Hand,
Die mir das Herz gestohlen,

Das purpurrothe Busenband,
Das Sträusschen von Violen!

Dein grosses, blaues Augenspaar,
Woraus ein Engel blickte;
Die Stirne, die so freundlich war,
Und guten Abend nickte;

Der Mund, der Liebe Paradies,
Die kleinen Wangengrübchen,
Wo sich der Himmel offen wies:
Bring' alles mit, mein Liebchen!

[Where are you, vision that stood before me
while I was dreaming in the garden,
and bound my hair with rosemary,
grown in my garden?

Where are you, vision, that stood before me,
looked into my soul,
and with a warm girl's hand
pressed against my cheek?

Now I look for you, full of sorrow,
now by the linden in the village
now in the town, dear vision,
and I can't find you anywhere.
I look into every window
where only a curtain flutters,
and have never yet
seen my darling.

Come sweet vision of the night,
come with your angel's face—
and in the light garb of a shepherd
as you before appeared to me!

Bring to me with the swan-like hand
that stole my heart,

the purple-red bosom,
that nosegay of violets.

Your big blue eyes,
from which an angel looked out,
your brow that was so friendly,
and nodded good evening;

your mouth, that paradise of love,
your little dimpled cheek,
where heaven opens up,
bring all of it with you, my darling!]

This is one of the most performed and recorded of Mozart's lieder, found on virtually every selection in the Schwann listings. Irmgard Seefried's sublime and passionate rendition shows that it demands more from the vocalist than from her accompanist: the piano score is regularly timed and closely follows the vocal melody, which, in contrast, modulates from meditative to animated tempi. Working together on this song, Mr. Duffy and Mrs. Sinico would have been aware, moreover, at some level, of how it appeared to divine their own story and their private impressions. The persona in the song is the male analog to Mr. Duffy. He praises the same features of his beloved as those observed by Mr. Duffy and which he finds so tantalizing: her "large blue eyes," that angel-like gaze into his soul, and her hand pressed to his cheek (the soaring interval in Mozart's melody gives this bar particular point). Indeed, the very impulsive gesture that caused their relationship to unravel would seem to have been prompted by that precise moment in the text of the song: "Und eine warme Madchenhand Mir an die Wanger druckte?" [And pressed a warm maiden's hand to my cheek?].

"*Abendempfindung*" [Evening Thoughts] would have been especially attractive to Mr. Duffy, since it is full of melancholy feeling and dramatic power: it is Mozart's only through-composed song (in which the melody changes from verse to verse in sympathy with their emotional development). Even though composed in 1787, in its blend of heroic and the maudlin, it anticipates a sensibility that would not come into its own for another century. And as Maurice Brown observes, Mozart's design of the persisting piano figure—"a nocturne-like accompaniment"—makes it "the true forerunner of the nineteenth-century German *Lied*" (27). It is suitable for all voices, and its slow and sustained manner does not make technical demands requiring professional training. This is Joachim Heinrich Campe's text:

Abend ist's, die Sonne ist verschwunden,
Und der Mond strahit Silberglanz;
So entflieh'n des Lebens schönste Stunden,
Flieh'n vorüber wie im Tanz.

Bald entflieht des Lebens bunte Szene,
Und der Vorhand rollt herab;
Aus ist unser Spiel! Des Freundes Träne
Fliesset schon auf unser Grab.

Bald vielleicht (mir weht, wie Westwind leise,
Eine stille Anhung zu)
Schließ' ich dieses Lebens Pilgerreise,
Fliege in das Land der Ruh.'

Werd't ihr dann an meinem Grabe weinen,
Trauernd meine Asche seh'n,
Dann, o Freunde, will ich euch erscheinen
Und will Himmelauf euch weh'n.

Schenk' auch du ein Tränchen mir und pflücke
Mir ein Veilchen auf mein Grab;
Und mit deinem seelenvollen Blicke
Sieh' dann sanft auf mich herab.

Weih' mir eine Träne, und ach! schäme
Dich nur nicht, sie mir zu weih'n;
Oh, sie wird in meinem Diademe
Dann die schönste Perle sein!

[It is evening; the sun has set,
and the moon shines in silver radiance;
thus flee life's fairest hours,
flying away as if in a dance.

Soon away will fly life's colorful scenes,
and the curtain will come rolling down.
Our play is over! Our friends' tears
flow already on our grave.

Soon, perhaps (as the gentle west wind
is borne to me a quiet foreboding),
I will end life's pilgrimage
and fly to the land of rest.

If you will then weep by my grave,
look mournfully upon my ashes.
Then, O friends, I will appear to you
and waft you heavenward.

You too, shed a little tear for me
and pluck me a violet on my grave,
and with your soulful gaze,
look sweetly down on me.

Consecrate a tear for me, and ah!
do not be ashamed to consecrate it.
Those tears will be my diadem then:
the fairest pearls].

Mrs. Sinico's singing of *Abendempfindung* would have always been suited to the time of day when they collaborated, its profound but controlled melancholy an expression of the parallel pathoi of their lives (his religious, hers marital). As the voice expresses the pain of loss, of separation for her beloved, she appeals for pitying tears. At the same time, this voice presses a survivor's guilt on its earthly beloved. The relatively simple piano accompaniment provides a classically firm underpinning to the dramatic shifts in the singing voice, as it modulates from stoic acquiescence to maudlin self-pity. At the same time, it follows, echoes, and sympathizes with the vocal lyric through nonprogrammatic arpeggios, dramatic full chords, and changes from major to minor keys (F major, C major, G minor, B-flat major, and F major). The reader who attends to the exquisite qualities of these songs—the effects of an intimate collaboration of piano and voice, requiring consonances of intonation, timing, and emotional interpretation—will gain a moving appreciation of their moment for Mr. Duffy: that he was experiencing with Mrs. Sinico a "union [that] exalt[ed] him, wore away the rough edges of his character, [and] emotionalized his mental life" (*D* 111.21–23).

The prospect that these songs constitute the most emotional expression of their failed union casts a new light upon Mr. Duffy's first effort to deal with the news of her death. While on one level his shock is moral at her pathetic decline and fall, the songs allow us to apprehend its profoundly emotional and aesthetic aspects. On the most basic level, he had to have been struck by the contrast between the expressive quality in their relationship and the banality of her end. And as he reviewed their relationship on his homeward walk, he must have been struck by the prescient matter of each of these songs: *Das Traumbild*'s account of their relationship and *Abendemfindung*'s forecast of Mrs. Sinico's imminent death and his subsequent survivor's guilt.

These songs deliver their full thematic force in the final scene of the story, however, when Mr. Duffy revisits the course of his last walk with Mrs. Sinico. It is here that *Das Traumbild* returns to the narrative and possesses Mr. Duffy's spirit. As the persona in the song stands under the village linden and gazes in the windows of the town, Duffy under the gaunt trees of the Phoenix Park and looking at the distant city lights (the narrative's transposition of the linden tree and the lighted windows), he finds himself reenacting the lover's loss of his beloved, his search for her in outer darkness, and rehearses his hope for happiness, in this life and in the next, in her love, and as Mozart's lover, he hovers between hope and despair. Just as he accompanied her when she sang *Das Traumbild*, "he seemed to feel her voice touch his ear" (D 117.4–5), and the vision implied in the song now recurs as Mr. Duffy walks with his ghostly accompaniment. Rehearsing their last walk together, the song reenters his mind, and gives a refined shaped to his grief and guilt as it rehearses their former conversations and musical collaboration. *Das Traumbild* is Mr. Duffy's last song before this musical story lapses into a permanent silence.

If *Das Traumbild* informs Mr. Duffy's perspective, *Abendempfindung* sets the terms through which he hears Mrs. Sinico's appeal from the grave. This is his "Evening Song": "Evening it is. The sun has vanished." As he steps out into the night, the text of the song starts, subliminally, to dictate the terms by which he is about to end his relationship with Mrs. Sinico. Just as "the west wind [gives] a quiet foreboding" of her ghostly approach, "The cold air met him on the threshold; its crept into the sleeves of his coat" (D 116.6–7). And just "[a]s the light failed" (D 116.3) he encounters her spirit ("he thought her hand touched his" (D 116.3–4), which remains with him until the very end when in the total darkness "he could not feel her near him" any further (D 117.30–31). Mrs. Sinico's cry from the grave to him ("Gaze mournfully upon my ashes") expresses her memory of their relationship, the pain of its loss, and regret of the vanished hope of redemption: now that she is dead, either by gradual or precipitate suicide, he is lost. The song has been the fulfillment of his maxim that "every bond is a bond of sorrow." The prominence of memory in the song helps account for the repeated sequence of death, ceasing to exist, and "becom[ing] a memory" (*D* 116.24–25, 32–33). In these ruminations, he is acquiescing in the maudlin self-pity that permeates *Das Traumbild*.[22]

A third Mozart song, *Das Lied der Trennung* [The Song of Parting], which very likely encumbered Mr. Duffy's music stand during his relationship with Mrs. Sinico, makes a momentary appearance in the story. The cry of a heart wounded by rejected love, the voice wonders if he will be forgotten, and if so, does life have any hope? Mozart moves the self-pity of the song to a dramatic climax in the spiritual despair of the last two of the seven stanzas: "Wirst du wen anders meinen, / Wirst du mich einst vergessen, / Vergessen Gott und dich" (If you love another, / if once you forget me, / may I forget God and you!). Reflecting on her death and the loneliness that preceded it, Mr. Duffy is moved to an existential meditation. Since he had demanded that he vanish from her life (and attempted to ensure it by subsequently avoiding concerts and public transportation), and she had complied (by returning his books and music), he now considers the implications of their each having attempted to live "lonely" lives.

Mr. Duffy seemed to have succeeded in banishing her memory until this evening's news. Now that she has ceased to exist, she has returned as a particularly vivid form of memory, a ghost, and will remain as some form of presence so long as he has a memory of her. But there will be nobody to confer such a postmortem existence upon this childless bachelor (*D* 116.22–33). The song concludes: "Mich warnend anzuzeiaen, / Vergisst Luise mich, / Vergisst sie mich!" (When I come in the ghostly hour, / let it be a warning that Luisa has forgotten me!).

These poignant and penetrating songs give the breath of life to the occluded bond of feeling and of sorrow at the heart of the Duffy-Sinico relationship. For each of them music was the language of the soul: for Mr. Duffy it replaced the consolations of religious hope, and for Mrs. Sinico it was a temporary displacement of affectionate love. With Mr. Duffy on the piano and Mrs. Sinico singing the lyrics, these songs—their interpenetrating vibrations concealed in the acoustic images of the narrative—conjured the possibilities and in retrospect reverberate the doom of their relationship. With its night wanderer in search of a lover sensuously idealized, these songs harmonize too (as we shall see) with the voices of the lovers from the Canticle of Canticles. Linking these songs are the "half forgotten" gum and apple whose odors occasionally escape from beneath Mr. Duffy's desk lid, sublimated into the literary endeavors by which he has tried to control and aestheticize his amorous feelings. When Mrs. Sinico attempted to raise it (or lower it) from the platonic, or aesthetic, to the personal, emotional, and potentially physical, Mr. Duffy responded with a practiced emotional withdrawal.

Duffy's "nocturnefield" (*FW* 360.12)

These reflections on the subtle art of "A Painful Case" throw an unexpected light on a question that must have struck any close observer of Mr. Duffy's daily routine. Every workday he takes the tram from Chapelizod to his "private bank," in the Irish Industrial Benefit Building at 108 Lower Baggot Street, has early dinner on South Great George's Street, most likely at Ross's Refreshment Rooms, 49 (Jackson and McGinley, 96), and from there every evening walks the rest of the way home (*D* 112.24–25). Since he is an inveterate walker (his favorite pastime is "roaming about the outskirts of the city"), and by patronizing this eating house, he is well on his way home (about one of the four miles total). To do this by the most efficient route, he passes at the back of Dublin Castle, either by Stephen and Ship Street or Golden Lane, and via Bride Street to Winetavern Street or Patrick Street, and along the Quays (north or south) to Parkgate Street and Chapelizod Road. On the November night on which he reads the account of Mrs. Sinico's death, he follows this same routine all the way home from George's Street with the alacrity of a practiced walker (*D* 113.7–13).

This workday regimen raises a couple of questions. Why does he dine so far away from his place of work and from his boardinghouse? The narrator allows us no more than the intelligence that Mr. Duffy sought to evade the society of "Dublin's gilded youth" (*D* 109.2) and because he approved of the unpretentious service of the restaurant. Since, moreover, Mr. Duffy is "set free" from his work at 4:00 p.m., for at least the winter months (which include the November evening on which "A Painful Case" concludes), he negotiates the first portion of his walk through twilight and the latter three miles solely by the light of the gas street lamps.

It is worth observing, even at this late stage in this discussion of the technique and cultural moment of the story, that just as all of its action occurs in fading light, at nightfall, or at night, nighttime is very much on the implied narrator's mind. The word "night" appears ten times in the story: more often than any other common noun. It is both the most melancholy and the darkest story in *Dubliners*; and, of course an appropriate setting even for an innocent liaison. Similarly, musical terms pervade the narrative, especially in scenes describing the relationship between Mr. Duffy and Mrs. Sinico: for example, "sheet," "score," "voice," "listen," "vibrate," "perform," "concert," "rhythm,"

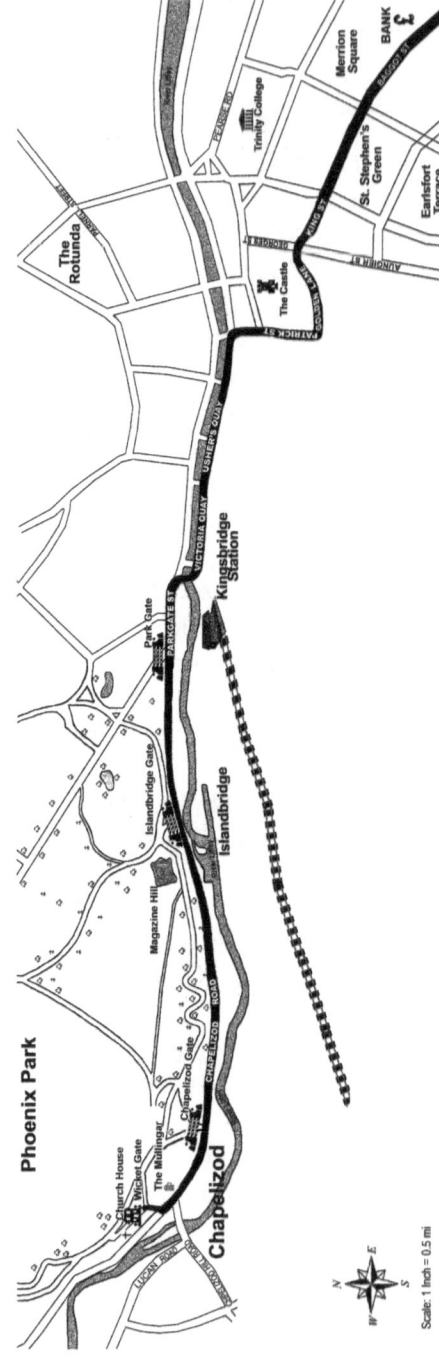

Figure 2.1. Mr. Duffy's Walks: Baggot Street–Chapelizod and Chapelizod–the Magazine Hill, Phoenix Park. Digital map by Arjun Sheoran, 2007.

"pace," "temperament," "note," "music," and "discompose." The entire action of the story follows the regular beat of Mr. Duffy's stout hazel.

Now, if he takes the most efficient way from the restaurant to his home in Chapelizod, his most usual route would take him along Golden Lane, the birthplace of Ireland's most famous composer, John Field (1782–1837). Joyce certainly knew that Field was born there, as he indicates in a letter to Constantine Curran, complaining that Dublin Tourism did not sufficiently recognize its musical citizens, William Balfe (1808–1870) and Field (*Letters* III: 449). (The authorities eventually complied, unveiling a commemorative plaque in 1988.) To identify the place Joyce had no need of official assistance, however: during his own youth, a descendant of Field taught music on Golden Lane (Bennett, s.v. "Field memorial"). The topographical metaphor is impossible to miss therefore. Having Mr. Duffy evade "Dublin's gilded youth" while unwittingly honoring the musician whose youth was spent on Golden Lane seems a deliberate irony on the narrator's part. The melancholy Mr. Duffy, the lonely pianist, regularly walks through an early hour of night past the birthplace of the composer whose distinctive cultural contribution is the musical form known as the "nocturne."

The nocturne developed by Field is "a romantic character piece for piano written in a somewhat melancholy or languid style, with an expressive melody over a broken-chord accompaniment," formally structured upon an ABA outline. Usually quiet and meditative, it suggests the gloom of night (*New Grove*, s.v. "nocturne"). Field was a virtuoso performer-composer: the supreme pianist of his generation, renowned for the sweetness and shading in his playing, the speed, evenness and purity of embellishment, strength and beauty of tone, and serenity in performance—and the originator of the style of pianism known as Chopinesque (*New Grove*, s.v. "Field, John"). Field's sixteen nocturnes are the most influential piano music of the early romantic period, adapted and brilliantly developed by Frédéric Chopin, whose emotional range was much wider than Field's. During his successful career from London, to Paris, Moscow, and to Saint Petersburg, Field was acquainted with all the leading composers of his time, including Muzio Clementi (his teacher), Joseph Haydn, Franz Liszt, and Chopin. This Irish virtuoso whose artistic home was Continental Europe is therefore one of Joyce's avatars.

In this connection, Stanislaus Joyce contributed something to the story besides the foundational incident and his dour disposition. His diary shows a vigorously skeptical mind, a pugnacious will, musical taste, and an unusual capacity for self-scrutiny. While admitting his intellectual limitations to rise to the challenge of Wagner, he records the pleasure he takes in Chopin's music: "he is, perhaps, the genius of Poland. . . . To me his music expresses deep, melodious melancholy, or with formal but most supple grace, a cold brilliant revelry" (*CDD* 46, July 31, 1904). Elsewhere in that same account, in contrasting his own "want of energy" with his brother's liveliness and "strange impulses," Stanislaus cites his preference for instrumental music over vocal, and for the smaller musical forms, including the nocturne, over the larger, including opera, favored by James (*CDD* 146–47). In an entry for August 31, 1904, shortly before his brother's departure, he records his reflections following a long walk that they had taken together that day:

> I have walked a good deal today (about twenty-two miles in all). . . . I left Jim at Sandymount at twelve and walked home. . . . I liked the night, it was clear and dry. My intimacy with Jim brings me in ways I like [*sic*]. I wrote a note to Pohlman's [music suppliers] for him in the G.P.O. on my way through town. I like the City at night, wide O'Connell Street . . . I go youngly through the late streets hearing a nocturne of Chopin's. Who but Chopin was able to write nocturnes? He lived by night. He is returned to Paris from some revel that has been brilliant, and is standing at this hour in his attic looking out at the open-dormer window. The huge pulse of life is lulled, darkness like a heavy cloud lowers overhead, and straddled roofs shine beneath him from recent rain. A melody is awake and moves with hushed weariness through the black harmonies of night, easily, almost inaudibly, changing to higher keys till light begins to be seen. . . . Neither dissembled drowsiness nor the changes from warmth into the cold night air could weaken my sense of gratification, for I was well pleased with the night. (*CDD* 72–73)

This passage is interesting for what it shows of the tenor of the fraternal relations between the brothers Joyce. In its exposé of his closeness to James, his melancholic temperament, their pleasure in walking, conversation, music, and sense of history and place, the passage informs the turn of mind that later produced "A Painful Case."

In writing "A Painful Case" as a literary nocturne, Joyce is creating the melancholic Mr. Duffy, the solitary walker, partially in the image of his dispassionate brother, and partly an expression of the alter ego to his own "joyous" self (similarly, as Stanislaus had an affinity for his nominal countryman "the genius of Poland," James had for the Doctor of Grace, after whom he was named). Like the nocturne, the story has an ABA outline: the first and third sections occurring in Mr. Duffy's lodgings and lonely routines, while the second deals with his relationship with Mrs. Sinico. All the events of the story occur outdoors, in fading light, or after dark. The inability of the main characters to develop their relationship beyond musical collaboration is its sad subject. The narrative technique of some passages in the story therefore adapts some devices familiar to musical composition. This helps account for the apparent rhetorical ineptitude exhibited in this passage where Mr. Duffy meets Mrs. Sinico at the Rotunda concert:

> Her face, which must have been handsome, had remained intelligent. It was an oval face with strongly marked features. The eyes were very dark blue and steady. Their gaze began with a defiant note but was confused by what seemed a deliberate swoon of the pupil into the iris, revealing for an instant a temperament of great sensibility. The pupil reasserted itself quickly, this half-disclosed nature fell again under the reign of prudence, and her astrakhan jacket, moulding a bosom of a certain fullness, struck the note of defiance more definitely. (*D* 109.28–110.3)

Commenting on this passage in his perceptive discussion of music in "A Painful Case," Jack Weaver observes that

> circularity, variation, and even musical retrograde (rhetorical *chiasmus*) are indicated by reversal of words as "defiant note" becomes "note of defiance." Since this is a musical occasion, uses of the word "note" also convey more than rhetorical meaning. The same must be said for the word "temperament," which suggests the manner in which the instrument is tuned. (19)

Listening to the rhetoric describing the progress of their relationship,

> Little by little he entangled his thoughts with hers. . . . Little by little as their thoughts entangled, . . she allowed the dark to fall [while in] . . . the dark discreet room, their isolation, the music that still vibrated in their ears united them. This union exalted him (*D* 110.26–111.22)

he finds that "the narrator's language contains balance, repetition, and a theme-and-variation structure" typical of musical composition (20).

Similarly, the final paragraphs of the story exhibit other rhetorical devices suggesting musical theme and variations: "he realised that she was dead, that she had ceased to exist, that she had become a memory" (*D* 116.24–25); "His life would be lonely too until he, too, died, ceased to exist, became a memory—if anyone remembered him" (*D* 116.31–33); "he felt that he has been outcast from life's feast . . . he was outcast from life's feast" (*D* 117.14–15, 19–20). And drawing attention to the acoustic quality of these last paragraphs, the narrative has Mr. Duffy attend to the double dactyls of the receding train ("the laborious drone of the engine reiterating the syllables of her name," *D*

117.25–26), before it retires musically: "He listened again: perfectly silent" (*D* 117.33). There is a formal and thematic congruency, then, between Mr. Duffy's daily routine, conducted as if it were a work of detached musical art, and his two patrons, joyous Mozart and melancholy Field.

Mr. Duffy's revulsion at her violation of the detachment required for art reflects Stephen Dedalus's position on the distinction between aesthetic and pornographic arts. For Mrs. Sinico the aestheticized moment is insufficient. She has been moved not to appreciate the moment in itself, but to some action outside the work: to convert the Mozart line into an actual gesture. Mark Heumann makes the analogous argument with respect to Mr. Duffy's literary preoccupations. By giving his feelings but a black-and-purple existence, he merely "writes himself": "why had he sentenced her to death?" (*D* 117.6–7). This is, of course, only partly true, because he resists Mrs. Sinico's suggestion that he publish his ideas. The humorous title of his commonplace book, moreover, indicates that he does not take himself as seriously as he expects others to do. The narrator goes one better: before Duffy meets Mrs. Sinico, much of his life could have been filed under the letter "B": his room stocked with books, bookcase, a bottle of gum, and bedstead; his colors black and brown; his work at a bank on Baggot Street; his lunch a bottle of beer and biscuits at Burke's; his dinner beef, cabbage, and a buff newspaper. In his daybook entitled *Bile Beans* he inscribes epigrams like "every bond is a bond to sorrow." This catalog is the narrator's writerly emblem of the "B-attitudes" in which Duffy, despite his efforts at personal liberation, is trapped.[23]

This reading of the story, then, depends on aesthetic considerations: the recognition of the relationship between the songs, their spirit and content; the relationship between their performers; and the manifold distinctions between life and art. In these respects, no less than its cunning management of free indirect discourse, dense intertextuality, and realization of what he hoped for in the musical settings of his own *Chamber Music*, it is what we would later come to recognize as the distinguishing characteristics of Joycean art.

Love, Marriage, and Moral Adjudication

"That high unconsortable one"

Chamber Music was Joyce's first creative work. A development of some early lyrics, gathered under the titles *Shine and Dark* and *Moods*, it originated in some of his epiphanies and his reading of Yeats, Paul Verlaine, and Ben Jonson. A careful arrangement of thirty-six lyrics written 1901–4 (but mainly 1901–2), it is, in Yeats's phrase that Joyce would make famous, "the poetry of a young man" (*Letters* II: 23). Joyce made several unsuccessful efforts to have this sequence published before turning it over to his brother Stanislaus, whose rearrangement of the poems finally found a publisher, Elkin Matthews, in 1907. By that time, Joyce had passed on to another phase in his own career and did not interfere with his brother's arrangement.

The Beinecke Library, Yale University, contains an autographed copy of *Chamber Music*, dated June 1905, following the last sequencing of the poems in which he took a personal interest. Within the following two months, as we have seen, he wrote "A Painful Case." There is good reason to infer, from a comparison of *Chamber Music* and "A Painful Case," why Joyce was no longer so concerned with the order, or indeed the fate, of *Chamber Music*, as he told Stanislaus on October 9, 1906 (*Letters* II: 172), and subsequently explained, "I have certain ideas I would like to give form to: not as a doctrine but as the continuation of the expression of myself which I now see I began in *Chamber Music*" (March 1, 1907, *Letters* II: 217).

We know that an enthusiasm for vocal song—for example, the love songs of the Elizabethans, John Dowland, William Byrd, and Thomas Nashe (*P* 233.6–7)—was among Joyce's artistic interests at the time he was writing *Dubliners*. He copied out some of these ayres and sang them on social occasions. During the first half of 1905, shortly before he wrote "A Painful Case," he was drawing to the close of *Stephen Hero*. In chapter XXII (May, *Letters* II: 88), he wrote:

One evening he sat [silent] at his piano while the dusk enfolded him. The dismal sunset lingered still upon the window-panes in a smoulder of rusty fires. Above him and about him hung the shadow of decay, the decay of leaves and flowers, the decay of hope. (*SH* 162)

Still fumbling with the images that had carried him through *Chamber Music*, he was on the verge of conceiving the new language of *Dubliners*. This passage is a prose reformulation of the images and rhythms of *Chamber Music* that Joyce had written during the previous four years. From its motifs of evening, silence, piano, and decay of hope, we can also infer the gestation of "A Painful Case," and, therefore, the close genealogical relations between *Chamber Music* and "A Painful Case."

If we observe the order governing the 1905 Yale manuscript, we can see that the "innocuous melody" of *Chamber Music* gives voice to a disappointed quest. William York Tindall summarizes:

The thirty-six poems tell a story of young love and failure. At the beginning the lover is alone. He meets a girl and their love, after suitable fooling, is almost successful. Then a rival intrudes. The hero's devotion gives way to irony and, at last, despair. Alone again at the end, the lover goes off into exile. (*CM* 41)

Between his composition of these poems and his reading of the page proofs, he had met Nora Barnacle, really fallen in love, and matured to the point that he could write, "It is not a book of love-verses at all, I perceive" (*Letters* II: 219). What Joyce most likely meant by this is that neither of the figures in *Chamber Music* is really a lover, but a pair of narcissists, one of whom considers himself an artist, and each of whom experiences the "other" but fails to respond in the assimilative manner we call "love." There is a relationship between the maturing of Joyce's artistry from the self-delusions of *Chamber Music* to the critical acuity of *Dubliners*, just as there is a personal maturing of the dreamy and self-absorbed Joyce in the loving presence of Nora Barnacle. In Stanislaus's tart summation, "As for his love poems, the fact is that when he did fall in love, he stopped writing them" (*MBK* 152). Just as *Chamber Music* features a young man's expression—full of self-regard, insecurity, and ineptitude—so does it idealize the young woman, who embodies a range of contradictions. Following a careful analysis of the collection, Father Boyle characterizes the woman in *Chamber Music* as

a clear Irish figure—lovely, graceful, shy, talented, passionate, affectionate, selfish, sensitive, possessive, intuitive, guilt-ridden, resentful, cold, determined—a woman of infinite variety. (28)

Her figure combines the Bride of the Canticle of Canticles, the Queen of Sheba, the Blessed Virgin Mary, Beatrice, Mercedes, Zoe, and the Vampire Lady. Tantalizing and mysterious, she is full of life and energy, shimmering with mysterious radiance and power.

As Tindall has observed, "*Chamber Music* must be regarded as the first trial of a method that was to produce his poetic, musically organized stories and *Portrait*" (58). These poems reveal Joyce's debt to Verlaine and the Elizabethans, especially Johnson. The lyric discipline acquired from these antecedents, converted to the services of prose, made Joyce an unexampled master of nuanced, symbolic narrative. Of this discipline, Hugh Kenner (paraphrasing Ezra Pound) observed, "If Joyce had not learned to write with this economy, he could not have written *Dubliners*" (32). Tindall goes on to illustrate this same point by showing the relationship between *Chamber Music* and "Araby" (56–57), the most evocative "failed romance" of *Dubliners*.

However, it is my contention here that of the five "failed romances" of *Dubliners*, "Araby," "Eveline," "Two Gallants," "The Boarding House," and "A Painful Case," this last is the most comprehensively indebted to *Chamber Music*. A close comparative examination of these two works shows how Joyce managed that transformation and was, then, free to let Stanislaus "bury the dead" and do with *Chamber Music* what he would. Joyce had moved on to the more serious work of *Dubliners*. Left to his own devices, then, Stanislaus arranged them as scattered love verses in the sequence I–XXXVI that has become the "standard" version.

Joyce's own original ordering of the songs of *Chamber Music* is, however, vital to understanding them as a whole and in relation to "A Painful Case." (Following Father Boyle's procedure [7–9], arabic numerals will indicate Joyce's order, and roman his brother's.) The 1905 sequence comprised thirty-four lyrics, with two added when he was in Rome in October 1906 (at the same time that he revised "A Painful Case"). The sequence is made up of two movements, the first upward to the consummation that is achieved in lyric XIV, and downward gradually through the subsidence of passion, external difficulties, ultimate disillusion, and finally, as in the two poems he calls "tailpieces" an Arnoldian listening to the noise of embattled waters (Boyle, 4).

But Father Boyle sees them as "an attempt at a portrait of himself as artist, as a projection of the woman he desired to meet in the world outside himself . . . and as a large philosophy dealing with human love" (28). The movement therefore is from innocence and virginity, through consummation, repentance, recrimination, and subsequent estrangement and despair. The first three lyrics introduce the lovers; their relationship begins in 4 II, gradually developing from the first hesitant approach up to the act of consummation (celebrated with religious tone in 17 XIV), declining thereafter, with a growing intellectualizing about the nature of love (34 XXXIV; Boyle, 7).

The first three songs in *Chamber Music* (lyrics XXI, I, III) compose a prelude to the sequence. They characterize the lonely artist hero. Lost in self-regard beside the river, he languidly plays sweet but funereal music on an unnamed instrument. This figure "who hath glory lost" (rejected grace), lives friendless ("His love is his companion"), and is "[T]hat high unconsortable one." The diction indicating the distanced, detached, remote, and aloof stance of this loner Joyce shifts but slightly to serve the portrait of Mr. Duffy: where "high" becomes "lofty," "scorn" becomes "careful scorn," "nor hath / Found any soul to fellow his" becomes "the soul's incurable loneliness," and "his companion" becomes "his soul's companion." The opening paragraphs of "A Painful Case" are elaborations of these core descriptors. The word "unconsortable," indicating that the hero's love relationship is but a temporary interruption of his solitary life, as Tindall observes, is key in *Chamber Music* (94). Similarly, though recast into the service of Catholic realism, Duffy's dilemma is that he still remains an emotional prisoner of his former lofty clerical aspiration. "That high unconsortable one" who "scorn[s]" the vulgar masses, this proud and gloomy Lucifer, has rejected the grace of his original election and become a forty-year-old Stephen Dedalus.

The second song (I) presents, again, this narcissistic figure of a personified but inverted ("bent") Love en route to Death. A bouquet of Pre-Raphaelite images (pale flowers, dark leaves, and weeping willows) adorns Love's brow: sweet, narcissistic, wan, and funereal. Transfigured in the first four paragraphs of "A Painful Case," they are marshaled to a detached view of Duffy (dark-haired and dark-named) alone in his Liffeyside Chapelizod playing upon his landlady's piano, or strolling Dublin's suburban environs. A particularly interesting aspect of Joyce's technical management of his materials here is his transformation of the poetic "And fingers straying / Upon an instrument" into the prosaic "His evenings were spent either before his landlady's piano or roaming about the outskirts of the city . . . these were the only dissipations of his life" (*D* 109.3–7). The expansion of the "straying"/"instrument" pairing into the multiple parallelisms of "evening"/"landlady's piano," and "roaming"/"outskirts" implies that Duffy's feckless narcissism and futile defiance are rooted in a subliminal attachment to the maternal image. This prepares the ground for the attraction he will feel for Mrs. Sinico and complements his claims to be independent of the feelings demanded by a woman and also to be detached from the life of the city. Of the instrument, we infer that it is stringed and represents some harmony between heaven and earth, implying that music expresses metaphysical or spiritual values, a major motif of "A Painful Case." The readers of "A Painful Case" who find in Mr. Duffy's mirror and lamp indicators of his onanism will be cheered to find their avatar in William York Tindall's Freudian reading of *Chamber Music* I as masturbatory (*CM* 182). The "shamebred music" combines the harpsichord on the frontispiece of the Elkin Mathews edition of *Chamber Music* with the pianos of Chapelizod and Sydney Parade. This comic outrageousness breaks down the deceptive elegance of *Chamber Music*, and moreover, points ahead to the synthesis of seriousness and jocularity that have become Joycean trademarks. These specific links between *Chamber Music* and "A Painful Case" are indications, moreover, that Joyce was a highly self-aware, and indeed, economic artist. "Like Mozart, Joyce knew what he was about from the beginning," observes Tindall, "his works, as TS Eliot remarked, are the same work, written again and again with increasing complexity" (62).

Lyric III completes the introduction of the solitary poet who, while attuned to the heavenly harps, seeks human love. A "religious wind" (Father Boyle's term) blows about him (10). Similarly, Mr. Duffy lives at an ecclesiastical address (Church House, Chapelizod), imagines himself as the proprietor of superior gifts, and in his twilight walks about the suburbs is a "lonely watcher of the skies." A similar religious or metaphysical doubling marks each work.

Song II introduces the lonely girl, playing her piano. Like the hero, she too is enthralled by narcissism, absorbed in her own music, and enfolded by the darkening twilight.

The twilight turns from amethyst
To deep and deeper blue,
The lamp fill with a pale green glow
The trees of the avenue.

The old piano plays an air,
Sedate and slow and gay;
She bends upon the yellow keys,
Her head inclines this way.

Shy thoughts and grave wide eyes and hands
That wander as they list—

The twilight turns to darker blue
With lights of amethyst.

Here the lonely girl—the hero's musical counterpart—plays the piano in the evening twilight. Like him, she is introverted and lacking in animation, as the words "wander," "sedate," "grave," "old," and "yellow" imply. The girl's "grave wide eyes" and the "deep and deeper blue" of the evening become, in "A Painful Case," Mrs. Sinico's "steady" and "very dark blue" eyes, with their defiant, and deliberate gaze (*D* 109.30–33). Similarly, the images of the twilight and lamp expand into "Many times she allowed the dark to fall upon them, refraining from lighting the lamp" (*D* 111.18–20).

Lyric IV is the lover's song as, responding to her music, he makes his evening visit at her home. The keywords here, "disconsolate" and "visitant," are transformed in "A Painful Case" into the imputations of Mrs. Sinico's marital unhappiness. Duffy's calls to the Sinico cottage, by contrast, are comically explained by the Captain's scarcely plausible inference that their visitant is interested in his teenage daughter.[1] Lyric V features the girl's singing voice. Her "merry air" has drawn him from the gloom of his book and room. Here, again, we see how these elements inform the depiction of melancholy Duffy's excursion from his translations and austere room in pursuit of his new "dissipation," Mrs. Sinico's singing voice. She is therefore the most reserved of Joyce's temptresses, the only one sufficiently endowed with "sensibility" (*D* 109.34) to entice stuffy Duffy from his study.

The subsequent set of songs (7–16: lyrics VIII, VII, IX, XVII, XVIII, VI, X, XX, XIII, and XI) raise the romance to its zenith (17: lyric XIV). In a series of songs that reflect pseudo-Elizabethan epithalamia (after Ben Jonson and Thomas Campion), Verlaine, and the Canticle of Canticles, the lovers pace the greenwood (lyric VIII), move from spring through summer, and prepare for a spiritual marriage and physical consummation. They are lightly touched with sensuality; but the lover, trammeled by his fixation on the maternal breast, and challenged by a third party, is at a loss about how to act towards his beloved. Beyond these broad anticipations of the Duffy-Sinico dating pattern (Duffy's emotional reticence, his awareness of the occasional presence of Captain Sinico and his apparent fear of social obloquy), there are a couple of notable transformations of elements from these portions of *Chamber Music* into "A Painful Case."

The pair find "quiet quarters" for their twilight walks (beneath the trees of the Phoenix Park, and perhaps in the Pinewood at Glendalough, by Poulaphouca's waterfall, Glenasmole, Glendhu, and in distant Donnycarney, all sufficiently remote points in Joyce's trysting map of Dublin); Mrs. Sinico is made unhappy by her seafaring husband's absence ("love is unhappy when love is away," lyric IX); and Mr. Duffy treats Mrs. Sinico as a mother rather than a lover responsive to her "almost maternal solicitude" (*D* 110.30) the prospect of her bosom "of a certain fulness" (*D* 110.2–3), and her acquiescent listening to his woes (*D* 110.31–111.29). By denying himself her embrace, he lives out the "sad austerities" (lyric VI) of the *Chamber Music* songs, and indulges in a maternal fantasy rather than a lover's embrace of the Other (lyrics VI, XVIII). Like the figures in lyric XX ("In the pinewood"), his relationship with Mrs. Sinico presages death rather than a renewed life (as the "enaisled" and coffin references imply). Only the jovial and mocking lyric IX ("Bright cap and streamers") anticipates the ironic glint of "A Painful Case."

Lyric XIV is the apex of the suite, a dense invocation of the Canticle of Canticles, and via epiphany #24 (Joyce, *Poems*, 184), a celebration of the consummation of sexual love. A compendium of the poet's various feminine figurations, the girl embodies the muse, the nation, the soul, the Church, and mother. She has therefore a genealogical relationship with Joyce's many versions of the universal feminine, romantic, realistic, and parodic: the girl on Dollymount Strand, Molly Bloom on Howth Head, and Gerty MacDowell on Sandymount Strand. In "A Painful Case," however, the climactic moment rudely interrupts one of Mr. Duffy's discourses, and the hitherto maternal Mrs. Sinico spontaneously springs from her auditor's chair and "caught up his hand passionately and pressed it to her cheek" (*D* 111.31–32). Just as lyric XIV is the turning point in *Chamber Music*, this is the point of reversal in "A Painful Case." And, as several commentators have noted, "A Painful Case" is the turning point in *Dubliners*.

The return sequence of songs (18–34: lyrics XIX, XV, XVIII, XIV, XVI, XXI, XXII, XXVI, XII, XXVII, XXIII, XXX, XXXIII, and XXXIV) traces the descent of the relationship from initial shame, through their parting, and to eventual despair. The lovers find themselves spiritually unmatched, their passions cool, and they are overcome with guilt and mutual recrimination. As the girl recoils under the pressures of social guilt and religious scruple, the poet withdraws to a detached and self-protective position. He rationalizes his fear of entanglement by imagining the female as a succubus. While he considers himself capable of living in a world that does not fulfill his heart's desires, he recognizes that she cannot manage without the succor of an imagined perfectibility. So as the "ghosting hour" of their relationship (and of the day and year) approach, he once more, and for the last time, mounts his agnostic pulpit, recapitulates their failed love, and prepares to accept the sleep of imminent death.[2]

A file of pallbearers, all but a couple drawn from the standing army of fin-de-siècle conventioneers, bears this paean of disappointed love to its final interment. A few make their way, resuited to modernist duties, into "A Painful Case." With the lovers' pain, for example, the environs are sympathetic—"the trees are full of sighs" (lyric XV)—whereas the Duffy-Sinico three-hour bond-breaking walk took place beneath the "gaunt trees" and "bleak alleys" of the Phoenix Park. Mr. Duffy's recoil at the prospect of "entanglements" and Mrs. Sinico's fright at his sententious dismissal of her affection, "she began to tremble . . . violently" (*D* 112.9), are surely recastings of the lines, "Dearest, through interwoven arms / By love made tremulous" (lyric XXII). And Mr. Duffy's agonized recapitulation of the affair and its ending, which is so passionate that it summons up, for a few moments, the specter of the dead. This is a reworking of the recapitulation of the tale of the "grave lovers" in lyric XXX and an expatiation of the "ghosting hour conjurable" (lyric XXVI) that provides the lovers in *Chamber Music* with the impression that they are players in a previously heard "mad tale."

Lyric XXII (Joyce's own favorite from among this group) indicts the girl's fear of passion—a true expression of her animal nature—as an expression of the sweet sentimentality of her religious view of nature. This belief in everlasting love hoodwinks her natural view of the changing moon; only a "hooded" Capuchin could consider nature perfectible. In "A Painful Case," it is Mr. Duffy who retains a view of the moon as "hooded," and who even after attempting a personal deliverance from celibate view of nature, is still a "comedian Capuchin." The hero of *Chamber Music*, with the wren (lyric XXIII), accepts that although life is brief and discordant, it is only dissatisfying to those who deny its terminus. In the final lyrics (XXXIII and XXXIV), as the seasons gather in the year, the lover hero accepts the loneliness that precedes death.

The two additional lyrics (XXV and XXXVI, termed "tailpieces"), more directly and emphatically declare the anguish upon which the original *Chamber Music* ended. In these poems, the hero is the abject and passive victim of nightmares in which he is abandoned and alone. The operative words in each lyric are "I hear": the musical harmonies of his previous life have conceded to the monotony of the elements and the metallic clangor of violent armies. The hearer is adrift in an indifferent and implacable universe. He now knows true despair. These terrifying images of metallic impersonality recur with abject emphasis in the final scene of "A Painful Case." Here too, the operative verbs are "hear" and "listen," and "the laborious drone of the engine reiterating the syllables of [Mrs. Sinico's] name" (*D* 117.25–26) makes plangent fun of his frayed emotional condition. Thus the displacement of the music that Mr. Duffy made with Mrs. Sinico by the steam pistons of the ten o'clock goods train from Kingsbridge hammering their way into the dark outskirts of Dublin City give us another take—and this time a tragic one—on the title *Chamber Music*. "A Painful Case" is the *Klagendeliede* of *Dubliners*.

"A Painful Case" is a selective redaction of one of the major themes of *Chamber Music*: the conflicts between the self, the world, and religion. Its understated surface conceals the obsessions with love, paralysis, and betrayal that underlie both *Chamber Music* and *Dubliners*. While technically inadequate to unleash its burden, *Chamber Music* transmits to *Dubliners* its author's command of symbolic forms in a manner that readers are more prepared to appreciate. This outline of the points of contact between *Chamber Music* and "A Painful Case," therefore, is a step toward identifying the genealogy of the *Dubliners* stories and showing why Joyce abandoned lyric poetry. As Tindall puts it, "If Joyce was dissatisfied with his poems shortly before their publication, it was because he had discovered in the poetic novel and story a more congenial and spacious form for embodying what obsessed him" (92).

In turning to seemingly realistic prose, Joyce abandoned the poetic diction of the 1890s: "sweet" and "soft," the most frequently used words in *Chamber Music*—representing subjective love—do not appear at all in "A Painful Case." In describing Mr. Duffy's postprandial taste, the narrator chooses the word "dessert" over the colloquial "sweet" (*D* 112.27). The economy and precision Joyce learned from Verlaine and the ironic elegance he saw in Jonson, he committed to the technical challenge of *Dubliners*. Added to the masters of short fiction whom he was reading thoroughly as he wrote these stories (Turgenev, de Maupassant, Moore), he was disciplining himself against automatic writing. The subtleties of *Dubliners* did not arise spontaneously. Readers who respond too eagerly to his relative dissatisfaction with "A Painful Case" need to be very careful about underestimating the standards he was already setting himself.

Several passages in "A Painful Case" blend images from the love lyrics of *Chamber Music* and the despairing mood of *Stephen Hero*. For example, we can detect how the images of the twilight, the lamp, and the "darker blue" of lyric II resurface in the sentence, "Many times she allowed the dark to fall upon them, refraining from lighting the lamp" (*D* 111.18–20), and in the consignment of "dark blue" to the color of Mrs. Sinico's eyes (*D* 109.31). Similarly,

Figure 3.1. Frontispiece, James Joyce, *Chamber Music* (London: Elkin Mathews, 1907).

there are many reverberations throughout "A Painful Case" of the whole suite of songs (Joyce's word for them) comprising *Chamber Music*. In designing "A Painful Case," Joyce returns to the autumnal setting ("The year, the year is gathering," lyric XXXIII), the narrative reserve, the blend of love and despair, and the dramatic rhythm of *Chamber Music*. The final paragraph of "A Painful Case" is an appropriately muffled redrafting of the cri de coeur upon which *Chamber Music* expires: "My love, my love, my love, why have you left me alone?"

Even though he had moved on artistically, Joyce retained an interest in the lyrics of *Chamber Music* as contributions to the tradition of the *lied* (March 1907, *Letters* II: 219). He evidently tried his own hand at this composite art, since he seems to have attempted, in vain, to have some of them prescribed for the 1909 *Feis Ceoil* (*CM*, 36 n. 41). He subsequently came to acknowledge his own limitations in this regard, however, describing them to Geoffrey

Molyneux Palmer (July 19, 1909) as "a suite of songs and if I were a musician I suppose I should have set them to music myself" (*Letters* I: 67). He warmly encouraged Palmer's efforts, only some of which, unfortunately, he ever heard; but thanks to Myra Russel, they are now available. Joyce would have been very pleased to find the excellent settings of some of these lyrics by distinguished composers such as E. J. Moeran and Samuel Barber (20–21).

For all the mileage that critics have traveled over the naughty double entendre of the title, nobody has observed that it is anomalous. In no sense does it refer to an intimate instrumental ensemble. Indeed, there is no evidence that Joyce had any interest in genuine chamber music: his Dublin was not Antonin Dvořák's Prague. As the harpsichord on the frontispiece of the original Elkin Mathews edition indicates (1907; Slocum and Cahoon, A3; figure 3.1), *Chamber Music* was conceived as a suite of Elizabethan ayres, or of songs for voice and "pianner" (*Letters* II: 219) in the tradition of the German lied perfected by Schubert and Schumann. This convention made its way into the drawing rooms of Victorian Dublin in the song settings of Thomas Moore and Sir Charles Villiers Stanford. It is therefore entirely consistent with the portrait of his would-be self in "A Painful Case" that Mr. Duffy would have a similar taste for the art song.

Canticle of Canticles

The last sentence of the first paragraph of "A Painful Case" is evidently designed to tantalize us with its odd assortment of odors:

> On lifting the lid of the desk a faint fragrance escaped—the fragrance of new cedarwood pencils or of a bottle of gum or of an over-ripe apple which might have been left there and forgotten. (*D* 108.10–13)

One of the features of Joycean listings is the appearance of an item that can only be partially accounted for, sending the readers back in search of a common denominator. In this instance, the denominator appears to be the faint fragrance emanating from the objects. The pencils and the gum are the tools of a man whose hobby is translation, since he probably drafts in pencil and writes his final version in ink, presumably gumming in later emendations and revisions. Sara Bershtel (and subsequently R. B. Kershner) have identified the apple as a recherché reference to Friedrich von Schiller's practice (reported by Johann Wolfgang von Goethe) of keeping decayed apples in his desk as a stimulus to his creative energies. In view of the many references throughout "A Painful Case" to German culture—an interest held both by the implied narrator and his subject—this is not unlikely. But this listing has another, and more apposite, rationale.

Thomas Kranidas observed many years ago that the narrator's selection from the contents of Mr. Duffy's double desk summons up images from the Song of Songs. These three items are distinguished from the other (unnamed) contents of the desk because of their "fragrance," and less obviously because they summarily gather images that permeate this unique book from the Old Testament. He admitted puzzlement about the narrator's point, beyond the general irony of the contrast between the sensuous—even sensual—allusion and Mr. Duffy's rigorous and rational self-rule (220).

The Song of Songs, which readers of the King James Bible know as the Song of Solomon, and Catholics call the Canticle of Canticles (*Jerome Biblical Commentary*, s.v. "Canticle of Canticles"), Joyce read as the *Canticum Canticorum Solomonis* (Vulgate) (*MBK* 259). It is an anthology of poems celebrating the joys of physical love. It is for this reason unusual among books of the Bible, and unique in that although it names twenty-one plants and fifteen animals, it makes no mention whatever of their Creator. Neither are the sexual joys it celebrates necessarily confined to marriage, although it appears to imply the prospect of a relationship that is exclusive and permanent. In view of Mr. Duffy's indifference to ordinary eroticism and detachment even from his own physical self, these references constitute a strange—even if partly occluded—presence in the story.

The fragrances of cedar, gum, and apple that might ascend from the desk of any clerkly Dubliner, could be taken by an imaginative reader with an Orientalist partiality as wafting from Northern Palestine, a land celebrated in the Canticle of Canticles: the clime of Lebanese cedars, myrrh, spikenard and honey, apples and pomegranates. These are the songs of at least three lovers—a king (traditionally Solomon), a rustic (Shulamite) maiden, and apparently her pastoral swain—each of whom is given to vivid self-expression. In the hands of the (evidently multiple) authors of these love poems, these synesthesic images praising the physical beauty of the beloved evoke images of intimate relations between the lovers and are apparently autoerotic or at least calculated to arouse the readers' voyeuristic proclivities. While most modern commentators regard the Canticle of Canticles as a loosely assembled collection of epithalamia, fantasies, choruses, love monologues, and dialogues, some readers (including Ernest Renan) have attempted to interpret them as the dramatization of a love triangle. Mainstream Christian and Jewish commentators, while wincing at the frank eroticism of the Canticle of Canticles, have attempted to read it either as an allegorical celebration of Jesus' love for humanity (or his bride, the Church), or as an expression of God's approval of sexual fulfillment within the bounds of marriage (since 3:6–5:1 implies a wedding day) (McKenzie, s.v. "Song of Songs"; *Jerome Biblical Commentary*, s.v. "Canticle of Canticles").

Any modern and open-minded reading of the text—such as one might expect from the implied narrator of "A Painful Case"—would have to concede that the primary residence of celebration is bodily (and at least premarital) love. Both of these readings are clearly accommodations to assumptions contrived by partisans of orthodox hindsight. Furthermore, as modern biblical archeology and comparative anthropology have discerned, many of the elements in the Canticle of Canticles derive from the Semitic oral tradition, itself influenced by Egyptian and Syrian love songs or rituals associated with marriage (and behind them, in the view of some anthropologists, primeval fertility rites). Embarrassed by its verve and physicality, the designers of the Catholic liturgy have admitted nary a verse from the Canticle of Canticles at any point in the calendar, or even into the modernized matrimonial ceremony. It sometimes appears among readings added by the partners in contemporary Catholic marriages, who innocent of the potential charge of impropriety that would have troubled their forbears, take comfort in the happy conjunction of vivid and sensuous poetry and biblical canonicity.

This is the context out of which the narrator of "A Painful Case" conjures up his three fragrant objects. The irony is, indeed, barbed: for the images beneath the lid of Mr. Duffy's desk—partly hidden, partly forgotten—reflect not only his repressed sexuality and his rejection of marriage, but also the scriptural or religious language that would have interpreted—however unconvincingly in the case of the Canticle of Canticles—the ultimate purposes of his bodily appetites. In other words, these references represent Mr. Duffy's alienation from his sexuality, from the religion of his youth, and from marriage itself, the sacramental institution by which the Christian tradition sought to reconcile them.

Whereas the Canticle of Canticles praises a veritable anatomical catalog of each of the beloveds' points of attraction (4: 1–5, 5: 10–16)—neck, belly, mouth, eyes, breasts, voice (the Canticle of Canticles itemizes twenty-five separate body parts)—in the tradition, apparently, of the Arabian *wasf*, Mr. Duffy allows himself to observe but four aspects of Mrs. Sinico's attractiveness: the marked features of her oval face, her blue eyes, her full bosom, and voice. Similarly, the narrator provides scant and uncomplimentary details of Mr. Duffy's physical appearance: his "long and rather large head," dry hair, and "unamiable mouth" (*D* 108.18–19). And again, whereas the Canticle of

Canticles rejoices in exotic food, wine, and intoxication as preliminary to loving conjunction, Mr. Duffy partakes of solitary plain fare, eats no dessert, despises intoxication, and recoils at the merest gesture that might intimate seduction. Nevertheless, once announced, the Canticle of Canticles—with its triangle of lovers (two dark, one light), its nocturnal searches through the city streets, its tensions and joys, separations and reunions, and its evocation of the exotic East—hovers above the action of "A Painful Case" as if it were an ironic reflection in this mirror of the presumed divine ends of our earthly loves. These images of sensuality, domestication, and repression converge in the narrator's summary observation of Mrs. Sinico's relationship with Mr. Duffy: "Her companionship was like a warm soil about an exotic" (*D* 111.17–18).

It is at this point that the relationship between one of Joyce's epiphanies and "A Painful Case" comes clearly into view:

> Her arm is laid for a moment on my knees and then withdrawn and her eyes have revealed her—secret, vigilant, and enclosed garden—in a moment. I remember a harmony of red and white that was made for one like her, telling her names and glories, bidding her arise, as for espousal, and come away, bidding her look forth, a spouse, from Amana and from the mountains of the leopards. And I remember that response whereto the perfect tenderness of the body and the soul with all its mystery have gone: *Inter ubera mea commorabitur.* (*Poems and Short Writings*, 184)

This epiphany—#24 of the forty that have survived—seems to have been written sometime in 1902 (since #19–23 are focused on the death of his brother George, which occurred on March 9 of that year, *JJII* 93–94). According to Stanislaus (who in this instance is admittedly guessing), it was provoked by a moment in Joyce's relationship with one of the Sheehy sisters (*MBK* 256–58). Returning to this epiphany some three or so years later, he transforms the gesture into that which ended the Duffy-Sinico relationship.

The vigilant eyes that both admit and conceal the inner life of the female figure are similarly transformed (via *Chamber Music*, as we have seen) into Mrs. Sinico's "dark blue eyes [whose] gaze . . . reveal[s] her . . . half-disclosed nature . . . under the reign of prudence" (*D* 109.31–110.2). Duffy sees but her iris swooning in the "enclosed garden" of Mrs. Sinico's nature. And their common imaginative link with the Canticle of Canticles identifies itself in the phrases, "telling her name and glories," the repetitions of "bidding," "arise," "spouse," and the allusions to Amana, the mountains and leopards, and the Latin Vulgate phrase that translates as "He shall lie between my breasts." This

last, bluntly censored as it enters Mr. Duffy's apprehension—for the concealed narrator does not allow us to apprehend what Mr. Duffy denies to
himself—becomes "her astrakhan jacket, moulding a bosom of a certain fulness" (*D* 110.2–3). Whereas these citations project a halo borrowed from this
minor (and distaff) biblical trope, in "A Painful Case" they cast around Mr.
Duffy's guarded stance an ironical nimbus. It is entirely apt that these texts,
which synthesize sacred and secular experience, should, in a story so close to
Joyce's own self-image as priest-artist, appear in the imaginative genealogy of
"A Painful Case."

Re-reading epiphany #24 many years later reminded Stanislaus of an amus-
ing and illuminating incident that occurred in Trieste in 1910. Accompanied
by Alessandro Francini Bruni, the two brothers attended an anticlerical comedy, *Il Cantico dei Cantici* by Felice Cavalotti (a nonentity commemorated by
a Roman street name). The vulgar abuse of this poem provoked Joyce's rage.
Stanislaus recalls

> In the interval, he told Francini, who was with us, that Cavalotti 'is a
> paunchy vulgarian whose highest ideal is a bellyful of *pasta asciutta*.'
> Francini agreed, and when we went home, they revenged themselves by
> reading *Canticum Canticorum Solomonis* in the Latin Vulgate in order
> to take the taste of *Il Cantico dei Cantici* off their mouths. (*MBK* 259)

As the form of this "revenge" reveals, Joyce's spiritual and aesthetic feelings were offended: the piece was philistine and blasphemous. The incident
evidently provoked an animated exchange between the three companions
during which Stanislaus's normally aggressive irreligion seems to have been
chastened. Concluding his account, Stanislaus observes that the Canticle
of Canticles is both a religious and a secular work, and offers an evaluation
with which his brother seemingly concurred, that it "may well be the greatest
[nuptial ballad] ever written" (*MBK* 259).

Joyce's appreciation of the Canticle of Canticles can be inferred from his
close and personal development of some of its tropes in *Chamber Music* (lyrics XIII, XV), as Stanislaus observes (*MBK* 258). Just as "A Painful Case" is
the central story in *Dubliners*, lyric XIV is the central song in *Chamber Music*,
"after which the movement is all downwards" (*Letters* I: 67). The Canticle of
Canticles appears in the narrative voices of three of the chapters of *Ulysses*
(12.1913, 14.371–72, 15.1327, 15.1333–34) and in the languages of Stephen (3.43),
Virag (15.2341), and Bloom (17.2050).

The ambivalent attitude of the Catholic Church towards the Canticle of
Canticles meant that it did not figure in Joyce's formal religious education.
It does not appear in Molly Bloom's interior monologue, nor in the language

of any of the conventionally Catholic figures in *Ulysses*. Even allowing for his usual hyperbole, Stanislaus is largely reliable when he reports that

> in Catholic homes and in Catholic schools the Bible is never read. In all the years from the time when I was at a nun's [*sic*] school at Blackrock to the time when I left Belvedere, never once was the English Bible, or Douay version, or Latin Vulgate opened or read or discussed in or out of class. (*MBK* 101)

Joyce may have come to the joys of the Canticle of Canticles independently, or, if the evidence in *Portrait* is historically reliable in this respect, by another route. More significant, however, are the imaginative implications, so far as the present investigation goes, of a passage from chapter IV. During Stephen's temporary retreat into repentance and self-accusation, when his imaginative energies were temporarily converted to spiritual discipline, he turned to a hyperscrupulous practice of the sacraments of penance and the Eucharist.

His devotion to these sacraments he strengthened by frequent visits to churches housing the Divine Presence:

> His actual reception of the eucharist did not bring him the same dissolving moments of virginal selfsurrender as did those spiritual communions made by him sometimes at the close of some visit to the Blessed Sacrament. The book which he used for these visits was an old neglected book written by saint Alphonsus Liguori, with fading characters and sere foxpapered leaves. A faded world of fervent love and virginal responses seemed to be evoked for his soul by the reading of its pages in which the imagery of the canticles was interwoven with the communicant's prayers. An inaudible voice seemed to caress the soul, telling her names and glories, bidding her arise as for espousal and come away, bidding her look forth, a spouse, from Amana and from the mountains of the leopards; and the soul seemed to answer with the same inaudible voice, surrendering herself: *Inter ubera mea commorabitur.* (*P* 152.5–20)

Now, if James Duffy's exposure to the Canticle of Canticles parallels that of Stephen Dedalus (and their uncommon creator), the allusions to it in "A Painful Case" suggest that he too, like Stephen, experienced a similar religious fervor in youth. The evidence in this section of *Portrait* provides the grounds upon which the spiritual director considered Stephen's self-imposed spiritual regimen as displaying an indication of his priestly vocation: "Perhaps you are the boy in this college whom God designs to call to Himself" (*P* 157.32–34).

The text that Stephen has adopted as the guide of his spiritual recuperation is Saint Francis Liguori's *Visits to the Blessed Sacrament and the Blessed Virgin Mary* (Gifford, *Joyce Annotated*, 207). This 244-page devotional manual comprises sixty-odd prayerful meditations directing the attention of the readers to the Real Presence of Jesus in the tabernacle. It consists of thirty-one visits, communion devotions, and a series of twenty-six "Loving Aspirations" to Jesus in the Blessed Sacrament. Saint Francis Liguori (1696–1787) was a distinguished moralist, a mystic, and singularly detached from the secular world. Early in this work he announces, in classic stoic manner, "Believe me, all is folly: feasts, theatres, parties, excursions,—these are the pleasures of the world, but pleasures which are filled with the bitterness of gall and with sharp thorns" (11). Doctrinally committed to a defense of the divine presence in the Eucharist, *Visits* undertakes to cultivate private eucharistic devotion, make reparation for blasphemies against this continuing manifestation of God's love for humanity, and amend our neglect of him in his various sanctuaries. This "old neglected book . . . with fading characters and sere foxpapered leaves" was available in several English editions during the 1890s. The most likely printing, however, that fell into the young Joyce's hands—and thence into the hands of his fictional alter egos—was the Dublin edition of 1841, under the imprint of the ubiquitous James Duffy.

These prayers and meditations strike modern readers—even observant Catholics—as embarrassing exhibitions of the pious sentimentality of another age. Conceived as fervent love letters between the putative visitor or communicant and Jesus, they are singularly weak on doctrinal solidity and saccharined over with the pale cast of piety. The author's devotion to the Blessed Virgin—which appears as fervent as that which he claims to inculcate towards the Blessed Sacrament—seems no less vivid or heartfelt. The devotional thus fails as a convincing apologia for the particular and unique manner in which God is present in the Eucharist, in contrast with the relatively distant heavenly existence of Mary or the saints.

Each of these meditations begins with a scriptural citation, the majority, as Stephen Dedalus records them, with verses drawn from the Canticle of Canticles. They are read personally and mystically and in accordance with the Catholic tradition of an allegorical hermeneutic. Representative excerpts read:

"Behold He standeth behind our wall, looking through the windows, 'looking through the lattices'" (Cant. 2: 9). Behold, O my soul, thy loving Jesus, burning with the same love with which He loved thee when dying for thee on the Cross, is now concealed in the Most Blessed Sacrament under the sacred species: and what doing? 'Looking through the lattices.' As an ardent lover, desirous to see his love corresponded with, from the Host, as from within closed lattices, whence He sees without being seen, He is looking at you, who are this morning about to feed upon His Divine Flesh. (139)

"A bundle of myrrh is my Beloved to me; He shall abide between my breasts" (Cant. 1: 12). The myrrh plant when pricked sends forth tears, and a healthful liquor from the wounds. Before His Passion, our Jesus determined to pour forth His Divine Blood from His wounds in so painful a way to give it afterwards all to us for our salvation in this Bread of Life. Come, then, O my beloved Bundle of Myrrh, O my enamoured Jesus; Thou are indeed a subject of grief and pity to me when I consider Thee all wounded for me on the Cross: but then, when I receive Thee in this most sweet Sacrament, Thou becomest, indeed to me more sweet and delicious than a bunch of the choicest grapes can be to one who is parched with thirst: "A cluster of Cyprus my Love is to me, in the vineyards of Engaddi" (Cant. 1: 13). (157–58)

A long tradition of Christian piety lies behind this kind of emotionalism. From the eighty-six homilies of Saint Bernard on the mutual affection of Christ and His bride, a Christian emulation of the eternal covenant between the Hebrews and God, to the ecstatic devotions of the Blessed (now Saint) Margaret Mary Alacoque's *Book of Devotion to the Sacred Heart of Jesus*, such effusions of piety were urged upon the laity. In this instance, they are the devotional and evangelical side of the allegorical interpretation of the Canticle of Canticles, and are very far removed from the theological and scriptural core of the Christian meditative tradition. Such "conversations" could only come from sexually naïve and emotionally arrested temperaments (as the repeated "virginal" references in the *Portrait* passage indicate).

To a young man of Joyce's intellectuality, sensibility, and knowledge of the world, his Dedalean representation of his short-lived spiritual arousal has a bemusedly sardonic edge. Joyce's own expressions of religious feelings are always circumspect and informed by the best minds that the Christian tradition bent upon the subject: those of Saints Augustine and Aquinas. His attachments, if any, are to the mystery of Christ's Incarnation and His consubstantial relationship with His Divine Father. The manner in which he was led to contemplate Liguori's reflections on the Canticle of Canticles must have given him much retrospective derisory self-criticism.

We can see the full expansion of this critique of Liguorian emotionalism in the "Nausicaa" chapter of *Ulysses*—where sexual naïveté, voyeurism, and the adoration of the Blessed Sacrament and hyperdulia ("Mariolatry") are vigorously, even blasphemously, satirized. In this chapter he is laying the axe to that particularly fibrous root of the popular religious culture he inherited. In the figure of Mr. Duffy he presents another cerebral stance that is not so liberating. Mr. Duffy's stern and earnest gloom, his rejection of Mrs. Sinico's sexual advance, and his agnostic despair, are thereby linked through the references to the Canticle of Canticles to his early religious formation and the "odour of sanctity" to which he once aspired. His lifted desk lid uncovers his repression of that once heartfelt, but subsequently embarrassing, phase of his spiritual past.

Just as the first paragraph of "A Painful Case" concludes with an Old Testament allusion to the marriage feast, the penultimate paragraph responds with a famous New Testament parable with the same theme.

The Marriage Feast

As Mr. Duffy gazes upon the lights of the city, observes the prostrate lovers in the shadow of the park wall, and reflects on his rejection of Mrs. Sinico's affection, he belatedly realizes that his stoic intellectuality has robbed him of the joys of life embraced by even the most "venal and furtive" citizens. Sensing their hostility as he stands alone in the enveloping darkness, "gnaw[ing] the rectitude of his life" (*D* 117.14), he broods on a maudlin metaphor, "he felt that he had been outcast from life's feast" (*D* 117.14–15, 19–20). The implications of his decision "to live as far as possible from the city" (*D* 107.3) return on him with fresh force as he contemplates "the empty distillery" (*D* 115.17). The "soul's incurable loneliness" about which he had previously theorized has, with the news of the death of the only person who might have loved him, now fills him with genuine "despair" (*D* 117.14).

Joyce's handling of this conclusion clearly owes a small debt to de Maupassant, whose stories he was reading in July 1905, as he sat down to write "A Painful Case." One of these stories, "A Little Walk," concerns the death of one Father Leras, a penurious bookkeeper who has for forty years led a monotonous and regular life. Dining out one evening on an impulse, and walking towards the Bois the Boulogne for the first time in his life, this committed bachelor observes the nightlife of Paris. Envying the bourgeois lovers in their carriages and disdaining the gross lives of prostitutes, he begins to recognize that the urge to live is often sordid and venal.

He realizes that his moral presumptions have come between him and a truly human existence. He realizes that he scarcely knows what love is, and is thrown into despair at the misery of his own existence.

> It seemed to him that the whole of humanity was filing before him, intoxicated with joy, with pleasure with happiness. And he was alone looking on at it, all alone. He would be still alone tomorrow, alone always, alone as no one else is alone. (377)

Joyce restrains himself from pursuing his narrative to the maudlin excess of de Maupassant's conclusion.

> He thought how good it must be when a man is old to find, on getting home, little prattling children there. To grow old is sweet when a person is surrounded by those beings who owe him their life, who love him, who caress him, saying those charming, foolish words which warm the heart and console him for everything. And thinking of his empty room, neat and sad, where never a person entered but himself, a feeling of distress overwhelmed his soul. It seemed to him that room was more lamentable than his little office. (377)

Yet Joyce appreciates the ironic potential in de Maupassant's switch of point of view at the denouement. The newspaper reports a body hanging from a tree in the Bois de Boulogne, evidently a suicide, "for which cause could not be determined. Perhaps a sudden attack of madness" (378). As he wrote to his brother, "Maupassant writes very well, of course, but I am afraid that his moral sense is rather obtuse" (July 19, 1905, *Letters* II: 99). In this instance, he exploits this technical switch to greatly understated effect, but disdains the melodramatic suicide and the overstated dream of a lost paternity, which, as we have seen, was on Joyce's mind. His repetition of the key phrase indicates Mr. Duffy's fixation on the notion of the eternal silence and darkness of damnation (the narrator tells us three times in the same passage that Mr. Duffy is in darkness).

His choice of metaphor in this dramatic context shows how his imagination is suffused with Matthean hues (more radical than Ernest Dowson; pace West and Hendricks, 703) reflected from his early clerical aspirations. He casts himself as the abject figure in Jesus' parable of the Marriage Feast:

> The kingdom of heaven may be likened to a king who gave a wedding feast for his son. He dispatched his servants to summon the invited guests to the feast, but they refused to come. A second time he

sent other servants, saying: "Tell those invited, 'Behold, I have prepared my banquet, my calves and fattened cattle are killed, and everything is ready; come to the feast.'" Some ignored the invitation and went away, one to his farm, another to his business. The rest laid hold of his servants, mistreated them, and killed them. The king was enraged and sent his troops, destroyed those murderers, and burned their city. Then he said to his servants, "The feast is ready, but those who were invited were not worthy to come. Go out, therefore, into the main roads and invite to the feast whomever you find." The servants went out into the streets and gathered all they found, bad and good alike, and the hall was filled with guests. But when the king came in to meet the guests he saw a man there not dressed in a wedding garment. He said to him, "My friend, how is it that you came in here without a wedding garment?" But he was reduced to silence. Then the king said to the attendants, "Bind his hands and feet and cast him into the darkness outside, where there will be the wailing and grinding of teeth." Many are invited, but few are chosen. (Matt. 22: 2–14)

The parable is a two-stage allegory of salvation history in which Jews and some Gentiles miss the joys of the eschatological banquet.

First, God's chosen people reject the prestige invitation, for which they are severely punished: historically (the parable is a reflection of the immediate aftermath of the Jewish War, AD 66–70). The Gentiles, some of whom fail to appreciate what they are offered, replace them: according to some commentators, this is a postscript added by the Matthean compiler to address the new, non-Jewish subjects of Christian evangelization. Even among these pagans, less prepared prospective Christians than the religious Jews, minimal standards of decorum, appreciation, and preparedness are nonetheless required. Grace may be a gratuitous gift, but it imposes some reciprocal obligations on the recipient. The parable shows, therefore, that whereas both Jews and Gentiles are offered salvation, many of them have rejected the divine call.

The banquet is a persistent biblical figure of the joys to which the believer is called and the messianic kingdom eternally delivers. It appears several places in Matthew (for example, 8: 11 and 26: 29), prefiguring the Eucharist. In this particular version, the parable of the marriage banquet, the Matthean compiler has ignored the inconsistency with Jesus' answer to the Pharisees (previously noted with regard to Mr. Duffy's lofty pseudotheological disdain of matrimony). He has, however, added the minatory tag about the "outer darkness" (which he has used before, 8: 12, and would again in 24: 29 and

25: 30). This is a well-established biblical trope, variously signifying chaos, evil, or separation from the divine presence. It is an especially forceful image in Job, for example, "The wicked man is in torment all his days. . . . He despairs of escaping the darkness . . . distress and anguish overpower him" (15: 20–24), and in a particularly forceful paradox: "Before I go whence I shall not return, to the land of darkness and of gloom, / The black, disordered land where darkness is the only light" (10: 21–22). For Saints Paul and John, Christ brought the light of grace to a world otherwise plunged in darkness (John 3: 19 et cetera, and Col. 1: 13 et cetera). Thus the phrase "life's feast" (D 117.20) refers to the eschatological reward that awaits the faithful and loving Christian, and "outer darkness" the realm beyond the orbit of redemptive grace. Its terrifying double image indicts those who refuse the invitation, whether Matthew's "useless servant" (25: 30) the Jews in his immediate historical context, the spoiled priest of Irish Catholic culture, or Joyce's Mr. Duffy. One way or another, they each refuse the call of God voiced in the person of Jesus.

This rich confluence of image and idea evidently informs the last three paragraphs of "A Painful Case." The images of feast, outcast, and "outer darkness," the ideas of the rejection of invitations to love and the resultant isolation and despair, clearly converge as emanations from Mr. Duffy's biblical imagination. The metaphor in which Duffy's regret is phrased, "he gnawed the rectitude of his life," seems less odd as a conveyance of the Matthean "grinding of teeth" expressing self-accusation. Similarly, the narrator's placing the scene at a remove from the city of Dublin, "the lights of which burned redly and hospitably in the cold night" (D 117.10–11), together with the eschatological implications of the park named Phoenix, suggest that Mr. Duffy is rehearsing his rejection of not only Mrs. Sinico's call to love, but also his previous rejection of the call to Christian belief and to the Catholic priesthood.

By the same token, then, the "despair" which he registers is not only personal, with respect to his rejection of the opportunity to share the human love offered by Mrs. Sinico, but also the invitation to the life of grace offered by Christ. His final situation is true despair: his entertainment of the prospect of incurable, and eternal loneliness. This force continues to resonate in the imagination of Joyce's Mr. Duffy even long after he thinks himself consolable only by Nietzsche's bleaker dicta. He seems to recognize and interpret the feeling upon which the story ends: "that he was alone" (D 117.34). He must know that he is having an epiphany of a demythologized Hell. In contrast with Gabriel Conroy, who is granted a preview of the Last Judgment and is offered the grace of repentance, James Duffy's paralysis resides in the closure of his soul to that prospect.

In addition, he is described, as is Father Flynn of "The Sisters," as "disap-pointed"; and that he "had neither companions nor friends, church nor creed. He lived his spiritual life without any communion with others" (*D* 109.8–9): his anti-Christian epigrams against the compatibility of love and human inti-macy; his conviction of "the soul's incurable loneliness" (expressly hopeless: since the absolute definition of damnation is the irredeemable separation from God); and his inability to seek forgiveness and repentance at the conclusion. In these theological—and eschatological—contexts, the narrator's comments, "He felt that he was alone" (*D* 117.33–34) and "he was outcast from life's feast" (*D* 117.19–20), imply not only distance from human companionship in this world, but also permanent alienation from the feast at the eternal table of the Lord in the hereafter.

To appreciate the links between the implications of this parable of the re-buff of a divine invitation and Mr. Duffy's residual clericalism, the argument must now consider a few further cultural assumptions derived from the Irish Catholic experience informing Joyce's portrait of James Duffy.

"in certain circumstances"

Throughout the story, Mr. Duffy imagines himself as a disembodied intel-lect: regarding his physical self with detachment and subjecting it to the firm discipline of an abstemious diet and a vigorous daily walk. A part-time in-tellectual, he is figured by association with his "square table" and desk (*D* 107.12), the compulsive arrangement of books, and folded newspaper. The "theories" he derives from such self-regulation fascinate Mrs. Sinico so much that she recommends that he commit them to writing. She is, by contrast, a bodily presence: described in terms of her dark blue eyes, her firm bosom, her looking "round" at the empty Rotunda (*D* 109.18–20), countering his ab-stractions with some of the "facts" of her life. The prosaic and dispassionate newspaper report of her fall, with the repellant bodily details of the manner of her undignified death shakes the security of his "lofty" abstractions. He can-not have missed, on rereading the account, the thrice-recurrent word "habit" cited among the circumstances that led to her death. Her consumption of alcohol and careless crossing of the railroad tracks had become such a daily routine, he learned. He must therefore have been chagrined by the prospect of their contrasting "habits": whereas his were the consciously cultivated self-imposed rules of a practiced ascetic, hers were the repeated lapses of a physi-cally and morally dissipated weakling, a "fallen woman." Whereas Mr. Duffy's walks are disciplined exercises, hers were of a "habitual sinner."

The newspaper account of Mrs. Sinico's death takes some time to pierce Mr. Duffy's moral armor. At first, he is revolted by the undignified details of her bodily injuries and the implications of the coroner's euphemistic avoidance of the language of social shaming—that she was a habitual alcoholic—whereas later he accepts (rightly or wrongly) that he is partially responsible for her disgrace and death. The language of the newspaper report, the phrase "in view of certain other circumstances of the case" (*D* 114.28–29), however, conveys more than this gross implication for Mr. Duffy. The Deputy Coroner's report echoes the terms in which Mr. Duffy considered that "in certain circumstances he would rob his bank" (*D* 109.14–15). In that instance, Mr. Duffy was engaging in an airy Nietzschean flight of moral fantasy. The coincidence of phrasing in the latter instance, however, presents him with an embarrassing and personal moral dilemma.

As they appear in the design of "A Painful Case," the Deputy Coroner's remarks imply complex ironies, dramatic and verbal. The delicate phrasing of his reference to Mrs. Sinico's chronic alcoholism is a professional cliché and a journalistic euphemism so revolting to Mr. Duffy (*D* 115.22–25). The Deputy Coroner's duty does not extend beyond establishing the immediate cause of death. In reporting the judgment, the *Evening Mail* cannot, in turn, without running afoul of the strict laws of libel, print what is found or admitted in open court. It does not, therefore, go beyond what the potential litigants, Captain Sinico and his daughter, admit of these "circumstances": Mrs. Sinico's "intemperate . . . habits" and nocturnal purchase of spirits (*D* 115.2–5).

Captain Sinico's testimony—that he and his wife had been happily married until two years before—is consistent with the narrator's observation that he thought that the object of Mr. Duffy's attention was not his wife, but his daughter (*D* 110.18–19), but contradicts the narrator's previous assertion that he had ceased to pay her attention for at least the previous four (*D* 110.19–20; 115.1–2).[3] Readers of "A Painful Case" are not privy to any moral misgivings that he might entertain arising from his contribution to her fall. We do infer that Mr. Duffy's rejection of Mrs. Sinico's feelings for him plays at least a contributory role in her decline and premature demise. He was, after all, meeting her more than once weekly for a period of at least several months, allowing their relationship to move from intimacy (*D* 110.6) to "intercourse" (*D* 112.6). We share with Mr. Duffy the knowledge of "certain (other) circumstances" contributing to her death to which the officers of the law, the relict of Mrs. Sinico, and the readers of the *Evening Mail* are not aware. Attentive readers of "A Painful Case" will have observed that the Deputy Coroner's phrasing will have the unintended effect of reminding Mr. Duffy of his former amoral bravado and eventually cause his moral comeuppance when he later revises his judgment and accepts personal responsibility for her drug dependence.

Within the verbal and imagistic structure of "A Painful Case," however, the Deputy Coroner's phrasing implies thematic links between Duffy's attempt to float his relationship with Mrs. Sinico above the coils of mortality. Throughout his friendship with her, as he allowed "the facts" of her biography to enter his thoughts, he imagined these intrusions in images consistent with classic male celibate suspicion of feminine temptation: "Little by little he entangled his thoughts with hers" (*D* 110.26, 111.16–17). Gripped in the ancient fear summoned by this archetypal image, Mr. Duffy recoils in panic from the pressure of Mrs. Sinico's cheek upon his hand (*D* 111.32). Thus, when reconsidering their relationship after rereading the newspaper account of her demise, he finds himself re-experiencing the moment when "her hand touched his" (*D* 116.4) and his assumption of moral responsibility for her premature end.

It is not otiose in this investigation of "A Painful Case" to observe at this point that Joyce returns to a Chapelizod bar for his setting of *Finnegans Wake* in general, and to "A Painful Case" in particular in the passage in II.6 (359.31–360.16). Mr. Duffy apparently patronizes the Mullingar House, what was to become Earwicker's establishment.[4] This brief interlude, which revisits the imaginary world of "A Painful Case," takes the form of a musical request program on the public-house radio. It follows the broadcast of an excerpt from a "fiveaxled production [of] *The Coach with The Six Insides*." This "Goes Tory by Eeric Whigs is To Become Tintinued in *Fearson's Nightly*" (*FW* 359.23–27). Then follows the song, "Good Night, Sweetheart," requested by Irish listeners for their emigrant friends. The harmony of instruments and the human voice, in images of the birdsong and the woodlands around Dublin, expresses the emotional bonds between domiciled Dubliners and the Irish diaspora. This passage illustrates the manner in which the realistic details of "A Painful Case" are metamorphosed into Wakese: for example, the "five or six working-men in the shop" (*D* 116.11–12), the yawning proprietor, and Mr. Duffy's effort to escape Mrs. Sinico's ghostly return become the "fiveaxled . . . [and] Six Insides," HCE/Shaun/Yawn, and the "Goes Tory" of *Finnegans Wake*. The male preserve of the cubed Chapelizod shop ("*The Coach with Six Insides*") is an appropriate refuge from a feminine ghost, associated with Mrs. Sinico's "full jacket" first glimpsed at the Rotunda. This same passage recalls Gluck ("gluckglucky"), *Chamber Music* ("badthumpered paeans"), and Wagnerians ("wheckfoolthenairyans"). Meanwhile, of course, the links between John Field ("nocturnefield"), Mozart's night song ("night's sweetmoztheart"), the digital arts of piano playing and literature ("clinkers . . . flourish as under-

Figure 3.2. Gaunt trees: Military Road, Phoenix Park. Photograph by Cóilín Owens, 2006.

wood"), Chapelizod and Tintagel, so vividly expressed in *Finnegans Wake* 359–60, are all implicit in the design and images of "A Painful Case." (Other links between "A Painful Case" and this passage will be noted as they arise.)

It is part of the verbal and topographical poetry of this story that this moment of moral enlightenment occurs as Mr. Duffy leaves the public house and walks through the Phoenix Park between Chapelizod and the Magazine Hill. Entering the park by the wicket gate in Chapelizod, he heads east for approximately 1.25 miles by Saint Mary's Hospital and via the Upper Glen and Military Roads to the Magazine Fort. On this winding pathway "under the gaunt trees," he recalls his last traversing of this route in the company of Mrs. Sinico (*D* 117.1–8); and it is on this same walk that he recalls the "circumstances" under which, by his rejection of her touch, he dismissed her from his life. The figures of the embracing lovers beneath the park wall rebuke his fear of fleshly embroil and heighten his despair.

Agenbite of Inwit

A pedestrian follower of Mr. Duffy from Chapelizod to the Magazine Hill will be gratified to find that along the way the Dublin Corporation has accommodated today's sightseers with a set of handsome benches (known locally as "Lovers' Seats"). Pausing on the spot where Duffy halted, one will not be able to view the city, its lights, the river, Heuston (formerly Kingsbridge) Station, or the rail yards because of commercial development and the high trees around and above Islandbridge Gate. Nevertheless, the effort to make an inventory of Dublin's "street furniture" produced, for the present writer, an unexpected consolation. A plaque informs the walking tourist that this was a unique spot in the topography of the metropolis, the only terrestrial point affording a panoramic view of the entire City of Dublin. The colonial authorities appreciated its advantage by fortifying the summit with the Magazine Fort, but the panoramic view available from the southeast slope of Thomas's Hill allowed ordinary folk to take pride in the Georgian grandeur spread along the skyline of their native city. In confirmation of the historical claim, this plaque directs the tourist's attention to the eighteenth-century engraving made in this very spot by the city's most renowned memorialist, James Malton (ca. 1766–1803).

The youngest of a family of distinguished artists, Malton made a set of twenty-five engravings of prominent buildings and city scenes, during the early 1790s. Under the proud title, *A Picturesque and Descriptive View of the City of Dublin*, they were collected and published in 1799 marking therefore the final years of the Irish Parliament. The last of these (dedicated to the distinguished Irish patriot and leader of that parliament, Henry Grattan), is entitled "View of Dublin from the Magazine, Phoenix Park" (1795). See frontispiece. In his accompanying note, Malton claims that this major view of the City of Dublin is unique: "It united the most of the leading features of the capital city that can be obtained from any one point of view." He draws attention to the many architectural features of the cityscape, among them the Four Courts, Christ Church Tower, the steeple of Saint Patrick's Cathedral, and the Infirmary at Kilmainham.

The engraving celebrates the elegance of Georgian Dublin—with its gentlemen, their horses and carriages, and its many fine public buildings on each side of what he calls the "serpentine windings of the Liffey" (before it was canalized). As a representation of city transport before the trains or trams of late Victorian Dublin, it does not, of course, include the salient aspect of the landscape to which Mr. Duffy's attention is drawn: Kingsbridge Station and the accompanying railway lines (1844). In other respects it anticipates by just over a century the scene featured in the penultimate paragraph of "A Painful Case." Accordingly, in the middle distance are several groups of riders and pedestrians, while in the foreground are two males observing the landscape and a male and two females, reclining and absorbed in mutual gazes. We can therefore infer that Duffy has stopped here not only because of his temporary emotional and physical exhaustion, but also out of a habit inherited from generations of pedestrian Dubliners. Thus as he takes Malton's literal vantage point, he may well be imagining the panorama of Augustan order and detachment (yet also the age of Mozart), and thus constituting himself as superior to the modern vulgarity he so despises.

This scene, potentially restorative to his conservative temperament, is however, enveloped in a darkness that corresponds to his present mood of quiet despair. Malton's sportive lovers are not fellow citizens enjoying the amenities conferred by free and happy citizens, but "prostrate creatures" (*D* 117.18), surrendering to "the coupler's will." The implied endorsement by this civic panorama is therefore both a mark of Joyce's pride in his native Dublin, while it also complements the sentence with which "A Painful Case" began: "Mr James Duffy lived in Chapelizod because he wished to live as far as possible from the city of which he was a citizen"(*D* 107.2–4).

A multifaceted topographical, historical, verbal, and dramatic metaphor summarizing the theme of "A Painful Case," therefore presides over the final three paragraphs of the story. Just as on this walk he recalls another four years previously, the pair of mutually embracing lovers underneath the parallel wall answers and rebukes his refusal of Mrs. Sinico's embrace.[5] The images are complemented and enlarged by the vista now visible to Mr. Duffy from the crest of the Magazine Hill: the shallow and sluggish river wending its way between Palmerston to the weir at Islandbridge, and veering from there past the rail yards before disappearing from sight under Kingsbridge (now Heuston Bridge); and the goods train slowly filing along one of the curved rails that serves the loading sheds at Kingsbridge Station and moving southwest into the dark countryside. In these multiple parallel and complementary images (male and female, natural and constructed, past and present, mythic and historical), we have a rich coalescence of the images of the tactile encirclement from which his celibate character shrinks: Emily Sinico's "touch" (the memory of his rebuke of her advance), their "entanglement" (his thoughts and her feelings), the "serpent" (the winding Military Road he has just traversed), "worm" (the departing train), the village he has just left (its public house and its two hot punches, its disused distillery and its worms, its name suggesting "lizard"), and the repression of his own genital identity.[6] All of these images specify, distinguish, and constitute the otherwise normal abstract evasion: "certain circumstances."

It is no surprise, then, that when Joyce returns in *Finnegans Wake* to this scene as a reenactment of the edenic offense, the metaphoric amplifications of the topos accommodate a rich revisitation: he expressly rejoices in a mapmaker's fantasy, amused again by his earlier imaginative transformation of the Glen and Military Roads, now renamed as the "Serpentine in Phornix Park" (*FW* 80.6), and its "serpumstances" (*FW* 297.07). Mr. Duffy's reaction to his impression that his entanglement with her is the salient circumstance in Mrs. Sinico's fall leads him not to renew his faith in either human nature or divine grace, but to surrender to the surrounding darkness and silence: to accept as his destiny "the soul's incurable loneliness." For Mr. Duffy, unless he repents, both his life and afterlife will be hell.

The hyperbolic image of the worm, then, although expressly provoked by the laborious train ("like a worm with a fiery head winding through the darkness, obstinately and laboriously," *D* 117.23–24), is overdetermined by other images in the narrative and in Mr. Duffy's preconscious. In the narrative memory, it ironically resummons the image by which Mr. Duffy's life before and after his relationship is characterized: "his life rolled out evenly—an adventureless tale" (*D* 109.15–16), and "Mr Duffy returned to his even way of life" (*D* 112.12–13). Its puffing engine, however, immediately summons his conscience-stricken memory of Mrs. Sinico. The demonic image that stalks his imagination combines the two conspirators in her fatal accident: the monstrous train and "the clutches of the demon drink" (*U* 13.290) that drew her under its iron buffer.

The figure of the demon here is an item from the biblically inspired phantasmagoria that haunt Mr. Duffy's imagination. Originally an "evil spirit" in Old and New Testaments (McKenzie, s.v. "demon, demonology"), the demon passed into Christian literature as a manifestation of the devil or one of the lower orders of malignant supernatural beings (*OED*). In Christian moral theology, the demon became synonymous with a failing or sin that through indiscipline became an ineradicable habit. The weakening of individual will was imagined as surrender to an external force outside the self. Thus a person conceding to the "habitual sin" of anger, sloth, or alcoholism was metaphorically considered to be "possessed" by a demon. His contemplation of "the squalid tract of [Mrs. Sinico's] vice" (*D* 115.25) as he gazes out his window and at the derelict distillery (*D* 115.16–17) may remind Mr. Duffy, as it did the narrator of "The Sisters," of the "faints and worms" (*D* 10.5) of which it is now empty. To the moralistic ex-Christian James Duffy (who is himself possessed by another demon, melancholy), the metaphoric usage "demon rum" or "demon drink," which was especially prevalent in the late nineteenth century (*OED*), evidently bares its saurian teeth at transfixed Duffy.

There may be yet another, more specific, Christian source outside the text. It may also derive—in either the narrator's or Mr. Duffy's memories—from their exposure to Giovanni Pietro Pinamonti's *Hell Opened to Christians, To Caution Them from Entering It*. The relevant passage appears in *Portrait* as part of the famous sermon on hell:

> —The second pain which will afflict the souls of the damned in hell is the pain of conscience. Just as in dead bodies worms are engendered by putrefaction so in the souls of the lost there arises a perpetual remorse from the putrefaction of sin, the sting of conscience, the worm, as Pope Innocent the Third calls it, of the triple sting. The first sting inflicted by this cruel worm will be the memory of past pleasures. O what a dreadful memory will that be! . . . They will repent indeed: and this is the second sting of the worm of conscience, a late and fruitless sorrow for sins committed. Divine justice insists that the understanding of those miserable wretches be fixed continually on the sins of which they were guilty and moreover, as Saint Augustine points out, God will impart to them His own knowledge of sin so that sin will appear to them in all its hideous malice as it appears to the eyes of God Himself. They will behold their sins in all their foulness and repent but it will be too late and then they will bewail the good occasions which they neglected. This is the last and deepest and most cruel sting of the worm of conscience. (*P* 128.23–129.22)

This is an elaboration on the image that appears in Jesus' description of God's eternal punishment of serious sinners, who will be "thrown into Gehenna, where 'their worm does not die, and the fire is not quenched'" (Mark 9: 47).[7] Mr. Duffy is particularly struck by this "last and deepest and most cruel sting of the worm of conscience."

As J. R. Thrane and James Doherty have demonstrated, Joyce drew extensively on Pinamonti's text, having heard the horrific description of eternal punishment first from Father James Cullen during a retreat in Belvedere College. At the time of the writing of *Portrait* and "A Painful Case" there were several editions of this text potentially available to Joyce: a Dublin edition from 1840 (Grace), two English editions (Richardson, 1845, 1846), and a Dublin edition (1884/1889). All of them exhibited the grotesque woodcuts depicting "The Sting of Conscience" that may well be the source of the images of "worm," "gnawing," and "fiery head" that inform the penultimate paragraph

Figure 3.3. Three woodcuts: Frontispiece, "I was the brother of dragons and the fellow of ostriches" (Job 30: 29), and "The Sting of Conscience," *Hell Opened to Christians* (Derby: Thomas Richardson and Son, 1845, 1846).

of this story. The most recent Dublin edition appeared as one item in a collection of pamphlets on the lives of various saints, the proper preparation for a Christian death, and various devotions, prayers, and reflections on the virtues of the Blessed Virgin. The collection was *Duffy's Standard Library of Catholic Divinity* (2 vols.), published by the historical James Duffy.

Three Cases of Pain

The most obvious point about "A Painful Case" is the apparent blatancy in its depiction of Mr. Duffy's emotional disability. Behind this cliché, the technique of the story implies a congerie of ideas and forms that it owes to the Christian understanding of love in its broad and narrow, ideal and juridical senses.

Christian moral theology makes a tri-fold distinction with respect to the central idea of love. The highest form is God's creative love of which the universe is the apprehensible manifestation. To the extent that we can return it to God, and with the aid of divine grace, we realize this form of love in our lives, αγάπη (agape). This is contrasted with the second form of love termed φιλία (philia): the disinterested and natural love for another, as found between parents and children, or between members of a tribe or society, or the bond that informs the feeling of universal human brotherhood. These two are distinguished from ἔρος (eros), the bodily love of one person for another that manifests itself in emotional and genital engagements. The Christian view of love implies mutual relationships between these three aspects of human aspiration, spiritual, intellectual, and emotional.

It is clear that Mr. Duffy has rejected love in each of these three senses. First, by his apostasy, he has rejected the gift of God's love—agape—proffered to him generally through the Irish Catholic tradition and in the special form of a priestly vocation. The final paragraphs of the story disclose his epiphany of despair at having put himself, deliberately, and through practiced habit, beyond the agape of God. Second, by withdrawing from social engagement—from his family, from the workers whose cause he notionally supports, from Mrs. Sinico's friendship, and from the ability to rejoice in the lovers' embrace beneath the Phoenix Park wall—he turns away from the natural love which binds these relationships, philia. Throughout their friendship, we are given to understand, Mr. Duffy has impressed Mrs. Sinico with his freethinking and his short-lived efforts on behalf of the proletariat. In these respects, he has disconcerted her inherited notional agape (as a presumably conventional Irish Catholic), while recalling the eros that her husband has banished from her life.

The dramatic turning point in the plot of the story, of course, is where Mr. Duffy recoils from the prospect of such an eros in a relationship that he would have liked to hold at a distance appropriate to philia. Therefore, in his effort to have philia take the place of both agape and eros, in both Mrs. Sinico's and his own life, Mr. Duffy has failed. These broad distinctions delimit the moral schema of the world of the story. Within these borders, Joyce has, moreover, devised a more detailed apparatus fitted for the judgment of daily affairs by moral standards derived from Christian principles.

The Christian moral code is a system of normative inferences derived from the teachings of Jesus Christ and the church's subsequent theological interpretation of them. Jesus did not have an ethical system, but embodied a radical moral stance: detachment from materialism, a call to repentance, and the love of God (agape) and the neighbor, especially the poor (philia). Christian moral theology was not systematized until the Middle Ages, where it combined Aristotelian logic and biblical exegesis. In its fullest sense, Christian morality—called πραξις (praxis)—is the mutual interaction of intellectual deduction, actual practice, and prayerful reflection.

It is clear that from the first draft Joyce had the firm intention of casting his material as a moral tale. Although nothing in the incident in Stanislaus's account required such a treatment, the story that took shape in Joyce's imagination had all the requisite ingredients. His emendation of the original title from "A Painful Incident" to "A Painful Case" indicates, however, that in rereading his story he recognized a paradigm that he had encountered in the course of his own moral education and had perhaps been unconsciously emulating: that of the casus conscientiae, the term inherited from medieval confessional usage for "a case of conscience."

This revised title expands the reference from one "incident" to two "cases": the death of Mrs. Sinico and the anguish of Mr. Duffy. The principal irony in the story derives from the contrasting relationship between these two. Of the suffering that drove Mrs. Sinico to alcohol and death we know only from hearsay and from circumstantial evidence. Of Mr. Duffy's anguish we know a great deal, from the life he has chosen to lead and from his mental habits. The central issue in the story is the relationship between one painful case and the other: between Mrs. Sinico's violent physical death and Mr. Duffy's moral pain in taking responsibility for that death. We do not have much evidence, beyond some circumstantial facts and the brief testimony of her family, regarding how responsible for her death was Mrs. Sinico herself. Whereas the manner of her death is a public embarrassment to her family and to the railway company, to Mr. Duffy it is a private one. We are not witnesses to whatever moral misgivings might have assailed Captain Sinico regarding his degree of responsibility for his wife's death. Evidently their daughter is personally distraught, since her testimony suggests that she had for some time attempted to help her mother out of her addiction.

The newspaper report of the death of Mrs. Sinico announces a "case" in three senses, two medical and one legal. With respect to her psychological dependence on alcohol, she was a medical case even before the accident. In this respect, the causes of her alcoholism we can infer are her husband's exclusion of her from his affections and her social isolation especially following the failure of her relationship with Mr. Duffy. We are told, whether or not reliably, that her alcoholism began two years previous to her death, which was two years after the separation from Mr. Duffy. We know nothing of the sources of her other proclivities towards alcoholism, whether genetic or social, except that she had a sensitive and high-strung disposition. That she was a "case" in this sense is admitted by her daughter, who tried, unsuccessfully, to rescue her from its effects by having her join a Temperance League.[8]

In a more particular sense, her case is medical with regard to the immediate cause of death. The medical examiner concludes that the fall produced by the impact of the buffer of the train did not produce injuries sufficient to cause death in a person of normal health. It was not moving fast at the time. He infers that she had a heart attack brought on by the shock of the impact. This would be surprising in a woman of her relative youth (forty-three years), except that she was at the time apparently under the influence of alcohol. Her death was therefore "probably" (*D* 114.20; a key word, as we shall see) the result of three related factors: her nervous disposition, her alcoholism, and the shock of the impact of the buffer of the Kingstown train.

The newspaper report is a "case" in another sense, too: insofar as it is conducted by the City Coroner's office with the assistance of the DMP and attempts to establish legal responsibility for the accident. The hearing occurs before the deputy coroner, a jury, and in a court open to the press. Its legal counsel represents the railway company; the driver and porter testify; a police sergeant and a constable represent the public good; and family members the private interest. Respecting the physical circumstances there are no mysteries. Despite the gates on the level crossing where Sydney Parade Avenue traverses the railway line, she started over the tracks as the train began to move out of the station.[9] This implied no negligence on the part of either the driver or stationmaster. (There are small gaps in the testimony, however: Who moved the body from the train lines to the platform? And why was this done before the constables arrived?) The solicitor earns his fee by reminding the court that

Figure 3.4. Sydney Parade Station and Level Crossing. Photograph by William York Tindall, from his book, *The Joyce Country*. Copyright 1960 by Pennsylvania State University Press. Reprinted by permission of the publisher.

the company had installed pedestrian bridges, gates, and crossing notices, each of which Mrs. Sinico had voluntarily ignored. The deputy coroner's final statement closes the legal case.

The larger "case," of course, is Mr. Duffy's. The story is primarily about his pain, which is neither legal nor medical, nor even that of the relict Sinicos, their painful public embarrassment. The pain of his "case" is moral. That moral case resolves itself into two aspects: to what degree is he responsible for the death of Mrs. Sinico? And what moral decision has he made in his life that—both before and after his relationship with her—has led to his final unhappy isolation? With respect to the first of these, Mr. Duffy originally regards Mrs. Sinico's death as her responsibility alone. From this point of view, his only moral pain is his private embarrassment at allowing himself to be associated with such a reprobate. Upon further consideration, however, he revises this judgment, and considers that due to his rejection of her appeal for love, his awareness at the time that she was rejected by her husband, and his having permitted their relationship to grow to the degree that she had developed an emotional dependence on him (a "case" in yet another sense, an infatuation, OED 3b: thus, its "pain" Mrs. Sinico's anguish at Duffy's rejection of her), that he was to a considerable, even primary degree at that point, responsible for her descent into desperation and death. He had allowed the pretense that he would not be an adulterer to become an excuse for avoiding the moral responsibility he had acquired by allowing his relationship with her to develop, whereas he knew that the Sinico marriage was one in name only: after eighteen years it had produced but one child, the now adult Mary. The paucity of evidence from four years in Mrs. Sinico's life holds those who would rush to judgment—as many have—accused of some brand of social prejudice. And just as the presumption of Duffy's selfishness may be said to underlie his first judgment, his prideful inflation of his role in her life may underlie his second.

Whereas the *Evening Mail* headline refers to a "case" in the medical or legal senses, then, Joyce's title refers primarily to Mr. Duffy's moral "case." Readers are therefore, in this respect, invited to consider how "A Painful Case" is a casus conscientiae, a "case of conscience" in the historical sense understood by handbooks of Catholic moral teaching. Such handbooks became standard devices in Catholic seminaries since the Counter Reformation, and would have been familiar—at least through selected examples—to a man of James Duffy's time and education, as they were to James Joyce.

The Jesuit Giraffe

These handbooks consisted of a series of specific scenarios representing concrete cases requiring the application of general moral principles. This method of the moral training of Catholic students and especially seminarians preparing for lives as confessors, by the careful examination of a sequence of cases promoted the approach to Catholic moral teaching and practice known as "casuistry." The name casuistry derives from the Latin for "case," *casus*, which itself derives from the verb *cadere*, "to fall."

Formally considered, casuistry is not ethics in that it does not examine fundamental principles, but merely enquires into the application of these principles in specified instances based on accepted or established conclusions of moral theology or ethics. Casuistry is based on established Catholic moral teaching, while taking into account the personal, social, political, and economic experience or circumstances under which a particular moral question arises. It undertakes to adjudicate between the conflicts of principle or duties afflicting what became known as "the perplexed conscience."

In their comprehensive and balanced history of the subject, *The Abuse of Casuistry*, Albert Jonsen and Stephen Toulmin question the reliability of the account found in the *OED*: "Often (and perhaps originally) applied to a quibbling or evasive way of dealing with difficult cases of duty." They point out that the historical association of casuistry with "Jesuitical sophistry" is prejudicial (150–51). This is largely due to Blaise Pascal's famous attack on casuistry in his *Provincial Letters*, where he took the moral high ground while ignoring the Jesuits' pastoral commitments. Pascal rightly recognized the inherent tendency of probabilism to slide toward moral skepticism, and in a culture that values individual liberty and prudence before classical principles, every opinion eventually comes to be viewed as good as any other (171). One result of his brilliant but unfair attack is that the claims and methods of the casuists have been "widely and deeply misunderstood; as a result most modern readers assume that casuistry is as dead or disreputable as astrology" (10). This was grossly unfair and a deliberate misreading of brilliant moralists such as Juan Azor, SJ, whose magisterial treatise on circumstances, *Institutium Moralium*, demonstrated in case after case that circumstances do indeed usually affect the very nature of an action such as a business contract or a bank robbery (154). It is with just such casuistic glee that Joyce surprises his readers in having his otherwise conservative and high-minded James Duffy admit his partiality to such a heinous crime: "He allowed himself to think that in certain circumstances he would rob his bank" (*D* 109.13–15).

Casuistry has its origins, in another sense, in a few passages in the New Testament. One is the incident of the Pharisees criticizing Jesus' disciples for plucking ears of corn as they went, not that they were taking what did not belong to them, but that they did so on the Sabbath. Was not this plucking, the Pharisees asked, considered "work" (Mark 2: 23–28)? The more famous example is when Jesus is asked whether or not it is lawful to pay tribute to Caesar (Luke 20: 20–26). And again, Saint Paul confronts the question of the consistency between Christian faith and the consumption of food left over from pagan sacrifices (1 Cor. 8). Casuistry has roots in classical literature, notably in Cicero's *De Officiis*, which was widely studied by students of Christian ethics in the middle ages. Jonsen and Toulmin summarize elegantly and aptly to our present purposes:

> Classical rhetoric provided the elements out of which later casuistry developed: the concentration on an *issue* about which there was an unresolved controversy, the introduction of *maxims* which were relevant to the issue, and presentation of set *arguments* that were appropriate to either side of the issue, the emphasis on the *attributes* of persons and actions, and the move to *closure* in arriving at a verdict or judgment. Rhetoric and casuistry were mutual allies. It is not surprising to find the Jesuits, who were dedicated to teaching classical rhetoric in their colleges, became the leading proponents of casuistry. (88)

The modern history of casuistry is one of extremes. On the one hand, the Jansenists took a rigorist view that the strictest judgment was always to be preferred. On the other, the Laxists took the permissive view that in cases of doubt, prudence (*phronesis*: a word that recurs in casuistic discourse), the easier course, was to be preferred. Between them were various moderate positions, best represented by Saint Alphonsus Liguori's prudent "probabalism." This term and position, made famous by its irenicism in a long-running and acrimonious debate, held that "when there is a question solely of the lawfulness or unlawfulness of an action, it is permissible to follow a solidly probable opinion in favor of liberty even though an opposing view is more probable" (*Catholic Encyclopedia*, s.v. "probabalism").

Joyce's dozen years of Jesuit education ensured that he garnered a primer in these methods and terminology of moral evaluation with which the Society of Jesus was particularly associated. A community of "worldly Christians" in the best sense of that phrase, the Jesuits perfect the vocation that is active rather than contemplative, training its members in education and pastoral work. To this end, every member of the Jesuits was trained in the technique of the moral evaluation of everyday situations cultivated through the regular analysis of casus conscientiae. During this training, whether as professed (potential academics) or as spiritual coadjutors (pastoral ministers), they were regularly and formally instructed in the processes of case evaluation. In Jesuit schools, moreover, their lay students heard lectures and were invited to conferences on the evaluation of moral cases, so that their graduates were all conversant with the procedures of casuistical reasoning (Jonsen and Toulmin, 150). The curriculum of both Clongowes Wood and Belvedere Colleges followed the spirit of the Jesuit *Ratio Studiorum* (quoted by Sullivan, 46–47) that was impressed by casuistic training in both religious and secular subjects. Joyce would have been exposed to moral and religious training in the Sodality of Mary at Belvedere, where various *casus* would have been read, studied, and discussed (Curran, 38).

References to this educational method appear throughout Joyce's work. *Dubliners* begins with Father Flynn's "putting difficult questions to me, asking what one should do in certain circumstances" (*D* 13.7–8), and originally concluded with the spiritual accountancy of Father Purdon's casuistically inspired sermon (*D* 173–74). *Portrait* exhibits the shrewd rector putting "curious questions" regarding theft, the proper administration of the sacraments, and apparent scriptural inconsistencies (*P* 106.17–36), and "the tall form of the young professor of mental science discussing on the leading a case of conscience with his class like a giraffe cropping high leafage among a herd of antelopes" (*P* 192.20–23).[10] When Stephen Dedalus, moreover, repels Cranly's attempt to inveigle him into an adventitious argument, his rejection of the casuistic tolerance "in certain circumstances" of bank robbery (*P* 246.11–21) recalls James Duffy's similar rationalization of the same crime in "A Painful Case." Again, in a significant rebuke of Mr. Duffy's ethic, Stephen claims that he would rather be one of the beggars Mr. Duffy despises (*P* 246.9; *D* 108.28–29).

Thus, when James Joyce told Frank Budgen that he would be more correctly characterized as a Jesuit rather than a Catholic, he meant that he was trained in this method of ethical analysis; and it was primarily to this method at the core of his religious and secular training that Joyce was making reference when he told August Suter that the Jesuits taught him how "to arrange things in such a way that they become easy to survey and to judge" (*JJII* 27). Many interlocutors attest to Joyce's lifelong interest in engaging in casuistic moral argument. Alessandro Francini Bruni, for example, cites the "Jesuitical casuistry of which Joyce can boast himself master" (Potts, 36), and Paolo Cuzzi recalls discussions of Thomistic morality "about which Joyce theorized with precision and ingenuity" (*JJII* 340). These witnesses' observations complement Joyce's remark to Jacques Mercanton, towards the end of his life, that the Jesuits held before his impressionable youth the prospect of justice in the world (Potts, 240). Thus the casuistical habit of thought to which he was exposed during his education persisted at least as a kind of conversational game. This is one of the elements that predisposed him to Daniel Defoe. Defoe, one of the few authors whose entire oeuvre Joyce read, endows his characters—Moll Flanders, Colonel Jack, and Roxana—with a special partiality to casuistic moralizing.[11]

Joyce's continuous interest in casuistry informs the central moral question in *Ulysses*: how should Bloom handle Molly's adultery? It also arguably informs the indulgent solution that Bloom adopts, as Michael Mason argues. "A Painful Case" anticipates this particular aspect of *Ulysses* in a couple of ways: normal marital relations between the Sinicos have ceased as they have between the Blooms; as Captain Sinico tolerates his wife's relationship with Mr. Duffy, so does Bloom Blazes Boylan's with Molly; and as Captain Sinico plays the sailor to Duffy the musician, so does Bloom the putative Ulysses to the impresario Boylan. The congruencies are not limited to these examples, moreover. In *Finnegans Wake*, the cases of Burrus and Caseous and Burrus and Margareena (*FW* 161.15–168.14) and the exposé of polymorphous outrages of familial relationships (*FW* 571.28–576.9) draw again, and this time with highest virtuosity, on the casuistic manner of the analysis of marital cases.

Joyce's transformation of the jargon and detached logic of Canon Law into this virtuoso representation of the primal chaos behind orthodox, unremarkable, or "normal" family relations, is the efflorescence of the contrast between the style and content of the newspaper report of Mrs. Sinico's death and the brilliance of the imaginative world residing unobtrusively within the apparent plain-speak of the narrative framework of "A Painful Case." Joyce's particular source text for the casus conscientiae in *Finnegans Wake* has been identified as M. M. Matharan's *Casus de Matrimonio* (1893), consisting of some five hundred cases judging conjugal legitimacy and relations in accordance with Catholic casuistic traditions, a heavily marked copy of which was found among the books in his Paris apartment.[12]

It is unlikely that Joyce had this copy of Matharan since his schooldays. But there were numerous authors in print at the time, several of them with multivolume collections of moral cases systematically examined: books by Jean Pierre Gury, Augustinus Lehmkuhl, or Gennario Bucceroni, designed for readers like those who formed Joyce's youthful moral imagination. Representative of this is Edward Génicot's *Casus Conscientiae: Propositi ac Soluti* (2 vols., Louvanii: 1906 [entirely in Latin]), or the dual-language text, *Cases of Conscience for English-Speaking Countries*, by Thomas Slater, SJ (2 vols., N.Y.: Benziger, 1912). These reference works were typically organized by subject: delivering sets of problems and solutions pertaining to the theological virtues (faith, hope, and charity), the Decalogue, the commandments of the Catholic Church, marriage, business affairs, personal associations with non-Catholics, heretics or atheists, reading forbidden books, and miscellaneous other topics that evidently appeared frequently in confessions, such as the abuse of alcohol, domestic violence, or Christian obligations to the poor.

These handbooks stated the problems concisely—in two or three direct sentences, the penitents identified by Latin pseudonyms—followed by an often long and detailed judgment, citing relevant authorities: Saint Francis Liguori (the Catholic Church's most eminent moralist), canon law, scripture, and papal pronouncements. The cases took into consideration innumerable particular (exacerbating or extenuating) circumstances: the social class, age, education, and temperament of the penitents, their level of affluence, personal maturity, and responsibilities; the time and place of the action; and the degree of responsibility exercised and its motivation (Jonsen and Toulmin, 119). The cases bore titles like "Unwilling to Return to Her Husband," "A Troubled Wife," and "A Husband in Difficulties," or "A Particularly Complex Case." The cases ranged from moderate challenges to principle, evidence, and logic, to baffling conundrums. They always engaged at least two conflicting principles and a set of particular circumstances that, defying easy resolution, required "discernment" (a favorite Jesuit word) (Jonsen and Toulmin, 151).

Joyce wrote "A Painful Case" for a Dublin Catholic readership that for the most part was accustomed to thinking in moral absolutes. Whether they personally practiced the virtues or not, they were regularly embarrassed by reminders of the saints who did so heroically, and generally acknowledged the objectivity and degrees of sin as Catholic authority defined them. They were raised to think that they could be categorically and dispassionately judged, and that the admitted complexity of many moral questions did not imply that they were either beyond answer or that they were utterly dependent upon values that were relative, or the products of social convention or political power. They were required to examine their own conduct scrupulously and periodically admit to its deficiencies in confession. Joyce did not come to this culture as a detached anthropologist, but as a dissenting insider, deeply and permanently at war within himself with that which shaped his feelings, imagination, and judgment.

As the passage cited above (29) from Stanislaus's diary attests, Joyce had a precise appreciation of the superior merits of Catholic spiritual and moral discipline over the alternatives. His story is designed with an ear to the moral nuance that is less easy to hear in a secularized and egalitarian society. In a culture that lays so much stress on individual liberty, inculcates righteousness over obligation, and that tends to regard all ethics as "situational," it is difficult to appreciate the matrix from which this story emerges. Readers conditioned to a moral climate that allows criminals to claim that they made "mistakes," passes off deceptions as "miscommunications" and "typographical errors," and identifies moral with legal obligations are not in a good position to appreciate the fine moral ironies of Joyce's story.

The hypothesis, then, is that the implied narrator of "A Painful Case" bemusedly imagines himself, "in the absence of Mr. Leverett" (*D* 113.22), as an ingenious giraffe, cropping the moral leafage beyond the average reach. Meanwhile, on the veldt below, where antelopes and hares bound, coroners (appropriately) perform the relatively simple task of assessing the probable cause of failure of the heart.

Casus Molestus

Posed in the form of a casus conscientiae, then, "A Painful Case" would have begun in Joyce's imagination as this embryonic paragraph:

> Jacobus, quidem caelebs melancholicus sed ingenio acuto praeditus ac liberalitus educatus, quadraginta anni aetate provectus, amicitiam vicinam uxore neglecta et infelice, Amelia, incipit. Adiuvato studio communo atrium musicae classicae et litterae, familiaritas sua per complures menses crescebat. Quamquam causam apertam sperare propinquitatem sexam oriri ea non dedit, significare eam cupere, Jacobus celeriter a coetu suo se removit. Magno animi motu discederunt. Quattuor anni postea, legit quod per temporem intervallum Amelia ebriosa fierat. Haec condicio iudicium suum tantum debilitaverat ut vesperi caderens sub rotis machinae pompae, statim necata est.
> Utrum Jacobus de morte Ameliae rationem reddet?

In translation, it would have read:

> James, an intelligent, educated, but melancholy bachelor, aged 40, entered a close friendship with a neglected and unhappy wife, Emily. Nurtured by their common (and mutual) interest in serious music and literature, their friendship escalated over several months. Even though he gave her no express grounds to expect the relationship to become sexual, when she indicated that she desired it, James peremptorily withdrew from her company. They had a highly emotional parting. Four years later he learned that Emily had become an alcoholic. This condition had so impaired her judgment that one evening she fell under the wheels of a train and was killed instantly.
> Is James responsible for Emily's death?

"A Painful Case," a pseudo casuist's detailed exposition of the "certain circumstances" surrounding this case, sets forth Joyce's solution. Setting aside the express consideration that James Duffy is not a conscientious Catholic, the story provides these considerations in the moral argument.

James Duffy is an apostate from the highly orthodox Catholicism of his youth. In part 1 of the story (*D* 107.2–109.16) we see that he has redefined his spiritual life apart from the community of Christian believers. He retains some of the ascetic practices assimilated from his youthful religious training; this and his intellectuality lead him into a reactionary and elitist position regarding the condition of his fellow citizens. It is not that he is morally unaware of them or views them cynically; he is intensely self-conscious, and retains a glimmer of hope that prepares him to encounter and accept a sign of grace (agape), however unlikely, that might manifest itself in others. He is punctual and scrupulous in his work, respects honesty, and despises sentimentality in private and public life. He is a moral relativist, but not a deep cynic. Thus while unwilling to patronize beggars, he makes an effort, against his temperamental inclination, to put his intellectual talents at the disposal of the proletariat. He respects social customs that mark the beginning and end of life, while retaining a private distance from family life that might expose him to the deeper commitments and threat to his personal independence that it might entail. He is intellectually alive but emotionally underdeveloped— and sexually naïve.

In part 2 (*D* 109.17–112.11) his one gesture towards social outreach (his temporary engagement with the workmen) is superseded by his relationship with Mrs. Sinico. In allowing his intimacy with her to escalate on the rationale that it is purely intellectual and cultural, he has repressed its inevitable sexual component. The naïveté of the celibate has made him complacent: "Neither he nor she had any such adventure before and neither was conscious of any incongruity" (*D* 110.24–25). He recognizes from the outset that she has a husband, and allows Captain Sinico's tolerance of the relationship, based upon his misunderstanding of the reason for Duffy's presence in their home, to pursue the relationship. Thus, he finds himself meeting Mrs. Sinico more than once weekly without regard to her inevitable emotional investment in a relationship with music at its center. He has exercised a *droit d'oreille*: committed adultery in all but its narrowest physical sense. Since he knows that Captain Sinico is no longer sexually intimate with his wife, Duffy can claim that he cannot be accused of "alienation of affection." He thinks that his relationship with Mrs. Sinico can be an expression of the anti-Augustinian encomium, "Do what thou wilt, but love not." He punishes Mrs. Sinico for her breach of this unstated rule.

In parts 3 and 4 (*D* 112.12–115.14) he takes refuge in Schopenhauer and

Nietzsche, appropriating their intellectual positions as endorsing his denial of love. He considers himself an exclusive partisan of philia, denying both eros and agape. The news story of the inquest dramatizes the unforeseen effect of his rejection of eros. Emotionally struck by the absolute nature of her own death, he finds that the citation of ostensibly extenuating circumstances does not mitigate the horror; rather, in view of his own contribution to those circumstances, his sense of moral horror is enlarged. In the unwitting citation of his own phrase, "certain circumstances," he sees a parody of his own previous casuistical rationalization of a putative bank robbery.

Parts 1–4, therefore, set up the casus conscientiae and establish the terms by which it can be adjudicated morally. Part 5 (*D* 115.15–117.34) argues the case from both sides. The question is not about Mrs. Sinico but about James Duffy: it is not whether or not Mrs. Sinico committed suicide, but whether James Duffy is morally guilty (fully or partially, or not at all) for her death. We get only Mr. Duffy's point of view, and as an interested party, he is not the best judge. However, since he has trained himself in detachment—he views himself as a third party—he is more able to act as moral adjudicator than most persons.

His first position is shocked silence. However, before he renders any judgment, he has spent at least a full hour on his walk home considering the issues before rendering it. On the one hand, he can be held fully responsible, if not for her death, then for the conditions that led to it. As a free agent she entered into her relationship with Mr. Duffy (her references to her husband during their first two meetings and her agreement to meet Mr. Duffy a third time make this clear). As a free agent she began her life as a solitary drinker (she was as aware as any normal adult would be of the "hobbling wretches" around her, and, moreover, had not cooperated with her daughter's efforts to have her join a temperance association). And again, as a free agent she undertook a dangerous crossing of the railway lines at night despite the clearly posted warning notices with which she must have been long familiar (she lived close by the station, and must have, therefore, been conversant with the train, its schedule, and hazards). She had no rightful claim upon Mr. Duffy's emotional or moral support, since she was married to someone else and since Mr. Duffy had never deceived her as to his personal intentions beyond sharing their common interest in music and ideas and did not conceal his relationship with her from her husband. Mr. Duffy was a model of sobriety and self-possession, and in no way led her into a life of drug dependence. He is therefore blameless with regard to her death, whether it was accidental, due to contributory negligence on her part, or still less, if suicide it is. From this liberal or laxist view, he stands exonerated of moral guilt for her death.

On the other hand, Mr. Duffy then moves to consider the counter argument (the clarity, niceness, and detachment and precision of his thinking contrasts with the crude gestures and material preoccupations of the men in the bar). He knew from the outset that she was a married woman, and a woman, moreover, with a refined and sensitive nature. He should have known that in articulating so much about his own inner life—his ideas and taste and capacities as a musical sophisticate—and on so regular a basis, he was bound to cultivate emotional expectations in her that he was unwilling or unable to meet. A fully grown man cannot claim innocence or naïveté about the "alienation of affection" he was encouraging in continuing this relationship so long as he did. And when she took the next natural and inevitable step, he treated her with abrupt cruelty. He attempted to justify his withdrawal by appealing to the social opprobrium that would follow his living with her in open adultery. While he did not recognize marriage as a sacrament, but as a voidable civil contract, and considered himself a freethinker, he still rationalized his withdrawal by reference to social conventions that he did not honestly respect. He lacked the moral courage to act on these convictions.

She was declaring her affection for a man who had with full clarity, declared himself independent of social or religious conventions, and thus could do so with some confidence that he would respond to her overture as a free agent and trusted friend. It was she who would suffer the greater social censure, since she had a husband and a daughter, whereas he was (in contrast with Parnell) a very private citizen. She was therefore taking the greater social risk. Her daughter depended, moreover, on her personal reputation for her profession as a private music teacher, and therefore Mrs. Sinico was in the greater jeopardy by a public break with her husband. And as a nominal Catholic, at least, she could be accused of "living in sin." Objectively, whatever her personal unhappiness in her marriage, and even if she could get a civil divorce, she was undertaking to become an adulterer and breaking the sixth commandment. Living openly and continuously with Mr. Duffy would have excluded her from the sacraments and the life of the church and endangered her eternal salvation.

The apostate Mr. Duffy had led her into some disrespect for this classic pillar in Christian morality. But in undermining her confidence in the church (by his Schopenhauerean preachments), building up her feelings for him, and then withdrawing his personal and intellectual support, he made a direct contribution to her decline into depression, alcoholism, and despair. Her experience of his company had made her life with her husband totally intolerable. She was trapped into a "sentence of death." Duffy's false rectitude had sent her there: from dependence on him to dependence on alcohol, to loss of self-respect, so that she became careless about whether or not she lived or died. By not delivering on what he implicitly promised, Mr. Duffy was responsible for her death. His example was a powerful "occasion of sin" for Mrs. Sinico. Thus, from a strict, or Jansenist, point of view, and on several counts, he is mortally guilty.

These contrary judgments on his mind, Mr. Duffy's thoughts then, in the final two paragraphs of the story, turn to the larger question of the value and happiness of his own life. The repeated references to his being "outcast from life's feast" (*D* 117.15, 20) denote a double judgment, secular and divine. Mr. Duffy's habitual practice of the ethic of individualism has deprived him of the virtue that animates anagogically the natural and supernatural orders. And rather than recognize the opportunity for repentance and renewal of his life, he turns away in despair from either prospect.

These judgments, coming after Joyce's careful establishment of character, circumstance, and moral transgressions, support the inference that one of the reasons that he changed the title from "A Painful Incident" to "A Painful Case" (*JJA* 4.95) is that the latter accommodated the reference to a casus conscientiae. The story establishes the conflict between moral principle ("thou shall not commit adultery") and the "certain circumstances" that attend the particular Duffy-Sinico relationship. The fact that this particular phrase appears three times in the story (*D* 109.14, 15, 114.28–29), and each time uttered in extenuation of what is normally considered a shameful felony (bank robbery, suicide), underlines one of the salient elements in all casus conscientiae: the specific circumstances that confirm, mitigate, or even nullify the gravity of the offense. The "certain circumstances" of which we read in "A Painful Case" lead Mr. Duffy—and most of his readers—to the conclusion that he is guilty of a greater sin—murder or assisted suicide—for not having committed adultery! In "A Painful Case" Joyce has returned to his masters a casus conscientiae sufficiently convoluted to challenge their moralizing ingenuity.

Around this substantial core Joyce has woven a pattern of allusions to several allied moral questions. Under what conditions should beggars be ignored?[13] What should a Catholic woman do when she finds herself in the constant company of an atheist? Under what conditions can a conscientious Catholic read books that are on the *Index Librorum Prohibitorum*? What possible conditions might justify a bank clerk in robbing his employer? What obligation does a railway company have to protect its customers from injury or death? Is it permissible for a husband to deny his wife sexual relations? Are restaurateurs permitted to overcharge? Are displays of personal bodily affection permitted in public places? While no doubt the implied narrator of "A Painful Case" would give different answers to these questions than would even the most tolerant of the authors mentioned above, they arise in this story because of its methodological relationship with casuistry and because of Mr. Duffy's fraught relationship with the kind of conscience it formed in him, and in his creator.

The appearance of many words and phrases in the story that are part of the language of casus conscientiae is further evidence that it constitutes a paradigm for "A Painful Case." The word "fall" (translation and etymology of L. *casus*, ex. *cadeo*, "to fall") appears in its several variations attributed to Mrs. Sinico: "a deliberate swoon" (*D* 109.32–33), "another collapse" (*D* 112.9), "allowed the dark to fall" (*D* 111.19), "You saw the lady fall?" (*D* 114.8), and "injured in the fall" (*D* 114.18), metamorphosing into Duffy's perception of "his moral nature falling to pieces" (*D* 117.7–8), underline the relationship between this story of moral falling, the word "case" in the title, and the casus conscientiae of which it is an exemplum. Again, as if one were reading a genuine casus, one finds throughout the story several instances of the moralist's characteristic diction: "prudence" (*D* 110.2), "misjudgment," "probably" (*D* 114.20), and, of course, "circumstances."

And yet again, we see that Joyce has woven into the texture of "A Painful Case" the key word "case" in each of these separate meanings as numbered under the substantive "Case" by the *OED*. Whereas, as we have seen, the story is principally concerned with legal and moral cases (*OED* #6, facts sub judice and #7, case of conscience), it also considers a medical case (#8), and takes into consideration a detailed set of particular circumstances (#5, a situation, plight, or set of external circumstances). And so far as it is concerned with Mrs. Sinico's infatuation with Duffy, it exemplifies her "painful case" on him (3). Last (and least), there is the exceptional case that proves the rule: that emblem and index of Mr. Duffy's intellectual life, his bookcase.

A Spoiled Priest

Wordsworth's Presence

Among the many unidentified books in Mr. Duffy's library are works of music, drama, religion, and philosophy. He does not keep books for show. Nor does he buy books without reading them. Their unorthodox arrangement—not by author or subject but by bulk—implies that he has taken them in hand. A respecter of book culture, he has assorted their ideas and pleasures—their metaphorical weight—with reference to his memory of their physical heft. The largest, we read, is the "complete Wordsworth," and the slimmest the *Maynooth Catechism* (D 107.17–108.3). The first of these is *The Complete Poetical Works of William Wordsworth*, with an introduction by John Morley (1888), which ran to 995 double-columned pages, while the latter was but 64 pages.[1]

The juxtaposition of these two volumes in the narrative, even though separated by the rest of his unitemized collection, implies something about the process of Mr. Duffy's spiritual or intellectual growth, from his childhood faith in Catholic Christian orthodoxy to the atheism implied by the addition to his library of Nietzsche's *The Gay Science* (D 112.16). Between these beginning and end points in his intellectual life, then, we can trace the graph that runs through Wordsworth and Schopenhauer. Beginning with the *Maynooth Catechism*, a brief summary of the doctrines inferred by the Catholic Church from the providential revelation made by the transcendent Judeo-Christian God, he moved to Wordsworth's Neoplatonic vision of an immanent Presence, from there to Schopenhauer's immanent and impersonal Will, and finally to Nietzsche's denial of metaphysics, his total nihilism. This is the trajectory of Mr. Duffy's spiritual hegira that can be gleaned from the implicitly instructive inventory of his bookshelves.

The second of these milestones, *Wordsworth's Poetical Works*, Mr. Duffy no doubt first encountered during his adolescence. Wordsworth was among the poets on which Joyce was examined in 1894 (Sullivan, 237; Bradley, 108–9, 163–64). Mr. Duffy's purchase of *The Poetical Works* indicates that he was interested enough in the introduction to Wordsworth provided by T. W. Lyster's *Select Poetry for Young Students* to pursue the matter beyond the syllabus of the Intermediate Examination required for entrance into a career in the bank.

Reading the first half of this volume, especially "Tintern Abbey," "Intimations of Immortality," and *The Prelude*—the fruits of the poet's single creative decade (1798–1808)—he would have experienced a profound liberation from the Tridentine catechetical discipline of his childhood education. For the Wordsworth of these great and moving poems, the natural landscape opens on the sublime, which, following his exertions, the observant walker beholds in subsequent meditative reverie. These works—especially *Lyrical Ballads* (1798)—are celebrated for their introduction of a new freshness, sincerity, and directness into English poetry.

Turning away from the classicism and rationality of the eighteenth-century Enlightenment, Wordsworth was the poet of joy, "breathing grandeur upon the very humblest fact of human life" (lxv). Reading Morley's introduction, Mr. Duffy would have found hope for the rebirth of his soul:

> Wordsworth . . . by his secret of bringing the infinite into common life, as he evokes it out of common life, has the skill to lead us, so long as we yield ourselves to his influence, into inner moods of settled peace, to touch "the depth and not the tumult of the soul," to give us quietness, strength, steadfastness, and purpose, whether to do or to endure. (lxvi–lxvii)

He would, moreover, have found a schema of the passage ahead. He would have recognized that he had just passed through childhood, the age of sensation, and that what lay before him were those of youth, the age of simple ideas and emotions, and manhood, the age of complex ideas and emotions. He would have encountered a sense of soul independent of divine revelation and a fragment of the supernatural, but possessed of a preternatural inner life that preceded his own physical birth and which drew its sustenance from a pervasive Presence. In Wordsworth, then, Mr. Duffy would have found a spiritual alternative to the transcendent, personal, and paternal God of his spiritual childhood.

Reading the masterpieces of Wordsworth's young manhood, Mr. Duffy would have been cautioned by John Morley's introduction as to the hazards ahead. This essay directed his readers towards Wordsworth's oeuvre as the autobiography of an unduly optimistic soul: politically, from radical to reactionary, religiously from pantheist to doctrinaire Anglican, and morally from social conscience to complacent celebrity.

If Mr. Duffy had indeed read Wordsworth's complete works, he would have been chastened by the prospect of the decline of a great poet who between the *Lyrical Ballads* and *The Excursion* gradually surrendered his independent vision for an orthodox one. As Morley's view implied, there is a correspondence between the ecclesiastical verse of the late Wordsworth and the social attitude that supported capital punishment as a deterrent to crime among the lower orders and opposed Catholic Emancipation as according undue empowerment to the superstitious and illiterate Irish millions. And gazing at the dark green and gilt spine of the bulkiest book on his shelf, he might have recognized the obverse of his own view of himself, as moving from the received ideas of the *Maynooth Catechism* through the simple ideas of Romantic youth (Wordsworth) and the advanced ideas of Schopenhauer and Nietzsche, and an explanation of his own unhappy final state.

Had he pursued the matter to the end, then, Mr. Duffy's confidence in Wordsworth's spiritual optimism would have been shattered by these failures. Darwinian bloody mindedness would have interposed itself in any event. By mid century the stage décor was being rearranged to assist the next act. In a personal hegira mirroring the historical progress of ideas during the nineteenth century, Mr. Duffy's reading—the specifics of which will be discussed in pages to follow—would have caused him to lose confidence in his Romantic mentor. Duffy's modernity is in substantial ways reactionary. His modernity, although earned and not simply modish, depends upon the rejection of the three major nineteenth-century ideas that Wordsworth so feelingly represented to readers of his poetry: doctrine of nature as Presence, the Neoplatonic role of the imagination, and the true source of human joy as the communion of one with the other.

Thus the Mr. Duffy whom we meet has already disabused himself of any notions that he might have garnered from Wordsworth. There is no evidence in the story that he responds in any felt way to the natural world. He lives attached to, yet at enmity with, the modern metropolis: dependent on its art and books, yet in a vehement reaction to its popular and consumer culture. He has, moreover, a vehemently un-Wordsworthian attitude towards beggars.

Nietzsche's two volumes, Wordsworth's poetical works, and the *Maynooth Catechism*, therefore document, in retrospective arrangement, the three stages of Mr. Duffy's spiritual progress, corresponding to the stages of adulthood, youth, and childhood. But as with many other aspects of the story, this progress is ironic, since Mr. Duffy's final condition is worse than his first. He has adopted one set of ideas for another and is no happier for it. The gradual

evacuation of theological, metaphysical, and social communions in "A Painful Case" cumulates in its last word: "alone."

These intimations of Wordsworth's evanescent presence in "A Painful
Case" are linked to an unexpectedly illuminating aspect of the portrait of Mr.
Duffy's angst. Early in the summer of 1905 (May-June), Joyce wrote a brief
account of English literary history for the students at the Trieste Berlitz School.
In this piece he awards Wordsworth, along with Shakespeare and Percy
Bysshe Shelley as poets of the first rank (*contra* Stephen Dedalus's Lord Byron,
P 80.33–81.1), offering in support a citation from the unlikely lyric, "Where
art thou, my beloved son?" (aka "The Affliction of Margaret _____") (*JJII*
205). This otherwise undistinguished poem (*Poetical Works*, 205–6), in which
a bereaved widow addresses the chimera of her lost son, appealed to Joyce
because it was for him, as it was for Wordsworth, an articulation of paternal
love.[2] There is a profoundly personal relationship, then, in Joyce's mind and
spirit, between the anguish of his separation from John Stanislaus Joyce and
from God the Father, articulated in his creation of the fatherless and sonless
Catholic apostate James Duffy.

Devotional Duffy

Mr. James Duffy was evidently raised an observant Catholic, since among
the books of this sophisticated, middle-aged man is the *Maynooth Catechism*
(*D* 108.1–2).[3] Schoolchildren of his time—and therefore, the vast majority of
his presumed original readers—memorized its entire 64 pages: this required
much more handling than its thin paper covers could sustain, so that the stu-
dious Master James Duffy bound it for himself. This compendium of official
Catholic Church answers to dogmatic and moral questions he would therefore have retained out of a nostalgic attachment to his school days rather than
for any desire to seek its counsel. He would have been able, therefore, without effort, to respond to such questions as "What are the Four Last Things?"
with the short list, "The Four Last Things are Death, Heaven, Hell, and Judgment."

Were this fictional James Duffy to return as one of Joyce's historical readers, he would not have been amused to discover himself in his creator's story,
which concludes with a preview of the third of these "Last Things." The
others, as attentive readers of the time would have (with a little prodding)
recognized, are those with which Joyce opened and closed the book: "The
Sisters" (Death), "Grace" (Heaven), and "The Dead" (Judgment). He would
also be annoyed to discover the grim humor that his creator was extracting

from an apparently innocent coincidence: he had a historical precursor in the eponymous premier Catholic publisher (1809–71). As Joyce was composing "A Painful Case," "James Duffy" was a household name in Catholic Ireland.

The historical James Duffy made his name and fortune in publishing devotional and patriotic books in cheap popular editions: most notably *Donlevy's Catechism* (1848), the standard religious primer before the *Maynooth Catechism* and the Young Ireland ballad anthology, *The Spirit of the Nation* (1843), the century's best seller. His *Library of Ireland* defined the Irish Catholic outlook between Catholic Emancipation and the Land War, publishing tracts, pamphlets, schoolbooks, and missals, in Barbara Hayley's condescending phrase, "invent[ing] a new kind of cosy family Catholicism" (42). The leading publisher of pious books and periodicals, he brought the "Devotional Revolution" into literate Irish homes, publishing Cardinals Wiseman, Moran, and Cullen's sermons, Cardinal Newman's lectures, and (perhaps historically where it all began for Joyce) Gobinet's *Instructions for Youth in Christian Piety Taken from Sacred Scriptures, and the Writings of the Holy Fathers.*

This latter text (two volumes in one) was published in 1867, and as Father Bruce Bradley's informative discussion indicates, was generally familiar to students at Belvedere through the preaching of Father James Cullen, SJ. From Father Cullen's marginalia in the surviving copy at Belvedere, it is clear that he used it extensively in delivering the annual retreats (one of which impressed Joyce so deeply). It provided an outline of the spiritual life for young Catholics, dealing systematically with the natural and supernatural virtues, the Christian vocation, the sacraments, and the effects of punishment for sin (122–28).

Launching his short-lived *Duffy's Irish Catholic Magazine* in 1847, he set to counter the contempt for Ireland's pious traditions from both French atheism and "the floating uncertainties" of German idealism by publishing works imbued with the twin fervors of Irish nationalism and Catholic faith.[4] He published all of the leading Irish writers of the nineteenth century, including William Carleton, James Clarence Mangan, the Banims (John and Michael), and Charles Kickham. This "major pioneer of print capitalism" may have profited from sentimental publications, but he was uncharacteristically Irish in his strict work ethic, denying his 120 employees or himself any holidays. The house that bore his imprint in Joyce's time published *A Catalog of Standard Catholic Publications authorized Catholic prayer books, works relating to Ireland, and world of history and fiction* (1903), Arthur Griffith's *The Resurrection of Hungary* (1904), and D. P. Moran's *The Philosophy of Irish Ireland*

ADVERTISEMENTS.

JAMES DUFFY & CO., LTD.,

Catholic Publishers,

Booksellers, Printers, and Bookbinders.

38 WESTMORELAND STREET, DUBLIN.

JAMES DUFFY & CO. beg to inform the Hierarchy, Reverend Clergy, Heads of Colleges, Convents, and Religious Institutions, that they keep, with their own Publications, a large assortment of Books issued by the principal publishers, also Foreign Books published on the Continent and in the United States.

Prayer Books in Various Bindings. Cheap Editions of Standard Catholic Works. English and Foreign Catholic Publications kept in stock or procured.

Books for Gifts, Prizes, Bazaars, &c., supplied on the best terms.

Missals, Breviaries, Diurnals, Rituals, &c. Latest Editions. Any book published in Europe or America procured to order if not in stock.

Importers of Crucifixes, Rosaries, Scapulars, Statuary, Religious Pictures, Medals, &c. Vestments, Stations of the Cross in Oleograph, Chromo, Iron, &c., Ecclesiastical Brass Work.

School Books and National Board Publications. Special Terms to Colleges and Schools.

Printing and Bookbinding executed in our Works. Estimates for Printing sent gratis. Bookbinding in all styles done by competent workmen.

Catalogues will be forwarded Post Free on application.

JAMES DUFFY & CO., Ltd., : 38 Westmoreland Street,

Figure 4.1. Advertisement for James Duffy & Co. *Irish Catholic Directory*, 1909.

(1905) (*Encyclopedia of Irish History and Culture*, www.pgil-eirdata.org and s.v. "James Duffy").

The multiple ironies in naming his protagonist—a reclusive brooder on a succession of authors reflective of nineteenth-century intellectual trends (from Wordsworth to Nietzsche, and Hauptmann)—after a figure so identified with sentimental devotionalism and the antagonist of floating idealism and atheism would not have escaped Joyce's intended original readers. In Mr. Duffy's adulthood he evidently abandoned this childhood faith ("He had neither . . . church nor creed," *D* 109.8), and disdained its moral corollary, the weaker Christian virtue of charity: "He never gave alms to beggars" (*D* 108.28–29).[5]

Despite his intellectual dissent, Duffy's modern rationalism (his self-analysis), and his self-assertion (his firm walk), he remains encased within his early emotional formation as a subscribing Christian. In describing Mr. Duffy's mental and psychological progress, the narrator uses the language that is consistent, constant, and familiar to Mr. Duffy: he thinks about "his spiritual life" (*D* 109.9). However he expressed this inner experience to Mrs. Sinico, it had an effect on her contrary to his own expectations and interpretation: whereas it made her "fervent" (*D* 111.26), it provoked in him a deeper sense of despair and isolation, since despite his spiritual communication with her, his inner voice spoke of "the soul's incurable loneliness" (*D* 111.28). He evidently told her of his spiritual anguish, thinks of the intellectual and cultural interests he shares with Mrs. Sinico as "sacred" (*D* 115.20–21), which made her his "soul's companion" (*D* 115.26).

Of his former faith and its moral dictates he retains a firm moralizing streak—he views gluttons and alcoholics with unconcealed disdain—and along with it some quaint superstitious habits, represented by his "carrying a stout hazel" (*D* 108.28–29, 113.8). This gesture towards druidic divination and the occult powers of the pre-Christian priestly class in Ireland (see Mac-Killop, s.v. "hazel"), indicates that the numinous still plays a residual role in his otherwise postreligious mindset. This detail accords with the observation of several critics that the Duffy-Sinico love triangle ironically reflects the Celtic tale of Tristan and Iseult.[6]

If the selected titles from his bookshelves represent the history of the serious interests that displaced the authority of Catholic teaching, the most obvious inference is that he seems to have moved from a childhood faith through "doubtful" frame of mind, through a Cartesian divergence of mind/soul and body: "He lived at a little distance from his body, regarding his own acts with doubtful side-glances" (*D* 108.23–25), to a Wordsworthian pantheism and

notional transcendentalism, then (as I shall argue below) to a Schopenhauerean demythologization of Christian belief and allied romantic spiritual-
ism, and eventually to the rejection of every "church [and] creed" (*D* 109.08),
and their eventual replacement by the abandonment of the metaphysical in a
thoroughgoing Nietzschean atheism.

By the time we meet him, there are few shreds of these former faiths remaining to Duffy: his erstwhile dutifulness now shrunk to a couple of ges-
tural minima—appearing at familial funerals and Christmas gatherings—and
the regimen of his personal life. Although he is a loner, his life is as regulated
as that of a monk whose life is "ordered." When confronting the existential
crisis in his life—the discovery of Mrs. Sinico's death—his response is a confusion of postures and valuations that he has adopted during spiritual hegira: he vacillates between social disgust at "a commonplace vulgar death" (*D*
115.23), partially repeated and prayerlike ejaculation, "Just God, what an end"
(*D* 115.18,28), and a Nietzschean disdain for her feminine weakness: "she had
been unfit to live . . . one of the wrecks on which civilization has been reared"
(*D* 115.28–31). The attitudes he subsequently strikes range from the dispassionately rational, "she had ceased to exist" (*D* 116.24) to the entertainment
of her spiritual presence even after death: "She seemed to be near in him the
darkness" (*D* 117.3–4).

It is safe to infer, therefore, that the presence of *The Maynooth Catechism*
in James Duffy's library is a Joycean metonymy for the Christian, if not clerical, vocation that Duffy, like his creator, imagined for himself in his youth.
The present investigation aims to uncover the multiple cultural models with
which Mr. Duffy struggles.

Father Duffy

It is surprising that the criticism of "A Painful Case" has not pursued the implications of the relationship between Mr. Duffy's celibate intellectuality and
dedication to a daily routine, which taken in concert with many apparently
incidental details of his circumstances, indicate that he has a clearly marked
clerical personality.

Joyce invested his fictional alter ego Mr. Duffy with many attributes of
the clerical mind. One of Joyce's most intellectual characters, Duffy is neither liberal nor liberally educated. His tastes are cultivated but narrow: confined, so far as we are explicitly informed, to the plays of Hauptmann, some
of Nietzsche's philosophical works, and the music of Mozart. His "exactitude,"
rationality, and "theories" render him unsympathetic to the "hard-faced real-

ists" (*D* 111.5) among the workingmen and to the pathetic "facts" of her life with which the overwhelmed Mrs. Sinico responds (*D* 110.29–30). The workmen are preoccupied with wage claims and she with a neglectful husband, whereas Mr. Duffy surrounds himself with a palisade of abstractions. This he fortifies with allocution and epigram, betraying a penchant for sermonizing (*D* 112.19–22) or imagining that he is conducting an "interview" (*D* 112.2), rather than engaging in openhearted dialog with his lay inferiors. Mr. Duffy sometimes catches himself in the role of a sole retreatant attending to his own sermon on the Gospel of Onan: "he heard the strange impersonal voice which he recognized as his own, insisting on the soul's incurable loneliness" (*D* 111.27–28). At other less self-conscious times, his penchant for Latinate diction and rhetorical excess shows itself in his silent and habitual rehearsal of moralizing cadences ("He saw the squalid tract of her vice, miserable and malodorous," *D* 115.25–26) betrays the overcompensation of a loner and the frustration of thwarted preacher.

Such an impression is certainly conveyed by his dark name (*dubh*) and gloomy disposition (*D* 108.16), his twilight walks, his remote residence, and his self-willed distancing from workmen, lovers, and the rough-and-tumble of city life, his daily routine, his emotional coldness, his "confessing" his values, his emulation of the ascetic tastes of the monk, his moral scrupulosity, and the terms in which the narrator intimates his inner life: that "he lived his spiritual life without any communion with others" (*D* 109.8). He continues to regulate his behavior as if he belonged to an "order," whereas the solitary requires no such ruled communitarian consideration. Mr. Duffy exhibits another aspect of "orderliness" that Joyce admired in the clerics he knew well: he told August Suter that the Jesuits taught him "how to survey and to judge," how to manage the symbolic order (*JJII* 27). The narrative cites this sequence of variations that link the word "order" with Mr. Duffy's character and behavior: "physical or mental disorder" (*D* 108.14–15), "inordinate" (*D* 111.5), "orderliness of his mind" (*D* 112.13), and "ordered a hot punch" (*D* 116.9), with apparent deference to the implied theme of "holy orders" or "ordination."

Mrs. Sinico's politely expressed regret about the "empty benches" (*D* 109.23) must have therefore wafted before the nose of the diffident stranger a faint whiff of ecclesiastical must. The implications of this nuance grow when their subsequent intimacies are described as between a penitent and priest-confessor in the enclosed purview of the confession box (*D* 110.31 and *D* 112.3), they occurred in "her little cottage" with its "dark discreet room" (*D* 111.20), and in a "ruined confessional" (*D* 112.3). In the same vein, the metaphor conveying the style, content, and parameters of his relationship with

Mrs. Sinico—"she became his confessor" (*D* 110.31)—betrays the frustrated, or abandoned, clerical vocation (the metaphor is Duffy's, the reversal of roles the implied narrator's).[7] Finally, the break in their "intercourse" (*D* 112.6) and Mr. Duffy's admission to his fear of "entanglements" occur in the most public walks in the Phoenix Park—between the Parkgate and Chapelizod—rather than in the "quiet" and "stealth(y)" auspices of their previous excursions (*D* 110.15–17).[8]

The narrator inlays his post-Christian portrait of Mr. Duffy with images drawn from several Catholic sacraments: communion, confession, ordination, and (as we shall see) matrimony. The major elements in the Christian myth contextualize his story: from Mr. Duffy's neglected apple to Mrs. Sinico's fall, her habitual sin, and his search for "redeeming" qualities in his friends (*D* 108.23).

"a redeeming instant"

No critic has registered my puzzlement at the clause describing Mr. Duffy as "a man ever alert to greet a redeeming instinct in others" (*D* 108.22–23). I admit to mental boggle at this quixotic use of "redeeming." Redemption, "buying back," whether legal or theological, implies a rational and contractual, and never an instinctual, process. Could it mean—in a broader, metaphorical sense—that Mr. Duffy is sensitive to evidence of a generous or indulgent spirit in a person he had previously considered less worthy? If so, the rest of the sentence, "but often disappointed," indicating that these hopes were intermittently held, appears to be an imprecise qualification. Turning to the manuscripts, I note that Joyce's original clause read, "a redeeming instant in the lives his soul spurned" (*JJA* 4.99). The meaning of this statement is immediately clear: Mr. Duffy was ready to acknowledge even a momentary sign of virtue or character in others, whatever their previous reputations to the contrary.

The dramatic instance of this "redeeming instant" in "A Painful Case" is, of course, Mrs. Sinico's gesture in breaking the platonic nature of her relationship with Mr. Duffy. It is worth observing that in the second revision of the story, Joyce refined the narrative on this point. The first draft was crude and melodramatic: "Mrs Sinico threw her arms round forward into his lap and seemed to faint" (*JJA* 4.109), whereas the second (and final version) reads, "Mrs Sinico caught up his hand passionately and pressed it to her cheek" (*JJA* 4.155). This fully accords with her character and the restraint in her relationship with Mr. Duffy, and, moreover, accommodates Joyce's other intentions (as we shall see) in the design of "A Painful Case."

It would appear that this slip entered the record when Joyce, writing the fair copy in 1906 (or perhaps listening to someone read a previous version aloud for his transcription), wrote "a redeeming instinct in others but often disappointed" (*JJA* 4.141), which slipped his own notice and that of subsequent textual editors.

In the Joycean lexicon, "disappointed" sometimes bears a particular freight that needs to be weighed at this point. Father James Flynn, in "The Sisters" is described as "a disappointed man" (*D* 17.19), Father Arnall describes hell as a world of "cruelty and disappointment" (*P* 118.22–23), and Stephen Dedalus calls Kingstown pier "a disappointed bridge" (*U* 2.39). These usages suggest that they bear, for Joyce, some theological implications relevant to the present elucidation.

In his Epistle to the Romans (5: 5) Saint Paul announces, "spes autem non confundit: quia caritas Dei diffusa est in cordibus nostris per Spiritum sanctum, qui datus est nobis" (and hope does not disappoint, because the love of God has been poured out into our hearts through the holy Spirit that has been given to us). This wording appears in the American Standard Version (1901), an adaptation of the English Revised Version (1881–85). It replaced the antiquated language of the King James and Geneva Versions ("And hope maketh not ashamed") and the Catholic Douai ("And hope confoundeth not"), so that subsequent versions for English-speaking Catholics and Protestants have become similarly familiar with this wording. The Revised Standard, Confraternity, New International, and New American Bibles all render the Vulgate *confundit* in some form of the verb "disappoint." This is an enthymemic form of an argument, which he develops, in further detail elsewhere in this same letter (8: 1–39).[9] Here Saint Paul is arguing that the gift of the grace to believe, once accepted, provides a confidence in fundamentals that will buoy the Christian up in the midst of ordinary difficulties. God's love of humanity is a guarantee that the individual Christian's hope for redemption is no illusion. The orthodox Catholic understanding of this statement is that the apostle is not making a psychological point (pace Pelagius) but an ontological or spiritual one. His primary frame of reference is not to the order of nature, but that of grace. Indeed, a person's feelings have no bearing on the actual spiritual condition of the soul. The unblinking fundamentalism of Saint Paul's view (original sin had not by then been defined) is that Christ's passion and death have reversed the order of the universe. The trope is not, of course, originally the Apostle's. It has many precedents in biblical language, for example, "In you they trusted and were not disappointed" (Psalms 22: 5), "Has anyone trusted in the Lord been disappointed?" (Sirach 2: 10), and "Those who hope in me will not be disappointed" (Isaiah 49: 23), which he is expressly citing.

So when the concealed narrator of "A Painful Case" inserts this trope in the text, he is advancing the theological theme, one of many similar instances in Joyce's work where the same term appears with reference to hope in Christian redemption. In his introduction to the hellfire sermon, Father Arnall sketches the signal function of the virtue of hope to Adam and Eve after their transgression: expelled "into the world, the world of sickness and striving, of cruelty and disappointment . . . God . . . promised that in the fullness of time He would send down from heaven . . . the Eternal Word" (*P* 118.21–31). These images remain a powerful presence in Stephen Dedalus's imagination and help account for his private joke in the "Nestor" episode of *Ulysses* "—Kingstown pier, Stephen said. Yes, a disappointed bridge (*U* 2.39). His personal crisis provoked by his mother's death has intellectual, emotional, and spiritual dimensions: he has been brooding in particular over his loss of the Christian hope that, despite all her suffering, she retained to her last breath (*U* 1.198–279). "The one true thing in life" that she represented to him while alive is now put to another test: whether it survives into "that other world" to become one with the creative love of the Divine Word. In this particular instance, he has been distracted by Armstrong's blundering reference to Kingstown pier (*U* 2.33), a familiar trysting place. In the "mirthless laughter" of these preadolescents, he imagines them (alphabetically) as girls: "Edith, Ethel, Gerty, Lily" (*U* 2.36). Why then does this provoke Stephen to give his enigmatic definition?

There is evidently an imaginative link in his mind between the metonymy of the "disappointed bridge," the L-shaped Kingstown pier, the name Lily (from "The Dead"), and the gnomon (from "The Sisters"), all signifying the world's imperfection: a particularly resonant retrospective arrangement. Thus Mulligan's taunt, that Stephen has "the cursed jesuit strain in you, only it's injected the wrong way" (*U* 1.209), refers to his paralysis of spirit resulting from the conflict between his religious formation—his inculcation with the counsels to perfection—and his adult skepticism. By contrast, Leopold Bloom, lacking the gift of faith, which is Stephen's inheritance, is free of such high expectations. Thus her discovery of Bloom's agnosticism leaves Mrs. Riordan "disappointed" (*U* 15.1715), and the catechist considers Bloom's cheerful secularity as an insurance against being "disappointed" (*U* 17.349).

The narrator explicitly compares his actions to those of a priest: "moving his lips as a priest does when he reads the prayers *Secreto*" (*D* 113.17–18), as if

Figure 4.2. The Wicket Gate, Phoenix Park, Chapelizod. Photograph by Cóilín Owens, 2006.

he were recapitulating, unawares, a habit acquired during clerical training.[10] Similarly, he has been accustomed to thinking of his public appearances in hieratic terms: "perform[ing]" funereal duties (*D* 109.11) and "assist[ing]" at meetings (*D* 110.32). This image of expected deference recurs during the interlude in the bar where he has evidently cultivated the expectation that he be "served . . . obsequiously" (*D* 116.10), rather than engage in the camaraderie normally afforded by one's "local." (Mr. Duffy reappears in *FW* 360.4 as "jemcrow, jackdaw, prime and second with their terce"). Here he disdains the "communion" of others, as he does again on entering the Phoenix Park by "the first gate" (*D* 117.1). It appears that Mr. Duffy prefers this wicket gate— which admits but one pedestrian at a time—to the main gate at Chapelizod (a small distance east of the village), which accommodates both pedestrian and vehicular traffic.[11] In the context of his residual quasi-clerical self-image, he retains the habit of following the injunction to "Enter through the narrow gate; for the gate is wide and the road broad that leads to destruction, and those who enter through it are many" (Matt. 7: 13) (cf. figure 3.4).

This particular allusion helps establish the theological or biblical perspective on the regression of Mr. Duffy's "spiritual life" (*D* 109.8). From the "lofty" perspective of his high-ceilinged room (*D* 107.8), he imagines Mrs. Sinico's admiration of his intellect, "that in her eyes he would ascend to angelical stature" (*D* 111.24–25): this means that he allows her to admire, but not to love him. It also implies that the loftiness that in the Christian dispensation begins with love and humility has become, in Mr. Duffy's case, grounds for his condescension to those with less intellectual endowment. He is an ascetic not out of humility, but out of pride. He declares himself unencumbered by bourgeois comforts (the burden of his walls being "free" of pictures), and lives under quasi-monastic high ceilings in a room decorated in primary colors (black, white, and red), denying emotional indulgence or engagement. But in his case, what might have begun as Christian detachment has become perverted into a disdainful elitism.

But at the same time, a man whose mental lexicon embraces theological metaphors like "bore witness" (*D* 112.13), "redeemed" (*D* 108.22), "disappointed" (*D* 108.23), and "doubtful" (*D* 108.25), and who is haunted by the "prophecy of failure" (*D* 109.19), the failure of the light (*D* 116.3), and the prospect of final "despair" (*D* 117.14), considers himself, whether he would admit to it or not, as having a soul, and thus a "spiritual life." The contents of his desk bear witness to the pattern of unrealized aspirations that marks his life: the unfinished Hauptmann translation, his desultory writing habit, his unsharpened pencils, and his forgotten apple. Without quite doing so, Mr. Duffy admits to these disappointments in his Schopenhauerean/Nietzschean observation on "the soul's incurable loneliness" (*D* 111.23). In these respects, Mr. James Duffy seems to share the "disappointment" of Father James Flynn.

Since the mental language is Duffy's, the Matthean reference reinforces the dramatic torque: his mind is well stocked with biblical and sacramental metaphors. The context from which he drew the reference illuminates something of Mr. Duffy's mindset: "At the resurrection they neither marry nor are given in marriage but are like the angels in heaven" (Matt. 22: 30). Jesus, answering the skeptical Pharisees, asserts that marriage does not persist into the next life. Like the angels, in whose lives sex plays no part, our glorified bodies will not have sexual desires. Saint Paul develops the implications of this by distinguishing the "natural" and "spiritual" bodies. The Christian understanding of the Resurrection denies both the naturalistic view of our lives and the platonic notion of the survival of the soul only (see 1 Cor. 15: 35–50). Mr. Duffy has taken a gnostic view of Jesus' answer by denigrating the body. He is taking a very lofty view of human relations. This disdain resurfaces as he observes the "furtive" lovers in the final scene: he has returned to the mindset with which his story began.

The narrator's adroit handling of the language of "A Painful Case" illuminates this contrast between Mr. Duffy's self-image as a morally superior quasi-cleric and his shrinking detachment from the crude materialism of the "hard-faced realists" among whom he is cast. From this judgment the detached narrator does not appear to demur, delivering sentences with but one or two words of romance provenance to leaven their coarser Germanic and Norse grain: "They [the patrons of the Chapelizod bar] drank at intervals from their huge pint tumblers and smoked, spitting often on the floor and sometimes dragging the sawdust over their spits with their heavy boots" (D 116.13–15). At the same time, in sentences like "The books on the white wooden shelves were arranged from below upwards according to bulk" (D 107.17–19), the precise balance and Anglo-Saxon clarity of the voice is an indication of its clinical detachment. Like "interval" in the previous example, the only word of Latin origin, "according" (*accordare < cor*: heart), is neatly packed into a sentence that turns on the phrase "from below upwards" and which is kept in place by the complementary bracketing of "books" and "bulk." This diction, blunt and precise, summarizes the external physical manifestation of Mr. Duffy's intellectual world.

When readers encounter Mr. Duffy's mental language, by contrast, the ratio between words of Romance or Germanic descent is reversed: "Mr Duffy abhorred anything which betokened physical or mental disorder" (D 108.14–15), and in this case, the consonance between the "abhorred" and "disorder" emphasizes the cultivation of his recoil. Similarly, when he tells Mrs. Sinico that "The workmen's discussions . . . were too timorous [and] the interest they took in the question of wages was inordinate" (D 111.3–5), the Latinate diction of his supercilious understatement seems deliberately calculated to impress a woman whom he knows hears nothing similar from her husband's lips. There is enough of the poet and frank observer of degradation in Mr. Duffy to allow him, when roused, to think in Anglo-Saxonisms appropriate to the occasion. We see evidence of this when he imagines the company Mrs. Sinico is likely to have kept before her death: "He thought of the hobbling wretches whom he had seen carrying cans and bottles to be filled by the barman" (D 115.26–28).

When he turns to moralizing, despite his reading of modern German authors, he slips back into the language reflecting his youthful exposure to Latinate diction: of Mrs. Sinico's drinking, "He saw the squalid tract of her vice, miserable and malodorous" (D 115.25–26); and of the embracing couples beneath the Park wall, "Their venal and furtive loves filled him with despair" (D 117.13–14). These instances typify the narrator's selective use of Mr. Duffy's mental language, implying the manner of his observations and that the source of his proclivity to moralizing lies in his early exposure to ecclesiastical Latin. Thus in the final scene the narrator twice translates what Mr. Duffy actually heard—from the puffing of the steam engine to what it (rather melodramatically) reminded him of, "Emily Sinico, Emily Sinico"—and into the narrator's parody of Mr. Duffy's characteristic vocabulary: "he heard in his ears the laborious drone of the engine reiterating the syllables of her name" (*D* 117.25–26). Again, in *FW*, in the voice of "jemcrow, jackdaw," the consonants and vowels of Mrs. Sinico's name float through the radio baize as "after Sunsink gang (Oiboe!)" (*FW* 359.36). As recirculations of images from "A Painful Case," they are appropriately combined with references to sunset, Dublin's Dunsink Observatory, Italian admonition, and the oboe).

Meanwhile, the narrator of the story, also attending to these themes and rhythms, ends his account with the repeated phrase, "perfectly silent" (*D* 117.33). This dactyl and trochee, a variation on the double dactyl that Mr. Duffy hears in the engine's departing puff, makes savage mockery of the original object of Mr. Duffy's spiritual aspiration: the ideal of Christian perfection. He would not take the wide gate of Mrs. Sinico's destruction.

In this final paragraph we have therefore the spiritual epiphany of "A Painful Case": when Mr. Duffy is finally alert to, but unable to greet, his own life's "redeeming instant."

Ascetic Duffy

A few days after he dismissed Mrs. Sinico from his company, Mr. Duffy received a parcel containing his books and music, bearing an ostensibly ecclesiastical address "Mr. James Duffy, Church House, Chapelizod, Dublin." This "old somber house" (*D* 107.5–6), originally the residence of the officers commanding the Phoenix Park garrison, stands today, exactly as it did in 1900: stark and detached, its front door elevated above the footpath. Joseph Sheridan LeFanu (1814–73), another recluse, sometime resident of Chapelizod, and an editor of the *Evening Mail*, fictionalized this same domicile in the gothic mystery, *The House By the Churchyard* (1863), a novel in John Stanislaus Joyce's possession (see Jackson and Costello, 70–72 and map, viii).[12] Some readers have observed, but only in passing on to more apparently appetizing topics, that Mr. Duffy furnishes his room with an eremitic austerity and that he deports himself with priestly mien (for example, Connolly, "A Painful Case," 108–9; Tucker, 121). He lives reclusively, furnishing his bare and lofty room as would a medieval monk his cell or scriptorium: furnished

Figure 4.3. Church House, Chapelizod. Photograph by Cóilín Owens, 2006

in primary colors, in white wood and black iron, and his high square desk and manuscript inscribed in black and purple ink. His monklike physical and figuratively brown mental habits make him into an inconspicuous figure of nonconsumption: his brown-tinted skin (D 108.17), his "tawny" moustache, his cedarwood pencil and gum bottle (D 108.11), brass pin, over-ripe apple (D 108.12), and buff *Mail* (D 113.9), his expressly medieval "saturnine" disposition[13] and regulated "habit" (D 108.25), and even down to the "plain honesty" (D 109.3) of his culinary taste, his disdain for small talk, and abstention from desserts (D 112.26–27). He is one Duffy whose name matches his bilious temperament.[14]

The discipline that has become ingrained in Mr. Duffy's habits and character he has inherited from fifteen hundred years of monastic practice. The Rule of Saint Benedict (ca. 500) is its classic formulation, adaptations of which form the bases of the constitutions and rules of the major religious orders in the Catholic tradition, the Franciscans, Benedictines, Cistercians, Dominicans, and in the Counter-Reformation, the Jesuits. With the object of offering a practical guide to those who pursue the ideal of Christian perfection, versions of this rule are voluntarily followed by devout laity associated with these orders (including May Murray, a Third-Order member of the Franciscans, *JJII* 136). On the premise that Christian perfection means more than the avoidance of sin—the obligation of all Christians—these regimens cultivate, through daily discipline, the positive virtues of humility, charity, and obedience. These physical and psychological disciplines provide the framework within which a true inner life can be cultivated, allowing the soul to progress through the four stages of spiritual refinement. Thus while from the outside, the discipline of the "ordered" life seems restrictive, reactionary, and life-denying, from the inside, the detachment from the material world allows the soul to progress from the primary stage of "purgation" to the final stage of "unity" with the life of grace.

The regimen of a monk's life imposes lifelong observation of regular hours for sleep, work, meals, and prayer. All physical habits—clothes, tonsure, physical appearance, and deportment—are communally standardized. The monastic discipline requires that all aspects of the daily routine be observed with scrupulous attention to regularity and punctuality so that every minor breach of deportment, such as moving with undue haste about any task ("precipitation"), allowing one's eyes to wander from the task at hand ("custody of the eyes"), not keeping one's bedclothes smoothed without wrinkle, or not fulfilling one's daily tasks with attention to the finest detail, are entered into a logbook that is completed at noontime every day.

Similarly, the monastic rule imposes strict regulation of reading and ideas, derived from daily study of the monastic rule, reading of scripture, attendance at the daily community Mass, and the five-times-per-day chanting of the divine office. Until recently, all of this was conducted in Latin, in which all but the lowest rank of monks—the lay brothers—were proficient. These intellectual and physical structures allow the monks to discipline their spirits through twice-daily periods of meditation (thirty minutes each), allowing the monks to ascend through the stages of spiritual growth outlined in Adolphe Tanqueray's *The Spiritual Life*, the standard textbook on the subject.

The monks lead communal lives, sharing their property, ideas, prayer, meals, and work. Thus no "particular friendships" are permitted; and monastic practice enjoins monks to each have an individual monitor who observes them in a detached and objective manner, pointing out their faults. Thus the monastic life inculcates a degree of detachment from the social and material world and from the self-interest and personal vanity that forms so much of the principle upon which the commodification of values in an individualist and capitalist culture depends. The monastic rule goes much beyond that of an academic institution, army, or prison, therefore, in requiring not only physical and mental compliance with the rule, but also spiritual acquiescence in every respect, so that every impulse at resistance, resentment, uncharitable feeling, has to be noted, communally admitted, curbed, and extirpated. Only through such a regimen can the soul be freed of the myriad attachments that constitute the fabric of the unreflective secular world.

The "ordered" life thus provides the conditions under which "imperfections" can be eliminated from one's life and the Christian virtues of detachment, humility, charity, and prayer can be cultivated. Detachment from all appetites, good in themselves, allows the monk to develop his full human nature as a creature of God. Along with the other major religions, the Christian tradition has understood this call to perfection as only possible to the person who lives apart from the appetites of greed, sloth, self-indulgence, and sensuality. In rare cases is this seen possible outside of the celibate state. Only those living apart from the pleasures of sexuality and the responsibilities of parenthood can expect to fulfill the Christian injunction, "Be ye perfect even as your Heavenly Father is perfect" (Matt. 5: 48). Joyce could therefore appreciate Renan's remark that "the monk is . . . the only true Christian" (272). That the Christian ideal can only be realized in the solitary life of the monk (the word derives from the Greek μονοⵉ, "alone") is a long and deeply rooted element in Christian tradition. Thus the sentence upon which the reader loses sight of Mr. Duffy, "He felt that he was alone" (*D* 117.33–34), conveys, beneath its flat surface the indelible and accusing image of his former aspiration to the life of the monk.

James Joyce was never a Jesuit scholastic. But he was a close observer—and for a time during his adolescence, a devoted admirer—of the Jesuit version of the intellectual, communal, and spiritual discipline inherited from the Rule of Saint Benedict. His membership in the Sodality of Our Lady gave him an elementary introduction to this ideal and rule, since it required daily reading of *The Imitation of Christ* (Thomas à Kempis) and daily fifteen-minute meditations. This exposure would have given him a good sense of what kind of discipline led to the development of the "silentmannered priest" (*P* 158.17) he subsequently dismissed from his gallery of *futurabilia*. He parodies the encomia of this moral and spiritual discipline in *Portrait* (147–53). Stephen Dedalus's subsequent resolution to live in "silence, exile, and cunning" (*P* 247.4) is therefore in one sense an adaptation of the conditions laid upon any monk or Jesuit: separation from family, nation, and the babble of the marketplace for the love of God. The Jesuits he knew at the National University—Fathers Joseph S. Darlington and Charles J. Ghezzi—were exiles for Christ, as were his avatars in Europe from medieval Ireland, Saints Fursey and Columbanus.

Joyce was naturally familiar with the differences between the religious rules and spirit of the Jesuits, Dominicans, Cistercians, and Franciscans in contradistinction with the secular (or diocesan) clergy, as discrete references to them in "The Dead," *Portrait*, and other contemporary accounts indicate: the austere Cistercians' sleeping in the shadow of their coffins (*D* 200–201), intellectual Cranly as "the [Dominican] white bishop" (Byrne, 43–44), the charitable Franciscan confessor of *Portrait* (141–45), and Fathers Flynn and Conroy ("The Sisters" and "The Dead," respectively), of the diocesan clergy. He understood that each of these major orders in its own right sought a practical way for its members to realize the object of a Christian life: the salvation of self and of the world. His portrait of James Duffy applies colorations from Joyce's own cultural formation, implying a similar adolescent captivation with its ordered modes of thought and feeling, and helping account for the cast of his particular alienation. It is therefore appropriate that Duffy reside in Chapelizod, where he is one-third of the way between Dublin City Centre, with its despised bank and "gilded youth," and the village of Maynooth, with its seminary and catechism. At the height of the crisis provoked by the newspaper paragraph, his gesture of "gaz[ing] out of his window . . . on the Lucan road" (*D* 115.15–18) is therefore a fitting emblem of his present social and material disquiet, moral bewilderment, and residual nostalgia for the spiritual clarity of his youth.

Extended into the relatively secular Catholicism of modern Ireland, these manifestations of a celibate-clerical character suggest, in the view of the present argument, that Mr. Duffy may be considered as an instance of the syndrome recognized as the "spoiled priest." Indeed, a survey of literary representations of this type leads to the conclusion that, despite its narrative shortcomings,[15] Joyce's Mr. James Duffy is the most penetrating exposé of the type in Irish literature. By contrast with the treatments by Carleton, T. C. Murray, and even John McGahern, which are variously comic or grotesque caricatures, Joyce's story provides the most acute observations of the melancholic mentality of a man who suffers from the impression that he refused to hear the voice of God: "You did not choose me, but I chose you" (John 15: 16).

Irish Clerical Culture

During the century between the founding of Maynooth (1795) and Joyce's youth, Catholicism in Ireland developed enormously: religious observance exceeding canonical requirements was almost universal, hundreds of ecclesiastical buildings—cathedrals, churches, and schools—were founded, and there was an unprecedented growth in Irish clerical numbers. This accelerated after the Great Famine, when in contrast with the precipitous fall in the general population, the numbers of clergy reached a proportion unmatched in Irish history (or, for that matter, anywhere else in the modern Catholic world, a trend that persisted until the 1960s). Under the determined leadership of Cardinal Cullen after 1850, the Irish Catholic character took its formidable shape: while it was the most heartfelt, observant, and energetic regional Catholicism in the English-speaking world, it was also firmly ultramontane, intellectually and politically conservative, and clerically controlled. The religious landscape that the young Joyce learned to pace was thus heavily "Cullenized" (*Encyclopedia of Irish History and Culture*, s.vv. "devotional revolution," "religious orders," "Roman Catholic Church").

Several congregations of brothers and sisters—notably the Irish Christian Brothers and Sisters of Mercy—were founded for the alleviation of poverty and ignorance. All the major continental orders and societies of religious— the Passionists, Redemptorists, Oblates of Mary Immaculate—had houses in Ireland. Whereas there had been but 120 nuns or religious sisters in Ireland in 1800, by 1900 there were 8,000 (Corish, 203). By Joyce's time, then, many Irish Catholic families had one or more members among the clergy. Having a member of the family consecrated in this way conferred a degree of social standing, relative financial security in an impoverished society, and the presumed spiritual benefits.

In a poor and orthodox Catholic society such as Ireland was between 1830 and 1960, social expectations for roles and professions were fixed. Unlike contemporary Ireland and America, career changes were practically unknown; education was expensive and available to but the few; and failing to complete a costly educational program could mean the ruination of a family's fortunes and reputation. Withdrawing was more than an embarrassment: it was a disgrace.

It was expensive to send a son for a clerical career, and entry to some of the more elite orders of sisters—the Sacred Heart Sisters, for example, by contrast with the Sisters of Mercy (which Joyce's sister Margaret joined)—required sizeable dowries for their daughters. Undertaking a clerical career required a substantial social and economic investment: there were no grants or foundations to underwrite such an education. The family therefore incurred a substantial debt if a son or daughter undertook a course of clerical training, entered a convent or seminary, and later decided to withdraw. Since the training was not readily transferable, the social embarrassment was unavoidable

and the debt unredeemable. Thus the social pressure on a seminarian to persevere was very strong.

Clerical culture, moreover, set its members apart from the lay mainstream.
This was due to the rule of celibacy and to moral authority that the profession conferred. Living outside the marital and familial bonds accepted by the
majority of the laity, a priest had unique access, on the one hand, through
hearing confessions, to their individual private lives. On the other hand he
was a uniquely public figure. Often the most—sometimes the only—educated
member of the community, through the Sunday sermon he had a virtual mo-
nopoly of the public attention. Those in religious training were exposed to
intellectual currents beyond the semiliterate laity. Clerical training required
a grounding in scholastic philosophy, church history (including a historical
treatment of heresies), and surveys of hermeneutics and church dogma. It required minimal intellectual, spiritual, and moral standards. This training, and
the aspiration that underlay it, set its members apart from the great majority of Catholics who were bound to the church by historical loyalty, popular
piety, and a certain degree of private skepticism and puzzlement about those
who took it that seriously.

Thus a person who having undertaken such a life and then abandoned the
course of study it required would be doubly set apart, socially and spiritually,
and would feel himself to be so, from the general run of his normal coreli-
gionists. Even more than a member of the clergy, an aspirant to the clerical
life who had failed in that course—for nothing like this would be a private
matter—would be set aside. If not already temperamentally predisposed to a
solitary life, the experience and training would cultivate such propensities.

The requirement that all members of the Catholic priesthood (and, of
course, members of religious orders or communities of either gender) be
celibate brought together these terms: so that psychosocial types who were
discomforted by heterosexual, familial, society might have thought themselves aptly fitted for the priesthood or religious life. While celibacy is a social
requirement for those who undertake a communal life, it has been a universal
requirement for the secular Roman Catholic priesthood since the First Lat-
eran Council (1123).[16] Celibacy, of course, serves as a screening device: since
the observance of sexual continence is beyond the capacity of the average
man, it helps ensure that only those of strong character and high principle
would enter the priesthood.

On a practical and psychological level, it allows the priest to give his un-
divided attention to the faithful, while also on a spiritual level, is a sign of

the priest's dedication to the life of the eternal spirit. Celibacy is also a public mark of the hieratic aspect of Christian ministry, a visible sign of him as "a man apart" from the ordinary Christian, and an intermediary with God. In this respect, members of the Catholic priesthood retain a historical link with the Jewish rabbinate—inheritors of "the order of Melchizedek"—while at the same time, as members of a nonhereditary class, their celibacy is a sign of God's grace available to all. Their celibacy is therefore an outward corollary of the indelible sacramental mark by which they are consecrated to God. In these respects, the Catholic priest is primarily a man endowed with unique sacramental powers and not a communal appointee, a "preacher," or social worker. In the Catholic tradition, the rule of celibacy has been the most manifest, and impressive, public sign of this distinctive vocation. Revulsion with or antipathy to conventional heterosexual expression rather than the love of God, the aptitude for a prayer life, or the desire to render service to the community, might, under these historical circumstances, have been occasionally perceived as the salient aptitude for a life in the Catholic priesthood.

A Spoiled Priest

A person who had attended a Catholic seminary or entered a monastery or convent but did not persevere to ordination or to final profession was termed in Hiberno-English, a "spoiled priest/nun." An educated layman with a reserved, withdrawn, or haunted look was assigned to the stereotype of the spoiled priest (Dolan, s.v. "spoiled priest"). The subject of a presumed repudiation of the vocation to the church, especially the priesthood, was considered a social embarrassment or worse: he was disowned by his family and rejected by his friends, so that if he did not seek the oblivion of emigration, he became a recluse or wanderer, sometimes becoming a polymath away from his native countryside. This figure from Irish folklore should not be confused with a man who of his own accord abandoned the priesthood, an ex-cleric, laicized priest, or former member of a religious congregation or order. This last is the opposite of a spoiled priest in that he is a man who became a priest when he should not, whereas a spoiled priest is a man who should have become a priest but did not.[17]

A "silenced priest," by contrast, is an ordained Catholic clergyman who has been suspended from his ministry. Such figures were held in special regard and popularly believed to possess special powers enabling them to cure sicknesses, or overcome the devil and evil spirits. When all other resources failed, the "silenced" priest was often approached in time of trouble. Father Keon in

"Ivy Day in the Committee Room" is apparently an example (*D* 126.1–127.4). George Bernard Shaw has a portrait of one in *John Bull's Other Island* (see Hickey and Doherty, s.v. "silenced priest").

Joyce's fictional universe accommodates examples of all of these clerical types, although their proportion of the population decreases as his work matures. The complexities attached to the social designation of the type are illustrated by the figure of Father Bob Cowley in *Ulysses*. Joyce adapted the name from his father's erstwhile secretary, Bob Cowall (*JJII* 20 n). From his brief appearances, in "Wandering Rocks" (*U* 10.740–952) and "Sirens" (*U* 11.353–1272), we learn something of his appearance, character, and talent, but nothing definite of his professional aspirations or history. His "red lugs and a bulging apple" (*U* 11.353), "brilliant purply lobes" (*U* 11.484) and his presence in the Ormond Bar in the middle of the afternoon imply that he is another member of Dublin's coterie of habitual drinkers. This appears to be confirmed by his improvidence, in that he is so far in arrears in his rent that he seeks Ben Dollard's advice in fending off the process-servers (*U* 10.887–954). He accompanies Simon Dedalus on the piano in his performance of Mozart's "*M'Appari*" (*U* 11.573 ff.). He is known to Bloom, Simon Dedalus, and his friends as "Bob" (*U* 5.180, 10.741, 883), but to the narrator of "Wandering Rocks" and "Sirens" as "Father Cowley" or "Father Bob Cowley" (*U* 10.740, 882–952, 11.774). His wearing a moustache confirms the implication of his friends' use of his Christian name that, at the very least, he is not a practicing priest (Gifford, "*Ulysses*" *Annotated*, 278).

In this respect his appearance in "Wandering Rocks" (*U* 10.740–42, 881–954) is set against that of the very sacerdotal Father Conmee (*U* 10.1–205). What are we to make of the contrast, then, between his two appellations? It is possible that the narrator, in acknowledgment of his sacerdotal ordination, and despite his resignation or suspension, continues to identify him formally, while allowing his social friends to think of him as "Bob" (Bloom: 5.180) or address him in this familiar manner (for example, Simon Dedalus: 10.741, 883; Ben Dollard: 11.449). It is equally possible to consider that he is a spoiled priest (Gifford, "*Ulysses*" *Annotated*, 88; following the Benstocks, 72). If he is one, the narrator's calling him by the derisive name "Father" is (like "Pisser" Burke's nickname) an indication of the mild malice with which his Catholic friends think of him even as they call him "Bob" to his face. Meanwhile, Bloom's mentally addressing him as "Bob" is an indication of his unfamiliarity with the significance of what the epithet "spoiled priest" means to his Catholic fellow Dubliners. In any event, in the disorderliness and alcoholism of his life, his ability to play the piano, his partiality to Mozart, and his moustache, he is both like and unlike the spoiled priest of the present inquiry, Mr. James Duffy (whom nobody calls "Jim").

Jackson and Costello trace the clerical lineage on both sides of the aisle. Joyce must have heard his father describe his own mother, Ellen Joyce, as "a spoiled nun," since she was for a time a postulant in the Presentation convent in Cork (21). Stephen Dedalus hears his father describe Dante Riordan as "a spoiled nun and that she had come out of the convent in the Alleghenies" (*P* 35.24–25).[18] Of Joyce's immediate family, his sister Margaret became a Sister of Mercy, whereas his brother Charlie was for a time a seminarian in Clonliffe College, the Dublin archdiocesan seminary. Stanislaus refers to this brother as a "spoiled priest" (*CDD* 21; cf. *MBK* 137, 140, 189). Joyce was sufficiently interested in spiritual autobiography to read, in December 1904, Ernest Renan's *Souvenirs*, which en passant, gives an affecting account of the formation of his clerical character, even after leaving the seminary at Saint Sulpice and abandoning orthodox Catholicism. In a letter to his brother, to whose tough-minded anticlericalism he was inclined to play, he derided Renan for his sentimental attachment to "dear old Grandmother Church" as "*un prêtre manqué*" (December 3, 1904, *Letters* II: 72).

Irish popular opinion would have been inclined, until recently, to share with Joyce his admission that he was a "spoiled priest" (Fallon, 70). Thomas Merton's reading of *Portrait* led him to much the same conclusion: "Joyce certainly looks like an Irishman who resisted a vocation to the priesthood" (211). Caroline Gordon broadens the charge in making the unreserved judgment, based on the severest interpretation of the Catholic understanding of grace (see Schleck below), that it is not

> a picture of the artist rebelling against constituted authority, but rather the picture of a soul that is being dammed for time and eternity caught in the act of foreseeing and foreknowing its damnation. (213)

One can only trust that divine mercy takes greater account than does Gordon of the irony in Joyce's portrait of his own youth.

Vocation

In the mind of the orthodox Catholic, nature—even in its socially conventional forms—is the medium of God's grace in the world. The Irish folk stereotype is therefore based on the theological assumption that the subject has rejected the grace of a vocation to the clerical or religious life. Father Charles Schleck defines a vocation as a call that God addresses to a person in the form of special grace that moves or inclines him to embrace the life to which he is called. This grace would seem to be the formal element of vocation rather than the call of legitimate ecclesiastical authority, which, though required, is merely a confirmation of the genuineness of the interior call. (*New Catholic Encyclopedia*, s.v. "vocation, religious and clerical")

Considered formally, a genuine vocation must fulfill three complementary sets of conditions: on the part of the subject, the church, and God. The subject must have the intellectual, psychological, physical, and moral qualities, and the proper intention. The subject should suffer no legal or natural barrier to the ministry, should be suited by family background, health, emotional stability, personal piety, balanced judgment, intellectual capacity, and morality—the ability to live chastely—to live a clerical or religious life. This implies that the subject should not exhibit any obvious impediment, such as extreme difficulties with continence, ill temper, habitual lack of docility, domineering personality, or lack of judgment. Properly constituted ecclesiastical authority must acknowledge those qualities and extend the invitation to the subject. The Catholic Church has the authority to authenticate, test, approve, direct, train, and profess or ordain candidates. A vocation requires a genuine internal call from God acknowledged in the soul, whereby the subject responds spiritually to the action of grace upon the soul. It is a pure gift from God that is furthered by meditation and prayer, and detachment from purely secular activities. Without this call, undertaking this course of action is a grave sin, and an obstacle to one's own salvation and the salvation of others.

Once heard, the rejection of a vocation may be sinful. On this point, theological opinion is divided. In answer to the question, is one bound to respond positively to a vocation, there are two opinions: if the clerical life is not a requirement but a Christian counsel, it cannot oblige under pain of sin; whereas if it is a unique gift of God, it cannot be rejected without incurring the pain of sin. The morally informed and intentional rejection of a recognized call cannot but be gravely sinful.

The folk tradition, without worrying itself about these distinctions, therefore, and assuming that anyone who embarks upon a course of study leading to the clerical life has de facto a vocation, considers that the failure to complete that course of study has rejected the gift, and moreover, shows the signs of it subsequently in her or his social deportment.

These considerations indicate that Stephen Dedalus in *Portrait*, although possessing the requisite intellectual and moral qualifications (this last, temporary, following the retreat), and hearing the summons from the appropriate ecclesiastical authority, the spiritual director of the college, lacks the true interior spirit, the crucial element, the genuine desire to serve God and man by the life of the evangelical counsels or the service of the altar. While offering membership in the Jesuits for Stephen's consideration, the spiritual director reminds him of this principle: "you must be quite sure, Stephen, that you have a vocation because it would be terrible if you found afterwards that you had none" (P 160.1–3). It is of course one of the major ironic reversals of *Portrait* that Stephen, while refusing to have his imaginative energies serve the church, co-opts its sacramental language in the service of his imaginative vocation: he would be "a priest of eternal imagination" (P 221.14).

The bravado of that self-ordination does not exorcize Stephen's residual daemons, the source of his "moody brooding" of which Buck Mulligan complains (U 1.235–36) and which Florry Talbot infers from Stephen's liturgical tones: "I'm sure you're a spoiled priest. Or a monk" (U 15.2649). As the present argument holds, Mr. Duffy shows in his mental and social habits symptoms consistent with the folk stereotype of the spoiled priest.

The Catholic idea of vocation is grounded in the Gospel account of the man of the ruling class who put this question to Jesus:

> "Good teacher, what must I do to merit eternal life?" Jesus answered him, "Why do you call me good? No one is good but God alone. You know the commandments; 'You shall not commit adultery; you shall not kill; you shall not steal; you shall not bear false witness; honor your father and your mother.'" And he replied, "All of these I have observed from my youth." When Jesus heard this he said to him, "There is still one thing left for you: sell all that you have and distribute it to the poor, and you will have a treasure in heaven. Then come, follow me." But when he heard this he became quite sad, for he was very rich. Jesus looked at him [now sad] and said, "How hard it is for those who have wealth to enter into the kingdom of God! For it is easier for a camel to pass through the eye of a needle than for a rich person to enter into the kingdom of God." (Luke 18: 18–25; cf. Matt. 19: 16–30 and Mark 10: 17–31)

A clerical vocation is not easy to follow, since even if one does not have riches like this young man, it requires that one "deny himself, and take up his cross, and follow me" (Matt. 16: 24). But this young man rejects the call for the sake of his wealth. Jesus elsewhere observes, "Some are incapable of marriage because they were born so; some because they were made so by others; some, because they have renounced marriage for the kingdom of heaven. Whoever can accept this ought to accept it" (Matt. 19: 11–12). From this, Saint Paul infers that to respond to the Lord one must be detached from family and wife, because one's primary attention cannot be directed to both at the same time (1 Cor. 7: 25–35). The young man of whom we hear no more is a counterpart in the Gospel to Judas, who hearing the Lord's invitation and following it part of the way, later lost the original motivation for the sake of thirty pieces of silver, only to realize that he had betrayed both himself and his Lord, and died in despair, the only sin for which, by definition, there is no forgiveness.

Refusal of the Call

The rejection of grace, the moment by which the spoiled priest of Irish Catholic culture is initiated, is thus a particular instance of the "Refusal of the Call" in archetypal theory. This refusal, instances of which can be found in international myths and folktales, is essentially a refusal to give up what one takes to be one's own immediate interest for the sake of a larger or deeper vision. Joseph Campbell explains in his *Hero of a Thousand Faces* that the Hero's adventures begin with the Departure, initiated by the "Call to Adventure," a variation on which is "The Refusal of the Call." In Campbell's words,

> Refusal of the summons converts the adventure into its negative. Walled in boredom, hard work, or "culture," the subject loses the power of significant affirmative action and becomes a victim to be saved. His flowering world becomes a wasteland of dry stones and his life feels meaningless—even though, like King Minos, he may through titanic effort succeed in building an empire of renown. Whatever house he builds, it will be a house of death: a labyrinth of cyclopean walls to hide from him his Minotaur. All he can do is create new problems for himself and await the gradual approach of his disintegration. (59)

When Lot's wife had been summoned forth from her city by Jehovah, she was punished for looking back by becoming a pillar of salt (Gen. 19: 26). Those who having started the journey, vacillate, stand under judgment:

> Because I have called, and ye refused . . . I also will laugh at your calamity; I will mock when your fear cometh; when your fear cometh as desolation, and your destruction cometh as a whirlwind; when distress and anguish cometh upon you. (Prov. 1: 24–27)

As the Latin slogan had it, "Time Jesum transeuntem et non revertentem" (Dread the passage of Jesus, for he does not return). This is the legend that applies to the Wandering Jew, who is cursed to remain on earth until the Day of Judgment, because when Christ had passed him carrying the cross, this man among the people standing along the way called, "Go faster! A Little speed!" The unrecognized, insulted Savior turned and said to him: "I go, but you shall be waiting here for me when I return" (quoted by Campbell, 63).

The deliberate refusal to respond to the deepest passion of the soul for the sake of some temporal advantage exhibits an inability to grow psychologically, to pass from childhood to adulthood. This is the inability to put off the infantile ego with its circumscribed sphere of emotional relationships. As Campbell puts it, "the timorous soul, fearful of some punishment, fails to make the passage through the door and come to birth in the world without" (62). The psychological oddity of the spoiled priest exhibits the effects of this disappointed promise and the potential unrealized, in curious fixations, trivial rituals, images of an ideal at one time desired but now despaired of, and in a disdain for those who never sensed such possibilities in their lives. The figure is an outsider from ordinary community life, disdaining its squalor, self-condemned to a Limbo of unrealizable hopes.

That Joyce was an acute observer of the cultural resonance of this type can be inferred from the general tenor of *Portrait*. There was a period in his own youth when he was especially religious. It was more extensive than might be inferred from the text of *Portrait*, since it appears to have run from at least the retreat of 1896 to the fall of 1897 (Bradley, 122–36); and having been touched by this experience, he was permanently to some degree in its thrall. His brother, a man of definite opinions, and endowed with a much more forthright temperament, observed of James:

> The truth seems to be that he who has loved God in youth can never love anything that is less than divine. The definition may change, but the sense of service due to something outside himself *sub specie aeternitatis* abides. In boyhood my brother had felt God to be a living presence, devotion to which had given a serenity that proved illusory. When belief in the Trinity went the way of all dogmatic beliefs, the capacity for devotion did not go with it. Not only was he still capable of setting an ideal aim above his happiness and his career; such an unquestioning sacrifice was even essential to his character. (*MBK* 153)

The Cultural Type

In arguing that James Duffy is Joyce's version of the spoiled priest type, it is worth pointing out that this figure has many precedents and successors in Irish life and cultural representation. Many figures that played distinguished roles in Irish political and cultural life began their careers as potential clerics. They include Gaelic poet Seán Ó Coileáin (1756–1816), novelist William Carleton (1794–1869), balladeer Jeremiah Joseph Callanan (1796–1829), Young Irelander John Blake Dillon (1816–66), boys' writer Captain Mayne Reid (1818–83), anthropologist Augustus Keane (1833–1912), architect Sir Richard Morrison (1767–1849), music collector and policeman Francis O'Neill (1849–1936), dramatists M. J. Molloy (1917–94) and Brian Friel, and Nobel laureate and politician John Hume.[19]

The type appears in folklore, and popular and serious literature, drama, and film. A remarkable example of the historical and literary type can be found in the case of Tomás Mac Casaide (fl. ca. 1760), whose autobiographical poem, "*An Caisideadh Bán*" has entered the folk tradition (see "The Spoilt Priest," *Field Day* 1: 303–4, 325). He trained to be a priest in the Augustinian friary at Ballyhaunis, County Mayo. But because of his irregular behavior, he was expelled before his ordination.

He then embarked on a picaresque adventure around Ireland as a rake, lover, drinker, sailor, beggar, sermonizer, and trumpet-player. For a time he joined the French army, only to desert, and spend the rest of his days tramping the roads of Ireland. His many poems celebrate these adventures, and although he is vehemently anticlerical, and writes with erotic abandon, he retains a sensibility formed by his seminary training, concluding each of his poems with a prayer for salvation.

> Bhí mé i gcoláiste go ham mo bhearrtha
> Agus san árd scoil ar feadh cúig bliana,
> Go bhfuail mé oideachas agus comhaire ón eaglais,
> Ach faraoir cráite do bhris mé tríd!
> Is rímhór m'fhaitíos roimh Rí na ngrásta
> Nach bhfuil sé i ndán go dtiochad saor,
> Mar is mó mo pheacaí na leath Chruach Phádraig
> Mar gheall ar ghrá a thug me d'iníon mhaoir.

> [I was at college until my tonsure and for five years in the seminary. There I received education and moral training from the church, but alas, I rejected it! And I greatly fear the judgment of the King of Graces, since my sins are as great as the half of Croagh Patrick, because of the love I gave to a steward's daughter].

An illuminating parallel case from the same historical period is the subject of Francis MacManus's novel, *Men Withering* (1939): about the eighteenth-century poet and spoiled priest, Donnacha Rua Mac Conmara [Red Dennis MacNamara].

William Carleton's story, "Denis O'Shaughnessy Going to Maynooth" (1831) is an unblinking view of the priestly vocation as a social invention. Denis is trained by his father in pompous, pseudolearned disputation that is taken as a sign of his aptitude for the priesthood. He learns the part well: affecting a superior manner, dressing the part, riding a horse, and sporting a fob watch. The clerical models he learns to emulate are spiritually empty, vain, and gluttonous, and prey on the peasantry. Denis is never presented as having any spiritual feelings, and his romantic relationship with a young woman, coinciding with the death of his father, results in his abandonment of his seminary studies. This decision does not cause him any crisis of conscience, nor does he suffer any social obloquy upon his departure from Maynooth. This caricature is but a rough variation on the spoiled priest type.

A folk variant of the type is "The Student Who Left College," to be found in Douglas Hyde's *Legends of Saints and Sinners* (155–72). Patrick O'Flynn disappears from the seminary, and spends a century in the company of the *sídhe* (fairies). There he enjoys the bliss of a land that is heavenlike except that he sees no sign of God, the Blessed Virgin, or any of the saints. He returns to the seminary only to find that he recognizes nobody and none there remembers him. His name is found on a list of those who left a century before. Unaccountably ordained, he dies immediately. Angels bear Father O'Flynn to heaven.

Patrick O'Flynn is a spoiled priest to the extent that he experiences a magical and pagan alternative to the life of grace he expected. His surprise is not so much in its joy as that it was not preceded by pain, suffering, and death, the essential prerequisites of the Christian heaven. In its improbable conclusion, the folk story, in contrast with the standard type, reconciles the opposition between Christian and pagan elements.

Canon Sheehan begins his story "A Spoiled Priest" (1905) with this note:

> This is the term used in some parts of the country to express the failure of a student who has just put his foot within the precincts of the sanctuary, and been rejected. Up to until a recent period such an ill-fated youth was regarded by the peasantry with a certain amount of scorn, not unmingled with superstition. Happily, larger ideas are being developed even on this subject; and not many now believe that no good fortune can ever be the lot of him who has made the gravest initial mistake of his life. (9 n)

The hero of the story that follows is mysteriously dismissed from Maynooth: "A student refused Orders was something too terrible. The star had fallen in the sea" (13). This causes a depression in his village and plunges his parents into the deepest disgrace. A letter arrives asking to see his father once more before leaving for America. This refused, he disappears from their lives forever.

There is one young boy in the village, however, who admires the ex-seminarian, and remains loyal to his memory. Years later, he becomes a priest himself, and investigates his friend's fate. Encountering a strange doctor at the deathbed of an old woman, he discovers that this is, indeed, the same person: he had become a successful man of the world. They part. Eventually, through the grace of the priest's prayers, the doctor abandoned his worldly life and became a Carthusian monk in Italy. The priest received a letter that read:

> Embittered and disappointed, I left Ireland many years ago. Not one kindly word nor friendly grasp was with me in my fare well . . . [I was] bitter and angry towards God and man. I had but one faith left—to do good in a world where I had received naught but evil . . . But while you spoke . . . my heart thawed out towards God and man. (22)

While Canon Sheehan's objectives are earnest, he lacks the technical skill to realize his two dissonant objectives. The story is vehemently critical of the clerical culture of Maynooth—which is represented as inhumane and hypocritical—but is implausible and sentimental. It fails to confer any of the characters with an inner life that might allow us to infer the presence of the Holy Spirit.

T. C. Murray's realistic Abbey play *Maurice Harte* (1912), a copy of which was in Joyce's Trieste library (Ellmann, 121), is a powerful exposé of the social pressures bearing upon contemporary seminarians. The eponymous hero allows the social pressure to complete his studies to so violate his conscience that he has a nervous breakdown. As a social realist, Murray is less interested in the forces at odds in Maurice's spirit than in the relationship between religion and social status. From one perspective (Mrs. Harte's), providing the material necessities of life is an undertaking beside which the conflicts of conscience seem incomprehensible. And from another (Maurice's), hypocrisy exacts insupportable social and psychological prices. Murray's treatment of the contention between the claims of loyalty and conscience has an imaginative resonance that causes the play to transcend its limited social origins.[20]

It may be a coincidence that during the summer of 1905 in which Joyce conceived the figure of James Duffy that Canon Sheehan published his sentimentally extended gloss on the folk convention (Joyce had participated in a discussion of Sheehan's previous clerical novel, *My New Curate*, while at the Royal University, on June 16, 1901; Costello, 173). It is less likely a coincidence that the figure also appears in the first story of George Moore's collection, *The*

Untilled Field ("The Exile"), which was on Joyce's mind as he developed *Dubliners* (one of which, "The Clerk's Quest," he considered "damned stupid").

Considered in the light of these two figures—Canon Sheehan's Kevin O'Donnell and Moore's Peter Phelan (who without much soul-searching also leaves Maynooth)—it is clear that Joyce's James Duffy improves on each of them substantially, in exposing the inner life of his figure. Their representations are simplistic, sentimental, or merely emblems in a tale, their spiritual or inner lives unexplored. Joyce is vastly more equipped than any of these writers to deal with this subject. From personal experience he has a sound appreciation of the vision of life that attracts the would-be cleric. From close observation of his acquaintances, he has a superior understanding of a character type that responds to the vision. He is more than adequately familiar with the philosophical and theological concepts and distinctions required for the task. He is incomparably well read in relevant literary representations of the type. He has clear grasp of "the cultural moment." His technical virtuosity enables him to invoke a world of ideas and feeling that within the apparently realistic narrative, allows him to represent the stages in the development, or decline, of the inner life—spiritual and intellectual—of his protagonist.

Owen Aherne

As the foregoing survey indicates, Joyce was predisposed in many ways—by communal and family traditions as well as by his personal education—to respond "as if hypnotized" by Yeats's "The Tables of the Law." Even though Joyce was then in his "skeptical-mystical-cynical phase" (Voelker's words, 25), his praise had Yeats arrange for a reprint (Foster, 278). In Yeats's story, Owen Aherne, possessed of "a fanciful hatred of all life . . . half borrowed from some fanatical monk" (Joachim of Flora), and caring neither for wine, women, nor money, had thoughts for nothing but theology and mysticism. His attachment to Joachim's mysticism leads Aherne to lose the capacity to feel the joys and sorrows of ordinary life and to a Gnostic denial of Christian humility and even the capacity "to anger God and then win his forgiveness" (Voelker, 27). Thus, disdaining the spiritual service of human society in the priesthood, he refuses the biretta (Yeats, 293). Voelker notes that Joachim and his disciples were one source for the figure of Mr. Duffy; and therefore his story derives from Joyce's "struggle to get free of Yeats's spellbinding vision" (26).

Thus Duffy's austere room is a parodic reduction of Aherne's rare and precious book kept in a case carved by Benvenuto Cellini (Voelker, 29). Yeats's Aherne behaves much like the spoiled priest of the tradition outlined above:

He wore a black, closely-buttoned coat, short hair, shaven head, which preserved a memory of his priestly ambition, and understood how Catholicism had seized him in the midst of the vertigo he called philosophy. (Yeats, 305)

Dizzied into a mystical imbalance ("I have lost my soul because I have looked out of the eyes of the angels"), he has despaired of God's mercy ("I am not among those for whom Christ died," Yeats, 305). Drawing on a wider range of detail from his family's Irish Catholic tradition, Joyce has taken Yeats's Owen Aherne and, by creating Mr. James Duffy, "lifted him out of a richly-colored Romantic canvas and set him in a photograph" (Voelker, 29).

"A Mere Accident"

Closer to Joyce's mind—and to the inner spirit of one version of this type— as he constructs the imaginative rationale of Mr. Duffy's bitter celibacy is Moore's novella, "John Norton" the second of the three works that make up *Celibates* (1895). In "The Day of the Rabblement," Joyce had publicly censured *Celibates* as decidedly retro, announcing that Moore was "draw[ing] on his literary account" (*CW* 71, 1901). This sneer from an upstart did sting Moore, especially since "John Norton" was a revision of "A Mere Accident" (1887). Implicitly admitting the censure at his inability to emulate Flaubert and adapt his style to each new book, Moore thought Joyce "preposterously clever," and as Adrian Frazier observes, moved directly to the greater experimentation of his next work, *The Lake* (1905) (317–18). By the time Joyce turned his own hand to fiction, he had been reading Moore attentively for several years, and "A Painful Case" is a particular appropriation of a story Moore had already unsuccessfully revised.

The first of the *Celibates* trio, "Mildred Lawson," interested Joyce sufficiently to have him undertake an Italian translation (December 1904) and recommend it to Nora's reading (January 1905, *Letters* II: 75, 78). When Joyce then, the following July, turned to his own study of a celibate personality temporarily disposed towards the clerical life, he was provided in Moore's revision of "A Mere Accident" with some elements of semisacerdotal character, details of setting, the rudiments of the plot, and the hint of an ironic title.

John Norton is an intelligent and cultivated young man, the heir to a country estate. His instinctive misanthropy and conservative tastes cause him to move into a Jesuit residence, where he can play the role of ascetic while surrounding himself with the gilded spines of writings of the Fathers of the church, Palestrina's scores, stained glass windows, and medieval architecture. When not in residence, he indulges in exotic foreign travel—Moscow, Beyreuth—and when a permanent guest in the cloister, he plays the role of a monk. His room is furnished in a manner emulated by Joyce's Mr. Duffy:

> He would have no carpet. He placed a small iron bed against the wall; two plain chairs, a screen to keep off the draught from the door, a small basin-stand, such as you might find in a ship's cabin, and a *prie-dieu* were all the furniture he permitted himself. (314)

An à la carte disciple of the Oxford Movement, he's an aesthetic ascetic. He is attracted to Catholicism, not because it gives hope to the poor and ignorant, but because of its dogmatic clarity, its moral courage in rebuking modern decadence and material complacency, its intellectual tradition, and the elegance and grace of its rituals, music, and architecture. Thus he rationalizes his repressed homoerotic tendencies—he feels no attraction to women, and is revolted by their flaunting of sex—by savoring the sensuous fruits of an earthly and unearthly estate.

In order to keep the disturbance of women out of his emotional and intellectual life, to resist change and development, John Norton has chosen to be a bachelor and celibate. Identifying with the Christianity of the Middle Ages, he reads Saint Augustine, Tertullian, and Marbodius—whose poem against the "poisoned honeycomb" of women he quotes with approval. An intellectual as well as a spiritual dilettante, he will never progress with his ambitious *History of Christian Latin* (279). His dreams are a blend of repressed homosexuality, religious Gnosticism, and aestheticism: contemplating "the beautiful slim body in which Divinity seemed to circulate like blood," and gazing on the figure of the Crucified, he realized that "it was this very hatred of natural flesh that had precipitated a perilous worship of deified flesh" (300).

Against this instinctive misogyny, he acceded to his mother's pressure to preserve the family estate, entangling the affections of an eligible neighbor, Kitty Hare. He regaled her with accounts of his religious tastes and proclivities, especially his reasons for declining what appeared to her (as well as his mother) as a vocation to the priesthood. In the course of the narrative, Moore develops rather well the reasons for Norton's blundering approach to Kitty (he precipitated the crisis in her affections by suddenly lurching from a succession of platonic perambulations to an overcompensating, aggressive, and unheralded kiss). His momentary lapse in the midst of these lofty disquisitions into precipitate passion—his kiss was also violent—caused him such revulsion that he immediately withdrew from her company. Alone on the downs, she was raped by a passing thug. In her distraction at the horror of this experience, she fled to her room, barring the door behind her. Returning to apologize, Norton knocked loudly on her door. This so terrified Kitty that she fell out the window to her death—the "mere accident" of the title.

His violent kiss had broken the tenor of their relationship, which up to that point was platonic and confessional—a suggestive model, therefore, for Joyce in "A Painful Case." If Norton is insufficiently developed, Kitty is even less convincing as a character, so that her suicide is inadequately motivated. Norton too easily accepted that he was responsible for this calamity. This trauma so filled him with remorse that he renewed his resolve to turn his world into a monastery (281, 307), thus making his emotional problems permanent.

> He clasped his hands across his eyes, and feeling himself on the brink of madness, he cried out to God to save him; and he longed to speak the words that would take him from the world. Life was not for him. He had learned his lesson. Thornby Place should soon be Thornby Abbey, and in the divine consolation of religion John Norton hoped to find escape from the ignominy of life. (368)

"A Painful Case" is evidently Joyce's redaction (and rebuttal) of Moore's "A Mere Accident": in its broad plot, its management of conflict, and even the phrasing of the false epiphany. More particularly in the present argument, the comparison helps elucidate the thesis that in the figure of James Duffy—imagined in the shadow of the would-be Jesuit John Norton—we have a version of the spoiled priest type in the Irish cultural tradition. Moore's Norton is not a spoiled priest, but a layman who has felt himself attracted to the clerical life. Fearing that he does not have a true vocation, he holds himself back; his intellectual and spiritual projects have been disappointments; but insufficiently detached from its celibate requirements, he remains permanently marked with the taste and conscience of a clerical character. So although he has not entered the seminary, does not belong to folk culture, and does not suffer any obloquy for his failure, nevertheless, his failure is of the same type as that which marks his immediate literary descendant, James Duffy.

Richard Wagner and Arthur Schopenhauer

We know how deeply Joyce was attached to Wagner and to the legend of Tristan and Iseult. Timothy Martin's fine study, *Joyce and Wagner*, explains how its Celtic origins—evoked in the first lines of *Tristan und Isolde*—made a strong impression on him. Although the opera was not especially popular among literary Wagnerites, as Martin observes, "it may have appealed to the musically sensitive Joyce for precisely this reason" (95). He was interested in Isolde as an embodiment of the "eternal feminine": a priestess and healer, a bride in an unconsummated marriage, and the forbidden wife of a trusted friend. He was also interested in the ideas surrounding the Liebestod—the idea of a love that is at once destructive and redemptive, the idea of redemption in death, the notion that the grave is a womb—all depicted in the language of night (Martin summarizes, 95). These aspects of the legend feature significantly in Wagner's treatment, apparently the version that made the deepest impression on Joyce.

Tristan und Isolde figures in the composition of *Exiles* (1912–15) where the consequences of an adulterous love—the betrayal of King Marke by his nephew and vassal—found fertile ground (Martin, 95). David Hayman has shown that act 2 of the opera, in fact, served as a working model for act 2 of the play: both acts are nocturnal and framed by acts set in daylight. The betrayed husband arrives, interrupts the tryst, and reproaches the lovers: act 2 of *Exiles* is a *Liebesnacht manqué* (Martin, 96).

"Work in Progress" began in 1922 with the sketch of Tristan and Iseult, which eventually, after much revision, became book 2, chapter 4 of *Finnegans Wake* (383–99). As Martin shows, this myth was on Joyce's mind throughout the writing of the *Wake*, becoming "one of the strongest and most intricate parallels to the book's main argument" (97, and see 100–106 and 194–204). In preparation for this project, he read Joseph Bédier's version, but in the earlier stages of his literary career, the primary source of his enthusiasm was Wagner's version. He was also interested in the romance surrounding its composition. While writing this opera, Wagner was passionately attached to Mathilde Wesendonck, the wife of his Swiss patron. When the opera that this relationship inspired was completed, Wagner broke off the affair—if that is what it was. They renounced each other, stating that their love was impossible; and always spiritual, as in the Duffy-Sinico relationship.

There is some internal evidence in the denouement of "Eveline" that Wagner's *Tristan und Isolde* had entered Joyce's imaginative processes before he wrote "A Painful Case." There is some external and much internal evidence that this same opera plays a central role in the conception, design, and theme of "A Painful Case," and is therefore Joyce's first treatment of the adultery theme in his fiction. This modifies Martin's position, who dates Joyce's introduction to the opera in 1912 (94).

Joyce had, in fact, two opportunities to see *Tristan und Isolde* in Dublin. The Carl Rosa Opera Company mounted productions at the Gaiety Theatre in November 1901 and in September of the following year (Reilly, 26–27). His possession of a copy of Wagner's libretti at this time (see *Letters* II: 25) implies that he attended this opera in addition to *Lohengrin* (Byrne, 65).

Diarmuid and Graine

The story of Tristan and Iseult is a Celtic version of the international tale of a love triangle. From the point of view of the dramatic action, in contrast with its characterological or thematic content, "A Painful Case" is Joyce's modernist version of the archetypal tale of illicit love. While the tale attained its prestige in the medieval period as a premier expression of the ideals of romantic love, it had many precedents in ancient and classic literature, from the Arabian story of Kais and Lobna, Pyramus and Thisbe, Dido and Aeneas, and Romeo and Juliet. Its various medieval versions included Marie de France's *Lai du Chevrefeuil* (ca. 1160), Gottfried von Strassburg's *Tristan* (ca. 1210), and Sir Thomas Malory's *Morte d'Arthur* (ca. 1400). Its modern versions by Matthew Arnold (1852) and Tennyson (1859), and its Irish analogs, the Tales of Deirdre and the Sons of Usna and Diarmuid and Gráinne, were evidently of less interest to Joyce than the version he witnessed in Wagner's *Tristan und Isolde*.

He had an opportunity to see the Moore-Yeats collaborative play *Diarmuid and Grania* in Dublin in October 1901, where it was performed four times at the Gaiety Theatre, October 21–23 (Ellis-Fermor, 212). It was the prospect of this production that provoked his "Day of the Rabblement" (October 15) in which he attacked Yeats's partiality to Irish subjects. This play, about "a hot-blooded, cold-hearted woman who put a love-spell on young Diarmuid at her marriage feast to Finn, then after years of love in a valley with Diarmuid, gets a hankering for Finn again" (Frazier, 295–96), was a critical failure. It was roundly condemned by Standish O'Grady as "a heartless piece of vandalism on a great Irish story," and by D. P. Moran as objectionable because of its concentration on "degenerate and unwholesome sex problems," by Violet Martin as "a strange mix of saga and modern French situations" (Foster, 251), and Joseph Holloway as "a beautiful piece full of weird suggestiveness, but lacking here and there in dramatic action" (14). Joyce might have been interested in it on account of Edward Elgar's incidental music (consisting of three pieces, op. 42), or Moore's conception of Grania as a figure of Lady Cunard; but it is highly unlikely that Joyce, in view of his public opposition to the production, was present at all. The relationship between Joyce's story and this particular Irish subject is clearly mediated by Wagner's treatment and none of these versions.

The play was a failure on several counts: the patchy collaboration of Yeats's beautiful language, Moore's modern characterization, the inability of the English actors to pronounce the Irish names and deliver with conviction the impression that they were figures from a national saga. It satisfied nobody, prompting many cruel witticisms from Dublin wags, mainly at Moore's expense (see Foster, 251–53). Joyce's impression is unrecorded. But in turning his hand to "A Painful Case" some four years later, he set himself a similar task: to produce a modern story after the design and theme of a Celtic myth.

Moore is a candidate for Joyce's model of Mr. Duffy: a prominent ex-Catholic who in the spirit of Nietzsche, returned to Ireland with the object of re-paganizing it. His affair with Lady Maud—the wife of Sir Bache Cunard and mother of Nancy (1896–1965)—was well known around Dublin when Joyce wrote "A Painful Case." The sly allusion to the absent Captain Sinico of the Palgrave, Murphy Steamship Company could well point to Sir Bache of the Cunard Lines whose absence from home allowed the strange relationship between the homosexual Moore and his cultivated wife to develop. Through his associations with the *Dana* group in the summer of 1904, especially Oliver Gogarty with whom he briefly shared the Martello Tower in September, he would have been familiar with the gossip embracing these literary figures. Moore's affair with Lady Cunard was the central relationship in his *Memoirs of My Dead Life* (1906), portions of which appeared during the summer of 1904 in *Dana* under the running title of "Moods and Memories" (see Frazier, 344–48).

Joyce's dissatisfaction with *Diarmuid and Grania* must have been allayed some weeks later with the Carl Rosa production of Wagner's *Tristan und Isolde*. A model for "A Painful Case," it clearly offers a structural and thematic precedent for Joyce's successful modernization of the archetypal tale of illicit love and, moreover, a Celtic myth which had, in accordance with Joyce's own imaginative proclivities, a local habitation and a name.

Tristan und Isolde

First, as many readers have observed, Joyce has good reasons to set the principal action of the story in Chapelizod (*Séipéal Iosóide*), the then hamlet on the outskirts of Dublin named after the mythic heroine, Iseult (Wagner's Isolde) (Bennett, s.v. "Chapelizod"). The story is Joyce's first exploration of the love triangle, in that Mr. Duffy plays the role of Tristan to Captain Sinico's King Mark (Wagner's Marke) and Mrs. Sinico's Iseult. In this respect, Mr. Duffy's melancholia (his *tristitia*) links him nominally to his romantic antecedent.[1] Mr. Duffy pays suit to another man's betrothed, like Tristan is an orphan (his remaining parent, his father, dies in the course of the story, *D* 112.23), and fails to realize the fullness of romantic love. Like his royal antecedent, Captain Sinico is known by his honorific, is associated with sea voyages, and with stereotypical age and remove. And Mrs. Sinico is modeled on Iseult in her passionate longing and the potion of collaborative music. The story revolves around musical performance, travel, a surreptitious and quasi-adulterous attachment, and concludes with what we are invited to hear as a *Liebestod*. The theme of each is the relationship between passion and death, love and immortality, the potentially transformative power of human passion expressed in the art of music. The action moves between Isolde's chapel and Tristan's death as he dreams of his lost love in the forest of the Phoenix Park.

The subject of the eternal lovers who defy social arrangements, the fear of death, and divine judgment to boot, has been the subject of innumerable artistic representations. Joyce expands the tragic implications of his little sketch by a scheme of subtle citations of Wagner's incomparably grand expression of a love so passionate that it transvalues human existence and death itself. Just as Wagner's lovers encounter one another accompanied by the ominous chords of disappointed longing, so does Joyce have his pair encounter one another in "the deserted house" of the Rotunda (*D* 109.20). In "A Painful Case" Joyce has drawn on a fine use of language and a range of suggestive allusion comparable to Wagner's "psychomusical vocabulary." Thus, while this story, like all of the others in *Dubliners*, gives the appearance of a naturalistic text, its full force and substance can only be apprehended by close attention to its apparently offhand technique, which, like Wagner's music, to the first-time listener seems incoherent. Like Wagner's music, the order salient to the penetrative force of Joyce's fiction can be found in its symbolic leitmotifs. This requires careful attention to every aspect of their composition.

Like the opera, Joyce's story has a tripartite structure. Wagner's opera comprises three acts of approximately ninety minutes each, Joyce's story of three divisions of 2 pages (sec. 1 above: *D* 107.2–109.16), 3 pages (sec. 2 above: *D* 109.17–112.11), and 5 1/2 pages (sec. 3–5 above: *D* 112.12–117.34), respectively. Joyce's version dispenses with the minor characters, and, of course, turns Wagner's romantic tragedy into an apparently prosaic and ironic account of a failure to express ordinary human feeling. Just as the action in the first act of the opera occurs during the day, when the lovers meet one another and by taking the love potion commence their betrayal, so in Joyce's story, the pair meet one another and begin a relationship that is harmonized by their common interest in music. Just as Wagner's music celebrates the relationship between love and death (is the potion poisonous or a love-draught?), so in the Joyce story the Mozart songs are of doomed infatuation. Translated into Wakese, the parallel between these two composers appears in the radio request passage that recalls "A Painful Case": "the dewfolded song of the naughtingles . . . on the heather side of waldalure . . . you wheckfoolthenairyans" and "pour their peace in partial . . . whoe betwides them . . . night's sweetmoztheart" (*FW* 359.32–360.12).

Like Wagner's opera, where the action occurs aboard ship between Ireland and Cornwall, Joyce's story has James Duffy's "walking out" with Mrs. Sinico in his "reefer coat" (in sailor's style) in the absence of Captain Sinico. The second act of *Tristan und Isolde* takes place in King Marke's castle, where, as he is out hunting, the lovers' tryst proceeds apace. Similarly, the relationship between Mr. Duffy and Mrs. Sinico, beginning with the Rotunda concert and ending with their anguished walk in the Phoenix Park develops at the piano in Captain Sinico's Sydney Parade cottage, accommodated by his regular maritime absence. Music is the subject and medium of the lovers' growing relationship: the mood of desolation that permeates the opening scene of act 2, expressed by the English horn and the pianissimo strings, has its correspondence in Joyce's creation of the melancholic Duffy and neglected Sinico; and similarly, the unparalleled grandeur of Wagner's *Liebesnacht*, "Night of Love," is a precedent for the Duffy-Sinico collaborative performances of the poignant Mozart songs of love, parting, and death.

Again, most significantly from a technical and thematic point of view, just as all the action in act 2 of *Tristan und Isolde* occurs at night, so does the relationship between Mr. Duffy and Mrs. Sinico develop—from the Rotunda concert to their final walk in the Phoenix Park—in twilight or after sunset. These darknesses are both circumstantially necessitous and representative: they accommodate the subterfuge of public betrothal/marriage by the respective pairs of scheming lovers. In Wagner's work, the darkness functions as a symbolic reversal of social convention, of quotidian legal love. In Joyce's story, it is linked both with Mr. Duffy's social alienation and psychic isolation and with Mrs. Sinico's alienation from her husband and growing emotional attachment to Mr. Duffy.[2]

To continue the logic, just as the darkness that surrounds Tristan and Isolde's ecstatic *Liebesnacht*, wherein Tristan invites Isolde to follow him into the realm of eternal night where their love can be out of this world and eternal, so is the Dublin dusk that descends on Joyce's pair a counterpart to their doomed relationship, which is represented in the text by the occluded duets in their private performances of Mozart songs, the intellectual incompatibility of the pair, Mr. Duffy's celibate fixation, his disquisitions on "the soul's incurable loneliness," et cetera. Thus while Joyce's citations of Wagner's text are both general and specific (for example, Isolde extinguishes the lamp that would betray their lovemaking, and Mrs. Sinico "refrain[s] from lighting the lamp," *D* 111.19–20), the atmospherics function very differently: it is not the darkness of eternal love but a growing existential despair. As impressed as Joyce must have been by the *Liebesnacht*, Wagner's powerful romantic elaboration on sexual infatuation, of orgasm (*la petite morte*) he is too much in the thrall of Dante's view of Tristan's delusion (he places him in the Second Circle along with those whose moral sin was lust [*Inferno*, canto 5: 67]), bending his imaginative debt to Wagner to ironic ends in the portrait of the lugubrious Duffy's fear of any kind of human attachment.

Thus the schema governing Wagner's management of the darkness of the night in act 2 can be compared with Joyce's development of the Duffy-Sinico affair: it affords the practical opportunity for love, the subversion of Marke's possession of Isolde, and the chivalric code to which Tristan was sworn; it represents the lovers' imminent death that, in concert with Wagner's subscription to Schopenhauerean pessimism at the time he composed this opera, ensures the permanent love of Tristan and Isolde; and it represents the dream world that is brought to an end by the return of King Marke and his entourage at the rising of the sun. In "A Painful Case," it provokes differences between the pair—Mrs. Sinico's desire and opportunity for affection and Mr. Duffy's reserve (which he rationalizes as his "distaste for underhand ways," *D* 110.16); it is an expression of Mr. Duffy's disdain for "phrasemongers," vulgar journalists (he prefers the conservative—and buff—*Evening Mail* to its nationalist—and white—rival the *Evening Herald*, *D* 116.20), the thoughtless indulgences and social display of "Dublin's gilded youth," and the social conventions of the day; and in Mr. Duffy's "disillusion" (*D* 111.34) on discovering that his companion interpreted his talks as a potential lover rather than as an attentive and admiring auditor at a night school where she learns that all bonds are sorrowful. Joyce's readers had to wait for *Finnegans Wake* to see his full appropriation of the night journey of these archetypal Celtic lovers.

Meanwhile, just as King Marke's return temporarily shames the lovers at the end of act 2, so is Mr. Duffy shamed by the realization of Mrs. Sinico's physical passion and by his association with a pathetic alcoholic. As the dawn breaks over Cornwall and King Marke's jealous and violent attendant, the righteous Melot, who in accordance with chivalric conventions shames the lovers into abject silence and delivers the fatal wound, so is Mr. Duffy dumb-struck by the rude and dispassionate report of "To-day['s] . . . inquest" (*D* 113.21–22) before the anonymous Deputy Coroner and his jurors, with its testimony from the railway porter P. Dunne and the engine driver who, though following railway regulations and was therefore blameless, was the efficient cause of the fatal injuries. This James Lennon answers to Mr. Duffy's Christian name (*D* 113.29–114.2).

Act 3 of *Tristan und Isolde* takes place at Tristan's home in Brittany. The stylized tree in most stagings represents both the woods surrounding his castle and the masts of the sequentially approaching ships of Isolde and King Marke. Mortally wounded, in his delirium he imagines her ship's approach long before it actually appears, and tearing off his bandages expresses his desire to be united with her in the permanent darkness of death's night. When she does arrive, she sinks, transfigured in death, while singing the sublime *Liebestod* (Love death) upon the body of her dead lover. In "A Painful Case," Joyce transforms these elements to serve his purposes. Mr. Duffy's assimilation of the permanent end to his last shreds of earthly or heavenly hope takes place on his way home, in his rented room, and during his walk beneath the "gaunt trees" of the Phoenix Park. Whereas Wagner's lovers trust that their love-suicide will guarantee their eternal togetherness, Mr. Duffy moves through a sequence of moral attitudes beginning with his reflection on the final loneliness that drove Mrs. Sinico to her death and concluding that he is totally alone now and forever. An appreciation of the Wagnerian background to the final scene of "A Painful Case" thus illuminates Joyce's fictional objectives.

In act 3 of *Tristan und Isolde*, as Tristan sinks into death he sings three tortured monologues (so testing of the lead tenor that they are often abbreviated). Expressing the mental confusion and visionary hopes caused by his loss of blood and heroic desire, they progress through three subjects: his loss of bearings ("Where am I?"), his hallucination that Isolde is beside him (she does not arrive until after his death), and his realization of the imminence of his own death (recalling the drink and his own parents' deaths). Mr. Duffy's response to the news of Mrs. Sinico's death progresses in three similar phases. First, he is so abstracted that he forgets his dinner and begins walking mechanically home (the two-paragraph passage describing his discovery and reaction are the only paragraphs in the story, apart from the newspaper report, that give no clue about what he feels or thinks [*D* 112.28–113.18]). We then savor the fruits of this first phase of his reaction: his revulsion at the indignity of her death. The second phase in his response comes "As the light failed and his memory began to wander" (*D* 116.3) and he imagines that "her hand touched his" (*D* 116.4). This hallucination persists as he walks east along the Glen and Military Roads and "seemed to feel her voice touch his ear, her hand touch his" (*D* 117.4–5). For at least the hour preceding the departure of the 10:00 p.m. train from Kingsbridge, he imagined that he was again in her presence as he had been four years before. Thus, as Tristan sees his beloved in a vision before his death, Mr. Duffy apprehends Mrs. Sinico's presence, and in a Joycean trope, infers that she died for him. The final phase of his spiritual descent is focused on two deeply wounding images: of the two lovers beneath the wall of the Phoenix Park and the train slowly moving into the night. These images, both poignant and mocking, are at once reminders of the sin of Adam and Eve and the death that was their punishment. In these moments of Mr. Duffy's dismal despair, we have the obverse of the culmination of *Tristan und Isolde*, in which the lovers' apparent separation by their simultaneous deaths is reversed in Isolde's famous *Liebestod*. For just as the puffing of the train reminds him of Mrs. Sinico's death twenty-four hours previously (Kingstown and Kingsbridge trains link with King Marke, as they did historically with King George IV after whom they were named in 1821 and 1828, respectively, Bennett, s.v. "Dún Laoghaire"), an engine, like that which killed her, in a Wagnerian citation, joins in the metaphoric expression of her name.[3] The slow tempo of this goods train leaving the station recalls, but with a difference we have come to expect from Joyce's fine ear, the newspaper report of the "slow train" (*D* 113.26–27)—meaning the *local* train—that killed Mrs. Sinico. We infer that before the curtain of silence falls on the action, Mr. Duffy, too, is alive to these tonalities.

"A Painful Case" is, therefore, Joyce's first, and qualified, subscription to *Tristianisme*. He found in Wagner's *Tristan und Isolde* a musical model for his own aims as a manager of language: the capacity to deal with levels of consciousness and motivation, the moral, the magical, and the imaginative; and to put powerful mythological materials to the service of a critique of contemporary life. In these respects, he has the technical skill to have his apparently naturalistic text enclose the mythic references and thus defy the odds that overcame Yeats and Moore in their failed effort to align Celtic materials with "French situations." Nobody was going to deride anything Joyce wrote as "Tanqueray B.C." He could harness Wagner's opera to his subject of the spoiled priest because each work is concerned with the inner life of the hero: Tristan's romantic longing and Mr. Duffy's melancholic disappointment.

Like Mr. Duffy, Wagner rejects the physical world. As he wrote in "Music of the Future" (1860):

> Life and death, the whole meaning and existence of the external world, depend here solely on inner emotions. With its ability to move us emotionally, the entire action rises to the surface only because our inner-most soul wills it do so; and it comes to light in the form that it had already assumed within us.

Thus the inner mental processes of the lovers is the focus of *Tristan und Isolde*, as the spiritual life of Mr. Duffy, the spoiled priest, is Joyce's subject. Mr. Duffy's unrealized spiritual aspirations separate him from ordinary civic life and from common human feeling. Similarly, the love of Tristan and Iseult sets them sharply apart from others, especially in its repudiation of worldly values, including the ultimate worldly value, life itself (Martin, 94). Wagner's romanticism, under Schopenhauer's influence, pushes his lovers to escape from earthly boundaries through intoxication, potions, and the longing for oblivion. This romanticized darkness shields them from the pressures of or-dinary life and is the entry to the transcendental realm where love is eternal. As it was in classical antiquity, night is the gateway to death, the entrance to Hades, and the final resolution and redemption of love. Wagner renders Isolde, in act 2, as a figurative angel of death, extinguishing the lamp.

For his part, Tristan longs to escape from the barren day into the wondrous realm of night. Day is the world of chivalry with its medieval code of virtues including honor, reputation, and loyalty—the world in which he is a hero. His illicit love for Isolde causes him to abandon these values and embrace those of night and death. Wagner's lovers expect to remain so for eternity.

However, in Joyce's story, the leitmotif of darkness traces Mr. Duffy's dis-mal passage from social isolation to the "outer darkness" of spiritual despair. Joyce has thus recast Wagner's Schopenhauerean pessimist into a Christian mold where the afterlife does not accommodate earthly marriages, and in any event is denied those who take their bodily lives into their own hands.

Tristan und Isolde is an expression of Schopenhauer's *World*: the denial in the name of a purer and higher spiritual ideal of the will to persist in ordinary life. Under his influence, Wagner thought of love as the path to salvation that leads to a total pacification of the will. It is neither motivated by or directed to a divine being, nor directed towards humanity in general, but is an actual physical and emotional love based on the attraction between men and women. The whole dramatic and musical design of *Tristan und Isolde* reaches its apex in the final *Liebestod*. Timothy Martin puts it so:

> The association between erotic and metaphysical longing evident in the earlier operas is intensified in Tristan . . . that life itself is a painful exile from a peaceful place of origin, from an "*Ur-Vergessen*" accessible only in dissolution. (92)

Joyce was attracted to Wagner because he was uniquely able to express the inner meaning of his drama in musical terms and to integrate his psychological and dramatic ideas with musical expression. Music is the art most amenable to the articulation of the human longing for transcendence and perfection. Through his early religious training, Joyce had tasted of this promise, and losing his faith but following a literary rather than a musical vocation, he would naturally gravitate towards a kind of composite art such as we find in the experiments of *Ulysses*, "Sirens," for example, or its apotheosis in *Finnegans Wake*.

In the case of *Exiles*, as we have seen, Joyce makes explicit use of the Wagnerian or gnostic conception of our remove from our true spiritual origins. In Martin's words,

> Birth, in *Tristan*, is . . . a kind of "fatal slip," to borrow a Joycean formulation into human existence, and death presents the opportunity to retain the lost paradise, to escape temporality, rationality, and the burdens of identity. The intense sensuality of *Tristan* and its music has always impressed its listeners, but the desire for sexual gratification only begins to express the sort of longing that is the opera's real subject. (93)

As he matured artistically, Joyce repudiated Wagner's heavy sexualization of his subjects. But so far as "A Painful Case" is concerned, its relationship with *Tristan und Isolde* is as a device to expose the cost of sexual repression derived from a culture that laid the heavy burden of an idealized perfectibility on its young and turned some of its more gifted and sensitive members into spoiled priests.

"the grim Dutch touch"

In view of the evident structural and thematic relationship between "A Painful Case" and *Tristan und Isolde*, Mr. Duffy's pessimism, and Wagner's express debt to Schopenhauer—without which it is difficult to grasp his larger intention in the work—the question arises about the relationship between "A Painful Case" and Schopenhauer's philosophical pessimism. The question is posed internally, in any event, by Mr. Duffy's aphorisms, spoken and written: "We cannot give ourselves . . . we are our own" (D 111.28–29), "every bond . . . is a bond to sorrow" (D 112.7), and "Love between man and man is impossible because there must not be sexual intercourse and friendship between man and woman is impossible because there must be sexual intercourse" (D 112.19–22). Readers have looked in vain through Nietzsche's *Thus Spake Zarathustra* and *The Gay Science* for the source of Mr. Duffy's bon mots, despite Stanislaus Joyce's assertion that his brother borrowed them from his diary at a time when he had not yet read Nietzsche, and despite the clear evidence of the text itself.

Careful attention to the narrative shows that Mr. Duffy coined his aphorisms before his break with Mrs. Sinico or within two months of its termination (D 111–12), whereas it is not until four years later that the Nietzsche volumes are observed on his shelves (D 112.15–16). Nietzsche's historical antecedent and an aphorist of comparably gloomy trenchancy is Arthur Schopenhauer. The entries in Mr. Duffy's commonplace book could well be his pithy précis of the philosopher's most popular essays, an edition of which appeared shortly before he met Mrs. Sinico: *Essays of Schopenhauer*, selected and translated by Mrs. Rudolf Dircks (1897). Mr. Duffy's aphorisms reflect a few of the personality traits popularly attributed to Schopenhauer—his isolation, pessimism, and misogyny—and emulate one of the philosopher's stylistic penchants. Although his serious work demands of his readers a high level of attention and philosophical training—it is densely metaphysical and deeply learned—he is one of the few major philosophers who also writes well for a wider audience. His name appears forty-eight times in *The Oxford Book of Aphorisms*, exceeded only by Nietzsche among quotable philosophers. Somewhere between Wordsworth and Nietzsche, Mr. Duffy's shelves evidently contain something by Schopenhauer, perhaps *Studies in Pessimism* (T. Saunders Bailey, 1893), William Wallace's biography (1890), *World*, or most likely, the Dircks's selection.[4]

Schopenhauer was much more widely read in 1900 than he is today: by the end of the nineteenth century, he had begun to outshine Hegel, and Nietzsche's sun was just rising. Joyce's encounter with and temporary enthusiasm for the ideas of Schopenhauer seems to have been during his time at the National University (1899–1902). He evidently had read Schopenhauer's *World* by the time he graduated, because he spontaneously quoted the philosopher's criticism of academic jargon ("poetic justice") during his oral examination for his BA in the spring of 1902, as James Caufield notes (708–9). The circles in which Joyce subsequently moved—the *Dana* group (Fred Ryan, John Eglinton, Oliver St. John Gogarty, Padraic Colum, et cetera)—were all familiar, on a conversational level at least, with Schopenhauer's opinions and ideas.

Padraic Colum describes a long conversation with Joyce (ca. 1903) that began at the checkout desk of the National Library as Colum returned the Haldane and Kemp translation of *World*. It began with Joyce's description of his appetite for whores as an expression of "the will to live," and did not end until they had reached the South Circular Road, by which time Joyce had railed against the cloistered life with Schopenhauerean verve (46–48). John Eglinton's essay, "A Way of Understanding Nietzsche" (*Dana*, October 1904), cites Schopenhauer throughout. Joyce's own reading of Nietzsche, which dates from about this time (*JJII* 142), would, in any event, have reminded him of that philosopher's indebtedness to Schopenhauer—repeatedly acknowledged in *Thus Spake Zarathustra*, *The Birth of Tragedy*, *Daybreak*, and *The Gay Science*, all of which Joyce evidently read.[5] Among Joyce's books in Trieste was the Dircks's compact *Essays of Schopenhauer*: the candidate most likely, therefore, to be imagined among the volumes on Mr. Duffy's white shelves (Ellmann, 126).

By the time Joyce wrote "A Painful Case," his literary sensibility was heavily influenced by writers, aside from Nietzsche, whose works reflected a Schopenhauerean pessimism. In his adolescence he had read Thomas Hardy (*MBK* 74–75), and subsequently Walter Pater, Turgenev (*CDD* 62), Tolstoy's *Anna Karenina*, and Moore's "John Norton," each of which "A Painful Case" inscribes.[6]

It is clear, then, that Joyce was familiar with Schopenhauer long before he cites him expressly in *Exiles*, and before he wrote "A Painful Case." If the aphorisms he has Mr. Duffy coin do indeed reflect Schopenhauer's essays, then Joyce may well have been introduced to the philosopher by his intellectually adventurous brother who was temperamentally sympathetic with the philosopher of pessimism. The account that would have recorded Joyce's proximity to Schopenhauerean influences—his brother's daybook from 1902 to 1904—is, unfortunately, lost. Stanislaus's account of his relationship with his brother (*MBK*), which drew on these entries, is permeated with terms, attitudes, and ideas that suggest his temporary acquisition of some Schopenhauerean attitudes, and helps account for Joyce's underlying reason for partially basing the figure of Mr. Duffy on "Il Penseroso," as Stanislaus nicknamed himself (*CDD* 57).

Neither of Stanislaus's published accounts of those early years (*MBK* and

CDD) expressly mentions Schopenhauer; nevertheless, the manner of Stanislaus's critique of religious indoctrination (*MBK* 81–82), the vehemence with which he denounced "false religion" (*MBK* 137–40, 189), his reflections on the relationship between belief and an orderly life (*MBK* 108), between psychology and philosophy (*MBK* 181), the tenor of his ruminations on sexuality (*MBK* 153), and his partiality to Giordano Bruno (*MBK* 145) all exhibit evidence of a mind exposed to Schopenhauer's ideas and vocabulary.[7]

Other indications that he was a sometime reader of Schopenhauer appear in Stanislaus's many phrases and aphoristic turns (for example, "Life itself is a symbol," *MBK* 132), and the earnestness and occasional arrogance of his discourse. Similarly, Stanislaus's habitual proclivity to contrast his own talent with his brother's genius (*CDD*, *MBK*, passim) reflects the manner in which Schopenhauer handles the subject in his chapter "On Genius" (*World* 3: 138–66). The genius is endowed with highly refined powers of perception as well as the intellectual gift to see the universal in the particular. In one of his characteristically pithy aphorisms he puts it thus: "He who is endowed with talent thinks more quickly and more correctly than others; but the genius beholds another world from them all" (138). Similarly, as Stanislaus reports it, the terms in which James acknowledged his own genius have a Schopenhauerean directness and intensity: "Jim wants to live. Life is his creed. He boasts of his power to live, and says, in his pseudo-medical phraseology, that it comes from his highly specialized central nervous system" (*CDD* 51), and "[Jim] seemed to me the person in Ireland who was most alive" (*CDD* 146).

What is of primary interest in the present investigation of the sources of Duffy's character and ideas as a man whose early spiritual formation was "spoiled" by his encounter with Arthur Schopenhauer are Stanislaus's observations about friendship, homosexuality, and heterosexual relations (both procreative and recreational) that might have been written by Mr. Duffy (*MBK* 150–58), and his observations on his father's friendship with Mr. Kelly on the quality of one's spiritual life (*MBK* 118). He also makes many references to a topic that, by the frequency with which it appears, evidently figured significantly in the brothers' conversations: the relationship between James's character as an adult and artist and his childhood love of God (*MBK* 153), the relationship between the priestly and poetic vocations (*MBK* 109), and the Schopenhauerean theme of the godlike gifts of the genius-creator.

The standard biography of Schopenhauer in Joyce's time was William Wallace's (1890). It contains many elegant précis of the philosopher's central ideas (Wallace was the Professor of Moral Philosophy at Oxford University). Stanislaus—or James—had no need, in fact, to go beyond this widely read work to grasp the force of his intellect and personality. In developing the thesis of Schopenhauer's famous pessimism, this biographer emphasizes the philosopher's Dutch background and character. Wallace devotes a whole chapter to a description of his merchant family, their dour disposition, regular lives, and contempt for those of lesser industry or gift (22–26). Stanislaus is admitting more than he intends when, in claiming to recognize elements of himself (aka "Hail Melancholy") in Mr. Duffy—his hostility to socialism, his antipathy to drunkenness, and his habit of committing his aphorisms to paper—that he characterizes these borrowings as enabling "the grim Dutch touch" (*MBK* 160).

Schopenhauer and Religion

One of the main themes of *MBK* is the gradual estrangement of the brothers Joyce from the Catholic Church and Christian belief itself. Stanislaus is the more forthright of the pair, for as he observed of James, he was "[a]n unwilling unbeliever like Renan" (*MBK* 230). From this account, it is clear that they did not drift into unbelief, but between them read extensively in religious literature: James read Thomas Aquinas's *Summa Contra Gentiles* (*MBK* 243), the Catholic mystics (*MBK* 131), Saint Augustine's *Confessions* (*MBK* 155–56), studied a collated edition of the Gospels (*MBK* 100), and the theosophists (*MBK* 131). The brothers quarreled with the Catholic Church in similar ways: James by refusing to take his final examination in religion at Belvedere (*MBK* 88), Stanislaus by refusing to make his Easter duty, and each of them debating with the other the values of the counterclaims of their religious tradition and of modern science and scientific skepticism, and entering into the debates surrounding the historical Christ (reading the critical lives of Jesus by Strauss and Renan, *JJII* 193). They lived in a family divided on religious lines—between their deeply pious and observant mother and their brutal and cynical father—which was reflected in the religious values of their children: Margaret a religious sister, Charlie for a time a seminarian, and James and Stanislaus contentious agnostics.

"A Painful Case" arises from the brothers' common and mutually supportive estrangement from the religion of their youth. Mr. Duffy's self-education with respect to religious ideas is a fictional representation of their informed and independent spiritual *katabasis*. He has educated himself in accordance with the progress of religious or metaphysical ideas during the nineteenth century: from his childhood Catholicism, through a Wordsworthian pantheism, and via a Schopenhauerean atheism to finally a Nietzschean nihilism.

With respect to Schopenhauer—the most influential of these figures on his mode of life and thought—he had a nonreligious childhood and education, and therefore felt himself free to examine from a disinterested perspective the process of Christian socialization from which even his most admired geniuses—Immanuel Kant and Beethoven—were not free.

Schopenhauer could therefore without twinge of conscience declare that he did not believe in God or personal survival after death. He thought these beliefs incoherent and beyond discussion: there was an unbridgeable chasm between our experience and what lies beyond death. And about that which we know nothing, as he remarked in a famous statement, "we should remain silent." Nevertheless, in his chapter, "On Death and Its Relation to the Indestructibility of Our True Nature," he argues that "a germ" survives individual death, to reappear in another body. In this speculation, he appears on the one hand to embrace Hindu metempsychosis that holds that an individual soul moves from one body to another as it expiates the misdeeds of previous embodiments (*World* 3: 300–306). On the other hand, the import of his general theory of Will would appear to promise nothing more in the afterlife than a dissolution into the mass of undifferentiated energy that permeates the universe. He returns to the question again in his essay "On Religion." Here he argues that the church developed the notion of Purgatory in answering the challenge to its ideas about the afterlife raised by the notion of metempsychosis (*P&P* 2: 364–66).

Joyce would therefore have encountered Schopenhauer's flirtation with metempsychosis at least a couple of years before the debate on the Celtic belief in reincarnation gained currency in Irish intellectual circles. Alfred Nutt's *Celtic Doctrine of Rebirth* and Arbois deJubainville's discussions of Greek and Celtic ideas of reincarnation intrigued John Millington Synge, George Russell, and Joyce (Tymoczko, 43–49; Owens, "Wooing of Étaín"). In her authoritative study of *Ulysses*, Maria Tymoczko considers that Joyce was influenced by deJubainville's understanding of metempsychosis among the Celts as nonjudgmental, "an affirmation of eternal verities, eternal values, eternal types" (46). The relevance of these considerations here is that Mr. Duffy's reading of Schopenhauer offered him a vague alternative to the firmly moral view of the condition of the individual soul after death, although, as we shall see, he cannot free himself from the fear of what divine judgment will mean for him. Like Stephen Dedalus, whose wits were driven astray by visions of hell (*U* 10.1072–74), Mr. Duffy cannot achieve the emotional freedom that might liberate him to love another human being and if not create, at least procreate.

For Schopenhauer, the enabling force in the universe is an impersonal, implacable, and invisible Will. This force empowers all observable phenomena, from the distant stars to the individual human embodiment. This energy is not observable, but can be inferred from the appearances, the phenomena, of nature. Too abstract and indeed unimaginable to all but those with philosophic capacities to be accepted for general consumption, it has to be rendered in narrative or dramatic forms: mythologized. This mythologization we call religion. Religion is popular metaphysics. People have a need for an interpretation of life, and it has to be one they are capable of understanding. That is why it is always clothed in allegory. Ordinary people have no direct access to truth; the various religions are simply schemata by which they grasp it and picture it, but with which it is inseparably linked ("On Religion," *P&P* 2: 325; Dircks, 98). Religion is at best a symbolical form of the truth, a beautiful allegory, and at worst a *pia fraus* (*P&P* 2: 336; Dircks, 113).

The priestly class of all religions has recognized and grasped the enormous strength and the ineradicability of this yearning for the metaphysical. Claiming that extraordinary channels have directly communicated the solution to the great enigma to them, they pretend to possess the means of satisfying it. Once they have persuaded the public of the truth of this, they can dominate them and dictate the rules of behavior. Political rulers have either to enter into prudent alliances or allow themselves to be governed by them. Rulers who wish to retain their prestige and power have learned to give the appearance of religious earnestness. If, however, as the rarest of all exceptions, a philosopher (like Schopenhauer) comes to the throne, "there arises the most embarrassing disturbance in the whole comedy" (*P&P* 2: 362).

Religious acculturation, in Schopenhauer's view, is particularly powerful if education is entrusted to those who conspire on behalf of religion to beguile the impressionable.

> Thus if in early childhood a boy is repeatedly told certain fundamental views and doctrines with unusual solemnity and an air of the loftiest earnestness never before seen by him; and if, at the same time, the possibility of doubting them is entirely passed over or else touched on merely to point to it as the first step to eternal perdition, the impression will prove to be so deep that, as a rule, in other words in almost all cases, he will be wellnigh as incapable of doubting those doctrines as he is of doubting his own existence. (*P&P* 2: 326; Dircks, 100)

Turning to the English, whose political culture and civilization Schopenhauer admires beyond all, he makes the following observation that must have impressed the young Joyce, since his version of it emerges in one of his most famous statements about his early work:

> Look at this nation, more highly favoured by nature than all the others and better endowed with intelligence, understanding, power of judgement, and strength of character; see how debased they are beyond all others, in fact, how positively contemptible they become, through the stupid superstition of their Church which appears among their other abilities positively like a fixed idea or monomania. For this they have to thank simply the fact that education is in the hands of the clergy who take good care to inculcate on their minds at the earliest age all the articles of faith in a way that amounts to *a kind of partial paralysis of the brain.* (emphasis added; *P&P* 2: 327; Dircks, 101)

Reading Schopenhauer's criticism of British culture, a secular affair by the standards of Catholic Ireland in 1900, Joyce must have considered that his judgment about the paralysis of the rational and pragmatic British applied a fortiori to their subjects, the pious Irish Catholics, the benighted servants of two empires. His comments on the relationship between church and state and the paralyzing force of political and religious authority are the most widely accepted commonplaces of Joyce's criticism of the culture that formed him: his famous letter to Constantine Curran in 1904, stating his aims for *Dubliners*, "to betray the soul of that hemiplegia or paralysis which many consider a city" (*Letters* I: 55). That these attitudes and terms originate in, or at least were confirmed by, his reading Schopenhauer is nowhere in any account of his early independent intellectual formation.

With regard to the mystification of the young and the paralysis of their spirits of which Schopenhauer complains in "On Religion" (cited above), Stanislaus similarly remarks:

> The most demoralizing element of Christianity is the dogma of the Trinity. When taught to children it does the work of original sin, for the making of a contradiction in terms the fundamental belief of a creed has the effect of darkening their understanding in its conception of anything [*sic*], of puzzling it and of wearying it; and the making of a great sin not to believe firmly in a mystery they can rarely even state to themselves weakens their will and discourages any natural inquiry into whatsoever keeps knocking at their heads. (September 14, 1904, *CDD* 99–100)

If we are to read the clue given us in "A Painful Case" as to Mr. Duffy's spiritual hegira, we see him move, in the course of the four years that span the action of the story, from Schopenhauer's criticism of religion to his disciple Nietzsche. A survey of Schopenhauer's essays on religion exhumes a few salient perspectives that Mr. Duffy appears to have adopted. Schopenhauer claimed for his work the effect of taking his readers who were raised in a childhood religion to the state of modern maturity: as declaring that mankind had outgrown the clothes of its childhood (*P&P* 2: 392). His critique of religion is elaborate and historical, dealing with each stage of its development from primitive polytheism to modern Christianity. In the course of that discussion, he offers en passant, a trenchant attack on pantheism, and thereby on another figure from Mr. Duffy's past, William Wordsworth.

Schopenhauer explicitly rejected the notion of God's immanence in the world as a self-delusion. He gave two major reasons for this rejection: it fails to account for the evil to be discerned everywhere, and it attempts to explain the better known by appealing to the lesser known: the immanent Presence that haunts Wordsworth's major works (*World* 3: 403–4, 471–75, and "A Few Words on Pantheism," *P&P* 2: 99–102). Schopenhauer's pitiless and implacable Will packed too much metaphysical energy for the mystical and passive Presence that by then Wordsworth had abandoned. In his "Essay on Spirit Seeing," Schopenhauer denounced "the mediocre Wordsworth" for his late compliance with the Anglicanism of "a stultified and priest-ridden nation" (*P&P* 1: 271). The irrational and morally indifferent force that powered Schopenhauer's universe evacuated man's experience of nature of its sense of Presence and Joy. Thus however his adolescent soul absorbed Wordsworth's mild metaphysic and notion of a companionable nature, on turning to Schopenhauer, Mr. Duffy's attention would have been redirected to the discipline of the urban landscape, with its hard and frequented streets and sidewalks, the culture of books, theatres, concert halls, cafes, and offices, and of political pressures arising from commercial life.

In the light of these observations, Duffy's failure can be accounted as a reversion to his childhood fear of damnation. The power of this early indoctrination is greater than his intellectual maturity. The result is that he is both a *prêtre manqué* and a Schopenhauerean *manqué*. He lacks the courage of his agnostic convictions.

Schopenhauer's Aesthetics

The principle by which Stephen Dedalus distinguishes between the lyric, epic, and dramatic modes he seems to have derived—without acknowledgment—from Schopenhauer's *World*. James Walter Caufield expanded the observations of Morris Beja (31) and David Evans on this point to embrace the ideas of "epiphany" (*SH* 211) and *claritas* as terms for Schopenhauer's notion of the genius-artist's insight or transcendent vision (702–3) (cf. the chapters "On the Pure Subject of Knowledge," "On Genius," and "On the Inner Nature of Art," *World* 3: 126–66, 176–81). They made their first appearance in Joyce's "Drama and Life" essay (January 1900, *CW* 38–46) and later, of course, in *Portrait*.

In his very interesting brief essay, Caufield suggests that Joyce's portrait of Stephen seems indebted to Schopenhauer's characterization of a genius-type as alienated and isolated. Stephen's misogyny in particular, his observation "that every physical quality admired by men in women is in direct connection with the manifold functions of women for the propagation of the species" (*P* 208.31–34), although rejected as too unaesthetic to be true, nevertheless neatly sums up a major tenet of Schopenhauer's metaphysics of sexual love. Joyce's youthful misogyny expressed itself with a vehemence that bears the philosopher's lapidary mark: "woman is an animal that micturates once a day, defecates once a week, menstruates once a month, and parturates [*sic*] once a year" (*CDD* 11 n. 8). Stanislaus reports that until he met Nora Barnacle, he spoke indecently of women, regarding them all as marsupials or whores (*CDD* 15; *SH* 210). In his correspondence with Stanislaus, he reflected on his relationship with Nora (by then a mother of fifteen months), offering a more balanced private generalization, though still enabled by Schopenhauer's less informed speculation:

> A woman's love is always maternal and egoistic. A man, on the contrary, side by side with his extraordinary cerebral sexualism and bodily fervour (from which women are normally free) possesses a fund of genuine affection for the "beloved" or "once beloved" object. (November 11, 1906, *Letters* II: 192)

Joyce had good reasons to erase Schopenhauer from the record. Caufield concludes that Stephen Dedalus's citations of Aristotle and Aquinas are decoys placed to misdirect readers from Schopenhauerean tracks, and are thus a further aspect of the ironies (double in this instance) of *Portrait* (710–11).

Joyce's early admiration for Schopenhauer was stimulated as much by his vivid style and coherent argumentation as by his bold atheism and his advanced theorizing about the metaphysics of music and sex and his influence on the composer of *Tristan und Isolde*. Caufield's glosses expose Stephen's pretentiousness in attempting to give Schopenhauerean distinctions the imprimatur of his betters. By the time Joyce had come to revise *Portrait*, however, he had outgrown his temporary infatuation with Schopenhauer. Joyce told

Boris Furlan in 1913 that Schopenhauer could not compare with Aquinas's systematic reasoning that was "like a sharp sword" (*JJII* 341–42).

These observations open the question of the relationship between Schopenhauer and that singular Joycean *futurabilium*, James Duffy. If the story is a fictionalization of a man moving from the myth of priesthood to that of artist, it allows us to see another dimension of its autobiographical character. "A Painful Case" is also an image of what Joyce might have become had he yielded to Schopenhauer's pessimism, elitism, misogyny, and personal spiritual despair. But "A Painful Case" is at the same time a celebration of a milestone its author had already passed, and a marker of his appetite for life, his willpower, and faith in himself. Thus "A Painful Case" is both a retrospective and prospective portrait of an artist-intellectual manqué.

Schopenhauer the Icon

Schopenhauer's stock was high at the end of the nineteenth century. The first major western philosopher to openly profess his atheism, he gave it a respectability that encouraged educated people of like mind to express such convictions openly. At the same time, although the scientific view of reality had gained widespread acceptance, it left many with a sense that too much of experience remained a mystery—that it was unable to account for the metaphysical aspect of experience. Science was unable, by itself, to police the premises vacated by the evicted God.

Thus, just as he was the scourge of popular sentimental Christianity, Schopenhauer was the leading critic of the scientific rationalism, inherited from the Enlightenment. This he called "absolute physics," holding that it failed to account for the forms of knowledge acquired through personal insight, interpersonal relationships, and experienced and expressed in the arts, especially music. Bryan Magee observes that Schopenhauer appealed to agnostics who were unwilling to move the object of their faith from God to science (428). To those who remained skeptics about skepticism, and who therefore still entertained a sense of the persistent mystery of the universe, Schopenhauer offered the idea of a life force, both in the human individual as the unconscious, and of the universe in the form of metaphysical Will. This concept, a development of Immanuel Kant's relationship between the imperceptible *ding an sich*, the noumenon, and the appearance, or phenomenon, is his fundamental contribution to the development of modern philosophy.

By locating the motivating force in our lives in our subrational selves, Schopenhauer drew attention to the irrational and instinctive elements in our experience and capacity to make decisions. By identifying the organizing force in the physical universe as an analogously amoral and impersonal metaphysical energy, he was able to account for the residual yearning for transcendence felt by modern agnostics and at the same time the partiality to detached cruelty of some and the widespread sufferings of the majority of humanity. His skill as a writer—he is one of the most penetrable of philosophers—led to his disproportionate influence outside the circles of professional philosophers and theologians. Neglected during his own lifetime (1788–1860), he became a celebrity because of the recommendations of Wagner and Nietzsche, so that by the end of the century his name was synonymous with intellectual greatness and originality (Magee, 433).

One reason for Schopenhauer's popular reputation was the widely circulated myth of his personal life. His ferocious disdain of sentimentality and vulgarity was dramatized by his celebrated daily routine and famous image. For the English-speaking world, William Wallace's biography—primarily intellectual and replete with vivid quotations from his subject's works—had a wider readership than any of Schopenhauer's own writings. According to Wallace, during the last thirty years of his life, which he passed in Frankfurt, he followed a rigid daily routine (after the practice of his master, Kant). Rising daily between 7:00 and 8:00 a.m., he would bathe while his housekeeper prepared him a cup of strong coffee, after which he would work nonstop at his writing desk until noon. He would then play his flute for one hour and depart for lunch to his table at *Englischer Hof*. There he would dine alone, depositing a gold coin on his table in front of him—which he promised himself to deposit in the poor-box if he ever overheard his fellow diners converse on any topic besides horses, dogs, or women. After lunch, he would return to his boarding house for a rest and his daily schedule of serious reading. He was enormously well read in all of western literature, modern and classical, in its various original languages (his marginal notes are written in the corresponding language) as well as in the literature of the Orient in translation (he was the first major European to read widely in this field). This he did until precisely 4:00 p.m., when with unvarying precision, he would dress for his two-hour walk around the city. The figure of Schopenhauer was a familiar sight to citizens of Frankfurt: no matter what the weather, there he would be, striding along at high speed, armed with a stout stick and accompanied by his poodle, disdaining beggars and laggards who happened to cross his path. At 6:00 p.m. he would enter the public reading room to peruse the day's *Times of London* (for he was an enthusiastic anglophile, from Shakespeare to the daily news). From there he repaired to a play, concert, or opera: he held Mozart,

Beethoven, and Bellini as supreme.[8] He often departed the theatre or concert hall after the item that interested him most in the evening program selection, meditating upon it as he returned to the *Englischer Hof.*, there to dine alone on a cold supper with a bottle of wine. He never stayed out late (Wallace, 170–78).

Although this account of the curmudgeonly rigor of his famous routine is somewhat overblown—he was, in fact, a remarkable conversationalist on every topic that evening visitors to the *Englischer Hof.* might bring up—it is substantially accurate (Magee, 24). The myth is a caricature of a man who although the patron saint of pessimism, was memorably witty and erudite. This myth grew around a man who steeled himself in mind and body to face every weather without flinching, and developing a self-reliance without equal, disdaining those of weaker body, mind, or spirit. The caricature exaggerated his eccentricities and was part of the myth of a man whose life embodied the willfulness that made him one with the creation. In Wallace's words, Schopenhauer undertook this regimen to persevere in developing "a philosophy which is no church and no religion" (170).

It hardly needs reiteration that the routine followed daily by Joyce's Mr. Duffy (who "had neither companions nor friends, church nor creed," D 109.8), seems to be modeled on the famous regimen of a philosopher he evidently read and admired. This burlesque, which should not have been lost on readers a century ago, invites us to consider the ways in which Duffy has not only adopted Schopenhauer's fanaticism about regulated exercise, but has also adopted his attitudes and ideas: his taste for music and opera, his misogyny, his aphorisms, his multilingualism, and his atheism, so that by the time of Mrs. Sinico's departure he is prepared mentally to move with the nineteenth century and become a disciple of Schopenhauer's disciple, Friedrich Nietzsche.

Duffy's Misogyny

Why does Mr. Duffy recoil at Mrs. Sinico's advance? At this point in their relationship, they had established a rapport based on several commonalities: of age (both around forty), of class (both middle), of domicile (both citizens of a capital endowed with safe and walkable streets and parks), of literary and cultural taste (both similarly partial to European classical music), of temperament (both reserved, neither socially gregarious), ethnicity (both Irish Catholic), and opportunity (Mr. Duffy a bachelor, Mrs. Sinico in a *marriage blanc*). They are a bourgeois couple. However, Mrs. Sinico is the more emotionally declarative: she is sufficiently independent of her social background to have married an Italian, and is the mother of a grown daughter. Her musical talent complements Mr. Duffy's intellectual capacities. They have each indicated their relative independence of social conventionality, she by her exogamy, and he by his high literacy. This has left them similarly outside the most accommodating of Dublin's social circles. Their relationship could have taken a "French" direction; and would have, had Mr. Duffy not shrunk from the prospect.

The breakup strikes readers variously. Bernard Benstock considers that Mr. Duffy, for all his self-image as an independent thinker, is as much a creature of social convention as any other character in *Dubliners*: he is afraid of social disapproval and the possible consequent damage to his career at the bank (130). To Warren Beck, his withdrawal is due to an indifference to sexual feeling (232). There have been several attempts to read Mr. Duffy as a closet homosexual (Norris summarizes, 252–53), or a narcissist or solipsist (Henke, 35). Margot Norris concludes that whatever closet he's in, it has an opaque door (170). Gerald Doherty conducts a fruitless post-colonial house search. The principal weaknesses in these readings of the story are their underestimation of its literary subtleties. They are highly selective, insufficiently historicized, and indifferent to the cultural traditions that profoundly shaped Joyce's values. Mr. Duffy's rejection of Mrs. Sinico's advance arises from a profound and irrational conflict. While he has attempted to exorcize the religious sensibility and scruples of his youth by reading advanced thinkers, he is still appalled by the prospect of the final judgment that banishes unrepentant adulterers from the divine presence forever: "Blessed are the clean of heart, for they will see God" (Matt. 5: 8). To his semi-clericalized conscience, moreover, subliminally imagining himself as a spiritual inheritor of the dignity of the order of Melchisedech, cohabitation with Mrs. Sinico would be more like sacrilege than common adultery.

The misogynistic rhetoric that he has acquired from his reading of Schopenhauer has been misread as evidence of homosexual posturing, although there is no evidence that he is any more a homosexual than was Schopenhauer. In Schopenhauer's "The Metaphysics of the Love of the Sexes" (*World* 3: 336–75), he would have encountered the philosopher's view that adultery was more serious for women than men (351), and in the notorious essay "On Women" (*P&P* 2: 614–26), Duffy would have found trenchant expression of hurtful attitudes with grounds of resistance to heterosexual relations quite different from those proposed by queer theorists.

Schopenhauer's view of sexuality is rooted in his metaphysics of Will. A disciple of Kant, he engaged in the nineteenth-century German debate over the relationship between the world of experience (phenomena) and the intuited underlying reality (noumena). For Schopenhauer, the philosopher can reflect on noumenal reality without the need to resort to myth, which the ordinary person apprehends in the form of religion. For Schopenhauer, the underlying noumenal reality is primarily energy, the Life Force, or what he calls Will. The ordinary human being experiences the primal energy that drives the universe in sexual attraction and expression, orgasm (although he did not use the term). For Schopenhauer, sexual love is the agency whereby the noumenal enters the world of phenomena, and the common person's primary and direct experience of this primal energy. This hypothesis is essentially inexplicable, beyond sufficient reason, and is indeed, irrational.

However, the evidence of its reality is to be found in universal, nonrational human experience: in the global persistence of religious belief and the possessive power of sexual attraction (Magee, 217–18):

> [Sexual desire] is the desire that even constitutes the nature of man. In conflict with it no motive is so strong that it would be certain of victory. It is so pre-eminently the chief concern that no other pleasures make up for the deprivation of its satisfaction; and, moreover, for its sake both brute and man undertake every danger and every conflict. (*World* 3: 312–13)

Schopenhauer is the first major western philosopher to accord a central role—psychological and metaphysical—to sexuality. For Schopenhauer, man is the embodiment of sexual impulse. At the center of the world of phenomena is the unconscious and hidden will to live. The moment of conception is of profound significance: "its kernel and greatest concentration [is] the act of generation" (*P&P* 2: 316).

In chapter 44 of *World*, "On the Assertion of the Will to Live" (3: 376–81), he expatiates. Ordinary people are individuated embodiments of the will to live. We are driven onwards by this irresistible, irrational, and implacable force that takes no account of their particular interests or happiness. From the beginning of our lives we are programmed to follow this blind, and indeed, tragic course. It leads inevitably to frustration, disappointment, and pain. We are thus destined, not for happiness, but for suffering; and we pass on to our offspring the virus, with life itself. We serve, not our own interests, but those of the species to which we belong.

Although as individuals we are powerfully motivated to the expression of sexuality, the common experience is that whereas it is the source of brief pleasure, it introduces us to a life of subsequent protracted suffering. When we engage in sexual activity, we may imagine that we are on our way towards personal happiness. But individual happiness is not the object of this aspect of life any more than any other activity. Common experience tells us that this does not result. We are driven to seek partners to whom we are biologically attracted but with whom we are incompatible in the longer run. Marriage, moreover, which commits us to permanence, seals our fates to double disadvantage: we halve our rights and double our duties (*P&P* 2: 622). "Falling in love," advocated by popular culture, is irrational, a folly, madness. In this respect, as in many others, Schopenhauer anticipates Freud, who calls romantic heterosexual love "the psychosis of normal people."

Thus, as William Wallace puts it,

> The center and root of all existence is not an idea, but a nisus or effort towards being, a blind unconscious striving, which in universal movement sways to and fro, driving, yet not by preconceived ends, but by something which is not mere force and still less intellect, and is only definable as Will. (94)

We are but servants of the force that ensures the survival of the species to which we belong. Furthering the preservation of its life, in Stephen Dedalus's words, we do "the coupler's will" (*U* 3.47).[9] Schopenhauer vents his colorful invective repeatedly on this theme, in *World* 1: 421–26, 3: 376–81, and again in his essays:

> For has it not been observed how illico post coitum cachinnus auditor Diaboli? (Directly after copulation the devil's laughter is heard). Seriously speaking . . . sexual desire, especially when through fixation on a definite woman it is concentrated to amorous infatuation, is the quintessence of the whole fraud of this noble world; for it promises so unspeakably, infinitely, and excessively much, and then performs so contemptibly little. (*P&P* 2: 316)

Around the theme that suffering, and not happiness, is the true object of life, Schopenhauer has spun many of his most memorable parables and aphorisms:

> We are like lambs playing in the field, while the butcher eyes them and selects first one and then another; for in our good days we do not know what calamity fate at this very moment has in store for us, sickness, persecution, impoverishment, mutilation, loss of sight, madness, death, and so on. (*P&P* 2: 292)

In Schopenhauer's view, women exemplify his thesis more clearly than men. His classic misogynistic essay, "On Women" (*P&P* 2: 614–26), asserts that women (in contrast with men) are totally subsumed by their biological destiny that is the duty of childbearing. They are interested in the species, not in individual development. Consistent with this role, they are capable of a higher degree of sympathy with the young, the weak, and the aged, than are men. They are, in consequence, incapable of the degree of will or intellect found among males that can produce original art, create scientific inventions, or produce literary works of power and vision. Whereas a man says "I will," a woman says "he will." Not being possessed of the detachment and willful drive of men, they are given to deception, flattery, manipulation, and frivolity. This subservience renders them incapable of friendship with men, which is possible only between equals (Schopenhauer's frequent references to friendship always assume male references). Again, by contrast with men, women are naturally disposed to rivalry with one another. Nevertheless, they are nurturing of the immediate needs of children, men, and seniors: mothers in youth, lovers in midlife, and nurses in old age.

The force of lust is therefore the necessary axis upon which the relationships between man and woman turn. Man's intellect is in a perpetual contest with this expression of the lower nature: ideal aims and the desire for pleasure are fundamentally incompatible. Thus, as William Wallace observes, Schopenhauer yearns for the ascetic ideal, to be free of the sexual altogether (92). He suffers like the most extreme Manichean who sees himself trapped in an abyss of futile repetition and at the same time endowed with a sense of "better consciousness." Averse to both materialist and spiritualist solutions, he finds himself caught between brief bouts of willful energy and an inner emptiness: what he calls "boredom" (Magee, 219). Most people are engaged in one of two tasks, gaining a livelihood and disposing of the material burden that accumulates from this effort. Each aspect of this process has the illusory merit of fending off boredom, a condition that can lead to despair (*P&P* 2: 286–88). Meanwhile, vulgar cultural expressions keep the mass of mankind in a state of stupor, agitation, or distraction.

Only those with fierce determination or extraordinary gifts can escape this common fate to which popular culture pushes them relentlessly. It takes self-knowledge and courage to withdraw from the charade. Thus, he holds that "There is in the world only the choice between loneliness and vulgarity." Great souls are fated to loneliness; but loneliness is a prerequisite for peace of mind (*P&P* 1: 429). This is a theme to which he frequently returns, presenting the point in many piquant metaphors, such as "In solitude we are like a fish in water" (*P&P* 1: 429).

Mr. Duffy has many inconsistencies: he is a loner and a socialist, a Catholic Unionist, a scrupulous clerk, and would-be bank robber. Yet beneath these contradictions, he has consistent attitudes towards sexuality, women, and solitude. They are evidently similar to these salient aspects of Schopenhauer's ideas expressed in these chapters and essays. Mr. Duffy's most florid aphorism that he has committed to paper is a summary of Schopenhauer's view of sexuality: "Love between man and man is impossible because there must not be sexual intercourse and friendship between man and woman is impossible because there must be sexual intercourse" (*D* 112.19–22).

Similarly, Mr. Duffy's disdain of phrasemongers and impresarios for their inability to think clearly and who pander to popular taste (*D* 111.10–14), his condescension to "the hard-featured realists" among the workmen who were resentful of his insistence on clear and precise thinking (*D* 111.5–7), his withdrawal from Dublin's civic life, and the way in which he explained to Mrs. Sinico that their relationship had to end all reflect a Schopenhauerean metaphysical impersonality, tone, metaphor, and emphasis: "insisting on the soul's incurable loneliness. We cannot give ourselves . . . we are our own" (*D* 111.28–29).

The text of "A Painful Case" contrasts the terms "woman," and "lady" with salient reference to two divergent perceptions of Mrs. Sinico's character and class status. At the coroner's hearing the railway porter testified that he saw a "woman attempting to cross the lines" (*D* 114.4), a designation later confirmed by Captain Sinico's testimony of her "rather intemperate . . . habits" (*D* 115.3). On the other hand, the term "lady" in the newspaper headline is semantically consistent with the way in which Mr. Duffy had always thought of Mrs. Sinico (*D* 109.17, 19; 110.23–24), as a female endowed with culture and dignity, and a captain's wife.[10] Mr. Duffy's subsequent revulsion at the contrast between Mrs. Sinico the cultivated "lady" and the alcoholic and perhaps suicidal "woman" reflects a particularly vitriolic passage in Schopenhauer's essay "On Women." He denounces the sentimental elevation, in modern European culture, of "woman" to "lady." He sees this as disingenuous, in view of women's comparative weaknesses of character by contrast with men's, and socially unjust in its denigration of lower-class women (*P&P* 2: 622). The first stage of Mr. Duffy's reaction to the news of her death—that Mrs. Sinico was a person of low character with whom he is ashamed to have been associated—reflects this Schopenhauerean judgment.

The burden of these contextualizations of Mr. Duffy's affair with Mrs. Sinico suggests that he has found in the reading of Schopenhauer a rationalization of his celibate and melancholic temperament. It has replaced the earlier ones—of a would-be Catholic priest and romantic poet.

Schopenhauer's Continental Progeny

Mr. Duffy has arranged his books according to their bulk. In this he is following Schopenhauer's encomium on the superior merits of a small but well-ordered library (*P&P* 2: 491). The partial list we are given does not include, as I have been arguing, the most influential author in Duffy's intellectual life. Schopenhauer's absence is the highest form of presence, both in Mr. Duffy's mind and that of the implied narrator. This presence is indicated through the narrator's sometimes extensive invocation of four Continental writers who were themselves imaginatively engaged in "theologicophilological" questions raised by Schopenhauer: Ivan Turgenev, Friedrich Nietzsche, Leo Tolstoy, and Gerhart Hauptmann.

Lishny Chelovek

Turgenev's novella, "Clara Militch" (1882), provided Joyce with an immediate precedent for the management of paranormal phenomena. Paul Delaney and Dorothy Young have pointed out that the general outline and many superficial details of plot and characterization in "A Painful Case" are apparent borrowings from this Dream Tale. The protagonists are intellectuals, recluses, social failures, are interested in music, and have brief, unorthodox, and unhappy relationships with musical women that lead to their similar moral crises. Even though Joyce thought Turgenev "a little dull . . . and . . . theatrical" (September 18, 1905, *Letters* II: 106), he felt that he was one of the European writers from whom he could learn. A careful tandem reading of "Clara Militch" and "A Painful Case" demonstrates that the relationship between these two works is both more circumstantial, substantial, and interesting than the broad parallels already noted.

The salient element in Turgenev's story that bears upon Joyce's conceptualization and execution of "A Painful Case" is his conversion of Turgenev's protracted Gothic scenes into the compressed ghost paragraph sequence in "A Painful Case" (*D* 116.34–117.8). Turgenev's Yakov Aratov develops a notional love romantic relationship with Clara Militch, an actress and singer. They become mutually infatuated with one another's images. When she attempts to make this relationship personal, he withdraws, only to discover, three weeks later, that she has committed suicide. Becoming alarmed that his rejection of her attentions drove her to this desperate extreme, he undertakes a forensic investigation of her brief life. First, her diary confirms his suspicion. Then, his recapitulation of her personal background leads him to imagine her more vividly in death than he had before. In the final chapters of this novella, Aratov enters into an obsessive spiritual relationship with her recurring ghost—her voice, her image, her eyes, her hair—even to the point of a passionate kiss with her spirit across the abyss thrown between them by death. These paranormal experiences convince him that although the deceased Clara has forgiven him for his callousness, their relationship is based not on love but on power. He concludes that it is only in death that he can be united with his ideal counterpart. In the final chapter he is discovered dead, apparently in ecstasy, grasping in his hand a lock of her hair.

Gothicism aside, Joyce might well have been struck, originally, by the coincidence between the name of the performer at the historical concert that Stanislaus attended—Clara Butt—and Turgenev's eponymous performer (such verbal coincidences play a minor role in the structuring of Joyce's universe). His attention might also have been arrested by the various ways in which Turgenev portrays Yakov ("the Russian form of James," as Garnett instructs her readers, Turgenev, "Clara Militch" 4) Aratov's renunciation of ordinary joys. One of his friends protests, "why fall prey to asceticism? You're not going in for becoming a monk!" (12). More substantially, considering the larger vision underlying the pathos of Mr. Duffy's life, "Clara Militch" would have resonated in Joyce's imagination as an expression of Turgenev's flirtation with Schopenhauer. It expresses a Schopenhauerean understanding of sex as the multiplier of suffering and the manifestation of the power relations between the sexes rather than anything so sentimental and trite as mutual love. It also exemplifies Schopenhauer's understanding of paranormal phenomena.

The story moves Aratov to reconsider his precise understanding of the next world, and he is evidently deluded into confusing psychological projection with objective spiritual fact. In his famous essay on spirits, Schopenhauer undertakes an idealistic (or what was subsequently called a psychological) rather than transcendental explanation of spirits. Here he claims to be following Immanuel Kant's *Traume eines Geistersehers*. Beginning with dreams (congeries of images not produced by the external senses), he distinguishes dreams from conscious imaginings. His essay distinguishes nine kinds of spirit seeing, from dreams, ravings of madmen, and tricks, to group sightings, appearances before actual events occur, et cetera. Denying, of course, that spirits who manifest themselves to the living individually represent the dead, he concludes that "a spirit apparition primarily and directly is nothing but a vision in the brain of the spirit seer" (*P&P* 1: 309).

As A. Walicki has argued, Schopenhauer informs the larger issue in Turgenev's fiction, particularly his "Hamletism." This "disease of reflection," which Schopenhauer conceived of as the inescapable fate of every thinking creature, found its way into Turgenev's depiction of the ineffectual character type, *Lishny Chelovek*, the "superfluous man" (17). These "Russian Hamlets," Yakov Aratov in "Clara Militch" and Tchulkaturin in *Diary of a Superfluous Man*, establish the type that can be found with many variants in Tolstoy, Aleksandr Pushkin, Fyodor Dostoievsky and Anton Chekhov.

The Joyce brothers read and discussed *The Diary of a Superfluous Man* in August 1904 (*MBK* 167). James thought Tchulkaturin was very like Stanislaus (*CDD* 62). Their correspondence from the summer of the following year, at a time when Joyce was entering "A Painful Case" into the written record, discovers their comparing further notes on Turgenev (*Letters* II: 90, 118). Joyce rated Turgenev below Tolstoy but "useful technically" (*Letters* II: 90). One application of Turgenev's technique (as Michael Levenson argues) can be seen in Joyce's borrowing the form of *The Diary of a Superfluous Man* for the exit from *Portrait*: Tchulkaturin writes his diary between March 20 and April 1, and Stephen's entries run from March 20 through April 27.

It seems equally clear that just as the figure of James Duffy reproduces some of Stanislaus's traits—his dour demeanor, his intellectuality, and his musical taste—he also inherits some of Tchulkaturin's characteristics. Both are melancholy bystanders. Both are given to painful, detached, third-party self-examinations. Like his forbear, Duffy attempts to impress his lady through his library and expresses his literary ambition through a desultory diary. Having passed his life in the lower grades of the civil service, Tchulkaturin is an "underachiever" and a wet blanket. Mr. Duffy is an outsider too, but for different reasons: he is an intellectual who understands the need for a social revolution but is helpless to engage his talents on its behalf, as a passive reader of the newspaper, and especially as implied by the emphatic image upon which the story concludes, the voyeur despised by the anonymous but "entangled" lovers.

Tchulkaturin's objects in writing his ten-day diary are apparently both self-discernment and self-display. He aims to find out "what sort of a queer fish one really was after all," puzzling over the seeming contradiction between his own morbidity and his intolerance of morbidity in others. The unacknowledged Schopenhauerean imperative to assert and record an existence, however futile, is inscribed in his consciousness and paradoxically—despite his "superfluity"—calls out for vindication. More educated and literate than the provincials around him, his only means of self-assertion is the literary record of his diary. The single incident in his life that he considers worth a brief claim on his posthumous readers' attention is an unhappy infatuation. Reading *The Prisoner of the Caucasus* with his lady was never a promising ploy. The arrival of a dashing rival, an army officer, with whom he blundered into—and out of—a duel, doomed it surely. His consequent social disgrace led him to the conclusion that he was never anything but a bystander in the lives of his inferiors. Whereas every one of them might have had some individual distinction, "bad, or good, clever, stupid, pleasant [or] disagreeable," he glumly concluded that he was "superfluous and nothing more. A supernumerary, and that's all. Nature, apparently did not reckon on my appearance, and consequently treated me as an unexpected and uninvited guest" (15). Mr. Duffy, mentally citing the same Matthean reference to those excluded from the wedding feast (Matt. 22: 13), sees himself, in the end, as "outcast from life's feast" (*D* 117.15, 20).

This feeling of his own inconsequentiality threw Tchulkaturin into deeply melancholic and self-critical introspection:

> I analyzed myself to the last thread, compared myself with others, recalled the slightest glances, smiles, words of the people to whom I had tried to open myself out, put the worst construction on everything, laughed vindictively at my own pretensions "to be like every one else"—and suddenly, in the midst of my laughter, collapsed utterly into gloom, sank into absurd dejection, and then began again as before. (16)

Nevertheless, although Russia would have been just as well or badly off with or without him, he felt the need, as he anticipates his imminent death, to leave some account of "the wearing sense of life, of the persistent, restless consciousness of existence!" (5). He adopts a Schopenhauerean defiance of social obloquy: among his final diary entries (April 1) is the paradoxical self-affirmation that "[s]inking into nothing, I cease to be superfluous" (97).

In reading Turgenev's short novel, Joyce was encountering a figure that reflected a morbidity produced by a Schopenhauerean perception of metaphysical impersonality. Turgenev may have criticized the "Russian Hamlets" in social and political life, but he also justified and pardoned them. Because they are weak, self-centered, and unwilling to risk responsible action, they become socially "superfluous" and bitterly disillusioned. The feeling of universal tragedy, the pain of existence, increases with the growth of self-consciousness and is inseparable from thinking devoid of illusions. This was the chief motif of his cautious justification of "Hamletism" and was at the same time one of the guiding ideas in the philosophy of Schopenhauer (Walicki, 8). Although Turgenev's Tchulkaturin is not the decadent aristocrat that we see in Pushkin's *Eugen Onegin* (1830) or Ivan Goncharov's *Oblomov* (1859)—he is too "Hamletized" for that—he is the figure that gives the type of the superfluous man its name. Like the bored and passive intellectual who, although notionally partial to the peasants, allows the serfs and servants to do the work while he plays the part of a sophisticated slugabed, leads a detached and futile life.

In the light of this imaginative genealogy, Joyce's version of the "superfluous man" is like Turgenev's realistic depiction of a latter-day Byronic romantic hero. In his cultural tastes and intelligence, Joyce's Duffy is a "natural aristocrat"; he shares with his Russian counterparts some vestige of social conscience—witness his flirtation with the workmen's cause—but like the Russian type, his very intellectuality debilitates him. Unlike his Russian antecedents, whose paralysis rises from their irrelevant aristocratic roots, Duffy's is a delayed effect of the ideals by which, in his Irish Catholic youth, he was enthralled. In "A Painful Case" Joyce has transformed the *Lishny Chelovek* into the spoiled priest.

Nietzsche

"A Painful Case" is an account of the damnation of a soul. If it traces Duffy's descent from the spiritual aspirations implied by a clerical vocation, his rejection of that ideal of love of God and service of mankind, and, in turn, the offer of human love from Mrs. Sinico. His subsequent turning to Nietzsche's works, *Thus Spake Zarathustra* and *The Gay Science*, indicates the further disintegration of the remaining certainties in his life. Given the religious and cultural background against which he is in reaction, Mr. Duffy would seem particularly well disposed to these, the most expressly anti-Christian of Nietzsche's works.

Were Mr. Duffy not already a man who "had neither companions nor friends, church nor creed" (D 109.8), brooding with lonely disdain for compliant believers as he strode the dark suburbs in his reefer overcoat (a metaphorical "James Overman"), the mere action of reading these works would have severed his link with the church in which he had been raised. All of Nietzsche's works were—like Schopenhauer's—on the church's *Index Librorum Prohibitorum*, which meant that they could not be read without proper ecclesiastical authorization. The legislation governing what was licit for Catholics to read was well known in Joyce's youth. It had been reformed by Pope

Leo XIII and published in forty-nine articles, four of which expressly forbade books "which outrage God and sacred things." Permission to read Nietzsche could be obtained by scholars from the local bishop. Otherwise, reading books by heretics or apostates, or others who attacked Christian belief or institutions suffered, ipso facto, the penalty of excommunication (*Encyclopedia Britannica*, 11th ed. s.v. "*Index Librorum Prohibitorum*" and *Catholic Encyclopedia*, s.v. "censorship"). Even outside church circles, Nietzsche was regarded as a notorious lunatic, and only for the fact that he was largely ignored, might have been seen as a threat to civil society. In any event, this reading shows that Mr. Duffy has an independent mind: more daring than Father Flynn or Gabriel Conroy, his only intellectual peers in *Dubliners*.

In the works of Nietzsche on his shelf, then, Mr. Duffy would have found the mentality of a lonely fellow traveler. Nietzsche's early formation as a prospective Lutheran minister had filled his receptive imagination with biblical tropes, so that the terms by which he expresses his rejection of Christian faith are charged with the Old Testament patriarchy, misogyny, and rage against the philistine rabble. This converts into the rejection of the effeminate Christian ethic of love and a determination to destroy the superstructure of social respectability and institutionalized hypocrisy that permeate the Christian churches. In its place, Nietzsche imagines a superman who is at once disciplined (Apollonian) and emotionally deep rooted (Dionysian), a man who can live without the ancestral illusions of mind or spirit, whose defining power is his ability to say "I will."

In one of the earliest commentaries on this story, Marvin Magalaner documents several of the particular ways in which Mr. Duffy subscribed to Nietzsche's ideas in *Zarathustra*. A would-be *Ubermensch*, Duffy finds in this work a reinforcement of his notions of self-sufficiency and intellectual superiority. He has no need either for the ordinary run of society or for the company of women (37–40). In *The Gay Science*, moreover, Nietzsche had already developed the critique of religion continued in *Zarathustra*, which would have appealed to a man with James Duffy's particular religious and artistic temperament. Duffy would have been intrigued by Nietzsche's aphoristic style, his attack on the idea of vocation, Christian theism, and its major ethical inference, "the ascetic ideal." In generally similar ways, then, Friedrich Nietzsche and James Duffy are Schopenhauer's disciples.

Evidently drawing on his own early seminary training, Nietzsche considers "two kinds of causes that are often confused":

I learned to distinguish the cause of acting from the cause of acting in a certain way, in a certain direction, with a certain goal. The first kind of

cause is a quantum of dammed-up energy waiting to be used some-
how, for something; the second kind, by contrast, is something quite
insignificant, at most a small accident in accordance with which this
quantum "discharges" itself in one particular way: the match versus the
powder keg . . . Is the "goal," the "purpose," not often enough a beauti-
fying pretext, a self-deception of vanity after the fact that does not pay
to acknowledge that the ship is *following* the current into which it has
entered accidentally? That it "wills" to go that way *because it—must*?
That it certainly has a direction but—no helmsman whatsoever? We
still need a critique of the concept of "purpose." (*Gay Science* 225)

In this critique of the Aristotelian "final" at the expense of "efficient cause,"
Nietzsche is eviscerating the idea of a spiritual vocation. Writing autobio-
graphically as a former Lutheran seminarian, he recognizes that he mistook
his original direction as having a transcendental purpose (the voice of God
calling him) whereas he now realizes that his situation was a historical accident (that he was serendipitously born into a religious family et cetera),
or that it was one of his own choices to make or reject as he might. Again, it
is impossible to imagine that encountering this passage, Mr. Duffy was not
struck by its coincidences of personal, spiritual, and expressive dimensions
with his own situation as an Irish spoiled priest.

The Gay Science is his most explicitly anti-Christian work, best known for
his proclamation of the "Death of God" (in which he was preceded, of course,
by Schopenhauer). The Christian idea of God, alive in the minds of our forbears, has been euthanized, so that churches are now, as the madman claims,
the "sepulchers of God." Forcing his way into several churches, he sang his
requiem aeternam deo (119–20). Reading this dramatic fable, Mr. Duffy must
have reflected on his own spiritual hegira from the dogmatic asseverations
of the slim catechism to which he subscribed in his impressionable youth,
to the "empty benches" (*D* 109.23) and "ruined confessional" (*D* 112.3), the
emblems of the spiritual vacuity of his adulthood. These images, recalling
the "bare ruined choirs" of Shakespeare's discreet murmur at the closure of
the monasteries, are a similarly apt comment on the silence that has progres-
sively descended upon Mr. Duffy's soul.

In reading the accompanying attack on metaphysics, Mr. Duffy would
have encountered Nietzsche's denunciation not only of religion in the narrow
sense of the term, but also of its secularized expressions in the schools of political philosophy: utilitarianism, classical liberalism, and socialism. In reading Nietzsche's scabrous attack on benign freethinkers who imagine that they

can jettison theology while retaining Christian ethics, Mr. Duffy would have squirmed with embarrassment at his former sympathy with the workmen's group and seen in Nietzsche's words confirmation of his decision to abandon their caucuses.

In that same work he would have encountered a severe rebuke to the residuum of Christian moral discipline that remained with him. In *The Gay Science*, Nietzsche argues that the Christian God—in contrast with those of the Greeks—was possessed of qualities that were the opposite of our inescapable animal instincts. Our natural condition could then be reinterpreted as an indictable inability to attain perfection, original sin. The denial of our natural proclivities is then recast under the guise of what Nietzsche calls "the ascetic ideal." The power of this ideal—derived partially from Socratic idealism and partially from biblical theism—was first attacked by Luther's "every man a priest," in which sexual intercourse with a woman was not only permitted, but normal. This "impossible monk" thereby initiated a "peasants' rebellion," and usurped the dominion of the *homines religiosi*:

> He did not know what he was doing. . . . Luther shared the blame for the degeneration of the modern scholar, for his lack of reverence, shame, and depth, for the whole naïve guilelessness and conventionality in matters of knowledge—in short for that *plebeianism of the spirit* that is peculiar to the last two centuries and from which even pessimism has not yet liberated us. (222–23)

Christian morality is thus translated and sublimated into an impotent attempt to don intellectual cleanliness at any price. This, in turn, as he read, is about to be evacuated by a soporific universal material consumerism. Mr. Duffy's absorption of these sections of *The Gay Science* and his quailing at the vanity and license of "Dublin's gilded youth" (D 109.2)—presumably in the chic watering holes of Stephen's Green and Grafton Street—must have gnawed heavily at the remaining moral sinews of the apostate but still emotionally observant Catholic. It is no wonder that, having traveled the route from that outlined by the *Maynooth Catechism* to his inference of Mrs. Sinico's nonexistence that he was disposed to feel that "his moral nature [was] falling to pieces" (D 117.7–8).

Reading *Zarathustra* and *The Gay Science*, Mr. Duffy would have encountered Nietzsche's ambivalent attitude towards women and the philosopher's search for truth. On the one hand, he could have rationalized his rejection of Mrs. Sinico's advance towards him as the justification of his masculine self-sufficiency, expressed in his aphoristic diary, his conviction of "the soul's incurable loneliness," and the aesthetic detachment of music. Women, on the other hand, are not capable of detached inquiry. "What is truth to a woman?" Nietzsche, following Schopenhauer's precedent, asks:

> Everything in woman is a riddle, and everything in woman has one solution—it is called pregnancy. . . . Man shall be trained for war, and woman for the recreation of the warrior: all else is folly. . . . The happiness of man is, "I will." The happiness of woman is, "He will." (*Zarathustra*, 89–90)

Women are fulfilled through the total surrender to love, to the will of another, and to pregnancy. These ends they achieve not by power of will, but by stealth. Their weaknesses—for adultery and drunkenness—were recognized by the ancient Romans as the only mortal sins they could commit. Nietzsche quotes Plutarch to the effect that "Women caught with wine were actually put to death; and certainly not just because sometimes women under the influence of wine completely forgot how to say no . . . to them it seemed like a betrayal of Rome, like the embodiment of the foreign" (*The Gay Science*, 58).

In his attitude towards Mrs. Sinico's physical attention to him, her willingness to engage in an adulterous relationship, her lack of intellectuality, her tearful pleadings at their breakup, and her eventual alcoholism and death, Mr. Duffy would have found rationalizations in *The Gay Science*. This work informs, therefore, the first and second stages of his reaction to her death (5 a, b; *D* 115.15–116.33): his disgust at her fall and indictment of her lack of self-control.

But his reading of that same work could also have informed the alternative conclusion that in rejecting her, he was, in the name of an ersatz ascetic ideal, turning his back on the only kind of happiness possible. Nietzsche was not consistent in his attitude towards women. Paul Smith observes:

> In *The Gay Science*, even as he seems to attack women for their disregard of truth, Nietzsche proposes that the search for truth has been the most debilitating and illusory project of the whole of Western philosophy and morality. Furthermore, he often aligns the productiveness of artists and real thinkers with the natural productiveness of women. Indeed, this the whole gist of *The Gay Science* as it tried to deconstruct the Western philosophers' concern for truth and to replace it with a Nietzschean conception of a free-floating, inspirational knowledge—a womanly knowledge, no less . . . the exact opposite of Duffy's kind of rational masculinity. Realists such as Duffy, a failed artist, would be

seen in Nietzsche's terms as too much tied to rationality, truth, and fact. (204)

This evaluation of his relationship with Mrs. Sinico appears to inform the third stage of his reaction (5 c. *D* 116.34–117.34).

In Nietzsche's works, then, Mr. Duffy would have encountered an attack on religion even more radical than in what he had read of Schopenhauer. Given Nietzsche's dismissal of metaphysics, he views religion not as a childish version of a higher and more abstract truth, but as a decoy that misdirects our attention from the actual causes of our afflictions. Rather than functioning as a kind of elementary metaphysics, religion has the effect of causing us to distrust our own experience and make it more difficult to make realistic judgments. Whereas for Schopenhauer, there is a direct relationship between the baleful Will that drives the universe and the irrational unconscious in the human character, for Nietzsche, religion is totally illusory and at fundamental odds with reason and science, our only means to true knowledge. Religion and magic are akin: both the offspring of our ignorance, fear, and psychological needs. Whereas for Schopenhauer, religion arises from the relationship between human beings and unknowable nature, for Nietzsche, it arises from social and psychological relationships: between people and within individuals.

Following their Jewish antecedents, the Christian priesthood gave to historical events transcendental values for which they had no warrant. By reading traumatic events in tribal history as manifestations of the will and judgment of a super being, they invented theological concepts and language—creation, salvation, judgment, guilt, redemption, sacrifice, piety—and ensured their own hegemony at the expense of the laity who were enjoined to deny the inferences that they might make from their own experience and practice an ascetic morality. Thus the priesthood became a parasitic class preying on the mass of citizens who, left to their own devices, would develop healthy and rational values and social relationships. In a reversal of terms, Nietzsche considers that the promise of the Kingdom of God is a sacrilege against a healthy natural existence.

Given his personal history, Mr. Duffy would have responded with chagrin to Nietzsche's rueful recollection:

This world, the eternally imperfect, an eternal contradiction's image and imperfect image—an intoxicating joy to its imperfect creator— then did the world once seem to me. Then, once upon a time, did I also

cast my fancy beyond humankind, like all backworldsmen? Beyond
humankind, in truth?
Yes, you brother, that God whom I created was human work and human madness, like all the gods! (*Zarathustra*, 56)

The apotheosis of the pathology of Christianity can be seen in the cult
of the saints, those exemplars of extreme and life-denying asceticism. They
gain notice by gratuitously exposing themselves to temptation and then—by
appealing to inhuman and unrealizable standards—resisting it. The perverse
thrill that results is one of the manifestations of the narcotic "high" that religion provides, robbing life of its joy and relieving its ennui:

a priest is and remains a human sacrifice . . . The people see such sac-
rificed, subdued, serious persons of "faith" as *wise*, that is, as having
become knowing, as "certain" in relation to their own uncertainty; and
who would want to deprive them of this word and of their awe? (*Gay
Science*, 209)

From its founder's opposition to Jewish patriarchy and elitism, Christianity inherited a particularly virulent form of misjudgment of the natural human condition: encouraging democracy, repression of instinct, jealousy of
the gifted, and the cultivation of servility. Christian culture thereby gave the
appearance of nobility to mere conformity. He wrote in *The Gay Science*, "Morality is herd-instinct in the individual" (114–15). For these reasons, Nietzsche
followed Schopenhauer in his partiality to Eastern religions as nonjudgmental and inculcating a respect for natural hierarchies.

Thus in reading Nietzsche, Duffy would have found much that he had
already encountered and apparently accepted in Schopenhauer, but the implications of their common atheism pushed closer to the helplessness and
cynicism of modernity. Nietzsche would have reminded Mr. Duffy, for example, that in entertaining and then rejecting Mrs. Sinico's attentions and
affections, he had, despite his self-image as a disbeliever, followed the pattern of misprized asceticism enjoined by the Christian cult of the saints. He
would also have encountered a similar misogyny: women fake their interest
in higher truths, seeking only to ingratiate themselves with men of genius,
and engaging in artistic endeavors only to realize their supervening biological
imperative. This would have confirmed him in his original evaluation of Mrs.
Sinico's attempt to convert a relationship based on the love of music into a
physical entanglement: "Why do war and rainy winds also bring on a musical mood and the inventive pleasure of melody? Are they not the same winds
that fill the churches and give women thoughts of love?" (*Gay Science*, 72).

Learning of her subsequent alcoholism would have given strong personal, but anecdotal support, to Nietzsche's historical prejudice that women were particularly partial to adultery and alcoholism. First Schopenhauer, then Nietzsche, had told him so!

Full Astrakhan Jacket

Even casual readers of "A Painful Case" have observed that it has apparent congruities with Leo Tolstoy's *Anna Karenina*, the most patent of which is the love triangle ending in suicide by train. Nevertheless, no serious reader has pursued the implications of Joyce's apparent invocation of this Russian masterpiece. In the line of argument developed in this study, however, that "A Painful Case" is primarily an expatiation of the processes of religious doubt and that the éminence grise of Schopenhauer presides over its intertextual descent, *Anna Karenina* deserves a more studied look.

It is clear that both before and during the time he was writing "A Painful Case," Joyce was familiar with *Resurrection*, *Youth*, and *Anna Karenina*. From persistent references then and thereafter during his writing career, Joyce ranked Tolstoy as the first among novelists. For example, on September 18, 1905 (shortly after completing "A Painful Case"), he wrote to Stanislaus: "Tolstoy is a magnificent writer. He is never dull, never stupid, never tired, never pedantic, never theatrical! He is head and shoulders over the others" (*Letters* II: 106). Joyce emulated Tolstoy in many ways. The scope of that debt—it extends through *Ulysses*—is much beyond the ambition of the present study, which will demonstrate how Joyce registers in "A Painful Case" his first homage to the Russian master.

Each work develops the implications of a double betrayal—Vronsky of Anna and Duffy of Mrs. Sinico: Anna turning to contraception, opium, and eventually suicide, and Emily Sinico to alcohol and possible suicide. Each work exposes the difficulties attendant upon any moral judgment of these sensational resolutions. It may be fanciful to imagine that Joyce's appreciation of the mild irony in Tolstoy's giving Anna's husband the "Karenin" because it derives from the Greek for "head" (*karenon*)—he is given to ratiocination and, moreover, has big ears—gave him the idea of marrying Mr. Duffy's Emily to one Captain Sinico (*caput*, "head," L.). Again, if it is a coincidence, it is a delicious one, to find that Mr. Duffy's private term of disdain for the conspicuous gourmands he assiduously avoided as "Dublin's gilded youth" (*D* 109.2), precisely the same phrase by which Stepan Arkadyevitch characterized Alexi Vronsky: "one of the finest specimens of the gilded youth of Petersburg" (1.11).[1]

Similarly, when Levin, on querying the hitherto unexamined source of his moral code, reflects: "What should I have been, and how should I have spent my life, if I had not had these beliefs, if I had not known that I must live for God and not for my own desires? I should have robbed and lied and killed" (8.12). This reminds us of the terms in which Mr. Duffy dramatized to himself his independence from the moral restraints imposed by the theism of which he was pridefully independent: "He allowed himself to think that in certain circumstances he would rob his bank" (D 109.13–15). And in view of what we know of the Mozart lieder that Mr. Duffy and Mrs. Sinico sang together, we might imagine that Joyce took the suggestion from the recurrent dream of her death in *Anna Karenina*.

These considerations, then, great and small, imply that Joyce paid close attention to Tolstoy's novel. They suggest that in "A Painful Case" he acknowledges that he is both Tolstoy's protégé and critic. Mr. Duffy, the would-be cleric, disappointed lover, and despairing agnostic is a Joycean makeover and riposte to Tolstoy's counterparts, the gilded youth Vronsky and spiritual questor Levin. In the course of Tolstoy's novel, in contrast with Vronsky's double betrayal, we behold Levin's disenchantment, suffering, and loss, and the rediscovery of the source of spiritual renewal in his abandoned or forgotten Christian faith of his childhood. "A Painful Case" may then be considered as Joyce's qualified homage to his master: the figure of Mr. Duffy, in his double betrayal and loss of spiritual faith, comprises the two sides of the central figure in the values of the novel: the gilded youth and the reflective moralizing landowner.

Anna Karenina is an extended meditation on the marriage bond: its social, psychological, legal, and moral aspects. In a social atmosphere permeated with emotional dishonesty—it's a vast tale of self-deception and small-mindedness—the ability of the characters to live up to the ideals of the marriage bond is the central moral question. And as the deepest character—Alexander Levin—confronts, on the eve of his wedding to Princess Kitty Scherbatsky (in a wonderfully comic interlude), the fundamental questions in life—faith, doubt, love—he realizes that he has never thought very much about them, yet is about to walk through the social ritual that presumes a system of permanent values (5.1). The ornate Russian Orthodox ritual, described in such loving and slightly bemused detail (5.1–6), serves to establish marriage as Tolstoy's "objective correlative" for the bond of love between God and man, embracing daily experience, hope, and benignity of spirit. It is a metaphor for the entire human condition—in that it is the central drama between the sexes and generations—and in its Russian Orthodox context, becomes a Tolstoyan metaphor for the tension between individual Christian vision and bureaucratic religion.

A metonymy for the human condition, marriage represents the ethical ideal, with adultery as its primary breach. As a moral meditation on the human condition, if fidelity and marital bliss is the ideal, adultery is the original sin, which to varying degrees, touches all. In the development of this major theme, Tolstoy weaves two main plots and several supporting variations. One of these ends with Anna's sensational suicide, and the other with Levin's domestic happiness and spiritual conversion. Whereas the former is the dramatic and public face of the novel, the latter is its private soul. Between them, they present two starkly contrasting ways of handling suffering and disappointment: a self-absorbed plunge into nihilism and a turning towards faith in God and divine mercy, and prideful vindictiveness or humility and kenosis. Whereas the manner of Anna's death has given the novel its shock value, it is clear that the intensity of Levin's conversion is the emotional climax in which Tolstoy is himself invested.

Similarly, "A Painful Case" is a meditation on marital failure and the pathology of a loveless celibacy. In Joyce's little story, there are two parallel plots: the failure of the Sinicos' hopes for a happy marriage and the failure of James Duffy's aspirations for the conciliation of his spiritual and intellectual potential. The first implies suicide; the latter, spiritual despair. The title does double duty in representing these causal and parallel shocks. As Levin is Tolstoy's alter ego, so is Duffy Joyce's. It is clear from these formal and thematic elements that there is a genealogical relationship between Joyce's and Tolstoy's works. Besides this evident generational link, it is also clear that behind this filial relationship lies a common ancestor: Schopenhauer's *World*.

Tolstoy began writing *Anna Karenina* under the influence of the Schopenhauerean idea of the weakness of women, their proclivity to adultery, the necessity of their domestication, and the contrasting strength of men in their capacity to identify with disinterested universals. The figure of Anna in the finished novel retains much of the condescending view that women are closer to the animal state than are men and that they are more given to luxuries. Even the more benign figures of Kitty and Natasha carry on without much more than a passing thought about metaphysical considerations. Men, by contrast, are more philosophically and spiritually inclined. Vronsky, for all his superficiality, once embarked on the course of his relationship with Anna, acts in a consistent and honorable manner.

Levin is the true moral hero of the novel. For him, family happiness and public responsibility are linked with ultimate meanings. Tolstoy's alter ego, he appears in the novel making two interruptions: of the vacuous government bureau presided over by Stepan Arkadyevich and again (in a manner reminiscent of Schopenhauer's disdain for official philosophers) as interrupting a similarly vacuous academic discussion with a blunt question about what happens after death. Levin moves from disbelief—at which Kitty, his wife, is naïvely appalled—to reflective questioning, and eventual faith. His conversion is the novel's true center. From the outset, we see Levin as a man of goodwill and emotional and spiritual openness. Taking his marriage preparation seriously, he approaches confession with reluctant hesitation. The ensuing scene—the hilarious interview with the priest (5.1)—while forcing him to confront his fundamental values—also indicates one of Tolstoy's major themes in the novel: the relationship between marriage and religious belief. Marriage may have its social and economic dimensions, but it inevitably draws its participants into existential and spiritual realities. In having Levin articulate his skepticism, Tolstoy points the direction that Levin will eventually embody: that of the serious spiritual quester.

His reflective predisposition leads him to especially acute reactions to the two major traumas of his adult life: the slow death of his brother Nickolay (5.20) and the screams of his wife as she gives birth (7.15). Each of these experiences—inscrutable death and appalling birth—causes him to examine the assumptions of the Christian orthodoxy he has thoughtlessly entertained since his childhood. His depression following Nickolay's death seems to bear out Schopenhauer's contention in "Man's need for Metaphysics" that the face of death intensifies man's wonder at his own existence. In the latter case, he finds himself bursting into spontaneous prayer that (in contrast with Anna's) indicates his potential acceptance of God's presence in his life. These incipient signs of his awakening cause him to wonder how everyone around him seems to subscribe to Christian values without any seeming perturbation of spirit.

At the same time, he considered that his own rebellion against religion as a university student was based on another complacency—that religion had outlived its day. This crisis drives him to search for a validation of his revulsion against materialism and of his vague but inextinguishable spiritual longings: if he did not accept the conventional Christian answer, what did he? So he read his way through Plato, Spinoza, Kant, Schelling, Hegel, and Schopenhauer, the philosophers who gave a nonmaterialistic explanation of life (8.8–9). However concerted this effort was, it did not satisfy him, because he found no solace in the recurrent vagaries of the philosophers who wrote of "spirit," "will," "freedom," and "substance"; and because he realized that they all began with assumptions he was unwilling to grant. Finding in Schopenhauer's notion of Will an idea with which he could sympathize if it were only Love, he was temporarily buoyed up by the prospect that his quest had ended. It had not.

However, when the moment of grace came, as it eventually did, Levin was spiritually prepared. After a day's work with the peasants, he has a respite from the labor as he gazes on the threshing floor, and in a momentary revelation beholds both the fullness of human endeavor and its tragic temporality. In this radiant scene (8.11), Levin apprehends for the first time the blessedness of life—in which the fruits of human labor and the light of heaven conspire to produce an image of divine grace. Levin's long apprenticeship in the social ascendancy, in political responsibility, and in the world of daily physical labor he bears with the peasants converge into a clear and radiant image of a universe beloved by its divine Creator. This is immediately confirmed by the example of Fokanitch, the upright old man who does not exact from his debtors what they cannot pay, of whom he hears it said, "He lives for the soul. He remembers God."

Levin is immediately struck by this example of Christian virtue in a mere peasant. He is filled with joy:

> At the peasant's words that Fokanitch lived for his soul, in truth, in God's way, undefined but significant ideals seemed to burst out as though they had been locked up, and all striving towards one goal, they thronged whirling through his head, blinding him with their light. (8.11)

In this moment of dazzling enlightenment, he is thrilled by the idea of living not for his own needs, and (in a Schopenhauerean sequence of inferences), not for what he understands, or feels attracted to, but for something beyond apprehension or definition. He realizes that the light of human reason cannot account for his relationship with the natural order, but that he shares in a sympathetic energy with the world around him (8.12). On further reflection, he then comes to realize that the religious tradition that he had imbibed at his mother's breast had already given him the answers that he had, all his life to this point, avoided. He realizes that self-interest would have moved him to rob and lie and kill, and in a leap that took him past Schopenhauer to a mystical Christian position, he is led to the unreasonable discovery that the fundamental law of nature was not baleful will, but indeed, love.

In this protracted meditation, Levin, from the perspective of a mature and responsible public man, a husband and father, examines the relationship between his childhood beliefs, his adult scientific understanding of the world, and his awareness of the counterclaims of the Christian and secular ethical systems. He recognizes that reason, if taken by itself, is the enemy, and thus is prepared to reaccept the faith of his childhood—to allow it to inform his

adult experience and maturity (8.12). He concludes that there can be no morality without faith—that we are not our own light—and that unless he finds
his own way back to the faith of his childhood, which he had left behind by
entering into a rational and scientifically minded view of the human condition, suicide is a rational solution to life's difficulties.

The climax of *Anna Karenina*, then, is Levin's conversion from modern
scientific skepticism to Christian belief. In the final section of the novel, Tolstoy provides the moral alternative to that which Anna's dramatic suicide
proclaims. He conciliates the faith of his childhood—which meant accepting
without really assimilating the deposit of Christian doctrine and culture—to
his experience as an adult in the midst of a morally challenging social scene
and an evolving political and economic order in which he plays a responsible
role. Levin has in the end reasoned himself beyond reason and into a spiritual
equilibrium between reason and instinct, personal history and cultural inheritance, reassured that the grounds of his final conciliation have all along been
latently within him, allowing him to distinguish between right and wrong,
and preventing him from lying, robbery, and homicide. Thus the ejaculation,
"My God!" heretofore uttered casually and out of habit becomes, in the light
of his spiritual enlightenment and his family's survival of the thunderstorm,
a real prayer (8.17). Fokanich's exclamation had become, for Levin, "a shout
in the street."

Now, although Joyce respected Tolstoy's "very genuine spiritual nature," as
he told Stanislaus, "I don't take him very seriously as a Christian saint" (*Letters* II: 106). "A Painful Case" affords the evidence that he was not among the
readers who thought the book ended with Anna's death. Just as Tolstoy has
Levin's story occlude Anna's tragedy, Joyce has Duffy's obscure Mrs. Sinico's.
As the climax of Joyce's rejoinder to *Anna Karenina*, Mr. Duffy's response to
the death of Mrs. Sinico expresses his horrified moral perplexity at her tragic
demise. He is the primary bearer of the pain in the title. In the light of *Anna
Karenina*, his pain has several sources and dimensions.

First, as a reprise of *Anna Karenina*, "A Painful Case" deals with a would-
be adultery. From this Russian norm the Irish Catholic Duffy recoils. Karenin
is an ambitious, but unloving man; putting status before intimacy, he lives out
a feigned marriage. Yet he tolerates Vronsky's attentions to his wife provided
that social appearances are upheld. Similarly, Captain Sinico tolerates Duffy's
interference in his ménage and maintains the appearance of normality both
in his work and in his testimony before the inquest. Just as Tolstoy's drama of
jealousy, passion, and power floats on the Christian assumptions about marriage, its ceremony, sacrament, and social obligations, so does the narrative

of "A Painful Case" look upon marriage from the outside, both in Duffy's interference in the Sinico ménage and in his final exclusion from the marriage feast of Christ's famous parable.

Second, whereas *Anna Karenina* was written as a stout defense of the family and as a polemical criticism of sexual (particularly women's) freedom, "A Painful Case" treats these issues with deft ambivalence. Tolstoy's novel entered the lists occasioned by "the woman question": the acrimonious public debate over women's education, enfranchisement, and sexual liberation. In this respect it is a polemical defiance of N. G. Chernyshevsky's *What Is to Be Done?* that advocated sexual freedom and the communal raising of children. Tolstoy took a conservative view of all these issues: marriage and childrearing were a woman's essential tasks, and family happiness was the highest human ideal. His novel was meant as a challenge, both artistic and ideological, to the ideas of the Russian nihilists (Pevear, ix). Thus where Kitty as mother, homemaker, and lover, exemplifies the womanly virtues, Anna's tragedy illustrates the consequences of uncontrolled female sexuality. Tolstoy's judgment of Anna mollified as he developed the novel, but her drug addiction and tragic death are the consequences of her adultery. Similarly, though with less sympathy, Mr. Duffy's moral judgment of Mrs. Sinico has three aspects: as a potential adulterer, as alcoholic, and as suicide. In contrast with Jesus'—and Schopenhauer's—injunction, he allows himself to usurp the role that belongs to God alone.

Third, in the figure of Mr. Duffy, Joyce gives us a portrait of the progressive loss of faith rather than the Tolstoyan conversion that we see in Levin. The portrayal of Mr. Duffy expresses Joyce's bemusement at Tolstoy's religious mysticism. Similarly, Joyce's implied skepticism about Duffy's brief flirtation with the Irish Socialists reflects his skepticism about Levin's dabbling in the lives of the peasants on his country estate as no more than political attitudinizing. This, of course, is but another aspect of the complex irony in the image of his pseudo self that Joyce projects in James Duffy. For just as Levin is Tolstoy's earnest self-portrait as a responsible landlord and nascent Christian, so is James Duffy an ironic self-portrait of the Joyce that had his youthful flings with socialism and with Schopenhauer. Joyce recognized Leo Tolstoy's inscription of his own name in the figure of Levin, by doing likewise with Duffy and having him pay court to a "lady" who lives, not in a Big House like Polyana, but in an ironically reduced "cottage" with the Tolstoyan name of "Leoville."

Fourth, this is not to say that Joyce approves of Duffy's choices or spiritual despair in preference to Levin's enthusiasm for the rediscovery of his long-lost faith. Both are self-deluded about keeping a true balance between nihilism and mysticism. From the start, the Duffy-Sinico relationship seems doomed. The "deserted house," the venue of their anticipated concert, "gave distressing prophecy of failure" (D 109.18–19) not only to the performance immediately anticipated, but threw a disconcerting shadow over their relationship. The subsequent narrative confirms this as the presence of death which, as we have seen, is the theme of their own musical collaboration (the Mozart lieder). It is the condition under which they consummate their final union, as Mr. Duffy in the solitude of the Phoenix Park contemplates Mrs. Sinico's death. Similarly, in *Anna Karenina*, death is as much the bond between Anna and Vronsky as adultery. Death accompanies Anna throughout the novel, from her first meeting with Vronsky, in their first embrace and their mysteriously common dream, and in their parallel exits from the action. Despite the social glamour of their lives, Tolstoy makes it clear that what binds them to one another is their sense of what Joyce's Mr. Duffy calls "the soul's incurable loneliness": their spiritual desolation, what Pevear calls "their metaphysical solitude" (xvi).

Fifth, each work expresses its author's temporary engagement with Schopenhauer's work and thought. For Tolstoy, Schopenhauer was a liberator from skeptical materialism, a way station on his journey to a full religious self-affirmation. In *Anna Karenina*, Schopenhauer is but a passing shadow (he is the guru presiding over Levin's reflections that making peasants literate turns them into worse laborers than they were before). His view of the relationship between human instinct—the heart—and the metaphysical order is a weighty element in Tolstoy's implied omniscient intelligence. Similarly, in "A Painful Case" Schopenhauer is the patron of Duffy's cynicism about social revolution in Ireland. For Joyce, as for Tolstoy, Schopenhauer provided an alternative to the pious Catholic orthodoxy of his youth: a road sign pointing the way ahead to Nietzsche, Bakunin, and Freud. And for Joyce's alter ego, James Duffy, Schopenhauer is a figure who takes him away from faith and to a life-denying despair.

Sixth, "A Painful Case" exemplifies Joyce's attentive and pointed assimilation of Tolstoy's marriage of reliable historical detail and structural symbol. His immense admiration for Tolstoy's narrative abilities is not diminished by his awareness of their ideological differences. He admires Tolstoy's ability to handle his materials as powerful symbols while also respecting their material temporality. For example, despite the major role as signifier the train plays in *Anna Karenina* (it links Saint Petersburg with Moscow, Vronsky with Anna, the porter's accidental death with Anna's, and it represents, for Tolstoy, the assault of industrialism upon the communal agricultural life), he is too much of a respecter of detail not to let us know that Anna is killed by the 8:02. In a similar vein, as we have already observed, the train Mr. Duffy observes leaving Kingsbridge does so at precisely the same time as that which leaving Kingstown on the previous evening had killed Mrs. Sinico: the ten o' clock. At the same time, Joyce emulates Tolstoy's figurative train in its conjoining the motifs of accident, love, and death, around which each fiction is designed. It is not amiss to point out here that Mr. Duffy's attitude towards trains is similar to Tolstoy's: fleeing the city that they enable, he retreats to the suburbs and makes it a point of honor, the tram service notwithstanding, to walk home from work.

Seventh, these observations invite further reflections on the ways in which Tolstoy remains one of Joyce's mentors as he moves on to his masterwork of Tolstoyan dimensions and scope, *Ulysses*. Joyce's technical skill disposes him more towards the expressiveness of a poet than of an epic storyteller, his deeply considered and dense intertextuality, his subtle and dexterous control of narrative voice. Tolstoy, on the other hand, is the master of the panorama, developing the web of social and economic themes in the express language of the grand storyteller. *Anna Karenina* remained important to Joyce after the writing of "A Painful Case" at the very least for its deeply humane treatment of Kitty's childbirth and Anna's recurrent dream of death: prefigurements of major passages in the vast comprehensiveness of *Ulysses* and *Finnegans Wake*.

Joyce no doubt appreciated Tolstoy's symbolic technique (his handling of the motifs of home, train, et cetera, in *Anna Karenina*), and beyond the narrow considerations of the present study, as George Clay summarizes:

> the open-ended cyclical structure and meaning of *War and Peace*, combined with its infinite detail—Tolstoy's microscopic focus combined with his universal overview; his cross-section of humanity; his naturalism, with truth as its goal; his comprehensiveness; his staggering variety of viewpoints; the way he provides the reader with so many different approaches to life that it is virtually impossible for any one set of values to dominate; his unending immediacy taking the place of suspense; his epochal outlook. (Orwin, 214)

These, at least, are the implications of the Duffy-Sinico relationship that ended with Mr. Duffy's eyes flagged by a headline about a death on the tracks, and began with their arrest by "a bosom of a certain fullness" molded by Mrs. Sinico's "astrakhan jacket" (*D* 110.2–3).

Schopenhauer's Progeny

Tolstoy first read Schopenhauer in September 1868 as he was finishing *War and Peace* and drafting *Anna Karenina*. During the four years it took him to write *Anna Karenina* (1873–77), he renewed his enthusiasm for the philosopher, going so far as to hang his portrait on his study wall. In a letter to his friend, A. A. Fet the poet, he described *World* as "a succession of intellectual delights," and "a whole world in an unbelievable clear and beautiful reflection" (Troyat, 316). He considered this work "genuine philosophy, whose task is to answer Kant's questions" (Magee quotes, 404). His enthusiasm for Schopenhauer subsequently cooled: although he considered him a sophist and a purveyor of much vulgar nonsense, he nevertheless concluded that Schopenhauer had taken us as far as philosophy can (Troyat, 316 n). His *Confession* (1884) recounts the process by which he arrived at his final position. In Magee's summary, there Tolstoy "tells us that it was the inability of even the greatest of philosophers to answer the only question that really matters in the end, namely, what is the point of living, that impelled him into religion" (404).

Although the philosopher's values do not bear upon the outcome of the novel, his influence can be discerned in a few significant ways in the shaping of its point of view, values, and particularly in the development of Levin's moral conscience. One can infer from Tolstoy's *Confession* that the figure of Levin passes through the three stages of his own spiritual development: from childhood faith to adolescent doubt—where he considered life a "stupid joke"—and on to his mature reconversion to Christianity. In this hegira, Schopenhauer is his admired philosopher who goes as far as is possible along the way without the gift of Christian faith. Reason has its limits; and Schopenhauer understands that the irrational has to be faced with self-defensive cynicism—as a joke—or with generosity of spirit—as faith. This is where Tolstoy departs from Schopenhauer, who has taken him along the road so far as he can go. Tolstoy ends with an Aquinian view that God is the answer to the ultimate questions. It is my contention here that in writing "A Painful Case," Joyce is retracing his version of these stages, in which Schopenhauer and, indeed, Nietzsche and Aquinas similarly figure.

On the most general level, Schopenhauer strengthened Tolstoy's capacities as an interpreter of the social world. Moving towards the mysticism of his later years, Tolstoy was increasingly skeptical of the limitations of a naturalistic perspective: the world of cause and effect in which characters act in accordance with reasonable motivations of which they are self-aware and which they control. It is very likely that Schopenhauer's fundamental perspective, that we know very little of the source of our own deepest emotions—the world of Will—and that therefore the reasons we give for our actions are as likely as not to be beside the real point. Tolstoy's characters are usually stated to be and are seen to act in ways that are self-deluding. Only Levin succeeds in transcending the self-deception that marks the characters in *Anna Karenina*. Only he makes a real intellectual and imaginative effort to see beyond the phenomena of the social world he has inherited. The rest of the characters are simply acting out the roles they have been assigned by historical circumstance. This is particularly true of Anna, whose inability to conciliate her personal desires with the rules of her class leads to her drug-taking and eventual suicide.

Tolstoy's view of the religious bureaucracy evidently coincides with Schopenhauer's, as the satirical treatment of Levin's confession indicates. Even Levin's open disbelief fails to derail the priest in the administration of his pious fraud. Nevertheless, Levin's eventual religious conversion recognizes that even such a predatory system plays a part in the divine redemptive plan. Levin thinks of this conversion as a process that passes from Schopenhauerean Will through Christian Love, which he sees as providing but a similarly thin metaphysic on his way to an idiosyncratic mystical Christian terminus (8.9). Tolstoy thereby takes his character beyond Schopenhauer, though not as far as Christian orthodoxy, for Levin is made in Tolstoy's image, with a faith in God, but is skeptical about Christ's divinity. Tolstoy, like Schopenhauer, was opposed to official philosophers, ecclesiastical bureaucrats, and occupiers of endowed positions from which to purvey dogmatic abstractions and administer rituals for the control of the unreflective laity. Both Schopenhauer and Tolstoy were themselves dogmatically anarchist. As Levin's reflections on childhood and reason indicate (8.13), he is close to Schopenhauer's idea that all cultures distinguished between virtuous and rational behavior.

The Schopenhauerean quotation that Tolstoy supplies as the novel's epigraph, "Vengeance is mine [to me], and I will repay," has drawn considerable critical attention. In *World*, Schopenhauer argues that no man is entitled to act in the role of a purely moral judge and retributor and to punish the actions of another, citing this verse from Deuteronomy (32: 32–36) as an application of his fundamental position that the true natures of all things, including those in the moral sphere, are beyond definitive judgment: God alone is the final arbiter of all human actions. Saint Paul had the same verses in mind when warning the Hebrews that "It is a fearful thing to fall into the hands of the living God" (10: 31), and that the Romans are not to arrogate to themselves the judgment of God (12: 19). Many critics have pointed out that this appears to be vindicated only with respect to Anna's suicide, where the impulse that drove her to adultery in the first place originates in the same irrational will that undermined her trust in Vronsky's affection and on to the railroad tracks. The punishment she suffers is immanent. The other nefarious characters (Betsy and Stepan, for example) are not punished for their philandering, and moreover, Levin is rewarded for his benevolence.

The epigraph is relevant, however, in two other aspects of the novel that bear upon Joyce's appropriation of *Anna Karenina* to his portrait of James Duffy. In writing of suicide (*World* 1: 514–20 passim), Schopenhauer condemns it as a tragic mistake because it allows temporary pain to obscure the possibility of "insight" (his term for what Joyce calls "epiphany"). However, we cannot judge any particular instance because, as he concludes, "human nature has depths, obscurities, and perplexities, the analysis and elucidation of which is a matter of the very greatest difficulties" (*World* 1: 520). As we have seen, Tolstoy's portrait of Anna's death qualifies as an individual case about which we know much but not enough to call it suicide. The epigraph and the case has a further bearing, then, on the manner in which Joyce portrays Mrs. Sinico's death and Mr. Duffy's attempt to give a moral judgment of his relationship with that death.

The epigraph has a further bearing on the action of *Anna Karenina* and, by implication, "A Painful Case." Since Anna's sin is adultery in a stratum of Russian society for which it appears to be the norm, and yet she is universally condemned for her transgression, she would seem to qualify for clemency by Jesus' application of the same encomium from Deuteronomy. Confronted by the woman taken in adultery who was about to be stoned, he dispersed her accusers with one of his most resonant lines: "Let the one among you who is without sin be the first to throw a stone at her" (John 8: 3–11). The force of this answer is not due to the talent of the evangelists (Christian quotes André Malraux, 211). This reverberation from the epigraph appears in several places in the novel (for example, 6.20 and 8.4: "It's not for us to judge, Sergei Ivanovich"). Anna may be guilty, but as Christian remarks, he does not allow her to be judged by other mortals (173).

These observations about *Anna Karenina* apply, in turn, to the equivalent action in "A Painful Case." Whereas Mr. Duffy recoils from adultery—although he disdains conventional morality (he would rob his employer were the opportunity to present itself)—he is quick to judge Mrs. Sinico's moral weaknesses: her alcoholism and apparent suicide. Ironically, on further reflection, he overcompensates and implicates himself in excess of what is justified by the evidence.

Resurrection

Joyce read Tolstoy's *Resurrection* in February 1905 (*Letters* II: 82) in the Louise Maude English translation (1899). So when he wrote "A Painful Case" in July–August 1905, it was relatively fresh on his mind. And it clearly impressed him, since he referred to it later that year expressing his admiration for superior physical, intellectual, artistic, and moral qualities of "the author of *Resurrection* and *Anna Karénin*" (*Letters* II: 107), subsequently purchasing a later edition that remained in his personal library when he left Trieste in 1920 (Ellmann, 130).

The title refers to the birth of the moral conscience of the main character, a member of the nobility named Nekhliudov (Tolstoy's alter ego). He is a young idealist who, while attempting to resist the blandishments of a corrupt society, seduces Katiusha Maslova, a servant girl. Years later, discovering that she is sentenced to four years servitude in Siberia as a prostitute, thief, and possible murderer, he is filled with remorse, considering that his thoughtless hour of pleasure many years before has led to her moral destruction.

He offers her marriage as a means of rescuing her from this severe penalty. In the course of his legal engagement in this undertaking, he finds that she is but one example of an entire underclass that are condemned by civil society and the legal bureaucracy to lives of undeserved misery. Thus, as his individual conscience is reborn, his personal quest becomes a social crusade. He soon identifies with the despised underbelly of Russian society. He discovers the wisdom of the Sermon on the Mount and sets himself against the entire social order.

Tolstoy's novel pursues the moral development of the main character: Maslova is but a passive figure throughout the work. The novel develops a rich set of contraries: rich/poor, country/city, free/unfree, dark/light, natural/artificial, the individual/the institution, the technical management of which was bound to interest Joyce.[2]

There is a clear relationship between *Resurrection* (part 1): and "A Painful Case." The broad parallels between the sexual misbehavior and repentance of Prince Dmitrii and James Duffy, can be inferred from the summary. They are especially interesting in the present inquiry regarding Mr. Duffy as an Irish spoiled priest and Tolstoy's development of Dmitrii Nekhliudov's character. In his youth, he was deeply religious, punctiliously observing the enjoyed fasts and attending church regularly, including the Holy Week services. For these spiritual enthusiasms he was mocked and called "Noah." His subsequent slide into dissolution led to his purchase of Masha's affections. This spiritual regress allows Tolstoy to dilate on the two kinds of love, eros and agape, those of body and of spirit.

These considerations are of lesser moment than the clear relationship between Tolstoy's treatment of the trial scene in *Resurrection* (1.5–10) and Mr. Duffy's reading of the inquest in the pages of the *Evening Mail*. The salient issues are that the moral turning point in each work, and Joyce recasts Tolstoy's heavily ironical legalese into cool and dispassionate journalese. In each scene the "resurrection" of the main character begins. Appalled by the transparent clichés of each legal procedure, each protagonist is moved to a reconsideration of the memories of his past relationship, which in turn leads to the moral crisis. Joyce's interest in the power of the rhetorical switches of gear to exemplified moral reconsideration was undoubtedly exemplified by Tolstoy's masterly management of Nekhliudov's revulsion at the abstract and heartless legal processes in which he plays the part of a compliant and complicit juror.[3]

Struck to the heart by the injustice to which he was witness, Nekhliudov appreciates the force of Jesus' criticism of Pharisaic justice, "He that is without sin among you, let him first cast a stone at her" (John 8: 7), one of the epigrams of *Resurrection*. In this respect, Tolstoy has reiterated the Schopenhauerean epigram with which *Anna Karenina* began. From this perspective, Nekhliudov undergoes a crisis and conversion similar to Levin's in *Anna Karenina*, and insofar as he also plays the part of Vronsky, his conversion from the life of a dissolute aristocrat, the character of Nekhliudov is a dialogic compression of the philandering Vronsky and the morally earnest Levin. From this perspective one can see how Joyce's James Duffy is a similar compression of Vronsky and Levin; and also a man who moves, in the final pages of the story, from a judgmental to a self-accusatory figure, recognizing his own complicity in the fall of Mrs. Sinico. Unlike Tolstoy's figure, however, who undergoes a spiritual regeneration, Joyce's Duffy falls further into anomie and despair.

In these respects, then, "A Painful Case" is an expression of Joyce's skeptical view of Tolstoy's espousal of Christian mysticism. In *What I Believe* (an apologia in the spirit of *Resurrection*), Tolstoy asserted that the way to knowledge of God was not intellectual, but ethical. Knowledge of God was not the result of metaphysical speculation, but of reflection on the human condition by a series of steps progressing from the purely rational to the ultimately mystical.

It begins with the rejection of the illusion of the finite world around one and end in the embrace of "infinite." Its practical application implied a moral evolution from the natural life of the body centered around self and family to life centered on the well-being of others. Both Levin and Nekhliudov are his literary personae in this quest.

Joyce is a disciple of Tolstoy's to the extent that he saw in his novels the unmasking of the arbitrariness, even falseness, of human institutions, the insignificance of natural life, and the inevitability of man's mortality. Out of the resultant nihilism came the Tolstoyan search for God. Only religious faith could fill that void. This tension between nihilism and despair is the central subject of Tolstoy's work. In Liza Knapp's words, "Tolstoy's writings, from the early works on, express this tension, even as they seek to alleviate it" (Orwin, 174).

Joyce's multiple citations in "A Painful Case" of Tolstoy's two novels of spiritual questing, which he evidently admired, underpin the argument in this reading: that James Duffy is not a naturalistic figure paralyzed by social forces, but a man on whom the breath of the Holy Spirit has been wasted. He has sold his spiritual birthright for a mess of pottage and has become, even before his death, a "lost soul." So even as Joyce rejects Tolstoy's mystical Christianity, he presents in the figure of James Duffy a man who can neither believe nor disbelieve. This is the source of his unique paralysis.

Gerhart Hauptmann

"In the desk lay a manuscript translation of Hauptmann's *Michael Kramer*, the stage directions of which were written in purple ink" (*D* 108.4–6). In crediting Mr. Duffy with one of his own accomplishments (he translated this and *Vor Sonnenaufgang* [*Before Sunrise*] during the summer of 1901), he is paying him two compliments: it credits Duffy's ability to complete a difficult task and also his sophisticated, current, and independent critical judgment. Writing to Hauptmann many years later (1938), he cited his own youthful translations as evidence of his devotion to the author of these plays, while admitting that he was then embarrassed by the potential appearance of these inept works under his name.[4]

Gerhart Hauptmann (1862–1946) is today regarded—at least outside Germany—as having more of a historical than permanent significance. With an oeuvre of over forty plays, he is the leading naturalistic dramatist in the German theatre. In some respects a successor to Ibsen—for so Joyce regarded him in 1901—his work embraced a wide range of social issues along with character studies and plays in which he expressed his metaphysical, religious, or mystical speculations. His sole work that survives into contemporary anthologies is *The Weavers* (1892), which Joyce considered a masterpiece (*Letters* II: 173).

Justly praised for its unflinching depiction of the hardscrabble life of the working poor, *The Weavers* is intensely German, rendered in the regional dialect with color and authority, representing the terrible conditions of manual workers in preindustrial Silesia. Regarding the sentence "The rainladen trees of the avenue evoked in him, as always, memories of the girls and women in the plays of Gerhart Hauptmann; and the memory of their pale sorrows and the fragrance falling from the wet branches mingled in a mood of quiet joy" (*P* 176.7–11), Stephen Dedalus may well have in mind Emma and Bertha Baumert, the pallid and sickly sisters from this play, and similar figures in *Drayman Henschel* (1898) or *Rosa Bernd* (1903). For their condition Hauptmann offers no solution but his compassionate portraits. Such figures, the victims of starvation, disease, and exploitation, represent *Elendsmarerei* (total misery), the persistent subject of dramatic Naturalism, and the reason for its ultimate undoing. Like today's "political correctness," its modish anxiety caused it to mislay its originally genuine moral compass and thus its long-term dramatic interest.

Although this work was already famous when Joyce, during the summer of 1901 while in Mullingar, undertook the translation of Hauptmann into English, it was not *The Weavers*, but *Michael Kramer* and *Vor Sonnenaufgang* he chose (*Letters* I: 398; *JJII* 87–88; Jill Perkins, 11 and 14 n. 7). *The Weavers* had appeared in Mary Morison's English translation in 1899 (London: Heinemann). Joyce's translation *Before Sunrise* has been published in a handsome edition, edited by Jill Perkins (Huntington Library, 1978); but the manuscript of *Michael Kramer* has disappeared (see Slocum and Cahoon, Ell aix). In choosing these dramas—Hauptmann's first success and most recent production—for his brave exercise (Joyce was self-taught in German), he was making considered judgments of their quality while also keeping an eye on the newly formed Irish Literary Theatre, whose company had earned a reputation for naturally expressive speech. Thus he rendered the Silesian dialect of *Vor Sonnenaufgang* into Hiberno-English. Joyce shared an enthusiasm for German drama with some of his university friends, Constantine Curran and John Marcus O'Sullivan (68: that was 1904), but had personal reasons for his attraction to *Michael Kramer*.

Joyce's interest in *Vor Sonnenaufgang* was no doubt because of its innovation as a naturalistic masterpiece in which the audience does not identify with the main character. We see the same technique in many of Joyce's stories, and of course, in "A Painful Case." He may have felt personally intrigued—or threatened—by the psychosocial premise (much contended at the time) of hereditary alcoholism.

Marvin Magalaner and Jill Perkins each discuss the ways in which the figure of Mr. Duffy's character and traits seem drawn from Hauptmann's Loth. Duffy clearly owes something to Loth's disowning of his childhood faith (Perkins, 104) and consequent dissociation from "sham religion" and "sham morality." Nevertheless, each retains from his early training a "highly intellectualized" concept of reality, cultivated through withdrawal from common society into the privacy required of the pursuers of truth. The "relentless absolutism" of Loth's moral crusade against alcoholism and his rational approach to marriage justifies his rejection of Helen and her consequent condemnation to "a death of shame" clearly sets the pattern governing Duffy's rejection of Mrs. Sinico. Again, Loth's sanctimonious lectures on the conditions of the working class to the compliant and unaffected Helen Krause, and his portentous talk about their being joined in death, would seem to have offered Joyce some pointers on the development of the relationship between his pair of would-be lovers. Hauptmann's play articulates—in a melodramatic manner, to be sure—the moral theme that reappears in "A Painful Case": the hazards of self-deception incurred by the intellectual moralist.

Neither Magalaner nor Perkins observes, however, that these elements are all grounded in distinctly Schopenhauerean values and character traits. Schopenhauer's intolerance of alcoholic excess and condescension to women find their common ground in the ironical representation of the respective treatments of Helen Krause and Emily Sinico. And Schopenhauer's insistence that a solitary life was a prerequisite for truth rings through both works with eloquent irony.

Ellmann considered that *Michael Kramer* was to Joyce's taste because he could sympathize with both the father's artistic dedication and the son's madness arising from his love for a waitress (*JJII* 87–88). It is not clear what Ellmann can have meant by the latter conjecture, since Joyce did not meet Nora Barnacle until 1904. It is more likely that Joyce would have been personally gripped by Hauptmann's dramatization of Arnold's conflicts with his parents. Michael Kramer's denunciation of his son's behavior—"These vagabonds of today think the whole world is a whore's bed! A man must recognize duties, I tell you" (*MK* 460)—he must have recalled similar words directed to himself by John Stanislaus Joyce. And more poignantly, he must have been struck by the scene between Arnold and his mother in act 1, when she makes a heart-wrenching appeal to him to abandon his profligate life, frequenting bars and houses of prostitution (*MK* 450–51), since Joyce was at the time in open rebellion against his mother's pious religiosity, a rebellion that was to climax the following spring in the scene depicted so unflinchingly in *Stephen Hero* (131–35; and see Costello, 177).

Joyce's enthusiasm does not appear to have been diminished by the play's dramatic weaknesses of which he was evidently aware. He wrote to Stanislaus in 1906: "[Hauptmann's] characters appear to be more highly vivified by their creator than Ibsen's do but also they are less under control. He has a difficulty in subordinating them to the action of his drama" (*Letters* II: 173). As many critics have observed, the characters Michaline and Lachmann contribute nothing to the dramatic development, functioning solely as listeners; nor is the potential for their interaction with one another exploited (Maurer, 81; Osborne, 144). Neither is the audience provided with any dramatic evidence—other than Lachmann's testimony—to support Michael Kramer's claim to actual creative talent, much less genius; and thus the grounds upon which he disowns his son—wasting his inherited artistic talents—are unconvincing. The audience is therefore left to infer that his sufferings are those of a father rather than those of an unappreciated artist (Osborne, 145), or that his artistic efforts are but self-therapy. Nevertheless, for reasons that have to do with Hauptmann's conception of Kramer as an artist with a religious temperament, Joyce found him fascinating, telling Stanislaus (in the same letter cited above) that "his way of treating such types as Arnold Kramer and Rosa Bernd is, however, altogether to my taste."

The play's representation of the conflict between a man of artistic genius and the mediocrities who drive his son to suicide must have impressed Joyce with some personal force since he was acutely aware of his own superior gifts, which we can discern between the ironies of *Portrait*. Joyce's chagrin at Yeats's rejection of *Michael Kramer* can be inferred, moreover, from the particular vehemence of "The Day of the Rabblement," in which he attacked Yeats's pandering to popular taste. This pamphlet was written on October 15, 1901, shortly after he submitted the manuscript to Yeats, and as already argued, Joyce's appropriation of Wagner's *Tristan und Isolde* to his purposes in "A Painful Case" was a creative response to the Yeats-Moore travesty, *Diarmuid and Graine*.

As Marvin Magalaner has observed, Joyce was predisposed to appreciate Hauptmann's blend of symbolism and naturalism because it resembled, in some ways, Ibsen's technique (40–41). His high estimation of *Michael Kramer* was shared at the time by such consequential figures as Thomas Mann, Bertolt Brecht, and Rainer Maria Rilke, who wrote, in 1900: "In my opinion this *Michael Kramer* is the greatest [work] that Hauptmann has thus far achieved; a masterpiece that . . . one will perhaps only understand and cherish decades from now" (Maurer quotes, 81). Hauptmann, with whom Joyce subsequently corresponded about this play, paid his then nineteen-year-old translator the highest compliment: a presentation copy of *Michael Kramer* inscribed to Somerset Maugham in 1938 bears the inscription, "Never has this book had a better reader than Joyce" (cited by Maurer, 81). My inference here is that Hauptmann's judgment is based on his penetrating appreciation of the text of "A Painful Case."

Acquainted with Grief

When Joyce turned his hand to composing the figure of James Duffy some five years later, we can well understand the general import of the manuscript of *Michael Kramer* lying unpublished in his desk. From what we know of Duffy, he too, like his creator, would have been attracted to the project of putting before an Irish readership this portrait of an artist in conflict with a philistine public. Magalaner has noted that Kramer and Duffy react similarly to vulgarity and inferiority. Their uncompromising attitudes in these respects turn them into recluses and towards the rejection of those who would be bound to them by normal human affection. Each character's inability to apprehend the cost of these rejections leads to the tragic outcomes. Mr. Duffy's inability to recognize the potential cost of his self-deceiving high-mindedness is, of course, a central irony in this particular intertextual relationship between *Michael Kramer* and "A Painful Case." His remorse, like that of Kramer's, comes too late (40–45).

There are several thematic and technical links between the works that, given the attention that Joyce paid Hauptmann's text in the course of his translation, are interesting in how they seem to have provided cues for Joyce's rapacious imagination five years later. The furnishings and ambience of Mr. Duffy's room are, like Kramer's, orderly (*MK* 454; *D* 107.8–108.3). They each have cane chairs, and as Lachmann observes, looking out of Kramer's studio window at his grove of poplars: "The rows stand there with so much dignity, that the grove has almost something of a temple about it" (*MK* 456). In view of the hieratic image with which Joyce surrounds Mr. Duffy, this appears to be a particularly suggestive observation. Similarly, when Kramer expostulates to Lachmann on the hermitlike discipline required of the true artist ("The original, the genuine, the deep and strong art grows only in a hermitage—is born only in utter solitude. The artist is always the true hermit," *MK* 465), we see that Lachmann's observations are not without point.

In the same vein, Kramer imagines his artistic work as if it were that of a priest, telling Lachmann and Michaline that his studio is "holy ground. Art is religion. If thou prayest, go into thy secret chamber" (*MK* 466). Not surprisingly then, the supreme subject for Kramer the hermit, consumed with the subject of human suffering, and taken with its relationship with the mystery of existence, is nothing casual or happenstance. He tells Michaline:

> if a man has the impudence to want to paint that Man with the Crown of Thorns—he needs a lifetime to do it, I tell you. And not a life, I tell you, of revelry or noise, but lonely hours, lonely days, lonely years, I tell you. The artist must be alone with his sorrow and with his God. He must sanctify himself daily I tell you! Nothing low or mean must be about him or within him! Then, I tell you, the Holy Ghost may come— when a man digs and strives in his solitude. Something may come to him then. (*MK* 465–66)

This sententious amalgam of Christian and Schopenhauerean imaginings permeates Kramer's image of himself. The major dramatic irony, of course, is that the "Holy Ghost" does indeed visit him when he reads his son's suicide note explaining that "he did not feel equal to life" (*MK* 529). Significant for the present purposes is the reflection that such an observation must have reverberated in Joyce's imagination as he developed Mr. Duffy's self-image as hieratic artist consumed with a post-Christian melancholia.

Nevertheless, all of these considerations are minor by contrast with the powerful meditation on the embroglio of relationships between creative aspirations, paternity, and the mystery of death in act 4 of *Michael Kramer*. In this "middle-class" play, Hauptmann allows himself the freedom from social engagement to dramatize the major spiritual epiphany that Joyce so admired. Its subject goes much beyond Magalaner's reductive formula "the fact of death, which sweeps away all lesser matters" (43). If anything, it reverses that cliché. The climax is a punctuated dramatic monologue—for that is what it amounts to—on the loss of his son in whom he had invested so many hopes. This catastrophe causes Michael Kramer to examine all the assumptions driving his life to this apparent disaster and disgrace.

In the process, Kramer moves from grieved anguish, to guilt, and through despair, to a final position of tragic joy. This is no facile passage, for in working through his spiritual crisis, Michael Kramer considers that the pain of withdrawal that his high conception of art required was focused on two major icons, the face of the suffering Christ that he was unable to satisfactorily complete and a copy of the death mask of Beethoven that hung on his studio wall. Meanwhile, he lived in the company of his handicapped son, whose disfigurement he had inherited from Kramer himself. His son's tragic death—the result of the forces of blind ignorance who flee from the indwelling spirit into alcoholic revelry—throws him back into a more deeply considered reflection on suffering and loss.

In his painting of the face of his dead son he makes, on the one hand, an express analogy between Arnold's anguished death and the representations of the sufferings of Jesus, incomprehensible because of his hypostatic nature, and those of that largest of human spirits, Beethoven (the "beethoken" of *FW* 360). To this point he had been dealing with it according to the highest standards—by his passion and cruel death, Jesus suffered for the sins of all mankind; and by so doing, made perfection, through grace, possible; amid the chaos of his personal life, his social isolation, and the tragedy of his lost hearing, Beethoven transformed his private anguish into the most profound and spiritually expressive music: a sublime rendering of human aspiration. Through his persistent, though never successful, attempt to render the portrait of Christ, Kramer pursues the impossible: a portrait of nature completed through grace.

Beethoven's death mask on the other hand, reminds him of the most concerted effort within his experience to express the desire for transcendence. In a futile effort to save Arnold from the life of a fop (and avoid becoming, in his words, "a lost soul," *MK* 479), he held the death mask of Beethoven before him, saying, "Look, look at this mask! Child of God, dig for the treasures of your soul!" (*MK* 481); and later, waking his dead son, and contemplating this same object, he exclaims to the world outside his open window: "Why do we cry our cries of joy into the immense incertitude—we mites abandoned in the infinite? . . . There is nothing in it of mortal feasts! Nor is it the heaven of the parsons! It is not this and it is not that" (*MK* 539).

Though both Jesus and Beethoven point in the same mystical direction, neither offers an exclusive or self-sufficient answer. They each offer redemption through suffering. Each came to his mission from the depths of an inner struggle cultivated through the long withdrawal from daily life. Each clashed vehemently with official definitions of art and religion. They each represent to Michael Kramer the highest human aspirations: to transcendence through solitude and suffering. This spirit transforms their deaths, making them immortal, though in different ways.

Hauptmann's play spoke to the young Joyce, then, because it presented a sensitive and intelligent man caught in a situation similar to his own. Possessed of a powerful religious tradition of which he was personally skeptical, he was beginning to imagine the symbolic tensions that would inform his own work. He must have been gripped by the dilemma represented by the contrasting icons in Kramer's studio: the never-completed portrait of human perfection in the face of Jesus, and the truculent face and deep-knitted brow of the dead Beethoven. Kramer's inability to finish the face of Jesus and the sterling presence of Beethoven's death mask—contrasting images of hypostatic perfection and of indomitable human will—cannot but have made on the young Joyce an indelible impression.

Joyce would have apprehended these objects as dramatic emblems of what would become a major theme in his work: the necessary imperfection—unless imagined as completed by divine grace—of the natural order. This is one of the reasons, I think, that he was so possessed by the play. In these contrasting icons we have an ur-version of a permanent Joycean concern that permeates *Dubliners*: the contrast between the square of perfection and the gnomon of the human condition. In Hauptmann's particular dramatization of the contrast, with its focus on the role of sorrow, he would have heard the Schopenhauerean note. Kramer's painting of his dead son's face and his modeling of a death mask are his responses both as a creative artist, and as a natural father who grieves for his dead son. These means, in turn, allow him to transform his human grief into a spiritual conciliation. These actions are all dramatized in the moving diorama of the last scene in which the women—Michaline and Liese—enter and perform the funereal rituals of lighting the candles at the bier, laying the wreath, and standing silently in mourning dresses as Kramer unburdens his soul to Lachmann.

Kramer's spiritual preoccupations are represented in these two objects, and his aesthetic resolution in the etching of his dead son. But Hauptmann's real subject is not Kramer the artist but Kramer the father. And this is what the final act dramatizes, and what apparently impressed Joyce so profoundly. And in confronting his son's death, his aesthetic preoccupations are put to the real test. He confronts this catastrophe with death-defying vim. Death, he asserts, is not final.

But before reaching this conclusion, Kramer had to pass through several stages in his assessment of death. First, before it intervened in his affairs, he thought of it in Schopenhauerean terms: "The whole thing seemed to me a devilish bad joke on the part of the powers that be, a wretched, futile kind of trick" (*MK* 534). When, however, it interrupts our daily routine, it exposes our material preoccupations as trivial. As Kramer tells Lachmann:

> When the great things enter into our lives, I tell you, the trivial things
> are suddenly swept away. The trivial separates, I tell you, but greatness

unites us. That is, if one is made that way. And death I tell you, always belongs to the great things—death and love. (*MK* 532)

Taking the argument further, he goes on to claim that

Death, I tell you, leads us into the divine. Something comes upon us and bows us down. But that which descends to us is sublime and over-whelming at once. And then we feel it, we see it almost, and we emerge from our sorrows greater than we were. (*MK* 533)

And in a burst of Schopenhauerean enthusiasm, he imagines that his rela-tionship with his son has moved out of historical time, so that he sees Arnold "as though he were my farthest ancestor" (537). This transforms his natural-istic view of each of their lives, concluding, "Death has been maligned. That is the worst imposture in the world. Death is the mildest form of life: the masterpiece of Eternal Love" (*MK* 538).[5]

Kramer realizes that his son has refuted his mediocre adversaries by tak-ing his life by his own hand, and has by virtue of his death risen to the realm of the divine. Lifting the veil from the face of his dead son, he observes, in a powerful simile: "his countenance is radiant with that heavenly light about which I flutter like a black, light-drunken butterfly. I tell you, we grow small in the presence of death" (*MK* 537). As he makes this reflective progression from material to mystical, from loss to accretion, from natural to transcen-dent, Kramer strides about his studio, as if moved to enact his own metaphor, around the bier and candles, and from his own easel to Beethoven's death mask, and from there to the open window, concluding with his climactic paean: "Why do we cry our cries of joy into the immerse incertitude—we mites abandoned in the infinite?" (*MK* 539).

Drawing on the spirit revealed in the persons of Jesus, Beethoven, and his own sense of communion with his dead son, Michael Kramer realizes that Arnold's death was not in vain. It appears to be futile, for Arnold harbors il-lusions about his capacities (e.g., he brandishes a gun that he is unable to use). Kramer's love for his son enables him to view this death as redemptive. This discovery transfigures, in turn, all his own incertitude, his suffering, and his dread of annihilation.

In composing "A Painful Case" as his son Giorgio was being born, Joyce must have been revisiting the excitement that he had experienced five years before as he translated, word for word, the summative epiphany of Michael Kramer's life. He read again, in his mind's eye, Kramer's excited boast to Lach-mann:

> I tell you, that time when my boy was born . . . I trembled on that day.
> And I wrapped up the man-child, I tell you, and I took him into my
> chamber and locked the door, it was like a temple, Lachmann. I placed
> him there before God. You fellows don't know what it is to have a son.
> I knew it, by the Eternal!" (*MK* 460)

If the Joyce of 1901 was moved by Arnold's argument with his distraught
mother, he was now in a better position to feel with his father's view of him.
He must also have recognized how Michael Kramer's spiritual resources allowed him to draw on both the Christian and Schopenhauerean interpreta-
tions of human suffering. For Michael Kramer's life has been taken up with
the alternative positions that all this anguish is a "bad joke" (*MK* 534) while at
the same time he attempts to paint the face of the Man of Sorrows. In the writing of "A Painful Case" as he was about to become a father, Joyce was drawing
on Hauptmann's model, which was both aesthetic and personal. In the figure
of James Duffy—a loveless and childless bachelor—he was presenting a figure
that embodied the fatal detachment of human, aesthetic, and spiritual values.
Duffy's fate is one pole in the ongoing Joycean struggle between faith, enlightenment, vision, and despair.

The invocation of Mr. Duffy's translation of *Michael Kramer*, then, has a
considerable bearing on how Joyce expects us to read Mr. Duffy's character, aspirations, and his meditation on Mrs. Sinico's death. To be sure, the
broad (and narrow) parallels between the works are there: the protagonists'
orderliness, solitude, conflicts between a personal and a parson's Christianity, between a sense of duty and faith in oneself (*MK* 459–60), religious and
aesthetic conflicts, failures in understanding and love. Like Kramer, Duffy is
an aesthete and intellectual; like Kramer, he impresses those around him with
the depth of what they take to be simple matters; like Kramer, he is given to
misogyny; and like Kramer, he has a melancholic disposition. Each of them
is beset by sudden arrival of death that seems to diminish drastically all other
considerations to the status of trivial distractions. But whereas Kramer succeeds in coming to a spiritual peace with the loss of his son, a peace drawing
on the images of Christ's love, Beethoven's will, and Schopenhauer's notion
of death as transfigurative, Duffy draws no such consoling hopes from the
religious or cultural traditions he shared with Mrs. Sinico.

For Schopenhauer, death is both the greatest human pain and the means
of our liberation into the eternal Will; and for the Christian, death is the main
sign of the limitation of our sinful human selves, but transformed, by the
resurrection of Jesus into the condition of eternal happiness in the presence
of the Creator. By drawing on each of these accounts, Kramer is conciliated.

But not so Duffy: he allows his intellectual sophistication to dim the gleams of promise, hope, joy, and love offered him variously by the Christian vision, by Mozart, Schopenhauer, and the relationship with Mrs. Sinico. He has drowned in Nietzschean cynicism and despair. Whatever we may think of Michael Kramer's final position, he is moved to compassion in the spirit of Schopenhauer. He does not consider himself to be alone. Mr. Duffy, by contrast—and in the spirit of his latest mentor, Nietzsche—has lost the capacity for compassion. Alone he remains.

As with Kramer, Duffy's reaction to the news of the death of one to whom he should have been beholden in love, passes through several stages. As we have seen, Duffy moves from denial (section 4, *D* 112.28–113.18), to moral revulsion (5 a; *D* 115.15–116.2), to an existential meditation (5 b; *D* 116.3–33), to a moment of mystical communion with the dead (5 c; *D* 116.34–117.8), and to a final despair (5 c; *D* 117.9–34). In the course of these reflections, he briefly considers that Mrs. Sinico's death is his fault, following Kramer's similarly brief consideration: "Perhaps I smothered this plant. Perhaps I shut out his sun and he perished in my shadow" (*MK* 537).

Joyce was evidently deeply impressed by Hauptmann's treatment of grief transformed into vision, for just as this last act of *Michael Kramer* informs the first and last stories of *Dubliners*, it also informs the resolution of "A Painful Case." Kramer's transformation from artist into father is informed by his religious conception of artist and enables him to reconcile himself with death as engaging a bodily and spiritual transformation. The import of "A Painful Case," therefore, can only be grasped when seen as an expression of what he considered to have inherited from Ibsen and Hauptmann: a "higher and holier enlightenment" (letter to Ibsen, March 1901, *Letters* I: 52).

Whereas the figure of the sorrowing Christ represents human perfection, Beethoven's death mask represents the highest human aspiration. Born of suffering and struggle, Beethoven's music mediates between the world of the senses and the transcendent. Hauptmann's conception of music here is apparently an implicit subscription to Schopenhauer's notion of music as the purest expression of Will. His profound and heroic music crosses the threshold between the phenomenal and noumenal spheres. The figures of Christ's and Beethoven's sufferings and death represent the parallelism, if not the equivalence, between divine and artistic redemptions. In making a portrait of Arnold in the presence of such icons, Kramer is executing several projects: expressing his acceptance of his son's death; forging a bond between them; breaking his artist's block by abandoning the incomplete portrait of Christ; asserting the role of art in conciliating heaven and earth; supplanting the parson; usurping the priest's dogmatism for an unorthodox vitalism; and asserting that there is a mutually sustaining relationship between natural life and spiritual values—transcendent or immanent—between human and eternal Love.

In *Michael Kramer*, then, Hauptmann transcends the Naturalism of his previous work. It draws on his own intense mystical experience by his father's deathbed. He witnessed there what he took to be the transfiguration of the dead and a manifestation of the glory of creation. In conferring on Michael Kramer an epiphany of the interdependence of the living and the dead, Hauptmann was admitting a debt to German idealism, Schopenhauer in particular. Kramer's attitude towards human suffering, his compassion for his dead son, his ability to face the moral and spiritual implications in an open-eyed way, especially in contrast with the women (who "want concealment," *MK* 532), are Schopenhauerean traits, traces of which we can discern in Mr. Duffy. Kramer has none of Nietzsche's hard-headedness, and for all his effort to free himself of sentimentality, neither has Duffy. Each of them reposes a greater degree of emotional reliance on the Christian understanding of spirituality than they would wish.

The wary agnosticism of Kramer's language is charged with imaginative energy drawn from the lexica of Schopenhauer's philosophy and Christian theology. It is therefore easy to appreciate why Joyce was so drawn to this work: for the problems it posed, the solution it offered, and its language. Thus, when Kramer struggles to find terms to explain his sense of salvation, despite the tragedy he has just experienced, he tells Lachmann that from the campaniles comes the news of him and his son, "Und daß keiner von uns ein Verlorner ist!" (*Samtliche Werke*, 1172), which Lewisohn renders as "that neither of us is a lost soul" (*MK* 539). We do not know, of course, what Joyce, in his lost translation of *Michael Kramer*, made of that *Verlorner*, but it is unlikely that it had no bearing on his choice of that freighted "alone" (as God abandons a lost soul, as Duffy abandoned and was abandoned by Mrs. Sinico) with which he ended "A Painful Case."

Conclusion

An Occasion of Grace

Along with Shem the Penman, Mr. James Duffy has the distinction of being Joyce's only mature celibate intellectual. He is thereby well equipped by his creator to cut through the meshes that trammel the souls of the general run of Dubliners. He is sufficiently endowed with intelligence and feeling to view with detachment his social formation. He is the figure in *Dubliners* who is least encumbered by a sense of family, national, or religious obligation. He is free to do what he wills. The central social drama in his quiet life is his failed liaison with Mrs. Sinico. It collapsed because whereas he imagined it as a platonic relationship animated by Mozart's music, she hoped that it could become as intimate as any human one could be: emotional, intellectual, and physical. This is the actualization of an apparently longstanding spiritual crisis of his inner life. For Mr. Duffy there was another, perhaps unconscious, agendum that required his denial of such hopes. The sophisticated technique of Joyce's story—which this long discussion has attempted to peruse—the "objective correlative" of the labyrinthine ways of Mr. Duffy's soul, reveals that agendum.

To this end, Joyce's portrait of this character is typically inlaid with literary and cultural allusion so that it is possible for readers to arrange James Duffy's life retrospectively and thereby uncover the contours of his inner struggle. Abandoning his early clerical aspirations, he has become a dilettante: dabbling in theology, poetry, music, drama, and philosophy. He supports these cultural hobbies through an occupation that does not engage his intellectual capacities or assuage his spiritual yearnings.

If we turn, once again, to the works of the philosopher who has been Mr. Duffy's principal guide through adulthood, Schopenhauer, we may be afforded one final look at that agendum.

As he ranges over many topics in *World*, there is one underlying perspective to which Schopenhauer continually returns and that would have appealed to James Duffy: his awareness of his own superior gifts and a self-conscious comparison with the manner in which other men of genius expressed theirs. In the chapter in the third book of *World*, entitled "On Genius," he identifies the salient quality in the man of genius—in contrast with the man (or woman) of talent—as the capacity, unimpeded by guarded self-interest, to realize full intellectual curiosity and expression. In an extended passage in this essay, he remarks on the particular childlike character of the genius. His discussion (which in some ways anticipates Freud) considers that during the first seven years of life, before the development of the genital system, the brain attains its full extension and mass (161). Among young children one finds the greatest levels of unimpeded desire for information: they have more intellect than will, that is, than inclinations, desire, and passion (162). In childhood, the intellect "eagerly apprehends all phenomena, broods over them and stores them up carefully for the coming time—like the bees, who gather a great deal more honey than they can consume, in anticipation of future need" (162). "Certainly what a man acquires of insight and knowledge up to the age of puberty is, taken as a whole, more than all that he afterwards learns, however learned he may become; for it is the foundation of all human knowledge" (162–63).

This hypothesis is best exemplified, in Schopenhauer's view, by the case of Mozart who throughout his life retained the spontaneity of a child. Citing George Nikolaus von Nissen's *Biographie W.A. Mozart's* (Leipzig 1828), he proposes that "[I]n his heart he nearly became a man, but in all other relations he always remained a child" (163). The exuberance and spontaneity of his music everywhere speaks of his pure, childlike genius. It exemplifies the proposition that every genius is even for this reason a big child, because he is able to look out into the world as into something strange, a play, and therefore with purely objective interest (163). For Mozart, the experience of the world was always as if apprehended for the first time, an epiphany. In the normal course of average lives, the mental aptitude of youth is afterwards lost, and the natural disposition for apprehending, understanding, and learning disappears (164). Unless one can retain into adulthood the childlike capacity for heedless play, one becomes grave, sober, thoroughly composed, and dully reasonable. Most people lose that energy, joy, and beauty and become melancholic creatures of routine. They sometimes look back with regret on their brush with genius: "Childhood is the time of innocence and happiness, the paradise of life, the lost Eden which we look longingly back through the whole remaining course of our life" (*World* 3: 162).

From this Schopenhauerean perspective, then, we can infer that Mr. Duffy seeks to recover in Mozart's music the sense of the original joy in life with which, because of his religious indoctrination during his adolescence, he became disenchanted. The account of his physical and mental habits in "A Painful Case" allows us to trace the successive efforts to recover this primal energy—the Wordsworth of his youth, the Schopenhauer and Hauptmann of his adulthood. Meanwhile, through his solitary concert-going, this gifted and self-conscious man attempts to revisit that prelapsarian world before the spiritual and moral intervention made by the sponsors of the *Maynooth Catechism*. Transported to a Mozartean Eden, he encounters Mrs. Sinico, where, for a time, they wander among its musical delights. But when his companion attempts to introduce the somatic appetite of the natural adult—an inference from the lyrics of Mozart's lieder—he recoils.

His particular paralysis derives from his inability to conciliate his three-way conflict: his dream of a joyful youth, his adolescent dream of Christian perfection, and ratiocination of his adulthood. His reading of Schopenhauer and Nietzsche, expressions of the intellectual appetites of a mature man, has revived in him the suspicion that he is marked with the consequences of original sin. Mrs. Sinico personifies this superstition along with the weaker Christian virtues excoriated by Schopenhauer and Nietzsche. Thus his inability to extricate himself from his residual Christian fear of the God the Final Judge has debilitated him as an aspiring atheist and as a lover of the human other. His revulsion at the prospect of sexual union with Mrs. Sinico is thus the result of his inability to choose between or reconcile Christian belief and modern skepticism. The dry shell of his social personality encloses a hopeless misogyny.

Thus, the schema of "A Painful Case" allows us to identify the succession of icons that he imagines, in retrospect, as successively presiding over the stages of his spiritual journey. They are the genius Mozart (his childhood), the suffering Jesus (his adolescence), the pantheist visionary Wordsworth (his youth), the metaphysical pessimist Schopenhauer (his early adulthood), and the prophet of nihilism Nietzsche (his full adulthood). Throughout this hegira, he has attempted to shore up his disintegrating personality with fragments collected from each of these stations. His inability to reciprocate Mrs. Sinico's love and his subsequent incapacity to assimilate the import of her death, so carefully delineated by the narrator of "A Painful Case," confirm that he has not succeeded in conciliating these conflicts.

His scruples and his scruples about his scruples prevent him from returning. Duffy has pressed through too many turnstiles since the spirit of "sweetmoztheart" enlivened his spirit. The music of Mozart and the words of Jesus are like the voice of Mrs. Sinico: not living presences in his life, but haunting ghosts of what might have been but cannot evermore.

At the center of the spiritual design of *Dubliners*, then, which treats with penetrating intelligence, ironic bemusement, and occasional fierce satire the conflicts between abject acquiescence in the received "faith of our fathers" and the persistent demands of a skeptical and maturing mind, rests the sad case of James Duffy. This story's understatement belies its profound discernment of the tensions between a residual attachment to the sentiment of childhood faith with its dream of relief, reward, and perfection, and the hazards of the natural order pulsing variably from hour to hour through joy, sorrow, and ennui. The spiritual scales of *Dubliners* hold in balance the cases of whether nature is hopelessly unfinished but nonetheless self-sufficient, or redeemable through a grateful and loving response to an unexpected visitation of grace.

From a Christian perspective, therefore, when Mr. Duffy's moment of potential grace arrives, he is unable to recognize and assimilate it. His impulsive rejection of Mrs. Sinico's proffered touch (at first justified as a decorous shrinking from sin) and his termination of their relationship (rationalized after a week's reflection as his removal of an "occasion of sin") amounts to a considered rejection of divine grace. Mrs. Sinico is Christ in female form, her sensual gesture, paradoxically, unveils the face of God. The parable of the marriage feast, in which Christ establishes a link between marriage, human sexual love, and the call to divine grace, links her gesture to the penultimate proffering of grace to Duffy. Still possessed of a univocal sense of evil, he refused the opportunity to respond to her with largesse of spirit. He does not recognize that, to paraphrase Stephen Dedalus, the path to eternal glory and triumph lay through life, error, and the fall (*P* 172.8–12).

The maudlin images and overblown rhetoric of the final paragraphs of the story imply that he has lost his equanimity and ability to assess and reverse the direction of his life. Mr. Duffy's painful case of conscience, his "agenbite of inwit," results from the self-judgment that his abrupt termination of his relationship with Mrs. Sinico is an unreported but nonetheless probable cause of the "sudden failure of the heart's action" (*D* 114.21). In this he is wrong. His reflections in the Phoenix Park, therefore, which focus on how he could have saved her, should, instead, have focused on how she could have saved him. Appearing to him in the form of a sinful Eve, she offered him a way through the valley of tears to grace and salvation.

Both Mrs. Sinico and Mr. Duffy are gnoma, then: she a representative of the sinful world, a victim of marital neglect, and twice denied in her aspirations to love and happiness, could yet be a medium of grace to one who might recognize his need of it. The surrounding symbolic order—where the Phoenix Park represents both an Eden of the fallen and a paradise of resurrection—furnishes the fraught arena accommodating this interpretation. When Mr. Duffy rejected Mrs. Sinico's gesture of human love he was still a disciple of Schopenhauer, and thus had not abandoned all hope as he later would when turning to Nietzsche. Thus the Christian ethos that adumbrates this brief sketch provides, by its vestigial presence, this option, both for Duffy and for the readers of his story.

Epilogue: annus mirabilis

By the end of 1906 Joyce appears to have become resigned to his dissatisfaction with "A Painful Case." Shortly after his return to Trieste from Rome the following year, into his life walked the marine paint manufacturer and man of letters, Ettore Schmitz (Italo Svevo). In this student of English he encountered a living alternative to the *figura* he had wrestled with in "A Painful Case."

This Italian-speaking, Austro-German secularized Jew was, to Joyce, an original character type. Although Schmitz was twenty years Joyce's senior, their temperamental and intellectual sympathies and similarities of background drew them together. Joyce must have been struck by the many ways in which Schmitz resembled his own unsatisfactory *futurabilium*, James Duffy. Schmitz had begun his creative life as an aspiring dramatist. And like Joyce (in Rome) and Duffy (in Dublin), he had been a bank employee by day, and writer and radical journalist by night. As an agnostic Jew who had endured instruction in the catechism while undertaking a nominal conversion (in order to marry his Catholic wife), and who was cheerfully indifferent to his apostasy, Schmitz exhibited for Joyce's observation the workings of a secular conscience. Schmitz, to be sure, regretted that he was a Jew who allowed himself to be baptized; but this was an ethnic and not a religious guilt. His attitude towards the Catholic Church was more hostile: he marveled—as would Bloom in the Westland Row Church—at the mindless consumption of "amazing rubbish in surroundings so splendid with wealth and meaning" (Weiss cites, 10).

Listening to expressions of such bewildered condescension, Joyce must have been privately amused. As he soon discovered, Schmitz had been liberated from his residual Jewish faith by reading Schopenhauer. The philosopher had taught him to view life as a comedy of illusions that could only be transcended through dedication to writing. According to his biographer, John Gatt-Rutter, therefore, the key to the "mystery" of Schmitz/Svevo's double life—a bank clerk and businessman, factory manager and writer, atheist and Catholic convert, private socialist and Italian irredentist—lies in Schopenhauer's grimly comic vision (4–6).

Thus when Joyce met him in 1907 he must have been struck by this man who in real life exhibited so many of the attributes with which he had endowed James Duffy: a middle-aged agnostic intellectual, an elite socialist, clerk and *littereur*, operagoer and Schopenhauerean. In the gifted Schmitz he met a man whose buoyantly humorous mental character, by contrast with the Irish ex-Catholic Duffy, was seemingly untrammeled by misgivings over his abandoned religious inheritance. Joyce's prior creation of the melancholy Duffy thus prepared him for the ways in which Schmitz could become the prototype of Bloom.

In the person of Ettore Schmitz, Joyce found a liberating alternative to the religious conscience and residual guilt that he could not find in any native Irish model. Thus the figure of Bloom bears some tinctures from the faded Duffy. When, for example, the cynical narrator of "Cyclops" ridicules him as an amateur philosopher, he lights on Bloom's partiality to some Schopenhauerean turns of phrase: "And then he starts out with his lawbreakers about phenomenon and science and this phenomenon and the other phenomenon" (*U* 12.466–67). Again, in Bloom's recurring pain at the loss of Rudy, we have a faint echo of Duffy's repressed paternal feelings implied by the Wordsworthian lament buried on his bookshelf. And again, Bloom's response to Rudolph Virag's rebuke, "Have you no soul? . . . Are you not my dear son Leopold who left the house of his father and left the god of his fathers Abraham and Jacob?" (*U* 15.259–62), is diplomatic: "I suppose so, father. Mosenthal. All that's left of him" (*U* 15.264). His diffident stance betrays a faint note of Duffian regret.

James Duffy cannot escape the power of his repressed religious and paternal aspirations. He registers profound anguish at his having "left the god of his fathers." Led by Schmitz's example, Bloom has, in Mr. Deasy's words, "sinned against the light" (*U* 2.361). And further, as secularized Jews, they have done so twice. In creating Bloom, therefore, in the image of a secularized Jew, Joyce has dared to go where he could not in the figure of Duffy. Duffy's rejection of the invitation to the marriage feast is a sin greater than those to which he is passing tempted—theft and adultery. The sin of despair, the rejection of the grace offered by the Holy Spirit, is as we have seen, the core of "A Painful Case."

Duffy's guilt at his exclusion from the marriage feast—and his sense of damnation at that prospect—is thus trumped by the appearance of Leopold

Bloom, for whom the sense of exclusion may be familial or social, but it is not metaphysical or spiritual. For Bloom, there is anguish enough in daily life besides that provoked by the prospect of final causes or imminent apocalypse. Joyce's dissatisfaction with the story was not resolved by any return to its manuscripts, but in his subsequent ability to refashion the debilities of this melancholy figure into the dialectic of *Ulysses* oscillating between the "moody brooding" Stephen and the buoyant Bloom. This liberation and renewal he owed in part to Ettore Schmitz, and is one of the reasons why 1907 was, for Joyce, his annus mirabilis.

Notes

Chapter 1. Introduction

1. As he witnesses the artfully cultivated devotional atmosphere surrounding the mystery of the Eucharist during morning Mass at All Hallows Church, Westland Row, the same phrase occurs to that bemused skeptic, Leopold Bloom (*U* 5.391). It is originally Ovid's (*Metamorphoses* 9.711).

2. During the weeks before beginning this story (June–July 1905), Joyce was finishing the manuscript of *Stephen Hero*, chapters 24–26. He had Stephen Daedalus reviewing

> the plague of Catholicism . . . [which] obscured the sun. Contempt of [the body] human nature, weakness, nervous tremblings, fear of day and joy, distrust of man and life, hemiplegia of the will, beset the body burdened and disaffected in its members by its black tyrannous lice. . . . He, at least . . . would live his own life according to what he recognized as the voice of a new humanity, active, unafraid and unashamed. (194)

These might well have been Mr. Duffy's thoughts when he was Stephen's age.

Chapter 2. The Dublin-Trieste Cradle

1. In an uncharacteristic error, Richard Ellmann reports it "rewritten" by May 8 (*JJII* 207).

2. As we shall see below, Ellmann's footnote shows that he does not recognize the significance of the letter on the constable's collar.

3. The best account of the process by which *Dubliners* was written and published is Hans Walter Gabler's introduction to the Norton Critical Edition of *Dubliners* (2006).

4. Jana Giles discusses Joyce's revisions from a creative writer's point of view, which complements the genealogical and intertextual purposes of this study.

5. Turgenev's "Diary of a Superfluous Man" (March 22) and Moore's "Home Sickness" utilize the same device very effectively.

6. "Hal Kilbride" reappears in *Finnegans Wake* (576.06), representing another Mr. Death for ladies who should have known better, King Henry VIII.

7. In his long letter of July 12, Joyce indicates this prospect with an allusion to Harriet Shelley's suicide in Hyde Park in 1816: "I . . . do not desire any such ending for our love-affair as a douche in the Serpentine" (*Letters* II: 96) that recurs in "A Painful Case" as Mr. Duffy contemplates Mrs. Sinico's death as he travels the Phoenix Park "Serpentine" walk.

8. In no draft is there any account of the unauthorized removal of Mrs. Sinico's body from the tracks to the platform.

9. Mr. Duffy's fear of alcohol—the lubricant of Mrs. Sinico's decline—reflects another aspect of Joyce's anxiety at the time he was writing "A Painful Case": his own proclivities in the same direction, inherited from his father, frequently angered Nora and Stanislaus (*JJII* 209–15).

10. Mary Lowe-Evans, in a blunt feminist body-slam, indicts not only this pair for Mrs. Sinico's death, but every male even remotely connected to the accident. Unaccountably, James Watt escapes the wreck.

11. Sunset in early November comes around 4:30 p.m.; Mr. Duffy's departure for the bar "as the light failed" (*D* 116.3), therefore occurs about three hours later.

12. By contrast with Moore, an estimable writer who must have crossed his mind as he wrote these sentences, Joyce handled such facts accurately and their symbolic superstructure inimitably.

13. In popular folk tradition, the soul's presence slowly diminishes during the thirty days following decease. Thus Hamlet's father's ghost appears within the month of his murder and Irish pious tradition requires a "month's mind" memorial Mass.

14. The Irish Rosicrucians and Theosophists were local variants on the Anglo-American Spiritualist movement. "A Painful Case" antecedes Sir Arthur Conan Doyle's belated enthusiasm for this fad.

15. Besides Myers, Joyce might also have read Schopenhauer's "Essay on Spirit Seeing and Everything Connected Therewith" (*P&P* 1: 225–309). This widely influential essay examines various paranormal phenomena, concluding that they can be attributed to what would subsequently be called psychological causes.

16. To provide for her habit, Mrs. Sinico was evidently visiting one of the several off-licenses along Merrion Road. Three were within a half mile of her home, and a further three within a mile. Since most public houses were either exclusively male or restricted the admission of unaccompanied females, Mrs. Sinico, by a combination of personal choice and social constraint, drinks alone.

17. On this point Bloom is unreliable. Had Mrs. Sinico been considered a suicide, she would not have been buried in Glasnevin. Moreover, as we read in "Ithaca," she was "accidentally killed" (*U* 17.947).

18. The Mozart entry in the 11th edition of the *Encyclopedia Britannica* has just this emphasis, as if implying a Nietzschean tragic joy.

19. The historical recording of "*Che farò*" that Clara Butt made for Columbia records can be found in *Clara Butt: A Critical Survey*, vol. 1, *The Acoustic Years*, Swarthmore, Pa.: Marston 520292. The recording will strike modern listeners as histrionic and lacking vocal precision and nuance, partly due to the pre-electric equipment, but mainly to the vocal style of the period. She cultivated an opulent and golden tone that went out of fashion after the Edwardian period. Nevertheless, Michael Aspinall seems justified in his estimation that this is "by far the best performance on records of this well-known aria" (liner notes).

20. The *Irish Times*—a partisan critic of Trebelli's—had some reservations about Butt's intonation. Nevertheless, today's listener can experience something of the frisson felt by the young Stanislaus Joyce on hearing this and the other arias that spring afternoon in 1902 from the Marston reissue.

21. Winifred Ponder's biography—to which Shaw wrote a brief foreword from which the quotation is taken (8)—is impressionistic and sentimental.

22. The doleful prognostication of "*Abendempfindung*" seems fulfilled in the visit that the mysterious "McIntosh" makes to Mrs. Sinico's grave.

23. In "Counterparts" (completed the month before "A Painful Case"), Joyce had characterized Farrington's alienation as his adoption of "B-attitudes" (see Owens, "Joyce's Farrington," 144–45).

Chapter 3. Love, Marriage, and Moral Adjudication

1. If the Sinicos are married eighteen years when Duffy meets Mrs. Sinico, their daughter is unlikely to be more than that age.

2. The four seasons of *Chamber Music* shrink to the winter setting of "A Painful Case." The number four otherwise organizes the temporal order of the story. The time-span of the action—between their meeting and Mrs. Sinico's death—is four years. Four p.m. divides Mr. Duffy's workday from his "dissipations." Their first "appointment" was their fourth meeting (*D* 110.12–13). During the period, both pass the age of forty, entering full adulthood.

3. In this respect, Captain Sinico's apparent naïveté about landlubbers complements Mr. Hill's cynicism about sailors "—I know these sailor chaps" (*D* 39.19).

4. Mr. Duffy patronizes "the public-house at Chapelizod Bridge" (*D* 116.8), outside of which he hears the tram "swishing" (*D* 116.20–21). There is a slight (and apparently inconsequential) ambiguity in the reference. The Bridge Bar and the Mullingar House—both in continuous existence before 1900, and on the north and south ends of the (now named) Anna Livia Bridge—are candidates for this distinction since the tram tracks between the Chapelizod and Lucan Roads doglegged over the bridge as it passed their doors. Of these, the Mullingar House is the more likely for both symbolic and practical reasons.

It is the closer to Duffy's residence on Chapelizod Road, its name derives from its former function as a "staging house" journey westward through Lucan and Maynooth to Mullingar (where, in the summer of 1901, Joyce had translated *Michael Kramer*, an achievement he credits to Duffy), and he returns to it in *Finnegans Wake*. To patronize this bar on his last excursion through the park, Duffy passes two other, more convenient, establishments. Both of these, Mrs. Peat's The Tap on Chapelizod Road and The Red Light (aka The Carlyle) on Park Lane (prop. William G. Gilman) just outside the wicket gate, catered to the Irish Artillery Regiment stationed in the park. To have Mr. Duffy prefer a bar with a male and Catholic proprietor (a reader of the *Evening Herald*), Joyce perpetrates a minor violation of the historical record, since in 1900 the owner and operator of the Mullingar House was a Mrs. Keys. During his father's youthful "jollifications" there, moreover, the Mullingar House was owned and operated by an English Protestant named Robert Broadbent.

In the course of providing this information, Jackson and Costello (71) correct the previous misidentifications of Duffy's residence on the south side of the river from which the inference that he drinks at the Bridge Inn was made (originally by Bidwell and Heffer, 126, and subsequently by Gifford, Jackson, and McGinley et al.) (see *Thom's Official Directory*).

5. The topical congruencies that compose the design of these paragraphs are prefigured by the image of the pair of rooms at opposite sides of the city, and of their lonely occupants brooding upon one another's absence, "Mr Duffy . . . gazed out of his window on the cheerless evening landscape" (*D* 115.15–16) contemplating Mrs. Sinico's abandonment, "sitting night after night alone in that room" (*D* 116.30–31).

6. The names "Chapel Lizard" (1654) and "Chappellizard" (1720) appear among its historical toponymics (Bennett, s.v. "Chapelizod").

7. Jesus is here citing the last verse in Isaiah: "They shall go out and see the corpses of the men who rebelled against me; / Their worm shall not die, nor their fire be extinguished; they shall be abhorrent to all mankind" (64: 24). The Prophet is here comparing the exclusion of those who reject God's commandments with the corpses tossed in the Valley of Gehenna outside the walls of Jerusalem. Thus the worm that gnaws Duffy's spirit as he views the City of Dublin from the Magazine Hill sounds some grave biblical bedrock.

8. There is no textual justification for the lowercase rendition of "League," which appears in both Scholes and Gabler's "corrected" editions. This creates a needless ambiguity, since the denotation of the uppercase usage is immediately clear to readers of the *Evening Mail*. In the original manuscript, Joyce wrote "temperance League" (*JJA* 4.121), striking "temperance" from the second full draft but retaining the uppercase for "League" (*JJA* 4.169). On this point, Joyce's handwritten versions of the story, the 1914 proofs, and first edition are unanimous.

The most likely "League" to which Mary Sinico might have made reference was the Pioneer Total Abstinence Association of the Sacred Heart. It was established in Dublin (1898–1901) by a Jesuit, Father James Cullen, and was the most successful of such movements in modern Irish history (Malcolm, 306–21). The Irish Temperance League (1858–), in contrast, was predominantly Presbyterian (Malcolm, 152). The use of the word "League" in the newspaper report is another indication of the copy editor's deafness to the nuances of Irish Catholic usage.

Were the Sinicos willing to pay, a private institution "for the care and accommodation of a limited number of Ladies . . . suffering from the excessive effects of Alcohol or Drugs" was available at "Verville," Clontarf (*Irish Catholic Directory*, 1909 advertisements, 100).

9. Sydney Parade is a subdivision of Merrion fronting South Dublin Bay between the Sandymount and Merrion Strands. It centers on Sydney Parade Avenue, a solidly middle-class residential street that runs for a half mile NE/SW between Strand Road and Merrion Road. It is handsomely stocked with detached and semidetached Victorian brick residences. In 1904, as *Thom's Official Directory* records, the ratable valuation of these residences ranged from £21 to £80, and bore names exhibiting their owners' sense of bourgeois comfort, for example, "Adelaide Hall," "Brighton Villa," and "Sans Souci." Many prominent Dubliners—barristers, doctors, businessmen, and public citizens—resided there (as do their social descendants today). Bloom's ideal country residence, "Bloom Cottage," has a £42 valuation (*U* 17.1501–80). There were therefore no "little cot-

tages" on this prestige avenue; but many houses with a fraction of these valuations could be found on the smaller streets between the Strand Road and the railway station. One of these, for example, was "Rose Cottage," at #1 Sydney Place, with a ratable value of £6. These modest abodes housed members of the lower middle-class, artisans, and blue-collar workers. The Sinicos evidently live in relatively humble circumstances.

A small irony arises, then, between the narrator's description of the Sinico abode (and concealment of its actual street address) and the newspaper's identification of it as "Leoville, Sydney Parade" (*D* 114.31).

Mrs. Sinico is killed as she makes her way along Sydney Parade Avenue via the widegate of the level crossing at the north entrance to Sydney Parade Station either to or from one of the nearest grocers licensed for the sale of spirits. All of these were on Merrion Road: two within a half mile of her home (#145, J. Tracey, grocer, and #188–92, Hugh Brady, grocer), and many more within a mile walk north towards Donnybrook (for example, John J. Johnson at #3, or Judith Ashford, tea, wine, and spirit merchants at #12 and 13; *Thom's Official Directory*). She might well be imagined to have patronized all of these by turn as much for the recreational walk as to spare her embarrassment as a too-regular customer in any one of them (cf. figures 3.4 and 4.2, and Matt. 7:13).

10. Following the Joyce family custom of giving one another raffish caricature (*CDD* 13–14), Joyce sometimes imagined himself as a cartoon animal: a spider, a grasshopper, or an earwig.

11. As G. A. Starr argues, in the development of these characters, Defoe drew heavily on the "Cases Matrimonial" appearing in John Dunton's *Athenian Mercury*, 9–33.

12. See Connolly, *Personal Library*, item 191, 23–28 and 30–31.

13. This question (with a recondite answer) recurs in *Finnegans Wake* 148.33–149.11 ff.

Chapter 4. A Spoiled Priest

1. The Dircks's edition of Schopenhauer's essays (1897) ran to 258 pages. This selection contains these essays of particular interest to Joyce or Mr. Duffy: "The Emptiness of Existence," "On Women," "Religion—A Dialogue," "Metaphysics of Love," and "On Suicide."

2. "The Affliction of Margaret _____" can be found in the Wordsworth edition on Duffy's shelf, 205–6. Joyce evidently had access to *Wordsworth's Poetical Works* while in Trieste, although it is not among the books listed by Gillespie.

In the middle of his disquisition on Shakespeare, Stephen Dedalus, hearing that "a gentleman [who] . . . says he's your father" has entered the National Library, responds "Give me my Wordsworth" (*U* 9.820–21).

3. Gifford identifies the 1883 edition familiar to Joyce (*Joyce Annotated*, 82).

4. See "A Catholic Literature for Ireland" (Deane, 1:1292–97).

5. Shortly before producing the first draft of "A Painful Case" (July–August 1905), Joyce was writing chapter 22 of *Stephen Hero* in which Stephen announces his apostasy to his mother (April 1905): "It's absurd: it's Barnum. He comes into the world the God knows how, walks on the water, gets out of his grave and goes up off the Hill of Howth. What drivel is this?" (133).

6. For example, Torchiana. As if Joyce did not already see the link, a topographical discussion of the relationship between Chapelizod and that tragic love story appeared in the *United Irishman* on October 19, 1901 (6). It was at about this time that Stanislaus told him of his encounter with the lady at the Clara Butt concert.

7. The confession box is designed to depersonalize the relationship between confessor and penitent. One historical reason for the celibacy of the clergy who heard confessions was the potential threat to the seal of the confessional posed by the potential "pillow talk" of a married clergy.

8. We read that "they met always in the evening and chose the most quiet quarters for their walks together" (*D* 110.14–15). A Joycean topography of Dublin suggests that one of these "quiet quarters" is Donnycarney. Cf. *Chamber Music* lyric XXXI:

O, it was out by Donnycarney
When the bat flew from tree to tree
My love and I did walk together;
And sweet were the words she said to me.

Along with us the summer wind
Went murmuring—O, happily!—
But softer than the breath of summer
Was the kiss she gave to me.

Donnycarney is where Father Conmee, reading Nones and Vespers, disturbs the lovers in "Wandering Rocks" (*U* 10.192–205, 842–43). Its name derives from *Domhnach Cearn-ach*, "Cearnach's Church." A quiet quarter, at the time on the northern fringe of the city, it was easily accessible because served by the Malahide tram.

9. Romans 8: 12–23 was read at the fourth and eighth Sundays after Pentecost during Joyce's time.

10. This term instructs the priest to say certain prayers in the Mass or other liturgical ceremony in whispered tones. Joyce originally wrote *In Secretis*, an error that persisted to the first edition (*JJA* 4.115, 161; *JJA* 6.138).

11. As the photograph shows of the stonework, this wicket gate originally accommodated vehicular traffic.

12. The "Irish Poe," who spent much of his childhood in the vicinity of Chapelizod, is the author of fourteen novels and numerous short stories. *The House by the Churchyard* provides some local color in *Finnegans Wake* (Atherton, 110–13).

Two of his "Ghost Stories of Chapelizod" (1851), which are early exercises in the project that was to become *The House by the Churchyard*, make a similar contribution to "A Painful Case." The author claims that they are collected from the oral lore of Chapelizod, a village he fondly remembers for its "melancholy picturesqueness." He delivers them with the simple directness of an oral informant.

In "The Village Bully," Bully Larkin mauled Ned Moran in a duel over "a buxom damsel." For Moran's subsequent death Larkin felt responsible. Entering the Phoenix Park one night by the "old gate," he was confronted on the path through the trees by the ghost of his deceased rival. Transfixed by the "unearthly gaze" of his dead victim, he was "incurably maimed" by the experience. He interpreted the apparition as inviting him to resume their pugilistic encounter "in Hell, where I am going." He was reduced to beggary and soon died miserably.

"The Sexton's Adventure" tells the tale of Bob Martin. Martin, the Church of Ireland sexton in Chapelizod, was dedicated to a "severe morality," censuring the high-spirited youth of the village for their disrespect. He had one fast friendship in the village: Philip Slaney, a saturnine publican. The relationship between this unlikely pair led to Slaney's over-indulgence in grog.

When Slaney committed suicide, Martin was accused of having made a drunkard of Slaney. The appalled Martin resolved never to touch whiskey again. One year later, walking home from a funeral on "a lowering autumn night," he passed Slaney's "public." Much to his surprise, he saw that it was lighted. Seated at the bar was the ghost of the suicide, filling his glass.

Martin bolted. The ghost pursued him hotly through the village, clinking bottle and glass, and inviting him to share a drink. When he reached his own door, the ghost tossed the liquor at him, whereupon it turned into "a stream of flame . . . which enveloped the pair."

Martin subsequently interpreted the event as his encounter with the Evil One who tried to tempt him to intemperance and thereby to damnation.

These sketches may have suggested some of the directions in the plotting of "A Painful Case." Duffy enters the Phoenix Park by the same gate as Bully Larkin, encounters Mrs. Sinico's ghost on the same path as Larkin did Moran's, and is similarly consumed with guilt and despair as was his predecessor. The unlikely friendship between Martin and Slaney, between melancholic and saturnine personalities, the alcoholic turned suicide, and the ambulatory and accusing ghost are features of "A Painful Case."

These curious and superficial elements suggest that Joyce's sophisticated story acknowledges the literally commonplace he shared with LeFanu. They are indications of Joyce's facility in weaving local lore and folk materials into a work of high ambition: at once mythological (*Tristan and Iseult*) and contemporary. In this respect, they admit some level of subscription to popular and elite aspects of the Irish Literary Revival. In another, of course, they underwrite his own serious "ghost story" discussed above ("Touched by Her Voice").

13. The spelling "mediaeval" in the corrected text (*D* 108.15) is not Joyce's. It entered the record of "A Painful Case" only with the 1914 proofs, where he apparently overlooked the compositor's alteration. Joyce spells it "medieval" in *Portrait* (169.05) and *Ulysses* (3.320 and 17.1524).

14. *Dubh* = "black." The surname Duffy is among the fifty commonest Irish surnames (MacLysaght, s.v. "Ó Dubhaigh"). As Flann O'Brien, in "John Duffy's Brother," his clever parody of "A Painful Case," observes: "there are thousands of these Duffys in the world; even at this moment there is probably a new Duffy making his appearance in some corner of it" (*Stories and Plays*, 91).

15. Warren Beck sees the story as a "hodgepodge" of inconsistencies and excessive exposition. It is too obviously calculated and abstracted, leading to a negative epiphany and a special kind of paralysis for the protagonist (219–36).

16. From its first centuries, the Christian Church held celibacy in special esteem. For evangelical and administrative reasons, this regard for celibacy—inherited from Saint Paul (1 Cor. 7: 7–8, 32–35)—expanded as a prerequisite for holy orders. The strict canonical precedent set by the Spanish Council of Elvira (295–302) gained wider acceptance until its universal prescription (*Catholic Encyclopedia*, s.v. "celibacy of the clergy").

17. Citing the Joyce brothers, Stanislaus (*CDD* 21, not 26) and James (*P* 35), the *Oxford English Dictionary* provides a misleading definition of a spoiled priest: "Nun or priest who has repudiated her or his vocation." As the references here are to two members of the Joyce family, Mrs. Conway and Charlie Joyce, neither of whom entered or abandoned the solemn vows of final profession or ordination, this misreads the historical record and conflates the contraries.

18. According to the community records of the Sisters of Mercy, Allegheny County, Eliza Ahearn (Sister Mary Euphrasia) was not finally professed when she left the Pittsburgh convent (private communication, March 1997). She was therefore a "spoiled nun."

19. Famous Continental figures of such diverse reputation and achievement who were onetime seminary students are Charles Gounod and Josef Stalin. They seem to have suffered no obloquy such as would have attended them had they been Irish ex-seminarians.

20. We get a brief cinematic glimpse of the type in David Lean's pastoral epic, *Ryan's Daughter* (1970), in the dour pub keeper, Ryan, played by Leo McKern. John McGahern's short story, "The Recruiting Officer" (*Nightlines*, 1970) is a fine portrait of a "spoiled brother." This subjacent story is told as if it were in the voice of one of the former Christian Brothers trudging in the opposite direction to Stephen Dedalus (*P* 165–66). His early indoctrination in Christian values and his subsequent dissociation from that severe regimen has left him with a paralysis of will. He had grown up with the religiously inspired idea that nothing in life is worth more than any other; and now he is left in a state of existential angst. Alienated from conventional society that is ruled by clerical sadists, he is disillusioned and disappointed. Abandoning his childhood faith, he has lost both a sense of community, any prospect of personal happiness, and hope of salvation. Like Joyce's Mr. Duffy, he is fully alone.

Patrick McGinley's Roarty, in the comic novel, *Bogmail* (1981) is a "spoilt priest," a fact that explains his learning and leadership qualities. But "too uneasy in his mind to be a natural leader. He saw the glory of the golden city and turned his back on it" (59). He leaves the seminary a confirmed Manichean, seeing the world as a battleground between the forces of good and evil. Seeing in the pub he owns a microcosm of that world, he considers it his duty to eliminate the rogue who deflowers his teenaged daughter. A heavily annotated copy of Saint Augustine's *De Malo* and the 11th edition of the *Encyclopedia Britannica* nourish his intellectual life. Trying to plan the perfect crime, he reads the entries on murder and homicide and calms his nerves with Schumann's Cello Concerto and Bushmills. He commits the murder by hitting his victim on the head with the 25th volume (SHU-SUB).

Recent versions appear in John B. Keane's novel, *A High Meadow* (1994). Edward Drannaghy ("the Ram of God") is a grotesque representative. The Irish Gaelic writer

Pádraig Ó Standún's novel, *2016*, develops a convincing portrait of what is no longer called a "spoiled priest." Quitting Maynooth for a woman who then rejects him, the main character, in old age, retraces his moral life. The novel successfully integrates the conflicts of conscience produced by social action. The novel ends fantastically with a vision of hell, where the devil complains of a lack of clients.

This brief survey shows that even in radically changed social circumstances, the type persists in the Irish cultural memory.

Chapter 5. Richard Wagner and Arthur Schopenhauer

1. Charles Wright (1966) produces a delightfully imaginative exploration of "A Painful Case" as a comedy of humors in his essay entitled "Melancholy Duffy and Sanguine Sinico."

2. One indication of this appears in a fine shift in the narrative. The account of their second conversation refers to Mrs. Sinico's family as "her daughter" and "her husband" (the latter three times in four lines, *D* 110.5–10). The possessives indicate a certain degree of pride and ostensible social security. On the other hand, as the Duffy-Sinico friendship accretes, these figures recede to the reduced status of "the daughter" and "the husband" (*D* 110.21–23). These Hiberno-English usages—ordinarily indicating a jocular familiarity—function here to reveal not only Mr. Duffy's lack of a personal interest in her family, but even Mrs. Sinico's emotional independence from them as her relationship with Mr. Duffy progresses.

3. It was not until he had completed the second full draft of the story (1906), that Joyce refined, into indirect speech, the train's tonal contribution to the story. No longer droning "Emily Sinico" "Emily Sinico" "Emily Sinico" (the dactylic stresses marked, no less!), it became a metaphoric voice, "reiterating the syllables of her name" (*JJA* 4.133, 179).

4. Schopenhauer's major work, *World*, translated by Haldane and Kemp (1883), comes in three volumes, and runs to over 1500 pages. The longest of its three volumes has 564 pages; and since it is therefore not as bulky as *Wordsworth's Poetical Works*, could be on Mr. Duffy's shelves. In the translation by E. F. Payne, today's readers have an excellent English-language edition of Schopenhauer's collected essays, *Parerga & Paralipomena*.

5. He temporarily postured as an *Ubermensch*, and in a card to George Roberts signed himself "James Overman" (*JJII* 142; *Letters* I: 56).

6. While writing "A Mere Accident," Moore read Huysmans's *A Rebours* and some of Schopenhauer. As Adrian Frazier observes, Schopenhauer's pessimism and misogyny inform the figure of John Norton (147–48). Moore was temporarily haunted by Schopenhauer's attitude towards women, and his faddish 1887 essay, "Pessimism a la Mode," is an instance of fin de siècle "parlour Schopenhauerism."

7. Joyce apparently read selections from Giordano Bruno in Father Ghezzi's Italian class (*JJII* 59–60; *P* 259.2–4). It is possible that he encountered this Renaissance Neoplatonist and "father of what is called modern philosophy" (*CW* 133) elsewhere, however, since Schopenhauer frequently cites him as a shaper of his own metaphysics. He follows Bruno in excoriating the "coarse, furious priests . . . his judges and executioners" (*World* 2: 13 n), and lacerating those incapable of making truly objective use of their intellects, "men of business, tradesmen, the born porters and carriers of life. To be sociable with

them is degrading . . . we make ourselves really cheap and common" (*P&P* 2: 71). Citing Bruno, Joyce makes a similar polemical point in "The Day of the Rabblement" (October 1901, *CW* 69).

8. They appear together in *Finnegans Wake* as "Bill Heeny . . . beethoken . . . [and] sweetmoztheart" (360.7–12).

9. Gifford glosses this reference as if Stephen is primarily making reference to the doctrine of predestination ("*Ulysses" Annotated*, 47). However, if the Schopenhauerean timbre in this phrase is taken into account, Stephen's crisis of faith is broader: between the personal God (who may or may not grant us free will) and the impersonal Will that drives men and women through the darkness in its ineluctable service, and pursuing the chimera of happiness in that service.

10. The term "lady" appears six times in the story, "woman" twice. In its report of the inquest, the newspaper report is punctilious in switching to the use of the term "deceased," which appears six times in reporting what happened after the point of fatal impact.

Chapter 6. Schopenhauer's Continental Progeny

1. Every translator from Constance Garnett (1886) to Richard Pevear and Larissa Volokhonsky (2000) has tendered the same English phrase. The term "gilded youth" deriving from French *jeunesse dorée*, indicates young men of wealthy families who, in the original context, assisted in Robespierre's downfall in 1794 (*OED*). All citations of *Anna Karenina* are to the Garnett translation, by part and chapter, since that was Joyce's version.

2. In book 1, chapter 39, moreover, the novel exhibits a tour-de-force of the management of the "defamiliarization" effect (the hilariously detached description of a religious ceremony that led to Tolstoy's excommunication from the Russian Orthodox Church, which Joyce was to push to such brilliant lengths in the "Lotus Eaters" chapter of *Ulysses*).

3. Maslova's four-year sentence to penal servitude may have suggested to Joyce the time marker that we have observed in "A Painful Case."

4. Writing to Hauptmann (February 12, 1938) to thank him for an inscribed copy of *Michael Kramer*, Joyce explained that much to his embarrassment, these "traductions" (as Ezra Pound humorously called them, *Pound/Joyce Letters*, 234–35) had fallen into mercantile hands in the United States (unpublished letter cited by Perkins, 11, 14 n. 7). He concluded his letter, otherwise written in German, with the comment, "An enemy hath done this." This quotation from the King James Bible (Matt. 13: 28) betrays Joyce's paranoia, his anxiety about the publication of works he did not intend for publication, and yet again his image of himself after that of Christ. The comment comes from the Parable of the Wheat and the Tares (Matt. 13: 24–30) that Jesus subsequently interprets for his disciples (Matt. 13: 36–43). A farmer, finding an infestation of tares in his wheat field, regards it as evidence of sabotage. He orders his harvesters to separate the weeds from his crop and toss them into a furnace. Jesus explains the allegory as distinguishing between the hearers of the authentic Word and the deceptions of the devil, which will be

apparent to all on the Day of Judgment. It is not surprising that this parable came to his mind as he reflected on the judgment of his fictional translator of Hauptmann's *Michael Kramer*.

5. In his first essay on James Clarence Mangan, Joyce (perhaps thinking of the poet's profile portrait in death) cites Kramer, "death, the most beautiful form of life" (*CW* 83; cf. *U* 15.2098).

Bibliography

Ainsworth, Godfrey. *James Joyce and Sr. Gertrude Joyce*. 2nd ed. Waverley, New South Wales: Franciscan Friary, 1999.

Atherton, James S. *The Books at the Wake: A Study of Literary Allusions in James Joyce's Finnegans Wake*. New York: Arcturus, 1974.

Beck, Warren. *Joyce's Dubliners: Substance, Vision and Art*. Durham, N.C.: Duke University Press, 1969.

Beja, Morris. *Epiphany in the Modern Novel*. Seattle: University of Washington Press, 1971.

Bennett, Douglas. *The Encyclopaedia of Dublin, Revised and Expanded*. Dublin: Gill and Macmillan, 2005.

Benstock, Bernard. *Narrative Con/Texts in Dubliners*. Urbana: University of Illinois Press, 1994.

Benstock, Shari, and Bernard Benstock. *Who's He When He's at Home: A James Joyce Directory*. Urbana: University of Illinois Press, 1980.

Bershtel, Sara. "A Note on the Forgotten Apple in James Joyce's 'A Painful Case.'" *Studies in Short Fiction* 16 (1979): 23–40.

Bidwell, Bruce, and Linda Heffer. *The Joycean Way: A Topographic Guide to "Dubliners" and "A Portrait of the Artist as a Young Man."* Baltimore: The Johns Hopkins University Press, 1982.

Boyle, Robert, SJ. "The Woman Hidden in James Joyce's *Chamber Music*." In *Women in Joyce*, edited by Suzette Henke and Eliane Unkeless, 3–30. Urbana: University of Illinois Press, 1982.

Bradley, Bruce. *James Joyce's Schooldays*. New York: St. Martin's, 1982.

Brown, Maurice J. E. "Mozart's Songs for Voice and Piano." *Music Review* 17 (1956): 19–28.

Butt, Clara. *A Critical Survey, Vol. 1: The Acoustic Years*. Swarthmore: Marston Records, 2000. 52029–2.

Byrne, John Francis. *Silent Years: An Autobiography with Memoirs of James Joyce and Our Ireland*. New York: Farrar, Strauss and Young, 1953.

Campbell, Joseph. *The Hero with a Thousand Faces*. Princeton: Princeton University Press, 1949.

Carleton, William. "Going to Maynooth." *Traits and Stories of the Irish Peasantry*, 2 vols. Dublin: Curry, 1842–44; reprint Gerrards Cross: Smythe, 1990.

The Catholic Encyclopedia. New York: The Encyclopedia Press, 1907–12.

Caufield, James Walter. "The Word as Will and Idea: Dedalean Aesthetics and the Influence of Schopenhauer." *JJQ* 35/36 (Summer/Fall 1998): 695–714.

Christian, R. F. *Tolstoy: A Critical Introduction*. London: Cambridge University Press, 1969.

Clay, George. "Tolstoy in the Twentieth Century." In *The Cambridge Companion to Tolstoy*, edited by Donna Tussig Orwin, 206–21. New York: Cambridge University Press, 2002.

Colum, Mary, and Padraic Colum. *Our Friend James Joyce*. New York: Doubleday, 1958.

Connolly, Thomas E. "A Painful Case." In *James Joyce's Dubliners: Critical Essays*, edited by Clive Hart, 107–14. New York: Viking Press, 1968.

———. *The Personal Library of James Joyce: A Descriptive Bibliography*. Buffalo, N.Y.: SUNY Buffalo, 1957.

Corish, Patrick. *The Irish Catholic Experience: A Historical Survey*. Wilmington, Del.: Michael Glazier, 1985.

Corrington, John William. "Isolation as Motif in 'A Painful Case.'" *JJQ* 3 (Spring 1966): 182–91.

Costello, Peter. *James Joyce: The Years of Growth, 1882–1915*. New York: Pantheon, 1993.

Curran, Constantine. *James Joyce Remembered*. New York: Oxford University Press, 1968.

Deane, Seamus, Andrew Carpenter, and Jonathan Williams, eds. *The Field Day Anthology of Irish Writing*, 3 vols. Derry, Northern Ireland: Field Day Publications, 1991.

Delany, Paul, and Dorothy Young. "Turgenev and the Genesis of 'A Painful Case.'" *Modern Fiction Studies* 20 (1974): 217–21.

A Dictionary of Irish History Since 1800. Edited by D. J. Hickey and J. E. Doherty. Totowa, N.J.: Barnes and Noble, 1981.

Doherty, Gerald. "Upright Man/Fallen Woman: Identification and Desire in James Joyce's 'A Painful Case.'" *Style* 35 (Spring 2001): 99–110.

Doherty, James. "Joyce and Hell Opened to Christians: The Edition He Used for His 'Hell Sermons.'" *Modern Philology* 61 (1963): 110–19.

Dolan, Terence Patrick. *A Dictionary of Hiberno-English: The Irish Use of English*. Dublin: Gill and Macmillan, 1998.

Donovan, Stephen. "Dead Men's News: Joyce's 'A Painful Case' and the Modern Press." *Journal of Modern Literature* 24, no. 1 (Fall 2000): 25–45.

Eglinton, John. "A Way of Understanding Nietzsche." *Dana: An Irish Magazine of Independent Thought*, 1904. Reprint New York: Lemma, 1970.

Ellis-Fermor, Una. *The Irish Dramatic Movement*. London: Methuen, 1964.

Ellmann, Richard. *The Consciousness of Joyce*. New York: Oxford University Press, 1977.

Encyclopedia Britannica. 11th ed. New York: Encyclopedia Britannica, 1910.

Encyclopedia of Irish History and Culture. Edited by James S. Donnelly Jr., Karl S. Bottigheimer, Mary E. Daly, James E. Doan, and David W. Miller. 2 vols. Detroit: Thomson Gale, 2004.

Evans, David. "Stephen and the Theory of Literary Kinds." *JJQ* 11 (Winter 1974): 145–49.

Fallon, Gabriel. *An Age of Innocence: Irish Culture 1930–1960*. Dublin: Gill and Macmillan, 1998.

Foster, R. F. *W. B. Yeats: A Life. I: The Apprentice Mage, 1865–1914*. New York: Oxford University Press, 1997.

Frazier, Adrian. *George Moore, 1853–1933*. New Haven: Yale University Press, 2000.

Gabler, Hans Walter. Introduction to *Dubliners: A Norton Critical Edition*, edited by Margot Norris, xv–xliii. New York: Norton, 2006.

Gatt-Rutter, John. *Italo Svevo: A Double Life*. Oxford University Press, 1988.

Gifford, Don. *Joyce Annotated: Notes for "Dubliners" and "A Portrait of the Artist as a Young Man."* Rev. ed. Berkeley and Los Angeles: University of California Press, 1982.

Gifford, Don, with Robert J. Seidman. *"Ulysses" Annotated: Notes for Joyce's "Ulysses."* Rev. ed. Berkeley and Los Angeles: University of California Press, 1988.

Gilbert, Stuart. *James Joyce's "Ulysses": A Study*. New York: Vintage, 1958.

Giles, Jana. "The Craft of 'A Painful Case': A Study of Revisions." In *New Perspectives on Dubliners*, edited by Mary Power and Ulrich Schneider, 195–210. *European Joyce Studies* 7 (1997).

Gillespie, Michael Patrick. *Inverted Volumes Improperly Arranged: James Joyce and his Trieste Library*. Ann Arbor, Mich.: UMI Research Press, 1983.

Gluck, C. W. von. *Orfeo ed Euridice: Opera in Four Acts*, libretto by Ranieri de Calzabigi, translated by Walter Ducloux. New York: Schirmer, 1957.

Gordon, Caroline. *How to Read a Novel*. New York: Viking, 1957.

Gordon, John. *Joyce and Reality: The Empirical Strikes Back*. Syracuse, N.Y.: Syracuse University Press, 2004.

Gorman, Herbert. *James Joyce*. New York and Toronto: Farrar and Rinehart, 1939.

Grove's Dictionary of Music and Musicians. 10 vols. 5th ed. Edited by Eric Blom. New York: St. Martin's, 1966.

Hauptmann, Gerhart. *Samtliche Werke*, Herausgegeben, Von Hans-Egon Hass. Band 1: Dramen, Frankfurt/Berlin: Propylaen Verlag, 1966.

Hayley, Barbara. "A Reading and Thinking Nation: Periodicals as the Voice of Nineteenth-Century Ireland." In *Three Hundred Years of Irish Periodicals*, edited by Barbara Hayley and Enda McKay, 29–48. Gigginstown, Mullingar: Association of Irish Learned Journals, 1987.

Hayman, David. "The Distribution of the Tristan and Isolde Notes under 'Exiles' in the *Scribbledehobble*." *A Wake Newsletter: Studies in James Joyce's Finnegans Wake* 2:5 (1965): 3–4.

Henke, Suzette. *James Joyce and the Politics of Desire*. New York: Routledge, 1990.

Heumann, J. Mark. "Writing—and Not Writing—in Joyce's 'A Painful Case.'" *Éire-Ireland* 16, no. 3 (Fall 1987): 81–97.

Holloway, Joseph. *Joseph Holloway's Abbey Theatre: A Selection from His Unpublished Journal, Impressions of a Dublin Playgoer*. Edited by Robert Hogan and Michael J. O'Neill. Carbondale: Southern Illinois University Press, 1967.

Hyde, Douglas. "The Student Who Left College." *Legends of Saints and Sinners*, 166–72. Dublin: Talbot, 1915.

Irish Catholic Directory and Almanac. Dublin: James Duffy, 1909.

Jackson, John Wyse, and Peter Costello. *John Stanislaus Joyce: The Voluminous Life and Genius of James Joyce's Father*. New York: St. Martin's, 1998.

Jackson, John Wyse, and Bernard McGinley, eds. *James Joyce's Dubliners: An Illustrated Edition with Annotations*. New York: St. Martin's Griffin, 1995.

Jackson, Roberta. "The Open Closet in *Dubliners*: James Duffy's Painful Case." *JJQ* 37 (Fall 1999/Winter 2000): 83–97.

Jerome Biblical Commentary. Edited by Raymond Brown, Joseph A. Fitzmyer, and Roland E. Murphy. Englewood Cliffs, N.J.: Prentice-Hall, 1968.

Jonsen, Albert R., and Stephen Toulmin. *The Abuse of Casuistry: A History of Moral Reasoning.* Berkeley and Los Angeles: University of California Press, 1998.

Joyce, James. *Before Sunrise.* Edited by Jill Perkins. Los Angeles: Huntington Library, 1978.

———. *Dubliners.* Edited by Robert Scholes in consultation with Richard Ellmann. New York: Viking, 1967.

———. *Dubliners: Text and Criticism.* Edited by Robert Scholes and A. Walton Litz. New York: Penguin, 1996.

———. *Poems and Shorter Writings.* 1991. Edited by Richard Ellmann, A. Walton Litz, and John Whittier-Ferguson. London: Faber and Faber, 1991.

———. *A Portrait of the Artist as a Young Man.* Corrected text by Chester G. Anderson and edited by Richard Ellmann. New York: Viking, 1968.

———. *Ulysses.* Edited by Hans Walter Gabler et al. New York: Random House, 1986.

Kenner, Hugh. *Dublin's Joyce.* Boston: Beacon, 1956.

Kershner, R. B. "Mr. Duffy's Apple." *JJQ* 29 (Winter 1992): 406–7.

Knapp, Bettina. "Joyce's 'A Painful Case': The Train and an Epiphanic Experience." *Etudes irlandaises* 13 (December 1988): 45–60.

Knapp, Liza. "The Development of Style and Theme in Tolstoy." In *The Cambridge Companion to Tolstoy*, edited by Donna Tussig Orwin, 161–75.

Kranidas, Thomas. "Mr. Duffy and the Song of Songs." *JJQ* 3 (Spring 1966): 220.

Levenson, Michael. "Stephen's Diary in Joyce's *Portrait*—The Shape of Life." *ELH* 52 (Winter 1985): 1017–35. Reprinted in *James Joyce's "A Portrait of the Artist as a Young Man": A Casebook*, edited by Mark A. Wollaeger, 183–205. New York: Oxford University Press, 2003.

Liguori, Saint Francis. *Visits to the Blessed Sacrament and the Blessed Virgin Mary.* Translated by Rev. R. A. Coffin. New York: Kenedy, 1853.

Lowe-Evans, Mary. "Who Killed Mrs. Sinico?" *Studies in Short Fiction* 32 (Summer 1995): 395–402.

MacKillop, James. *Dictionary of Celtic Mythology.* New York: Oxford University Press, 1998.

MacLysaght, Edward. *Irish Families: Their Names, Arms, and Origins.* New York: Crown, 1972.

Magalaner, Marvin. *Time of Apprenticeship: The Fiction of Young Joyce.* New York: Abelard-Schuman, 1959.

Magee, Bryan. *The Philosophy of Schopenhauer.* New York: Oxford University Press, 1997.

Malcolm, Elizabeth. *"Ireland Sober, Ireland Free": Drink and Temperance in Nineteenth-Century Ireland.* Syracuse, N.Y.: Syracuse University Press, 1986.

Malton, James. *A Picturesque and Descriptive View of the City of Dublin.* Reproduced from the edition of 1799 with an introduction by the Knight of Glin. Dublin: Dolmen, 1978.

Martin, Timothy. *Joyce and Wagner: A Study of Influence.* New York: Cambridge University Press, 1991.

Mason, Michael. "Why Is Leopold Bloom a Cuckold?" *ELH* 44 (1977): 171–88.

Maupassant, Guy de. "A Little Walk." *Short Stories of de Maupassant,* 374–78. New York: Book League of America, 1941.

Maurer, Warren. *Understanding Gerhart Hauptmann.* Columbia: University of South Carolina Press, 1992.

McBrien, Richard P. *Catholicism.* 2 vols. Minneapolis: Winston, 1980.

McCourt, John. *The Years of Bloom: James Joyce in Trieste 1904–1920.* Madison: University of Wisconsin Press, 2000.

McGahern, John. "The Recruiting Officer." *Nightlines.* London: Faber and Faber, 1970.

McGinley, Patrick. *Bogmail.* New York: Penguin, 1981.

McKenzie, John L. *Dictionary of the Bible.* Milwaukee, Wis.: Bruce, 1965.

Merton, Thomas. *The Seven Storey Mountain.* New York: Harcourt Brace, 1948.

Moore, George. *Celibates.* London: Walter Scott, 1895; reprint New York: Brentano's, 1926.

———. *The Lake.* London: William Heinemann, 1905.

———. *The Untilled Field.* London: T. Fisher Unwin, 1903.

Moore, George, and William Butler Yeats. *Diarmuid and Graine.* Introduced by Anthony Farrow. Chicago: DePaul University Press, 1974.

Murray, Thomas Cornelius. *Maurice Harte.* Dublin: Maunsel, 1912. Reprinted in *Irish Drama 1900–1980,* edited by Cóilín Owens and Joan Radner, 167–208. Washington: Catholic University of America Press, 1990.

Myers, Frederic W. H. *Human Personality and Its Survival of Bodily Death.* 2 vols. London: Longmans, Green, 1903.

New Catholic Encyclopedia. 2nd ed. 14 vols. Detroit: Gale; Washington: Catholic University of America Press, 2003.

New Grove Dictionary of Music and Musicians. 20 vols. Edited by Stanley Sadie. Washington, D.C.: Grove, 1995.

Newton, Ivor. *At the Piano: The World of an Accompanist.* London: Hamish Hamilton, 1966.

Nietzsche, Friedrich. *The Gay Science: Cambridge Texts in the History of Philosophy.* Edited by Bernard Williams. Translated by Josefine Nauckhoff. New York: Cambridge University Press, 2001.

———. *Thus Spake Zarathustra.* Translated by Thomas Common and revised by H. James Birx. New York: Prometheus, 1993.

Norris, Margot. *Suspicious Readings of Joyce's "Dubliners."* Philadelphia: University of Pennsylvania Press, 2003.

O'Brien, Flann. *Stories and Plays.* London: Hart-Davis, MacGibbon, 1973.

O'Brien, Joseph V. *"Dear, Dirty Dublin": A City in Distress, 1899–1916.* Berkeley and Los Angeles: University of California Press, 1982.

Orwin, Donna Tussig, ed. *The Cambridge Companion to Tolstoy*. New York: Cambridge University Press, 2002.

Osborne, John. *The Naturalist Drama in Germany*. Manchester: Manchester University Press, 1971.

Owens, Cóilín. "*Entends sa Voix*: Eveline's Irish Swansong." *Éire-Ireland* 28, no. 2 (Summer 1993): 37–53.

———. "'A Man with Two Establishments to Keep Up': Joyce's Farrington." *Irish Renaissance Annual* IV (1983): 128–56.

———. "The Wooing of Étaín: Celtic Myth and *The Shadow of the Glen*." In *Assessing the Achievement of J. M. Synge*, edited by Alexander G. Gonzalez, 57–74. Westport, Conn.: Greenwood, 1996.

Pevear, Richard. Introduction to *Anna Karenina: A Novel in Eight Parts*, by Leo Tolstoy. Translated by Richard Pevear and Larissa Volokhonsky, vii–xvi. New York: Penguin, 2000.

Ponder, Winifred. *Clara Butt: Her Life-Story*. London: George Harrap, 1928.

Potts, Willard, ed. *Portraits of the Artist in Exile: Recollections of James Joyce by Europeans*. San Diego and New York: Harcourt, Brace, Jovanovich, 1986.

Pound, Ezra. *Pound/Joyce: The Letters of Ezra Pound to James Joyce, with Pound's Essays on Joyce*. Edited and with a Commentary by Forrest Read. New York: New Directions, 1967.

Reid, Stephen. "'The Beast in the Jungle' and 'A Painful Case': Two Different Sufferings." *American Imago: A Psychoanalytic Journal for Culture, Science and the Arts* 20 (1963): 221–39.

Reilly, Seamus. "James Joyce and Dublin Opera, 1888–1904." In *Bronze by Gold: The Music of Joyce*, edited by Sebastian D. G. Knowles, 3–31. New York: Garland, 1999.

Renan, Ernest. *The Life of Jesus*. Translated by Charles Edwin Wilbour. New York: Carleton, 1861.

Russel, Myra Teicher. *James Joyce's Chamber Music: The Lost Song Settings*. Bloomington: Indiana University Press, 1993.

Senn, Fritz. "Distancing in 'A Painful Case.'" *La Revue des Lettres Modernes: Histoire des Idées et des Littératures* 834–839 (1988): 25–38.

Sheehan, Canon Patrick A. *A Spoiled Priest and Other Stories*. London: Burns Oates and Washbourne, 1905. Reprint Dublin: Clonmore and Reynolds, 1954.

Sloan, Barbara L. "The D'Annunzian Narrator in 'A Painful Case': Silent, Exiled, and Cunning." *JJQ* 9 (Fall 1971): 26–36.

Slocum, John J., and Herbert Cahoon. *A Bibliography of James Joyce [1882–1941]*. New Haven: Yale University Press, 1953.

Smith, Paul. "Crossing the Lines in 'A Painful Case.'" *Southern Humanities Review* 17 (Summer 1983): 203–8.

Standún, Pádraig. *2016: Urscéal*. Indreabhan: Cló Chonemara, 1988.

Starr, G. A. *Defoe and Casuistry*. Princeton: Princeton University Press, 1971.

Sullivan, Kevin. *Joyce Among the Jesuits*. New York: Columbia University Press, 1958.

Thom's Official Directory of the United Kingdom of Great Britain and Ireland for the Year 1904. Dublin: A. Thom, 1904.

Thrane, J. R. "Joyce's Sermon on Hell: Its Source and Its Backgrounds." *Modern Philology* 57 (1960): 172–98.

Tolstoy, Leo. *Anna Karenina.* Translated by Constance Garnett. London: Heinemann, 1901; reprint New York: Random House, 1939.

———. *Resurrection.* Translated by Louise Maude. London: Grant Richards, 1902.

Torchiana, Donald. *Backgrounds for Joyce's Dubliners.* Boston: Allen and Unwin, 1986.

Troyat, Henri. *Tolstoy.* Translated from French by Nancy Amphoux. Garden City, N.Y.: Doubleday, 1967.

Tucker, Lindsey. "Duffy's Last Supper: Food, Language, and the Failure of Integrative Processes in 'A Painful Case.'" *Irish Renaissance Annual* 4 (1983): 118–27.

Turgenev, Ivan. "Clara Militch." *Dream Tales and Prose Poems.* In *The Novels of Ivan Turgenev*, vol. 10, 1–101. Translated by Constance Garnett. London: Heinemann, 1896.

———. "The Diary of a Superfluous Man." In *The Novels of Ivan Turgenev*, vol. 13: 3–98. Translated by Constance Garnett. London: Heinemann, 1896.

Tymoczko, Maria. *The Irish Ulysses.* Berkeley and Los Angeles: University of California Press, 1994.

The United Irishman (newspaper) [Dublin] 1899–1905. 1901–5.

Voelker, Joseph. "'He Lumped the Emancipates Together': More Analogues for Joyce's Mr. Duffy." *JJQ* 18 (Fall 1980): 23–34.

Walicki, A. "Turgenev and Schopenhauer." *Oxford Slavonic Papers* 10 (1962): 1–17.

Wallace, William. *Life of Arthur Schopenhauer.* London: Scott, 1899.

Weaver, Jack W. *Joyce's Music and Noise: Theme and Variation in His Writings.* Gainesville: University Press of Florida, 1998.

The Weekly Irish Times (newspaper) [Dublin] 1899–1905.

Weiss, Beno. *Italo Svevo.* Boston: Twayne, 1987.

West, Michael, and William Hendricks. "The Genesis and Significance of Joyce's Irony in 'A Painful Case.'" *ELH* 44 (1977): 701–27.

Wordsworth, William. *The Complete Poetical Works of William Wordsworth.* Introduced by John Morley. London: Macmillan, 1888, 1928.

Wright, Charles D. "Melancholy Duffy and Sanguine Sinico: Humors in 'A Painful Case.'" *JJQ* 3 (Spring 1966): 171–81.

Wright, David G. "The Secret Life of Leopold Bloom and Emily Sinico." *JJQ* 37 (Fall 1999/Winter 2000): 99–112.

Yeats, William Butler. *Mythologies.* New York: Macmillan, 1959.

Zlotnick, Joan. "Influence of Coincidence: A Comparative Study of 'The Beast in the Jungle' and 'A Painful Case.'" *Colby Library Quarterly* 11 (1975): 132–35.

Index

Cóilín Owens is Professor Emeritus of English at George Mason University. He is the editor of *Family Chronicles: Maria Edgeworth's Castle Rackrent* (1987), editor of *Irish Drama, 1900–1980* with Joan Radner, and author of *Before Daybreak: "After the Race" and the Origins of Joyce's Art* (2013 and 2015).

The Florida James Joyce Series
Edited by Sebastian D. G. Knowles

The Autobiographical Novel of Co-Consciousness: Goncharov, Woolf, and Joyce, by Galya Diment (1994)

Bloom's Old Sweet Song: Essays on Joyce and Music, by Zack Bowen (1995)

Joyce's Iritis and the Irritated Text: The Dis-lexic Ulysses, by Roy Gottfried (1995)

Joyce, Milton, and the Theory of Influence, by Patrick Colm Hogan (1995)

Reauthorizing Joyce, by Vicki Mahaffey (paperback edition, 1995)

Shaw and Joyce: "The Last Word in Stolentelling," by Martha Fodaski Black (1995)

Bely, Joyce, and Döblin: Peripatetics in the City Novel, by Peter I. Barta (1996)

Jocoserious Joyce: The Fate of Folly in Ulysses, by Robert H. Bell (paperback edition, 1996)

Joyce and Popular Culture, edited by R. B. Kershner (1996)

Joyce and the Jews: Culture and Texts, by Ira B. Nadel (paperback edition, 1996)

Narrative Design in Finnegans Wake: *The Wake Lock Picked*, by Harry Burrell (1996)

Gender in Joyce, edited by Jolanta W. Wawrzycka and Marlena G. Corcoran (1997)

Latin and Roman Culture in Joyce, by R. J. Schork (1997)

Reading Joyce Politically, by Trevor L. Williams (1997)

Advertising and Commodity Culture in Joyce, by Garry Leonard (1998)

Greek and Hellenic Culture in Joyce, by R. J. Schork (1998)

Joyce, Joyceans, and the Rhetoric of Citation, by Eloise Knowlton (1998)

Joyce's Music and Noise: Theme and Variation in His Writings, by Jack W. Weaver (1998)

Reading Derrida Reading Joyce, by Alan Roughley (1999)

Joyce through the Ages: A Nonlinear View, edited by Michael Patrick Gillespie (1999)

Chaos Theory and James Joyce's Everyman, by Peter Francis Mackey (1999)

Joyce's Comic Portrait, by Roy Gottfried (2000)

Joyce and Hagiography: Saints Above!, by R. J. Schork (2000)

Voices and Values in Joyce's Ulysses, by Weldon Thornton (2000)

The Dublin Helix: The Life of Language in Joyce's Ulysses, by Sebastian D. G. Knowles (2001)

Joyce Beyond Marx: History and Desire in Ulysses and Finnegans Wake, by Patrick Mc-Gee (2001)

Joyce's Metamorphosis, by Stanley Sultan (2001)

Joycean Temporalities: Debts, Promises, and Countersignatures, by Tony Thwaites (2001)

Joyce and the Victorians, by Tracey Teets Schwarze (2002)

Joyce's Ulysses *as National Epic: Epic Mimesis and the Political History of the Nation State*, by Andras Ungar (2002)

James Joyce's "Fraudstuff," by Kimberly J. Devlin (2002)

Rite of Passage in the Narratives of Dante and Joyce, by Jennifer Margaret Fraser (2002)

Joyce and the Scene of Modernity, by David Spurr (2002)

Joyce and the Early Freudians: A Synchronic Dialogue of Texts, by Jean Kimball (2003)

Twenty-first Joyce, edited by Ellen Carol Jones and Morris Beja (2004)

Joyce on the Threshold, edited by Anne Fogarty and Timothy Martin (2005)

Wake Rites: The Ancient Irish Rituals of Finnegans Wake, by George Cinclair Gibson (2005)

Ulysses *in Critical Perspective*, edited by Michael Patrick Gillespie and A. Nicholas Fargnoli (2006)

Joyce and the Narrative Structure of Incest, by Jen Shelton (2006)

Joyce, Ireland, Britain, edited by Andrew Gibson and Len Platt (2006)

Joyce in Trieste: An Album of Risky Readings, edited by Sebastian D. G. Knowles, Geert Lernout, and John McCourt (2007)

Joyce's Rare View: The Nature of Things in Finnegans Wake, by Richard Beckman (2007)

Joyce's Misbelief, by Roy Gottfried (2007)

James Joyce's Painful Case, by Cóilín Owens (2008; first paperback edition, 2017)

Cannibal Joyce, by Thomas Jackson Rice (2008)

Manuscript Genetics, Joyce's Know-How, Beckett's Nohow, by Dirk Van Hulle (2008)

Catholic Nostalgia in Joyce and Company, by Mary Lowe-Evans (2008)

A Guide through Finnegans Wake, by Edmund Lloyd Epstein (2009)

Bloomsday 100: Essays on Ulysses, edited by Morris Beja and Anne Fogarty (2009)

Joyce, Medicine, and Modernity, by Vike Martina Plock (2010; first paperback edition, 2012)

Who's Afraid of James Joyce?, by Karen R. Lawrence (2010; first paperback edition, 2012)

Ulysses *in Focus: Genetic, Textual, and Personal Views*, by Michael Groden (2010; first paperback edition, 2012)

Foundational Essays in James Joyce Studies, edited by Michael Patrick Gillespie (2011)

Empire and Pilgrimage in Conrad and Joyce, by Agata Szczeszak-Brewer (2011; first paperback edition, 2017)

The Poetry of James Joyce Reconsidered, edited by Marc C. Conner (2012; first paperback edition, 2015)

The German Joyce, by Robert K. Weninger (2012; first paperback edition 2016)

Joyce and Militarism, by Greg Winston (2012; first paperback edition, 2015)

Renascent Joyce, edited by Daniel Ferrer, Sam Slote, and André Topia (2013; first paperback edition, 2014)

Before Daybreak: "After the Race" and the Origins of Joyce's Art, by Cóilín Owens (2013; first paperback edition, 2014)

Modernists at Odds: Reconsidering Joyce and Lawrence, edited by Matthew J. Kochis and Heather L. Lusty (2015)

James Joyce and the Exilic Imagination, by Michael Patrick Gillespie (2015)

The Ecology of Finnegans Wake, by Alison Lacivita (2015)

Joyce's Allmaziful Plurabilities: Polyvocal Explorations of Finnegans Wake, edited by Kimberly J. Devlin and Christine Smedley (2015)

Exiles: A Critical Edition, by James Joyce, edited by A. Nicholas Fargnoli and Michael Patrick Gillespie (2016)

Up to Maughty London: Joyce's Cultural Capital in the Imperial Metropolis, by Eleni Loukopoulou (2017)

Joyce and the Law, edited by Jonathan Goldman (2017)

www.ingramcontent.com/pod-product-compliance
Lightning Source LLC
Chambersburg PA
CBHW031054020726
47495CB00007B/1874